Herbert Kastle was born and brought up in Brooklyn. He has been an English teacher, an editor, an advertising copywriter, but he now devotes his time to writing. Mr Kastle is the author of many successful novels including *The Movie Maker*, *Cross Country*, *Hit Squad*, *Dirty Movies*, and *Sunset People*.

By the same author

HERBERT KASTLE

Hit Squad

GRAFTON BOOKS

A Division of the Collins Publishing Group

LONDON GLASGOW
TORONTO SYDNEY AUCKLAND

Grafton Books
A Division of the Collins Publishing Group
8 Grafton Street, London W1X 3LA

Published by Grafton Books 1979
Reprinted 1984, 1985, 1988 (twice)

First published in Great Britain as *Death Squad*
by W. H. Allen & Co Ltd 1978

Copyright © Herbert Kastle 1977

ISBN 0-586-20549-7

Printed and bound in Great Britain by
Collins, Glasgow

Set in Times

For Bob Sherman, who believed in it,
And for his Betty.

'We shall be wise to inspect violence now while our social contract yet permits diversity of opinions. Or we shall wait too long, and our contract will be lost and we, the violators and the violated, will in silent agreement bow to a higher, invulnerable force. Then order will be all.'

— *The Social Contract*
by Robert Ardrey

TELEPHONE PROLOGUE

VOICE ONE: 'Hello?'

VOICE TWO: 'Yeah, I'm calling from a booth. You alone?'

ONE: 'I can talk, but watch it. You never know. Keep it general.'

TWO: 'Still no contact. The prick just doesn't *go* anywhere. Except home. And I been thinking ... maybe we should drop it?'

ONE: 'We don't drop *anything*. The decision's been made. If we drop things after decisions are made, we'll fall apart. And we can't fall apart. Don't you understand how important this is?'

TWO: 'Yeah.' Sighing: 'We'll pick up on him tomorrow night. Maybe then.'

ONE: 'Whenever. But never talk that way again. This is war.'

TWO: 'Yeah.' Embarrassed.

ONE: 'You obviously don't see it yet, but we're going to change the history of this country. First you, me, the rest here in New York. Then others in other cities. Then ... the *works*!'

TWO: 'Well, I'll be in touch.'

ONE: 'Let's have some enthusiasm. You're a Paul Revere. A Minuteman. It's really that important!'

TWO: 'Okay, Mr Washington.'

ONE: Laughing: 'Now you've got it.'

LETTER PROLOGUE

Dear Editor:

There is a sickness in this city. I don't mean default or Welfare or every union being out for itself. I don't mean the muggers and perverts on our streets. I don't mean the low rate of conviction of criminals, and even those getting out to rob, rape, and kill again within a year or two. I don't mean the obvious weaknesses of our city, our society. Because we could handle all that, could cure *that* sickness, if the people who are supposed to be law-abiding, the people who run the gut level of our city, were doing their job. And I'm not complaining about ineptitude, laziness, just plain don't-give-a-damn. That would eventually lead to their being thrown out of office or off their jobs. I'm speaking of people in responsible positions who are *dishonest*. It's one thing for a mugger, a thug, a crook to commit a crime. It's another thing for a city official – and I include everyone from the mayor on down; I include cops and street cleaners, councilmen and city attorneys, firemen and inspectors for Health and other departments – it's another thing for *these* people, sworn to serve the public, to be criminals. New York City has rot at the core, and that's why we can't solve our problems. Too many officials are cheating on and stealing from the public. Too many are committing crimes for profit, power, or both. And too many have the positions, the tools, to cover their crimes as no ordinary criminal can. That's why they can't be stopped by ordinary methods. But they *must* be stopped!

Honesty and ethics. Anything done to return them to our life and times is acceptable. *Anything* ... so let the perpetrators beware!

Sincerely,
Mr Clean

ONE

The marauders came out of the north, from Harlem, first on Amsterdam Avenue, then on Park, moving into the land of white power and wealth, the magical and remarkably few streets of residential Manhattan affluence. They came in a new Firebird, bright red, easily identifiable, the license plates clean and lighted in the rear. They sat together in the front seat, three black youths with moderate Afros, the center man uncomfortable on a console, long legs spread to accommodate the four-speed stick shift, yet wanting to be with his fellows; his fellows wanting him there tight against them. For they were on desperate business and felt the chill of strange turf, despite wine and pot, piss and vinegar, a little cocaine spread thin amongst them.

'White *turkey*,' the driver, deeply black and burly, muttered as a young man scurried across the intersection, face turning in shock as the Firebird ignored the red light.

But why shock? It was two-ten A.M. and this was New York City and if Park weren't so broad here, so open and exposed here, they'd have shown him what shock was all about.

They were high and the strange turf couldn't restrain them for long and the streets grew narrower and darker as they turned east, to Second Avenue and then to First. The F.D.R. Drive hummed faintly even at this hour, and beyond lay the East River, dark and silent. Between First and the F.D.R. was a hunting ground.

They cruised the Fifties; the East Side Fifties where the cash was. The radio played soul, FM soul and few commercials, the music stirring them without their noticing it; the constant background to their lives, black rock soul.

They were high on what they'd drunk and smoked and sniffed. And on the warm summer night. And, more than

11

that, on justifiable hatred, justifiable robbery and mayhem and homicide; on the prey due them by their view of American history; on what they'd gleaned from the Black Power speeches, the fragments of black political talk, the articles and pamphlets not really read since they'd never learned how to read, really. They'd learned to justify, and all America conspired to make them strong in their violence. All America practiced thievery, chicanery, mayhem . . .

'Motherin' pigs,' the outside man, as tall as the center man but not as lean, not as light-skinned, said as they approached a police car parked to their right on the one-way street. But no cops were inside, or walking around, and their sudden tension dissipated in wild laughter and in the feeling that luck was with them tonight. Still, the burly driver had taken out his gun, and he didn't put it back in his belt. He placed it on the seat under his right thigh. The lanky center man took out his own gun. The outside man simply touched his, under his bright print shirt, then fingered the childhood scar on his chin, a thoughtful gesture. They had the pieces and they had the luck . . .

He saw them then. *'There!'*

The middle-aged couple was leaving an apartment house on the left side of the street, turning east toward Beekman Place, the F.D.R., the river, the continuing darkness.

The driver cut his lights and pulled into an empty space on the right curb, near a hydrant. The three youths watched as the couple stepped into the street some thirty feet in front of them and began crossing, the man a little ahead, removing something from his pocket.

'Keys,' the center man said, shoving at the driver. 'They goin' for a car.'

With that they were out and running. The woman heard them first, looking to her right, her mouth opening and her hand rising to her throat. The man was almost at a dark sedan and he too turned, then bent and frantically tried to fit the key in the door. 'Leave my wife alone,' he said, his voice shaking.

The driver had his gun aimed. He was almost on the

12

woman and he gasped, 'In front the car, bitch! One fuckin'
word, just one!'

The woman said, 'Arny,' weakly and went with the
driver.

The outside man had reached her husband and hit him in
the face with his left fist. The husband was tall and heavy
and merely grunted. The outside man, enraged, his manhood threatened, used his gun as a bludgeon, slamming it
twice into the side of the man's head. The man half turned,
sagging against the car. 'We'll give you all our money. Don't
hurt us.'

The driver had shoved the woman to the ground in front
of the sedan, in the space between parked cars, and felt safe
here. He grabbed her ass, intending to pull up her dress, but
she was an old bitch and said, 'Lord God!' just like his
mother. It turned him off, and he called to the others, 'Bring
him here!'

The outside man and the center man shoved the husband
between the cars. The outside man hit him again as he vol-
untarily knelt to lie face down beside his wife. The blow cut
into his ear. He said, 'Stop,' and reached for his hip.

The outside man had seen movies and TV shows and no
one was going to pull *that* shit. He put the gun to the nape of
the man's neck, tilting the barrel up toward the head, and
squeezed the trigger. Nothing happened . . . or so he thought
because the sound was so small. He'd never fired the ·22
automatic before. He thought it had misfired; bucked a little
and clicked a little but no bullets out the front. So he
squeezed the trigger twice more, and only then saw the *effect*
of those clicks. The man's head had snapped down, *splat*,
against the pavement; he'd stretched out, flattening, sighing,
emptying of movement, of life.

The woman was sobbing now; beginning to get noisy. The
center man said, 'That's it,' and put his gun to the back of
her head, pushing the barrel through the fluffed-out blonde
hair. He took a deep breath, and the outside man said, 'Go
on, Radford,' and the woman said, 'Dear Lord Jesus, don't
punish me for what I've done. Be merciful.'

'Do it, man!'

The center man pulled the trigger. His gun was a ·38 revolver and it made a hell of a lot more noise than the ·22 and bucked in his hand. The woman jumped and made a funny sound, like a hiccup. And stopped. The center man turned from her and reached into her husband's back pocket. He took out a wallet, showing it to the outside man. The outside man said, 'Shee*it*! I thought he had a piece.'

The driver was standing up, looking toward Beekman, the F.D.R., and the river. 'Cool it, Lester!' he said, as if the ·38 hadn't blasted. And as far as Fifty-second Street was concerned it hadn't. The houses slept. But then the driver crouched, looking over and past the car before him. 'Someone's down there.'

The center man said, 'Let's split!'

The outside man had the woman's purse. He wanted to take watches and rings, but he also wanted to see what was going on. 'Where, man?'

'The corner ... coming up on us. One dude, see? And ... shee*it*, another, there, the other side!' He ducked low then, pulling the center man down with him. The outside man stayed erect another second so as to spot the big dude on the left side of the street.

'What we do, Ju-Ju?' the center man asked.

'We wait,' the driver said, wetting his lips. He looked at his friends. Radford, the center man, was checking his piece. Lester, the outside man, was taking a watch off the husband's wrist; then he tugged the wife's right hand from under her body.

The driver looked over the car again. 'They about even, the one on our side a little back but close enough. You two take him and I'll take the big dude the other side and we finish fast together. I say when.'

He ducked down, watching the outside man pull a ring off the wife's finger. The light was dim here and he saw no blood and it was nothing, those two lying there and those two walking toward them. Nothing! They could take this whole honky city!

Ju-Ju, the driver, got up when the big man on the left side of the street was almost abreast of them. Ju-Ju began to run toward him. He heard his friends running too, and a high-pitched shout.

He said, '*You!*' leveling his gun, waiting for the hand to go up or whatever. The big dude ducked and there was a car in the way and Ju-Ju was out in the open and the big dude's voice, big too, called, 'Drop it! Police!' And Lester's ·22 popped three times on the other side of the street.

'The fuck you say!' Ju-Ju turned and heard two loud shots behind him. He cringed, thinking to feel his back torn apart, but he got to the other side, stepping on the woman, and ducked behind the dark sedan. He looked to see his friends bending over a fallen figure and said, still trying to keep his voice down because it would be worse if they had people looking out all the windows, 'Let's split!'

Lights were going on across the street, behind where that big dude was waiting with a gun; a fucking pig, and wasn't *that* luck!

His friends were running, keeping low behind the solid line of parked cars, and he was running with them, back to the only open space on *any* Manhattan street; the place kept open by a fire hydrant; the place where the Firebird waited with lights off and engine running.

Radford, the center man, got in first, lunging over the seats and into the back. Ju-Ju climbed over the stick shift, behind the wheel, and jammed into first as Lester, the outside man, slammed the door. He knew he couldn't U-turn fast enough on the narrow, car-lined street, and what if another car drove *in* as he tried to drive *out* against the arrow? Bad odds, so he floored the gas, scraping the front right fender on a Porsche and burning rubber and ducking and waiting for the pig to open up on them as they went by. When nothing happened, and when they'd hit the little end street called Beekman, and when they'd turned again and got back to Park, and when they were heading uptown, heading home-sweet-home, he finally put on the headlights, laughing explosively. '*Mothah!*'

And his friends laughing. And Radford in back saying, 'That was no pig, Ju-Ju, or he'd have gone for us! He faked you out, man! One gutsy mothah faked us out!'

They parked on 140th, near Eighth, after driving around near St Nicholas Park to make sure they hadn't picked up a tail. But that was just to be real professional, to play Kojak, man, because no way could anyone have followed them!

It was a little after three-thirty when they examined their loot: the contents of two wallets and a woman's change purse; two men's watches and one wild-looking woman's watch with a thick band that looked like solid diamonds; two men's rings, and three from the woman.

They had sixty-four dollars in cash. 'Nothing, man,' Ju-Ju said, but he was content and took his twenty-one and they flipped for the extra dollar and decided they'd cool the watches and rings for a few weeks. Ju-Ju kept the lady's watch and the two men's rings, letting Lester and Radford pick over the rest. When they began to fight about a dy-no-mite ring the woman had been wearing, he said, 'What sorta *turkeys* I got here? We gonna split whatever we get for the stuff, ain't we? We just holding it for each other!'

Lester muttered, 'Right on,' and let Radford have the big ring. They left the Firebird with the keys in the ignition and the doors unlocked so that it would be gone in a few hours.

Ju-Ju, the driver, felt good because they'd gotten away with what now seemed a crazy scene.

Lester, the outside man, felt good because he figured he'd finally proven he wasn't chicken.

Radford, the center man, felt bad even though he'd won the extra dollar. He was the only one who hadn't gotten to drive the Firebird. And he was the one who'd spotted it yesterday afternoon near Riverside Drive, parked with the keys inside while the woman ran into the liquor store.

Maybe it wouldn't be as hot as Ju-Ju thought.

When they split, he doubled back and got the keys and locked the doors. Then he walked the eight blocks to Corinne's and knocked. Her brother Clifton, about nine, opened up for him, rubbing his eyes, and said, 'Can't you visit early, man?' Radford said, 'Watch it, baby,' and showed him the piece. Clifton wanted to handle it and Radford said tomorrow, maybe, if he went to bed in the other room with

16

his two kid sisters, leaving Corinne alone. Clifton said, 'What happened to the bread, man? Don't I get a dollar no more?' Radford gave him his dollar and went to the small back bedroom, more like a closet, and got undressed and slid under the covers with Corinne. She stirred and said something and tried to go back to sleep. He shook her. She yawned. 'My momma's gonna kill you some night.'

'I won't sweat it, long as your poppa stays away.' He put her hand on his hard-on, whispering what he wanted, trying to pull her head down.

She stayed half asleep, grumbling, not into it ... so he told her what they'd done.

That woke her. She looked at him, eyes big. 'You kill them all, Radford?'

'Yeah. Three, I think.'

'Why?'

'What you mean, why? You know slavery? You know South Africa? You know *Roots*? You know *this*?' He gave the Black Power fist.

She smiled and kissed his knuckles. 'I think you're shitting me, Radford.' But her kisses traveled to his shoulder, his chest, and finally where he wanted them. She was a sweet little cocksucker, using her lips and tongue the way he'd taught her, and he had to stop her after a few minutes because he wanted *in*. He got her on her back and she locked her strong legs around him and he dug that hard little ass, that fifteen-year-old pussy, and came fast and slept like a baby.

But he was up early, thinking what they'd done and maybe they'd be caught. He dressed and left before Corinne awoke, and it was raining. He caught hell from his mother, but dodged when she tried the broomstick. He changed clothes in the bathroom, calling, 'Oyeah! Amen! Hallelujah!' when she and his sister Margot gave him the shit about being a no-good and God-turning-away and ending-up-in-prison and worse than that losing his immortal-soul. His fucking soul yet! I mean, man, who had such a rap now'days but old mommas?

He went down to the coffee shop and had hotcakes and

17

milk with ice in it, and then the radio said there'd been a 'massacre' – four people dead, one a police captain.

Radford stopped eating. *Four?* He didn't remember Ju-Ju saying he'd shot at the pig . . . who was *really* a pig and hadn't faked them out. But there'd been two shots from that side of the street and maybe one had been Ju-Ju scoring lucky.

Later, when they got together near the schoolyard, Ju-Ju said it wasn't him. 'No way, man! I never used my piece! What kind of fuckin' shit they tryin' to pull?'

Lester said, 'You sure? I mean, we each got a honky, Radford and me, and I got *two*. So if you're thinkin' . . .'

'Don't tell *me* what I'm thinkin', man! I'm thinkin' you're calling me a liar!'

'Cool it,' Radford said. 'What difference does it make? Three, four, no one knows who did it and no one's gonna know.'

'Yeah, right,' Lester said.

Ju-Ju spat at the schoolyard fence. 'Maybe, you know, *ricochet?*' He spat again, like he did when he was mad. 'When you iced that dude, the last one, maybe the bullet bounced across the street . . .'

Lester started jumping all over the sidewalk, doing his laughing bit. Ju-Ju turned and looked at him, looked hard. Lester bent over, wheeing and whooing, but backed off the real point with: '*Iced*, he say! Like he say it all the time. What's *iced*, man? It's blow away. Like on Kojak – blow away. Or like they used to say, waste.'

'I hear iced,' Ju-Ju said, walking away from them. 'I say iced. Someone make me say different?'

'Iced,' Lester muttered, and stayed back. He wasn't in Ju-Ju's league. Neither was Radford. Ju-Ju was a heavy dude in a fight.

Radford jerked his head at Lester. They caught up with Ju-Ju, staying about half a step behind. Radford said, placating, '*Maybe* ricochet. I mean, what else we got?'

Lester said, 'Don't let's worry about it. We get called in on the three, we don't have to worry about the four.' He paused. 'We all together on this, right?'

18

Ju-Ju nodded, and slowed so that they were walking with him.

Which was cool. Which got them together.

Radford said, 'When we going out again?'

'Not too soon,' Lester said. 'Right, Ju-Ju?'

'Wrong,' Ju-Ju said. 'I'm not going out, *period*.'

'You mean *never*?' Radford asked.

'That's what I mean, baby. I don't know about you, but I'm not asking for the slammer. Once was cool, but the odds gonna change next time – I got the *feelin'*? Can you dig it?'

'Yeah, well, if you say,' Radford murmured, thinking it was bullshit, Ju-Ju saying he was blood-related to the old Papa Doc from Haiti and had the voodoo gift and that's why his father always called him Ju-Ju instead of his true name, Albert.

Radford looked at Lester, and Lester was looking at him, and even though they didn't make faces or say anything, Ju-Ju said, 'You two do what you want. You get caught, you talk my name, *then* we'll see what I can do, voodoo or a bullet up the ass.'

'Hey, *man*!' Radford said, and Lester said, 'What you talkin' about, *man*!' and they were all three hot. Until Ju-Ju went into the store and bought an afternoon *Post* and they found out the cop who'd been killed was black. Ju-Ju said, 'I never saw no brother!'

Radford said, 'No *pig*'s a brother.' Lester said, 'Fuck him, Ju-Ju!' Ju-Ju crushed the paper in both hands and threw it into the street. 'Yeah, right.'

It began raining hard, so they decided to catch the show at the Apollo. And it was a good one – black dudes wiping out white racist pushers – but even so, Radford could tell Ju-Ju was down.

TWO

Thursday, July 17, P.M.

His shoulder ached. Touch of sciatica, the doctor said. *Maybe*, Ruthie said in that cynical way of hers. Doctors, she said, were usually full of shit; that's why they needed all that malpractice insurance. Yeah, *maybe*, but his shoulder still hurt. Little pain in the chest too, sometimes, and he worried about heart attacks even if the pain went away when he belched. Because he was fifty-eight in a young man's business and during the past two months his age seemed to have caught up with him. When he said this, Ruthie smiled her young woman's smile; his wife, sure, and concerned, but only twenty-seven and he'd have smiled the same way at twenty-seven.

Helen wouldn't have smiled; she'd been only two years younger than him. But Helen was dead of a massive coronary. Almost three years ago and he'd been lonely and found Ruthie and now his young wife smiled, thinking he was dreaming up illnesses the way young men did. Smiled, because didn't he have an eight-month-old son? Didn't he make love to her two, three times a week and want more but she wasn't always in the mood? Wasn't he her 'bull', a big man, not so tall but big in the shoulders, the chest, the head and hands? (He'd also been big in the belly, but she'd made him get rid of that with diet and exercise.)

Anyway, a kind of weariness, a dread of age and death, had caught him, and so he'd taken his vacation the first week in July instead of the scheduled September; had four full weeks coming to him, accrued, and it was great out in Amagansett; walks on the beach with Jen yelling her six-year-old lungs out – 'Daddy look at this!' and Daddy look at that and he loved being called Daddy after thirty-one childless years with Helen. Loved the chunky, dark-eyed little girl, though Jen was Ruthie's, not his by blood. But she was his by *heart* as much as the tiny brown-haired boy bobbing in the papoose pack on Ruthie's back. They had the beach and lobster dinners and more loving than in the city. After five days, when the pains were gone and the weariness and dread disappearing – when it was all beginning to come together – the captain called him at the cottages' office; five A.M. and he said, 'Come back *right now.*'

He'd tried to argue, suggesting Balleau and the new lieutenant and others. But Hawly said Deverney wanted his 'old pro' to head up the special squad. So he packed up his family and drove back to their uptown apartment and then to Manhattan West Homicide, and there'd been briefings and bullshit and calls made to the precincts concerned to clear the way for outsiders to come in. And here he was. And the city seemed dirtier, noisier, uglier, more dangerous than it had six days ago. And his shoulder ached and he pressed his chest and belched softly.

Jones drove the radio car as quickly as anyone could, as skillfully as anyone could, crosstown at three P.M. of a rainy workday. No sense using the siren; it wouldn't have saved more than a few minutes and Roersch didn't want the racket, the headache. Besides, what was the rush? The meat was long gone; witnesses wouldn't appear during those two or three extra minutes.

'I'm not going to like this one,' Jones muttered, driving down Fifty-second past the intersection of Second Avenue. 'Walking into the Third Detective Zone and telling them we're taking over. Especially on a big case. Has it ever been done before?'

He was a tall, lean-muscled, very black man who'd worn his hair defiantly Afro for a while until Deverney, an old-line bigot, had been promoted from captain of Manhattan West to deputy inspector and out of the station. With Hawly moving up to captain and the new lieutenant, John Murray, obviously moderate in his racial views, Jones had been cutting back the hair. He was a detective sergeant, as was Roersch; twenty-five years younger and not inclined to test the longevity pecking order. Besides, Roersch had helped get him the promotion.

'Yes,' Roersch grunted, rubbing that aching right shoulder. 'A few times. The last, far as I remember, was called the Manhattan Homicide Task Force.'

Jones stopped for the traffic signal at First. It was raining lightly. It began raining heavily before the signal changed. Jones edged slowly into the intersection, cursing pedestrians who, in the New York manner, ignored red lights. 'I'd like to get that idiot sucker there for jaywalking!'

'You want a flop to traffic division?' Roersch asked. 'I can have you back in uniform by Monday, the latest.'

'Hey, I know you pissed at having your vacation screwed, but don't take it out on the field hands, massa.'

Roersch saw patrolmen in yellow rain slickers standing around on the sidewalks: one on each side of the street; one between two parked cars, right side of the street. They'd had to hold down the crime-scene positions since about three A.M., despite the medical examiner and Forensic having done their work and carted away the bodies. They'd stood in light rain and heavy rain and Roersch hoped they didn't know they were doing it so a hastily formed special squad, dubbed M-4 for Massacred–Four, could look at the chalk marks that, in this rain, would be crayon marks. Because they'd consider it rinky-dink and bullshit and they were probably right.

Still, Roersch *wanted* to view the actual scene, not just the photographs Forensic had taken. He was an old-fashioned bull. He had his own personal Five Commandments. He worked his own way and it was good enough to have gotten him more collars and more solveds than anyone in any homicide unit in the city ... though it hadn't helped him pass exams and he'd just about given up on making lieutenant. But he was a detective first grade as well as a sergeant, which meant that special assignment to a case this big – certainly if he cracked it – would put him in line for what the Bureau called 'getting the money': the raise to twenty-three thousand dollars a year lieutenant's pay without the actual promotion. As the vacation feeling continued to wear off, getting-the-money grew in importance. After all, he had two kids ...

Jones was pulling toward a parking space on the right.

Roersch buttoned his raincoat, forgetting beaches and sea and relaxation, and said, 'Willis, we know each other too well to hide what's really bugging you. You think you're here because you're black. You're here because you're the best I've got.'

Jones backed into the parking spot. 'The fact the three suspects are black doesn't mean shit, right?'

'We've got other black cops.'

Jones cut the engine. 'I won't kid you, Sergeant. I'd like to be white, or at least Chinese, until they catch those three mothers.'

Roersch said, 'And I won't kid you, Willis. I'd like to be your thirty-three, or at least forty, until they find out how to keep us alive forever. Could we work a trade?'

Jones grinned then and got out of the car. They met on the sidewalk pulling up their collars, adjusting their hats. Thunder rumbled from across the river; from Brooklyn. Rain fell out of steel-gray skies. Jones asked, 'Just what did this Manhattan Homicide Task Force work on?'

'I forget most of it, but their big case was Charlie Chopoff, who cut the cocks off four little black boys, killing three in the process.'

Jones grunted as if he'd been hit. 'Did they get him?'

'They got someone – a Puerto Rican psychotic whose wife gave birth to a black child and helped flip him out completely. He's never been tried; still in a mental institution.'

Jones turned slowly away, taking the sheet of paper from his pocket listing the names and addresses of the few citizens who'd come forward as witnesses. 'Guess that's about all anyone can hope for in this bankrupt shitbox. Chances are we won't do as well. Because even if we pull off a miracle and catch those kids, they could be under sixteen. Then they'll get slapped on the wrist and do maybe a year to eighteen months ... for four murders, including a police captain.'

Roersch knew what he was feeling. Being a police officer in this city caught up with you every so often. Being a homicide cop was the worst. And Jones wasn't just bulling about what happened to juvenile killers in New York.

'Willis, Charlie Chopoff never struck again, so that special squad did their job. We will too.'

Jones nodded, back still turned, water beginning to darken the yoke of his tan raincoat. He crossed the street to where Captain Worth had died, paused to exchange a word with the patrolman, and went on to the entrance of a red brick apartment house.

Roersch walked to the officer standing between two cars. He flashed his gold shield, muttered his ID, and looked down at two white-crayon figures on the blacktop surface. The officer, young and pink-faced, said, 'You the one we've been waiting for, Sergeant?'

Roersch said, 'Guess so,' remembering details of the early report. Louise Sanders had died here. Forty years old give or take a year. Actress, though not very well known. At least not until last TV season. Then she'd landed the part that might have been the break of her career, playing the madcap landlady of a San Francisco rooming house in *Lilac's Daughter*, a situation comedy CBS had renewed for next season.

He looked at the smaller of the body outlines. Louise. Canceled. By New York's insanity.

The larger figure was her husband, Arnold Jaeker. (Sanders was Louise's professional name. She and Jaeker had been married 'some years', the early report stated. Further information was being gathered right now.) The Jaekers had been executed by gunshots in the back of the head; three ·22's for Mr and one ·38 for Mrs.

He took out the sheaf of onionskin paper, flipped to the second page, and looked for addresses. All he found was, '... reside in Los Angeles, California.'

They were visiting New York. No hotels on this street, so they were using the apartment of a friend, or visiting that friend.

He flipped to the last of six pages, where the witnesses were listed. Three. And none was acquainted with the victims.

He asked the patrolman if he knew whether anyone had come forward to explain the Jaekers' presence on East

24

Fifty-second Street. 'Got me,' the pink-cheeked youngster replied. Roersch found his pen and scribbled a notation on the back of the report. Then he said, 'You can call in now. Say M–4 checked out your scene.'

'M–4,' the youth repeated, smiling a little. 'Ten-4.'

Roersch ignored him, returning to the report. As far as the information went, none of the four victims lived on Fifty-second Street ... and no one had come forward to explain their presence here. Strange ...

Well, not so strange, if the *identities* of the victims weren't known to the residents of the street at the time the report was written. By this evening, when people returned from work, when they'd read their papers or seen the TV news, the situation was bound to change. Then there'd be calls to the local precinct, which would be switched to the special squad room at Manhattan West Homicide.

He stepped up on the sidewalk and walked about twenty feet further east, to where a strongly built patrolman stood back against a building and out of the direct drive of rain. Two young girls in smart, mid-length raincoats swung by, looking down at the white-crayon outline. The patrolman followed them with his eyes, sighed, and shifted his weight. Roersch flashed his shield and identified himself, then consulted his carbon of the report. This was where Richard Magris, thirty, had caught three ·22 slugs. One had torn through his throat, and that was the one that had finished him as police and an ambulance attendant had begun lifting him onto a stretcher. He'd lived the twenty-five minutes before the ambulance arrived, and long enough to gurgle what one responding radio car officer took to be, 'Marty, God ...' and the other thought might have been '*My* God,' the 'my' extended and distorted by that torn throat. Roersch asked the patrolman if anyone had come forward to offer information about Magris.

'No, Sergeant. But the responding officers left about five this morning. I relieved someone else at noon. Maybe one of them ...'

Roersch made another notation on the back of the report. He returned the departing patrolman's wave-salute and

25

crossed to the north side of the street, moving back west perhaps five feet at the same time. He stepped onto the sidewalk, nodding at the guard, going through his identification procedure quickly, automatically, looking down at the fourth body outline. A police captain had died here:

Thomas Worth, age forty-nine, soon to be promoted to deputy inspector, according to the P.C., and what came out of the police commissioner's office was gospel. Thomas Worth, one of the few non-Caucasians to reach such exalted rank, whose death was bound to cause a hell of a stink in middle-class black circles. That he'd been cut down by three black kids ... well, the confusion of rationales Roersch left to the Harlem revolutionaries and intellectuals. The criminals wouldn't give a damn.

Not so the police. What mattered to the police was that Worth had *belonged*. What mattered to the Bureau, as the detective division was known, was that Worth had been a bearer of the gold shield. What mattered to the patrolmen in their radio cars and on the beats was that he had been a cop for twenty-six years.

No cop killing was allowed to slip into the inactive files, and no one in charge of a cop killing was allowed to rest his ass as long as the case remained unsolved. The M-4 Squad had been formed to solve four murders ... or so the news media had been told. Actually, it existed to get whoever had killed Captain Worth.

'Scumbags,' the patrolman muttered.

Roersch glanced up to see a really well-worn officer, fifty or more, with a gut, ruddy jowls, and a nose just a touch too veiny-red for anything but the sauce.

'Glad I'm retiring,' the patrolman said. 'Live in Maspeth and now I'll be able to *stay* in Maspeth. Goddam coloreds pissing all over the goddam city ...'

Roersch interrupted, 'Captain Worth was colored, right? The detective who just spoke to you is colored, right? A lot of those you watch on TV and at the ball parks are colored, right?'

The officer stared at him. 'Hey, Sergeant. I'm not talking

26

about *blacks*. I'm talking about *niggers*. You know what I mean.'

'Do I?' Roersch murmured, sick of the subject. Soon it would be all whites against all blacks, and what the hell would happen then?

He drew out the report, trying to laugh at himself. It would never come to that.

Black crime was the villain. It was real, and it created enormous fear, and from that fear came enormous hatred. And he had to solve *this* black crime and get the money and may be consider Ruthie's plea that they leave the city 'for the children's sake'.

'And what happens if you collar them?' the patrolman was saying. 'Even if they're *not* juveniles, we get the lawyers and the tricks and the hung juries and the mistrials and the plea-copping and the appeals and they're back on the street in two-to-five and those four people are still dead.'

'You can't think of that,' Roersch snapped. 'You think of the courts, you won't be able to do your job.'

Ignoring the courts was the first of his personal Five Commandments. You did your work, made your collar, and in police terms had your solved. The other Commandments were:

Never believe anything about a case no matter who says it's so until you check it out for yourself. This includes material given you by full chiefs, the P.C., and J. Edgar's ghost.

Forget fingerprints, forensic medicine, and Columbo's instinctive ability to find vital clues. In fact, forget vital clues. Concentrate on *people* – everyone who might have anything to do with a case.

Keep your informants confidential. Treat them with care and respect. Otherwise you won't have any.

Avoid working on Mafia, organization, or racketeer killings. They rarely get solved; and who cares anyway?

These rules had helped him survive thirty-five years on the force, including more time than any city detective on

Homicide, four shootouts, three commendations, twelve major solveds and three times as many strong assists. Which along with a buck fifty could buy him a hot dog and a beer in today's New York.

Checking the report, he saw that Captain Worth was the only one of the victims who hadn't been robbed. He'd died with gun in hand, hit twice by ·38 caliber bullets, probably from the same gun that had killed Louise Sanders Jaeker. One bullet had passed through the heart, the other through the top of the head and into the mouth, where it had been recovered. The heart shot had obviously been first, since the head shot would have had to have been fired from straight above if Worth were standing. Either shot alone would have been enough to kill him instantly, and Roersch marveled at the marksmanship of the kid who had used that ·38. Especially on a black morning street. Especially rushed, coming across to rob and being confronted by a gun.

He was reading the witnesses' statements. Three kids had been seen by three witnesses – at *least* three witnesses, since others would hold back because of not wanting to be involved; hold back until he dragged them forward, or they came forward themselves. Looking around at all the windows, the hundreds of windows, he felt that there would be at *least* three more. And since the first three agreed on the basics of the case, chances were so would the others. Three blacks – called 'youngsters' by the woman, called 'youths' by one man and 'kids' by another – three black men, young, on a robbing and killing spree.

He asked the patrolman if anyone had come forward to offer anything about Captain Worth, and the man surprised him. 'Yeah, woman named Gleason.' He was opening a notebook. 'Good old Irish lady. Said she saw the captain get it. Pitched forward on his face at the first shot, she said, then jumped a little on the second.'

Roersch took her address, which was of the apartment house directly behind the crayon figure, where one of the three original witnesses, a James Lowery, also lived. He looked down at the outline again. Worth had come to final rest parallel to a parked car. Well, not *exactly* parallel. His

28

body had been slanted slightly toward the building side instead of the gutter side. His head – he had fallen face down – had been angled toward the building, and while Roersch knew that gunshot victims jerked in any and all directions and no sense was to be made from such information, he couldn't help but follow the direction that head seemed to indicate. There was a basement entrance a few feet further north; he walked there; a closed iron gate led to three down steps.

He tried the gate. It opened, and he went down the steps. There was a shadowy passageway with a door off to the right; then, further along, another door on the left; then, at the far end, probably at a yard or an air shaft, a rectangle of daylight.

He came back to the crayon outline. Worth hadn't been robbed because he'd been the last killed and lights had gone on in windows and the kids had known their time was running out and they'd split. They'd missed a prize; Worth had been carrying almost two hundred dollars in his wallet.

'What the hell was he doing here?' Roersch muttered. 'He lived in Westchester.' He looked at the cop. 'They find his car?'

'Not that I know. They were checking plates all up and down the street but he could have been in a garage on First or maybe on another street or used a cab, who knows? Detectives from the Third are still working around, I think. What's this with Manhattan West coming in ... M–4, I mean? That's not kosher. The Third was steamed. You shooflying them?'

Shooflies were police internal security; cops who policed other cops. 'No way. Just a central information unit to put this case together. The P.C. wanted it, so he got it. Let your friends at the precinct know, will you? We have a tough enough job without being called finks.'

'Yeah, can I call in now?'

Roersch nodded and put the report back in his pocket to prevent it from turning into a sodden mass. He looked at the crayon lines and felt water trickling down his neck. He also felt exhaustion creeping up on him. He'd been packing and

29

driving and working since five A.M., and his day was far from over.

He took off his hat, shook it briskly, and replaced it on his head. And bent over that body outline, glaring at it. He was bugged, bothered; something wrong here; something about the way the captain had died on this street. Something . . .

Other witnesses would explain Worth's presence here, would clarify his death, would add a few little details to make it feel right. And that would be the end of vague doubts. Or so he fervently hoped. He didn't want this case complicated in any way. Simple as it was, it was still going to be a bitch – to find those three kids, make the collar, get the solved. They could've come from Harlem. From Brooklyn's Bedford Stuyvesant. From anywhere upstate or Jersey or who the hell knew what black street in what black neighborhood in what borough, city, or state.

But he'd play the odds; he'd work Manhattan first. Had to get things organized. Put in a call to Joe Hooker at Fort Apache, the South Bronx's 41st precinct, which caught the worst robbery, mayhem, and murder squeals in all New York. Ask his advice. Call Jimmy Weir for an old-time talk-over. Call on Hawly's vast knowledge of police filing systems. Those three had to have records *somewhere*.

But first he needed decent descriptions. *Not*, as the woman witness had said, 'One was tall and skinny and another was broader and another, well, he was tall too.' And their car. So far he had three different colors – black, green, and red – from three different witnesses. But that was S.O.P. on a dark street; colors just didn't show. Two of the witnesses, the men, had said the car that had sped away had looked like a Camaro or a Firebird. *Both* had said it: Camaro or Firebird. The woman had said it was a two-door and looked bright red when it passed under the street light. She'd been firmer about the color than the men. He wondered if the new witness, Mrs Gleason, would corroborate any of this.

He also had to locate relatives, friends, business acquaintances of the three victims who'd been robbed to give him some idea of the items taken. He needed leads: jewelry to trace. A car to find. Three individuals, not faceless black kids, to hunt. He needed a case, dammit, *a case*!

Jones was saying, 'You okay, Eddy?'

He turned and glared and took hold and said, 'I also need patience, Willis.'

'Oh, *yeah*,' Kingfish replied. ' 'Cause what we got here, Andy, is one *scared* white neighbourhood. Even Opalescent Rose, stripped naked, couldn't get her black ass into Mr Lowery's apartment, dirty old man though he 'peared to be.'

'He refused to be interviewed?'

'No,' Jones said, himself again. 'Just kept the chain on the door and me in the hall. You'd better get Ross or Luria for this part of the job.'

'C'mon,' Roersch said, upset. 'I've got a new witness in that same house. And some questions for Mr Lowery.'

Jones hung back. 'Mind if I have a smoke in the car, Eddy? It don't take two for *this* tango.'

Roersch said, 'I mind, Willis,' and led the way into the lobby, where a doorman, well along in years and well back near the elevators gave them Mrs Gleason's apartment number.

Roersch thanked him and asked who'd been the doorman last night.

'No doorman. I'm on seven A.M. to four P.M.; Meyer's on four to twelve. Management couldn't get a midnight-to-seven man for what they pay . . . the risks of coming to work so late. Can't use the subway – that's just askin' for it – and you wouldn't believe what we get walking the streets . . .' He glanced at Jones. 'Well, some of the other houses give their late man an apartment, like the super, so's to be covered. But the smallest apartment here rents for five hundred, and that plus salary . . .'

The elevator arrived. Roersch and Jones stepped inside. Roersch pressed the button for five and Mrs Gleason. Jones hummed softly. Roersch recognized *Dixie* and smiled.

THREE

The Victims

He'd been married to Louise for a few months short of ten years, and back in Los Angeles it was thought to be as solid a marriage as could be, a real love match. Fine. Right. Love had been an important part of it. Love was *still* an important part of it . . . but not the kind of love that would set well with CBS, or with Louise's growing number of fans. It was more the *National Enquirer*'s thing, and if they ever found out they would crucify her.

Not that they actually had to *find out* anything, since they made up most of what went into their filthy rag. They simply had to have it *suggested* to them.

So Arnold and Louise Jaeker were extremely careful swingers, and even so her new eminence had made it terribly dangerous to deal with any but people who had as much to lose as they did. Imagine what would happen if it got out that 'Louise Sanders, the perky Mrs Lilac of *Lilac's Daughter* and at least part of the reason for its top-ten listing,' as *Variety* had put it – imagine what would happen if it became known that she needed threesomes and foursomes and vibrators and two-way broads, needed very young men and kinkier and kinkier sex to get off on?

At fifty-one, Arnold had had his share of wild stuff. But never anything like this. And he was beginning to like it, if not to need it, as much as she did. He could always satisfy the extra cravings – the hungers that came with the years – by using his position as senior partner in Jaeker–Morgan Agency to arrange a matinee with a sweet young thing. But Louise herself, eight years younger than he, satisfied his sexual needs most of the time. And blew his mind in the 'gigs' in which those young men and women did everything imaginable to her with their bodies, with vaginal and rectal inserts and vibrators.

He was right there in bed with them, an important element, as Louise looked to him for reaction, for shame and pain and jealousy ... and growing passion. And always, Arnold Jaeker finished by making wild love to his wife; her payment to him for having to watch his beloved ravished in so many ways.

They were flying to New York, ostensibly to meet with television bigwigs about Louise's future. But what they had really come East for was not the television bullshit, but for the special action today and tomorrow. They were set for two consecutive gigs in Marilyn's apartment. They hadn't had a gig in six weeks, and Louise was irritable and headachy.

They arrived at Kennedy at two-twenty Wednesday, July 16, and went by cab to the Prince George, which they favored for its out-of-the-way downtown location, and because it was not an in place with the theatrical crowd. Louise waited near the doors as Arnold signed the register Mr and Mrs A. Jaeker.

She was trembling by the time they reached their suite and he got on the phone to call Marilyn. Marilyn didn't answer, and Louise decided to take a hot tub to ease the tension. When Arnold entered the bathroom to unpack his toiletries, she was just stepping into the water. 'Sonofabitch!' she shouted. 'Can't I even have fucking *bathroom* privacy? Must you always be walking in while I'm bathing or pissing ...'

He retreated quickly, closing the door on her shrill, raging voice; then felt sudden anger of his own. He was a mild man. His first marriage had been to a mild, unassuming woman, and they had rarely raised their voices to each other. And they had never – not even when he'd left Verna for Louise – indulged in obscenities. Because Verna was a lady; well-bred, well-educated, well-balanced.

He opened his attaché case and took out the pint flask. He filled the tumbler-cap with Scotch and tossed it off; then filled it again and sat down on the striped couch. He sipped and grew calmer. Well, the mild, unassuming, well-bred, well-educated, well-balanced woman had bored the hell out of him. No getting away from it, they'd had thirteen years of

33

yawn. No one could say that about his life with Louise. She was a tough, willful woman, yes, but a talented woman as well. An *exciting* woman . . .

He thought of her bending over as she'd stepped into the tub, her breasts still firm without silicone or insets or anything foreign to their own full, round nature; her bottom long and lean, but still jutting saucily, touched with hollows in each cheek; her belly a little softer than it used to be, a little bigger than it used to be. But most of all he thought of her face (before it had suffused with rage), the tongue held between small, capped teeth as her foot touched hot water. That piquant, big-eyed, bow-lipped face. That face that had gripped him eleven years ago when they'd been introduced in the Universal Studios commissary, he squiring a client who'd just landed his own series, she newly separated from her moneyed second husband and trying, via an aging producer and would-be lover, to work her way back into the industry. At two the next morning, he'd eased out of her arms, dialed his home and whispered that he was 'stuck with Wallace Klempert and you know how he is when he gets bluesy and boozy . . .'

A year later, to the month, he'd married Louise.

He still loved her. He wanted her almost as much as he had that first night. He wanted her right now, with or without the gig.

He finished his Scotch and tried not to think the question that had been bothering him lately:

Did Louise want him? Did she care anymore?

She was available to him once or twice a week, but more passive in the act than he preferred. Only when they finished up a gig did the old explosiveness, the biting, clawing, sweating female he'd adored, return to him. Only after every imaginable obscenity had been imposed upon her body . . .

Which was one reason he'd been looking forward to tonight's gig as much as any of the three more active participants. They were all show-biz, and all very much in the public eye.

There was Marilyn Maigret, a regular on one of the top daytime serials, in which she played a self-pitying wife losing out to a woman doctor treating her alcoholic but salvageable husband. She'd been losing out almost a year now in the snail's-pace development of soap-opera plots. And since the self-pitying wife was becoming involved with a syndicate gambler, Marilyn's life on the show was assured for another year or two.

Morgan Breen was one of the better-looking, better-spoken young newscasters on local television. He was engaged to a network VP's daughter, and expected to make the jump to national prime time. His future looked as rosy as his clear, innocent cheeks.

Marilyn was a voracious dyke. In Los Angeles for a screen test, she'd attended a party at the Jaekers' penthouse apartment and followed Louise into the bathroom. It was Marilyn who had introduced Arnold and Louise to 'my close friend and a fellow closet swinger, Morgan Breen'.

Morgan was a frenetic cocksman with an outsized organ and the need to use it in more ways than the VP's daughter had ever dreamed of; or would, he had judged, tolerate. He was a voyeur, a mild sadist, a milder masochist, an extremely cautious pederast, with his strongest passion reserved for lying in bathtub while women urinated on his head and face.

Arnold had paid Marilyn's and Morgan's fares for weekends in L.A. several times over the past two years. They always parted amiably. They used and satisfied each other completely. All were equally concerned for their good names. So it was the perfect gig.

Louise came out of the bathroom. She apologized for her nerves and asked him to call Marilyn again. He did, and there was still no answer. Louise muttered, 'Shit!' and then, 'I might as well have my hair done . . .'

He made that call for her too, then went with her to Saks' beauty salon and sat in the waiting room, enjoying a cigarette. After a while, he rose and went to the counter and asked the beautifully coiffed but dumpy girl if Mrs Jaeker would be much longer. The girl said she could go inside and find out. He said, 'No, don't bother,' and returned to his chair.

He thought of Morgan with his ten-inch cock and the way he shoved it into Louise's mouth, sadistically, sitting above her, choking her, making her swallow his semen . . .

He lighted a second cigarette. And shook his head. Because he was turning on.

Thomas Worth no longer commanded a station house, and come fall they'd be kicking him closer to the exit with that deputy inspector promotion. Because after he made deputy inspector they'd get him to retire, probably on November second, his fiftieth birthday.

No one had told him this. No one had to. He'd been a cop since turning twenty-three, and that was a lot of years in which to develop instincts. A lot of years to develop quite a bank account, too . . . and several well-filled safety-deposit boxes.

He'd escaped the Knapp Commission even though all sorts of lower-echelon cops, already nailed for being on the pad, had come at him with deals in order to save their own hides by finking. A deal for protecting gambling operations on a one-for-six basis (he'd get a dollar for each six the gamblers took in – too good an offer to be real). Deals for shaking down certain after-hours clubs (which were already on his pad, and had shown him he was on the spot). Deals by overly anxious officers from other districts: he'd drunk one under the table and taken him to the bar's toilet and opened his shirt and found him wired like the inside of a television set.

Old Tom Worth had known he was in trouble, and had become a very good little captain until after the trapped takers, like Bill Phillips, and the inexplicable 'angels', like Serpico, had finished their testimony. And then, with a good third of his precinct working cheerfully and profitably along with him he'd gone back to making the gamblers and pimps and pushers and strong-arm men pay heavily for continuing the operations no one had figured out how to stop.

Four months ago things had changed again and he'd been transferred from his precinct into 'A senior executive position' at Headquarters – behind a desk and away from the action – and told to 'formulate a report on crime, violent and otherwise, according to precincts in Manhattan, the Bronx, Brooklyn, and Queens'. *What, no Staten Island?* he'd thought sourly.

When he'd asked *why* such a report, he'd been told that the P.C. might need it for an upcoming conference in Washington. *Might.*

An insult to his intelligence. They'd just wanted him jerking off until they could retire him as a deputy inspector, 'a credit to his race', as some shmuck or other would say at the farewell party.

This fucking country with its white racist shit! All the honkies roasting all summer at the beaches and winters in Florida; roasting themselves black as they could! What the fuck sense could you make out of a country like that? A country that called you black even if you were three-quarters white, as he was; even if you were *nine-tenths* white.

Made *no* sense ... even if it was good old black-is-black-is-beautiful pride that was responsible for keeping the shit alive and healthy nowadays; for making it grow even worse.

And who screamed that pride the loudest? People who had less reason to be proud than anyone he could think of – the loudmouthed radical, revolutionary, criminal trash out or Harlem and Bedford Stuyvesant.

But since there was no way to solve such things, he'd said the hell with it and gotten as far away as possible. Which was why he was here, on the train pulling out of Tarrytown, heading for Grand Central. Of course, he liked it better when he was going *from* Grand Central *home*, but either way it was a sweet ride, little more than half an hour, and no graffiti and obscenities and VIVA PUERTO RICO LIBRE and all the other tripe they spray-painted onto the subways. A clean train, the passengers almost all white, but the few blacks were *right*: well-dressed even if some were a little hip with denim suits and such crap; cool and clean and moneyed and scoring more points for their race than all the loud-mouthed Commies and Islams, and if he could only take Cassius Clay – yeah, *Ali!* – and shove a nightstick into his big mouth, he would! Because Ali was like the rest of them,

37

babbling away about some stupid black cure all. Jesus Christ, the goddam Negro race was full of fucking clowns! The whites might be bastards, might have started the goddam trouble, might end the world someday with their fucking bombs and whatnot, but they didn't have nearly the percentage of *clowns*!

He looked out the window. He looked at the green; the beautiful summer green; the manicured country. The train *clack-clacked* and the sound was good, because that *clack-clack* said that Clarise and the three boys and his doll Rita, his baby, his eight-year-old honey-colored beauty, were out of the city and the city school system with its shakedowns and beatups and constant threats of violence. *Clack-clack* said Tarrytown was the best of Westchester and Westchester the best of all New York State. Tarrytown was expensive houses in what was called 'an executive residential area' and goddam if it wasn't just that.

He lived on a lovely road with four other families, none of them black, not a black for at least five miles, and that one the director of his own brokerage firm. Old Tom was in his hundred-thousand-dollar house not because someone had put pressure on a neighborhood to open to blacks, but because he'd had the money and he'd had the personality and he had calmly purchased a house from a real-estate agency and a property owner neither of whom had ever before considered selling to a Negro. He had busted his own block, and not because he'd overpaid (he hadn't), but because he was who he was.

And who he was was due to the pad, what he took from the scum, mostly white, who lived off misery and human vice. Who he was he was proud of, and fuck the Knapp Commission. Maybe a third of the force had been on the pad, and more trying to get there. And if it had dipped below that, maybe real low, that was because they were scared.

Old Tom wasn't scared. He was cautious, but no one would get him because he could bring down half of Headquarters if he took a flop.

He would stay on in Tarrytown after retirement ...

though he wanted to score about another hundred thousand. Because it took more than education to assure the safety, the future, of his four children; not to say of his wife and himself. No little retirement cottage for them! No fucking middle-class shit for Tom Worth! He had close to three hundred thousand tucked away, tax free. He would draw on it to supplement his pension after November second. But ... was it really enough? He had aimed at half a million by retirement. He wanted the very best for all of them, *forever*. He had a knowledge of poverty, black poverty, and a fear of such poverty still haunted his dreams.

He turned from the window. He looked at the other passengers: people who ran corporations, invented systems for IBM, published magazines and books, produced television and Broadway shows, held seats on the Stock Exchange, pulled the strings that made this country jump. He was probably more respected, more listened to, than most of these American kings. Why? Because he was a captain of police, and this was a country whose asshole was *tight* with fear of violence. And cops were the only ones standing between the country, the money, the good things, and the tons of shit trying to drown it. Cops, dammit ... cops were the *best!*

And cops were entitled to what cops could get.

That was what Knapp and the others didn't understand. The pad wasn't taking from anyone but the enemy. And if the cops didn't take it, *no one* would, and the crooks would be stronger and richer and nothing would be any better, it would be *worse*.

He had no shame.

He had no sense of wrongdoing.

He had only an irritation with having been stopped before he'd accomplished his goal, finished building his pile.

In the past two weeks, however, his irritation had hit a low ebb; was in fact just about gone. Because that make-work report, that phony pile of used toilet paper, had revealed a vein of pure gold. Angie Tortemango of the Jersey Tortemango *familia*, favorite nephew and heir apparent of

39

Pasquale 'Paddy' Tortemango, a *don* of the first water – well, little Angie had gotten himself caught in a funny situation: screwing a broad in a local motel. Not exactly against the law, but it sure as hell could get him killed.

Old Tom had pointed this out to Angie the first time he'd visited the worried nephew's bachelor pad on East Fifty-second two months ago. He'd allowed Angie time for thought, and then set up a meet at Brooks Brothers, his favorite clothing store, where he combined shopping for a new suit with casual conversation ... about a casual one hundred thousand dollars. The money was to assure that Tom would eliminate that interesting section of the report so that no one else would be able to draw the conclusions he had drawn. He might be able to track down the original statements and destroy them – for an extra twenty-five thousand.

Tonight he was visiting Angie's place for the second time; payoff time. Angie had raised a down payment of twenty thousand. The next payment would be fifty, then fifty-five, for a grand total of one twenty-five ... because Angie wanted to go for the original records. Old Tom wasn't worried about locating them: they'd been turned over to him for his report.

He was seeing Angie at two A.M. He'd give Angie some comfort, some sweet talk, to take the edge off the shake-down: promises of services to be rendered in regards to his floating crap games and his work for Uncle Paddy selling dope and shylocking. Always leave them calm and satisfied was Captain Tom Worth's motto, especially when it didn't cost him a dime. And how could Angie know he wouldn't *be* a captain after November? But if Angie made bad sounds, angry noises, he'd told about the Xerox copies in the bank vault inside the sealed envelope marked TO BE OPENED IN THE EVENT OF MY DEATH, and the envelope inside *that*, stamped and addressed to Pasquale Tortemango. Angie would pray for old Tom's health night and day, because something else he couldn't know was that Tom never kept any evidence connecting him to payoffs. The *threat* of such evidence was enough.

Evidence. It hardly qualified as such. Yet it was worth about a thousand dollars a word.

The material for Tom's make-work report was concerned with all crime in the four major boroughs during a twelve-month period ending April fifteenth. It included family mayhem in the South Bronx, murder in Harlem, gang warfare in Bedford Stuyvesant, stickups in Kew Gardens; crimes leading to death, serious injury, and long stretches up the river. It also included raids on policy parlors, bookie joints, pushers' hangouts, and hookers' havens by those most tempted of cops, the gambling, narcotics, and vice squads who dealt with crimes that generally led to heavy bread for the boys in blue.

The charge against Angie was in the Manhattan folder – 'Possession of marijuana' – and was based on very weak evidence, a roach found in a motel room occupied by Angie and his 'ex-wife'. That phrase, 'ex-wife', in the arresting officers' report of interrogation of suspect had caught Tom Worth's eye right after the name 'Angie Tortemango'. First, how many Angie Tortemangos could there be? And second, *the* Angie Tortemango had never, to Tom's considerable knowledge, been married.

Okay. Maybe Tom didn't know everything. And so what if Angie had taken a broad to bed? A million guys had registered as Mr and Mrs with a million broads at motels all over the country during that twelve-month period, and how many were actually married?

But why had Angie found it necessary to explain to the arresting officers that the woman in bed with him, the woman registered as his 'Mrs', was his *ex*-wife? Because the broad's name was actually Tortemango. And the cops who had walked in on them had checked IDs and had found that Angie and his 'wife' had different addresses in different states. And, as one cop's report stated, 'Mr Tortemango was shaken, upset, hinted at bribery, and so a closer check of the premises was made and the remains of a hand-rolled marijuana cigarette found in a wastebasket. Mr and Mrs Tortemango both claimed the "roach" must have been there when they checked in as they didn't use drugs.'

41

How come cops in Angie's room?

He'd picked the wrong place on the wrong afternoon, though it later developed he'd been living dangerously for three months, meeting Maria Tortemango twice a week at that same X-rated West Side motel. The cops, eighteen inside and six backup, had raided the Don Juan on complaint of two citizens' groups. The charges were: using the premises for purposes of prostitution, for a shooting gallery (selling and using narcotics), for the showing of illegal and indecent films offending the public morals (closed-circuit TV pornography).

Watching a film, 'in a waterbed, nude, at the time we entered with passkeys secured from the office', were Angie and Maria Tortemango. The roach was found, their IDs were rechecked, the differences in home addresses noted, and questions asked. 'The woman, Maria Tortemango, became emotional and sick,' according to the report, 'and was allowed to leave. Mr Tortemango was taken into custody.' Which meant that Angie had probably said that if anyone was to blame it was him.

Okay. Small deal anyway, and the cops had probably known the charge wouldn't stick. But it fattened the report for the two citizens' groups, who got little enough satisfaction, since the Don Juan was open for business, with new porno cassettes, that very night.

At the precinct, Angie had been booked and 'released in his own recognizance'. He'd waited a few tense days before realizing that there wasn't enough evidence to be sent to the D.A.'s office ... especially since no one had recognized him. It wasn't the kind of action for which you expected to bust one of *the* Tortemangos ...

Reading all this minor tripe, old Tom remembered a Tortemango wedding that wasn't Angie's, and went to lunch and used a phone booth to call a buddy at the *Daily News*. When he hung up, he was smiling broadly.

Pasquale 'Paddy' Tortemango, fifty-seven, widower, had married Maria McCarthy, twenty-six, ex-model in Fort Lee, New Jersey, last summer. Angie had been best man, and had proven it later by fucking his new aunt. That explained Maria's being 'emotional and sick' at the motel bust. She and Angie would get a lot sicker if Paddy found out.

The train went *clack-clack*. Captain Thomas Worth began counting *clacks*. It would take a hell of a long time to count twenty thousand, but if each clack represented a hundred, then he'd only have to count two hundred. As he would tonight, when Angie handed over the sheafs of hundred-dollar bills.

He lit a cigar. He turned to his *Times* and snapped it open and folded it lengthwise in the special way that *Times* readers used. And saw the shadow and looked up as the young man walked by; walked to the end of the car and out of the smoker. Walked like a cop.

Tom hoped he *was* a cop and could afford Tarrytown and a short commute. But the train started its run further north and young cops willing to spend three hours a day in commuting lived above the switching yards of Harmon, in Ossining and Peekskill and other lunch-pail communities. And the opportunities for making extra money were shrinking and the young cops lived poor and the city was even poorer and the force had been cut to the bone and he worried because it was the thin blue line and let that line get *too* thin and the jungle would take over and the city would run red . . .

He closed his eyes. He didn't want to think about it.

It scared the shit out of him.

Richard Magris loved his work. He was associate editor of three Kromer Publications – a confession, a fact-detective, and a movie-TV magazine. He made what he considered good money, and added to it with articles he freelanced to his own company. Dick had been married eight years, had three children, and now, finally, in his thirtieth year, had experienced true sexual satisfaction combined with true friendship . . . which was true love, wasn't it?'

Well, close enough. Enough to fill him with song and poetry and burning desire.

There were problems; plenty of them. His wife Kathy, for one. He cared for her in his own way, though not in the way she cared for him. Still, she was a great girl and he wouldn't intentionally hurt her for the world. But he *was* hurting her with his coolness in bed; his inability to continue the act that had passed for sexual love.

There were the children, ages six, four, and three; two boys and a girl, and so much a part of him that he couldn't *conceive* of total separation.

There were his parents, still living on Eastern Parkway, even though the Brooklyn area was growing poorer, more racially tense, more unpleasant to visit. He'd planned to move them out to Queens, close to the Kissena Boulevard condominium in which he and his family lived. But what could he do now?

His wife, his children, his parents: he feared losing them. And he might. Even his loving, gentle father might turn from him.

Dick Magris was an ethical man and wanted to stop sneaking matinees and evenings, wanted to stop lying and come out into the open . . . but God, he was afraid!

Because his love was named Marty and it wasn't any cutesy girl's name; Marty was Martin Anders, twenty-three, the most beautiful creature Dick had ever known. Also the most important: Marty had shoved Dick headlong into homosexuality. Because of him, Dick had gone gay within the span of one long evening; or, more accurately, given in to his latent homosexuality (Christ, how often had he seen and used that cliché phrase!).

He was gay now. Definitely. But still locked tightly into his closet – at the office, at home, with his old friends, and with his parents. Still playing macho male and slowly twisting in the agony of his indecision. Listening to Marty and Marty's friends describe their liberations, knowing his own time had to come, yet going on as before, eight months after that first release. Going on because he was a good father (yes, there were other fathers), a good son (they were *all* sons), a terrible coward when it came to giving up the approval of the world at large for the world of love.

44

Marty was growing irritable. Marty wanted to be with him. Marty wanted a home, a stable relationship. Marty was fearful of the series of quick affairs that characterized too many homosexual lives. And Marty was beginning to see other men.

He and Marty were the same: ethical, stable, career-minded people. They'd met at an editors' convention in Philadelphia, though they worked in Manhattan just a few streets apart. Marty was a junior fiction editor at a soft-cover house, and they'd been placed at the same table for the opening-day luncheon.

It had happened rather quickly after that, helped along by several drinks in the hotel bar. It had happened because Marty at twenty-three had far sharper instincts than Dick at thirty. It had happened because the boy had removed his clothing as soon as they'd entered his room and asked if he wasn't beautiful. And he was.

Marty had come to him and knelt and allowed him no time for retreat. He had taken the shocked, stunned, almost catatonic husband-father-son to bed and undressed him and slowly, lovingly, begun to free him. By morning, an exhausted, completely satisfied Richard Magris had begun to do things in return. His head had been light, spinning; he had never known real sexual pleasure before this night. *Never*, in thirty years!

Still, he was one of the lucky ones. He had broken through early enough to salvage his life ... *if* he had the guts.

He sat on the rocking, roaring subway train, speeding from Queens to Manhattan, from Kissena Boulevard to Fifth Avenue, from lies to truth. Tonight he would be with Marty. Tonight was another of 'those goddam endless revision sessions', and Kathy wanted to believe him and didn't believe him even though he had help in his cover story from his editor, Paul Mahon, who was having an affair with a secretary and thought Dick was doing the same. He covered for Paul and Paul covered for him and Kathy no longer believed him. But Dick couldn't help it. Couldn't help wanting his lover's long-muscled body, a swimmer's body, and his bulging buttocks, and his rigid, uptilting, pink-red penis . . .

He realized the train was stopped at his station and leaped up and pushed through the crowd and out the doors. And bumped into a heavyset middle-aged man trying to enter. The man said, 'Goddam faggot prick!'

He turned swiftly and as the man passed him punched the back of his neck. And would have followed him inside the car and continued punching if the doors hadn't closed. The man was sagging forward against a pole. The man turned as the train began moving and stared out the window in shock. Richard walked alongside the train, looking right at the man, raging. He'd been called *faggot*. It was beginning to show.

Then he was in control again, realizing it was a common enough insult.

He walked the three blocks to his office, glancing up at a sky mostly blue but with a few grayish clouds that supported the forecast of rain later tonight. He passed shop windows and examined himself in them: five-ten, lean but not thin, wavy brown hair receding slightly in front, sharp-featured face he considered far from good-looking, conservative enough blue blazer and gray slacks – though cut well, snug and lean fitted. And he walked briskly . . .

His walk. Could it be his imagination, or had it changed? Eight months now since he'd met Marty. Eight months of his new sexuality.

*Wa*s it beginning to show?

FOUR

The two black men were brought into the basement head-quarters of M–4 handcuffed but still kicking and screaming. They were big men and it took all three uniformed officers to handle them. One, Sergeant Colburn, kept shouting above the obscenities, the motherfuckingpigbastards, 'Don't club 'em! For Christ's sake keep 'em conscious for Sergeant Roersch!'

It was eight-thirty in the morning and Roersch sat at one of the desks jammed into the small, windowless, yet over-lighted room. No fewer than four large overhead fixtures, one for each desk, had been installed according to Captain Hawly's 'make sure they get enough light' directive. Roersch was shielding his eyes as he read the Fives – forms D.D.–5 – the reports that had been pouring in under pres-sure from the P.C., the mayor, and a *promise* made by the governor at a news conference that 'this heinous crime will be solved and solved *quickly*!' Forensic had worked through the night. A unit from the Third Detective Division, under orders to send their reports on to Roersch, had worked equally long and hard. Jones, along with detectives third grade Lauria and Ross, had been relieved of all Manhattan West Homicide duties and would be reporting at nine ... which was when Roersch should also have reported. But despite working until almost midnight to clear channels, to organize this damned M–4, to contact friends in various pre-cincts, to clear funds for informers, to write and arrange for later mimeographing and distribution an appeal to every resident of East Fifty-second Street, to try and comfort a disgruntled wife, and most of all to get his own exhausted brain functioning properly, Roersch had been unable to sleep more than four hours.

He'd made a predawn breakfast for himself as Ruthie,

Jen, and eight-month-old Mark slept on, and when seven-thirty had finally crept around he'd watched the morning news, the sound turned low, but not low enough to miss the heavy comments made about the Massacred Four. Then he'd driven downtown and west to the old station house on Ninth Avenue and signed in. Hank Colburn, the desk sergeant, had said, 'You'll get 'em, Eddy! For the money, baby!'

He'd gone to the stairs at the back of the squad room and down to the holding pens, the four cells that smelled of sweat and pain and fear. Homicide suspects were held there pending arraignment; a maximum of four to a cell, sixteen prisoners in all, and that constituted a hell of a crowd in that small an area. They'd been full as he'd glanced to his right, nodding at the patrolman sitting on a tilted-back chair.

Roersch had turned left, down the hall away from the cells, and reached the open door to what had been a storeroom. He'd thrown a light switch, squinted in the sudden harsh glare, muttered, 'Be*yoot*iful,' and gone to the first of four desks arranged in a rough square, each desk facing the door. Because that was the one that held his nameplate from upstairs; the one already piled high with paper.

And there he was sitting, shielding his eyes, trying to organize the multiplicity of reports by subject before reading them, when the door burst open and men and voices filled the room.

He stood up. The uniformed sergeant yelled, 'Hold 'em, dammit!' The patrolmen struggled to hold the two blacks, who threatened to break free despite their wrists being cuffed behind them. 'A few good whacks with the baton,' one cop said, reaching down.

Roersch said, 'Easy,' and came around the desk. He went to the nearest of the prisoners and grabbed his face with his big right hand, digging his thumb into the tender flesh beneath the chin. The man looked into his eyes and grew still.

Roersch said, 'What happened to make you so crazy?'

The other prisoner shouted, 'They call us nigger bastards!' His face was long, very dark, twisted with something too deep to be called anger. *Madness* was closer. 'Fuckin'

48

niger bastards and our mothers whores and our fathers cocksuckers and they spit in our faces and say now we get it! They spit right in the car takin' us in. They grab my main man here by the nuts . . .'

The prisoner Roersch was holding was lighter, a little smaller, and the same madness filled his face, his eyes. 'Grab me and hurt me, man! Fag pigs! And nigger this and nigger that! What we do we do, but no one gonna rap us with that nigger and whore and cocksucker and say they tear off our balls so no more little niggers . . .'

Roersch turned to the patrolmen. 'Bullshit,' one said, but his young Irish face was suffused with more than blood; it held obvious, rampant hatred. '*They* use the word, not us.' He chewed gum as if it were alive in his mouth. 'We read 'em their rights.'

The prisoner Roersch was still holding forced harsh laughter. 'Our *rights*! Man, the only rights we heard had "nigger" in 'em. And tellin' us we killed some pig captain . . .'

Roersch tightened his grip, that thumb digging again. The prisoner grunted. 'So book us. We stole thirteen dollars.'

The second cop, darker, maybe Italian or Jewish, breathed heavily and said, 'They had an old guy – at least sixty-five, maybe seventy – had him in a doorway on Eleventh. We caught them in the act. They had a piece, a ·22 automatic. It could be one of the M–4 pieces, right? They had this old guy on his knees, his head broken, blood all over, tearing out his pockets. He's in lousy shape, the ambulance medic said.'

Sergeant Colburn said, 'Why'd you ask for Sergeant Roersch? Why bring them *here*, you dumb . . .?'

Roersch said, 'Okay, Hank.' He let the prisoner go and spoke to the young cops. 'You were in a radio car?' They nodded. 'You called in to your precinct?'

The Irish cop said, 'Right, and they checked it out and told us to bring them here.'

'Checked it out?' Roersch murmured. 'What the hell is there to check out? You got a prisoner, you bring him to your own precinct unless he's hurt and needs medical attention.' He paused. 'Who's your commanding officer?'

'Captain Weir.'

Roersch smiled, surprising the three cops. Jimmy Weir, his old buddy from Safe and Loft. Jimmy, who'd gone to Patrol Borough Manhattan North, and recently into a West Side precinct house. Jimmy, always good on tests; always good for a laugh. 'Take your prisoners in as usual.'

'The gun . . .' the darker cop began.

'The gun too. There are thousands of ·22 automatics in Manhattan, and even more ·38 revolvers. If we jump at every one, we won't even have time to go to the john. Hand the gun over to your sergeant and he'll get it to Forensic. If anything shows, *then* I'll get it.'

'Why'd our captain say bring 'em here?' the Irish cop asked stubbornly.

Roersch ignored the question. 'You made a good collar. You've either saved a man's life or solved a homicide. Your prisoners are scum, but they're not *nigger* scum. You understand that? You could blow your solved in court on a word like that.'

'We never . . .' the dark cop began.

'Off the pig!' the prisoner Roersch had questioned shouted. 'Fuckin' lying . . .'

Roersch looked at him. The man stopped, then leaned forward, neck muscles straining. 'Next time I hit the street, won't be no old man get a crack on the head. Next time . . .'

Roersch waved them out and got on the phone. He reached Jimmy and said, 'Hey, Captain, what're you doing so early?'

'We've got a crisis or two of our own, Eddy. Guess you're too busy for lunch at Danziger's?'

'Maybe in a few days. Unless you send me more Valentines.'

Jimmy laughed. 'I thought I'd solved your case for you.'

'Not quite. Your suspects were in their late twenties, early thirties. We're looking for teenagers.'

'Your witnesses could be wrong, Eddy. All cats look alike in the dark. Black cats, that is.'

Roersch said, 'Yeah,' because friend or no, you didn't come down on a captain, on *anyone* of superior rank, in the

New York City Police Department. And Jimmy wasn't anti-black for a New Yorker these days; he was actually liberal for a cop.

Jones came in as he was hanging up.

'Want some coffee, Eddy?' he asked, taking two containers from a paper bag.

Roersch nodded. 'Black, Willis, if you remember.'

'I remember, Sergeant.'

And then that stupid play on words had them both laughing; not very hard, but laughing.

Jones complained about the light, got on a chair, and unscrewed the bulbs in two of the four fixtures. 'Two hundred watts each, Eddy! Can you believe it?'

Lauria and Ross came in and were given piles of paper. The phones began ringing. They read and answered calls and Roersch asked for abridgements of the reports and began making notes on his own reading. Along with the four interviews he'd conducted yesterday, these reports began to show him where the original picture of the crime was going to be reinforced.

He also saw that his uncomfortable feeling about Captain Worth's death wasn't going to go away; not just yet, at any rate. Maybe tonight, when he'd be able to sit down at home and put together ...

His phone rang. He said, 'Sergeant Roersch.' The woman's voice asked, 'Is this M-4?' He said, 'Yeah, sorry, M-4'.

'This is Headquarters Sergeant. You're to report here within the hour. Ask for Policewoman Nolan's desk.'

He groaned. 'I'm up to my eyeballs in D.D.–5's, Miss Nolan.'

'*Officer* Nolan. The order doesn't come from me, naturally. And I presume it's a little more important than reports.'

'Who *does* the order come from?'

'I don't know. But it was routed through the P.C.'s personal secretary.'

Roersch said, 'Thank you,' and was heading for the door before he'd hung up.

He used the siren all the way, wondering if he was going to be given an important piece of evidence, a pep talk, or some Headquarters chief as a shadow commanding officer.

He didn't use the police basement garage, knowing from past experience how crowded it could get. He took a chance and parked on the street near the housing east of his goal, then ran to the entrance of Number One Police Plaza, the huge new building in Manhattan's Civic Center that had replaced the grim old headquarters at 240 Center Street. Struck by intermittent sunlight, its modern design, its clean red-brick facing, its spacious plaza seemed a proper subject for technicolor travelogues. Yet, somehow, there was nothing bright or cheerful about it.

Ahead was the Brooklyn Bridge; nearby were the Municipal, Federal, and U.S. Court House buildings; all around were either new or refurbished structures. Urban renewal at its best; a rebuilt, revitalized downtown area; yet to Roersch it seemed in shadow – the shadow of that iron-fisted building that housed New York City's Police Headquarters.

Almost everyone who was anyone in upper police echelons was located in this sixty-million-dollar monster: the police commissioner, first deputy, chief of operations, chief of detectives, director of personnel, chief of organized crime and a host of deputy commissioners and chiefs. He felt like a private called to the Pentagon in his fatigues. Yet he didn't envy these men their positions. Their money, yes, but not their being shut away from the streets, the action.

At least he *had* felt that way all his thirty-five years on the force. It was this thirty-sixth year that was breaking his balls.

The lobby was dominated by a twenty-foot-square brick sculpture hanging off the wall like a stone-age version of the Manhattan skyline. In the plaza beyond, the massive fifteen-thousand-pound red-steel disks of the Five-Borough sculpture added to the sense of power, of heavy-handed authority that was, after all, what the police represented.

He asked the uniformed cop sharing the big round information desk with the civilian woman where he could find Officer Nolan.

'We've got two, John and Donna.'

Roersch said Donna and was given an office number. A few minutes later he got off the elevator amidst a ton of gold braid and found the right office. The uniformed cop typing away was young and remarkably pretty. Roersch identified himself. She stood up, and was even prettier standing. When she turned to lead the way to an inner office, he decided he wasn't as old as he'd felt back at the station. The clouds were clearing, the sun was beginning to show, and it might just become a beautiful summer day after all. Imagine turning on for a cop's ass!

His attitude changed once she'd ushered him inside and stepped back, closing the door on him and the gold-braided officer behind the long desk. It was Deputy Inspector Deverney, once Captain Deverney of Manhattan West Homicide, not one of Roersch's favorite people.

Deverney rose, grinning. 'Congrats on the assignment, Eddy! You're a sure thing for the money. Have a seat; make yourself comfortable!'

Roersch said thanks and sat down in a small leather armchair. Deverney came around the desk, a big man, over six feet, yet that didn't describe his bigness. *Big as a house* described it. And not much was flab. He was about Roersch's age and had slicked-back gray hair and a pock-marked meaty face with eyes that turned ice-blue when he was pissed, which was almost always since he hated just about everyone who wasn't white, a Goldwater–Reagan Republican, and a cop. And he was pissed this very moment.

He walked to Roersch and behind him and around to the other side of the desk, a big gray shark swimming restlessly, ready for blood. 'You notice anything strange about this office, Eddy?'

'No name on the door.'

Deverney smiled a little. 'Anything else?'

'Your lady cop doesn't know who she's working for, unless she was told not to say.'

Deverney's smile flickered wider. 'There's nothing like an old detective, a *shadow*, we used to say. From the days when you could fuck anything in long hair.' He chuckled.

Roersch gave him the mandatory chuckle in response.

A moment passed and Deverney's eyes went icy again. 'We caught some shit on this case, Eddy. First we decided not to say anything about it, not even to you, because the more people who know, the bigger the chance it could leak to the news media. Then we felt you might need the information, though it doesn't figure to help you find those three freaks.'

He walked behind his own chair and around the desk again. 'The P.C. made the final decision this morning; phoned me at home and said to acquaint you with the facts. Said you might, in the course of your investigation, come across something that would lead you to suspect . . .' He was behind Roersch, and stopped speaking and stopped moving.

Roersch turned his head. Deverney walked on, reached his chair, and sat down. 'This Captain Worth was a real skell.'

Roersch raised his eyebrows. Deverney was using a word that cops used for the vilest sex criminals and turncoats, the lowest of the low. And he was using it on a murdered police captain known to be in line for deputy inspector. It couldn't be Deverney's well-known dislike of blacks, because that was balanced by his equally well-known love for cops, including many of those who had been caught with their hands in the till by the Knapp Commission. So what could Worth have done?

Deverney was opening his top drawer. He tossed a bulging ten-by-twelve manila envelope on the desk. It had brown stains at one edge. 'Worth was carrying this. Take a look.'

Roersch leaned forward and opened the envelope's metal clasp. He shook out four tightly bound packages of hundred-dollar bills.

'Fifty in a pack, Eddy. Twenty thousand dollars.'

Roersch nodded, understanding that Deverney assumed it was a payoff, but still not certain that *this* was what deserved the icy-blue eyes.

'He died with it *on* him, Eddy! It could lead to another series of investigations into police corruption like Knapp's, *including* Knapp! If the Daily Worker *Times* ever got hold of it, they'd put their kike heads together and figure everyone in this building had a piece of the action! They'd just *love* to bring us down . . .'

Now Roersch understood. Captain Worth wasn't a skell for having lived on the take, but for having *died* on it. This could prove embarrassing for other cops, also on the take, some perhaps within this impressive building. Was Deverney among them?

'How many people know about this?' Roersch asked.

'One of the two responding radio-car officers, who was smart enough to hide the money inside his tunic the minute he realized what it was.'

But not smart enough to pocket it, Roersch thought, wondering what *he* would do if *he* found twenty grand on a murder victim who probably had no right to it.

Probably.

'Any chance Worth legally owned the money?'

Deverney laughed sharply. 'Anyone who has legal right to such money uses a cashier's check, a personal check, anything *but* cash. And doesn't pick it up at two A.M.'

'But the widow might still raise a question.'

'Don't hold your breath, Eddy.'

Roersch wouldn't. He had brought it up simply to see if any question *had* been raised.

'The others who know are a full inspector, the P.C., and myself. The responding radio-car officer, Michaelson, didn't confide in his partner. Officer McCoy. So four people know about it. Officer Michaelson has been temporarily assigned as standby driver for the full inspector, pending his promotion to sergeant. He's a good man, Eddy. No worries about a leak there.'

Michaelson might not have made such a bad deal after all, refusing to pocket the twenty grand, protecting the department's good name by contacting a superior.

'Doesn't Michaelson's commanding officer know about the money?'

Deverney said, 'No. He contacted me directly. I know his father. Old Michaelson used to deliver eggs to our home. I helped get the son into the department. I figured the father was a white Jew, the son might be the same.' He was smiled in obvious self-satisfaction. 'Jesus, how right I was!'

Roersch nodded. The kikes were on the *Times*; the white Jews on the force.

'Whenever you run into anything relating to Worth,' Deverney said, writing on a card, 'call this number. You'll either get me here, or be told where I happen to be.' He handed Roersch the card. 'You're to conduct all investigation into Worth's activities on Fifty-second Street yourself. I mean, do it *personally*, Eddy.'

'Yes, but overlapping . . .'

'No buts. No leaks. No news stories about Worth except as the great black captain who was brutally murdered. The *prick!*'

Roersch put the card in his pocket. 'I'll do my best.'

'You'd better, Sergeant. For getting the money. For the promotion. And—' those glacial eyes dug into Roersch – 'for your ever-loving ass. This is very important to the P.C. Remember that. He'll be watching this case like under a microscope. And so will I.'

Roersch was sweating. He wanted to say, 'Maybe you'd prefer to give it to someone else?' but it was too late for that. *Five* men now knew about the twenty thousand.

Deverney stood up. Roersch followed suit. 'Good luck,' Deverney said. Roersch walked to the door and paused.

'How do I handle the reports?'

'I thought I made that crystal clear. There's to be no mention of Worth in relation to the twenty thousand.'

'I don't mean that, Inspector. Do you want a daily report on all progress, or what? And how do I handle my superiors at Homicide West, Lieutenant Murray and Captain Hawly? How do I explain reporting to you and not to them?'

Deverney shook his head. 'No one's going to be looking over your shoulder, Eddy. You don't report to me, and you don't report to them. Murray and Hawly will be told to leave you strictly alone. You're the commanding officer of M–4. If you run into problems with any officer anywhere, just call the number I gave you. We want fast action, and the lid clamped tight on that twenty thousand. Give us that, and you'll not only get the money, you'll retire a lieutenant.' He raised his right hand. 'I swear it on my mother's grave.'

The pretty cop looked up from her typewriter when Roersch came out. He wiped his face with a handkerchief. She said, 'I thought the air-conditioning was set just right.'

'I'd be sweating at the North Pole today.'

She turned back to her work.

'Good-bye for now,' he said. 'I'll be speaking to you again, when I call Inspector ...' He paused. 'What's your boss's name?'

'I don't know. If he wants me to know, he'll tell me. Like he told you.'

He grinned. 'You'll make captain yet, Miss Nolan.'

'*Officer* Nolan.'

'Donna,' he said, walking to the door and thinking of Ruthie and wishing they could go back to Amagansett and the beach and the hard bed in the cottage that smelled wonderfully of wood and salt water. A hot old man, by God. Hot to trot, and hot to get away from whatever was coming down on M–4. Because it was *something*. His hunch was growing, his instincts sharpening.

The lady cop said, 'Well, *that's* better,' and touched her short-cropped brown hair and smiled in a way that showed she'd picked up his horny vibrations.

He was flattered.

Back at the basement headquarters of M–4, he was hotter than ever. Because with all the ordering and installing of desks and phones and lights, no one had thought of air-conditioning, or even ventilation. The door was open to the dim hallway leading to the cells, which *did* have ventilation. But it didn't reach to the sweatbox their room had become. And it wasn't noon yet.

Jones looked across at him, face wet, chin actually dripping. 'As commanding officer, I think you should *do* something.'

Behind Jones, Detective Third Grade Ross, lean and lanky as a basketball player, and young enough to be one, said, 'Amen.' Behind Roersch Detective Lauria, short, dark, quick of body and mind, and even younger than Ross simply sang the first line of 'In the Good Old Summer Time'. Both were wearing what looked like wash-and-dry shirts in the wash stage.

Roersch thought of going upstairs, and asking Lieutenant Murray for help – fans or vents or whatever. Murray would then go to Captain Hawly. Hawly would go through channels, and in perhaps a week one workman would come in and start poking around. A week after that, he'd return with a city engineer and they'd find a way to link up to the cell area air shaft. The actual work would take another two or three days. By then M–4 would have become R–4 – the Roasted Four.

He dialed and said, 'Officer Nolan? Sergeant Roersch. Is your boss still around? Fine, let me speak to him.' A moment after that he was explaining the situation to Deverney, concluding with, 'The investigation will suffer, Inspector.'

Deverney said he'd see what he could do.

At twelve-forty, three workmen and a city engineer arrived. They brought two large floor fans with them, which the engineer positioned carefully – one at the rear of the room, and the other reversed at the front as an exhaust. It helped, a little. Then the engineer checked blueprints and spoke softly to his men, and the men began to smash the wall just a few feet to Roersch's left. The engineer, older and thinner than any city employee Roersch had ever seen, said, 'I apologize, Sergeant. I've been told about your assignment, and I certainly don't want to impede you in the slightest. But if you could move from your desk for just an hour . . .'

Roersch took a pile of reports upstairs to the bullpen, which held six desks. His was the only one with 'rank', partitioned by walls that ended four feet shy of the twelve-foot-high turn-of-the-century ceiling. There was also a doorway without a door. Still, he had a degree of privacy, and a frosted window onto the street.

And it was cool here. It was also quiet, until the occupants of the other desks began dropping in to ask about M–4. Then Lieutenant Murray arrived, followed by Captain

Hawly. They proceeded to chat with each other about how they would handle the case.

'Known Criminals File would be my first move,' Murray said, his handsome black-Irish face already beginning to go to fat, despite his being just forty years old. He was six-one and heavy boned and attracted a good deal of attention from women.

'No way,' Hawly said. He was short, husky, five years older than Murray and in excellent shape, with sharp features and crew-cut graying blond hair. An entirely different kind of Irishman, Hawly, with none of Murray's love for heavy food or strong drink. Still, he too was to be found at all the Irish 'socials' that raised money for the I.R.A. Quite a bit of that money came from his men, both as a sign of conviction and because it was wise to stay on the good side of one's C.O. 'These skells are too young to be known criminals. And too crazy. A pro wouldn't kill so casually.'

'They're blacks,' Murray replied. 'Race prejudice, Captain. Crow Jim.'

'Granted, it's happening a lot lately, but the age of these boys indicates the best bet is to check schools . . .'

Roersch nodded first at one, then at the other, and contained his impatience. He'd gone through the thinking this conversation represented in his first half hour on the case. Now he wanted to be alone, to *work*!

Roersch went out for a hamburger and iced tea at one-ten. When he returned at one-thirty, two men were carrying a crate through the bullpen toward the stairs. Roersch went to his desk and settled down to reading the Fives. A few minutes later, his phone rang. Jones said, 'The engineer would like to see you.'

Roersch went downstairs, where the elderly engineer met him in the hall. 'It's taking a little longer than I first estimated, Sergeant. I hope I haven't inconvenienced you, but we're about finished now. Just fitting the refrigeration unit into the air-shaft opening.' He stepped aside and pointed. 'I'll have to leave the cosmetics to someone else – the painting and such – but we'll clean up and be out of your way in a short while.'

Roersch stared. Where before there'd been wall, there was now a more-or-less square opening, and a freshly built platform extending into a metal air shaft. Two men were lifting the large air conditioner into the opening. When they finished, one of the three original workmen, thirtyish and black, began slapping a puttylike sealer into the gaps between unit and wall.

'Give it about half an hour to set,' the engineer said.

'It don't need that long,' the black workman said. 'Hardens like concrete in five minutes.'

Jones said, 'You oughta leave some of it here for when we catch the killers of Captain Worth. You read about that? We'll shove it down their throats ...' He stopped, because the workman had finished and was moving out of the room, moving away from his words.

'Hey, brother,' Jones said. 'I'm talking to you.'

The workman went past Roersch, his face set.

'You goddam scumbag!' Jones shouted, and started after him.

Roersch said, 'Willis.'

Jones stopped. 'You see the way that bastard acted? You see what they think of cops? It doesn't matter if it's black cops or dead cops or what. He's a city employee, not a crook, yet he hates ...' He choked on his words, his rage.

'I understand, sir,' the elderly engineer said as he left.

'The hell you do,' Jones snapped.

Roersch said, 'Help me carry some stuff down from my office, Willis.'

They were climbing the stairs when Roersch stopped. 'I think I should take you off M-4.'

'*No!*'

'Even that "no" shows you're in bad shape.'

Jones sighed. 'Sorry, Eddy. Just feeling what Fats Waller called Black and Blue. I want to stay on. Once we begin canvassing the ghettos, I'll be able to carry *more* than my weight. I've got good informants ...'

Roersch started upstairs again. By the time they reached

his office, he'd agreed to keep Jones. But then again, he'd never intended to drop him. It was Edmund Roersch he wanted to drop.

At two-thirty, Hawly phoned to say that newspeople were arriving in droves. 'We've got maybe twenty up here, including all three networks, so I think you'd better hold a news conference.'

Roersch said, 'Christ, Bill, today is organization day! I don't have anything to tell them!'

'Okay with me. But you'll still have to make a statement, even if it's only to say that there's nothing to say.'

Roersch groaned.

Hawly laughed. 'That's what commanding officers put up with. Just get a little makeup on – lipstick and eye-shadow will do – and trot your celebrity ass up here for the cameras.' Before Roersch could ask him to fill in, he'd hung up.

Roersch went up the stairs, straightening his tie, trying to revive his wilted collar. The bullpen was a madhouse. Hawly had allowed the newspeople inside and cleared an area near the partition. He saw Roersch and raised his voice. 'All right, ladies and gentlemen, here's Sergeant Roersch, Commanding Officer of M–4. Please make it brief, as we've got a homicide unit to run.'

Roersch came through the crowd, stepping over extension cables. He turned, and was blinded by half a dozen portable TV lights switching on. Someone yelled, 'Get the mikes up.' Four microphones were shoved under his chin, held by outstretched hands as reporters tried to stay out of the way of cameras.

The questions began to come. He answered:

'We're looking for three men, but we have no specific suspects. No, it *doesn't* mean we're stumped. We've just begun. I expect to have more to say tomorrow, or Sunday. Now if you'll excuse me . . .'

They wouldn't excuse him. A voice asked him to describe the suspects.

'Male Negroes, young, perhaps in their teens, driving what might be either a late-model Camaro or Firebird, possibly red.'

Another voice, female, asked if he'd explain what the victims, especially Louise Sanders and her husband, were doing on Fifty-second Street.

'I can't explain.'

'You mean no one has come forward ... doesn't that strike you as unusual?'

'No. People don't like to be involved in murders. But we hope *these* particular people will soon respond to a letter I'm having distributed later today.'

'Would you read that letter, Sergeant?'

'I don't have a copy on me.'

A sheet of paper was shoved into his hands. He squinted, and for the first time saw some point to this interview. He would reach a lot of people. He began to read:

'To the residents of East Fifty-second Street: Your police department is engaged in an effort to bring the murderers of four people to justice. These people were killed on your block, under your windows. One was an actress you enjoyed on television; another a police captain who spent his life protecting your life and property; all were innocent victims of a brutal robbery-murder. We know you will want to help us, because it is actually helping yourselves. Some of you might have seen something, or heard something, at the time of the murders. No matter how minor you think it is, please contact the special M–4 unit at the number listed below. Some of you might have been acquainted with the victims, none of whom lived on Fifty-second Street. If they were visiting you or anyone you know, please use the M–4 number listed below. Your identity will not ...' He stopped and looked into the glare. 'I repeat, your identity will *not* be made public.' He looked down at the sheet again, reading off the victims' names and the M–4 phone number. 'That's it,' he said, and the letter was taken from his hand.

'It's signed,' a voice called out, 'Sergeant E. Roersch, Commander M–4 Unit. What's the "E" for, Sergeant? And how come a higher-ranking officer wasn't put in charge of such a case?'

Hawly, standing nearby, said, 'Edmund. We call him

Eddy. He was chosen for this most difficult case because of his vast experience . . .'

The lights and microphones were moving toward the captain. Roersch stepped back gratefully, then went around the crowd toward the staircase. A lovely dark-skinned lady with close-cropped hair blocked his path. 'Could you say a few words about Captain Worth for our black citizens?'

'He was a fine police officer who served this city for over twenty-five years . . .'

'And lived out of it in Westchester County,' the pretty reporter interrupted. It was then that Roersch noticed the open purse and the tape recorder inside. He nodded. 'What was that?' she asked.

'Captain Worth's widow and four children live in Tarrytown, yes. He'll be given an inspector's funeral, and more than that he'll be given what any murdered police officer is given in this city – the complete dedication of his fellow officers toward solving the crime.'

'His being black was nothing special, you're saying?'

'Not to me. I'm sure it was to his fellow blacks, who were proud of his position . . .'

'Some of those fellow blacks had their heads broken at the Columbia University riots, where there were accusations made of Captain Worth's having acted in a brutal manner. Would you comment on this?'

'I know nothing about it. I assume the captain acted as his orders, and the situation, demanded.'

She smiled. It was a great smile, even if meant to be cynical.

'I think your readers, or listeners, would get better information in this area from a black officer, my second-in-command, Sergeant Willis Jones. Call him at that special number.'

'Are you saying that because you're white you can't . . .'

He started past her. She snapped her purse shut. 'Thanks, I'll call that black honky of yours.'

He kept going. She said, 'Sergeant.' He turned. She said, 'I'm sorry about that last remark. Police stations make me nervous. Genetics, I guess. I'll call your . . .'

But Roersch fled, because the lights were swinging toward him again.

He went downstairs, where he fell into his chair and ripped open tie and collar. 'After thirty-five years, had to make a jackass out of myself. But Willis-baby, you might just vote me your favorite person in all the world. *If* you can turn this girl's sharp tongue to better purposes.'

They worked. Roersch handed out assignments. At six-thirty, Roersch was alone. He leaned back and closed his eyes and tried to think his way past all the facts, the lack of facts, the race and bullshit, to a jumping-off point, a place from which he could begin to see how to catch his killers. He'd done this before, on other cases. It was his hunches, his instincts, the twists of mind that helped him bypass road-blocks, that made his record what it was.

But nothing got through the confusion, the gut feeling of disaster looming. And what the hell kind of disaster could that be? Either he ran down the three kids or he didn't. If he didn't, he'd retire as a sergeant, probably this year. If he did, he'd retire as a lieutenant, probably a few years later. Either way he was coming to the end of his career; had to accept it; time and tide wait for no man.

'Fuck time and tide,' he said, and picked up the phone. He'd fucked them by marrying Ruthie. He'd fucked them *good* by having a son at age fifty-eight.

Ruthie answered. 'I didn't realize what a big case they handed you! It's all over the newspapers and on television. They gave your name on the Channel 11 News – Jen and I yelled out loud! A big shot was being interviewed and he said the most experienced homicide detective was Sergeant Roersch ...'

He began to feel good about the news conference; it should make the ten and eleven o'clock programs. He said, 'Honey, keep your pants on. At least until I get home.'

She laughed. 'It'll be an honor to trick a famous man like you.' She still used the lingo of her hooker past at times. And it bothered him at times. This wasn't one of them.

'If I'm still able to by eight, eight-thirty.'

'That late? You've been going since five Thursday. You'd better get some rest, Eddy.'

'Yeah. Serve something good for supper.'

'How about little Ruthie, on toast?'

'That's dessert, baby.' He thought of her big butt, round breasts, skilled lovemaking. He thought of her childlike face twisted in passion, and he wanted her right now. He said, 'Kiss Jen and Mark good night for me,' and popped one for her and hung up before she could use that sexy voice on him.

He tackled the last of the Fives, which carried him to seven-thirty. He collected the abridgements, including his own, and put them in a plastic zipper folder and went upstairs. The night tour was on, Sergeant Harry Balleau in charge. Balleau was a perennial night man; he liked it that way. He even *looked* like a night person: heavy-lidded eyes behind yellow-tinted prescription glasses, sallow skin, and a stoop to his shoulders that made you think of a scholar bent over his midnight books. But the only midnight books Roersch had ever seen him bent over were *Playboy* and *Penthouse.*

'How's our big wheel?' Balleau said, looking up from a blue report sheet.

'Spinning uselessly. At least right now.'

'I'm covering your phones, Eddy.'

'You're doing more than that, Harry. You're M–4 as long as you're here and I'm not.'

Balleau nodded. 'Be a pleasure working with you again. Just get the captain to put it on paper.'

Roersch said it was already in the works.

Balleau took off his glasses and rubbed the bridge of his nose. 'What do you think about this Captain Worth? I mean, what do you figure he was doing on that street at that hour?'

'Don't know. But maybe someone'll tell me. Or tell *you,* tonight.' He began to walk away.

'Looks like a chick to me, Eddy. These coons gotta have their pussy regular. Wife in Westchester and girlfriend on Fifty-second. White stuff too, I'll lay odds.'

'Could be,' Roersch said, not turning as he went out. Balleau screwed around more than any two men Roersch knew, and was single only because his wife had found out and divorced him.

Roersch got in his car, fully intending to drive straight home. But he ended up on Fifty-second Street, parking at a hydrant near the end of the block, putting down his visor with its police department identification card. Not that it would do much good if a gung-ho traffic cop came along.

He went to one of the apartment houses on the south side of the street, near Beekman Place, and saw the small lobby, no doorman, a double row of nameplates with buttons beside them. And a speaker-receiver unit for communicating with the tenants, who could admit visitors on a buzzer lock-release system.

He began to read names, then stopped. Too late. Too tired. But he had to canvass this street himself, because of Captain Worth. Had to find the payoff man, because of Inspector Deverney. Had to put that angle firmly under wraps, because of the whole goddam police department.

And had to reach out and touch that payoff man, had to hear his voice, had to look at him and judge him . . . because of Eddy Roersch.

He crossed the street to a house on the north side. It had a larger lobby, and a doorman. The doorman looked at him suspiciously through the glass doors, already locked at eight P.M. This street was going to be nervous for quite a while. Roersch showed his badge. The doorman opened up. Roersch asked, 'What time do you get mail delivery?' The doorman said, 'Ten, ten-thirty.' Roersch said thanks and went to his car. Postmen were great sources of information. He would be here tomorrow to speak to this one.

FIVE

Friday, July 18, P.M.

VOICE ONE: 'Hello?'

VOICE TWO: 'Got your message. I'm calling from a booth. You alone?'

ONE: 'No, my sister's cooking dinner for me. But she's in the other room, so we have a few minutes.'

TWO: 'You said to call.'

ONE: 'I'd like to have coffee with you later. Make it twelve. That all-night diner on Fourth; know where it is?'

TWO: 'Yeah. But why not Kelley's, like last time?'

ONE: '*Never* like last time. And when you meet with *your* Number Two, make sure it's always in a new spot. Caution, my friend, caution.'

TWO: 'Uh . . . are you happy about how it's going?'

ONE: 'Of course. A mission accomplished, and a new one on the drawing board.'

TWO: 'But did you see the TV? This M–4's a big deal. I figure they're going to come up with money for rewards and informants and put the pressure on night and day . . .'

ONE: 'And catch the three black butchers who did it.'

TWO: 'I'd like it better if those mothers died in a shoot-out.'

ONE: 'That could very well happen. Though it won't change anything if they're put on trial.'

TWO: 'Guess not. Guess I'm still new at this. Got the tights, know what I mean?'

ONE: 'We're *all* new at it. But give it time. And remember that it's not for personal gain; it's for the survival of the nation. Remember *that*, Mr Jefferson, when you hear reference to the Bicentennial.'

TWO: Sighing: 'I will, Mr Washington.'

ONE: 'Glad you haven't forgotten who I am.'

Both laugh.

67

ONE: 'There, you're back to your old self.'

TWO: 'I suppose I'll get used to it in time. You can get used to *anything* in time, right?'

ONE: 'If it's in a good cause. Good men can do anything in a good cause. You couldn't do it, believe me, for selfish reasons.'

TWO: 'I don't know how the hell I got into it even for *these* reasons.'

ONE: 'Because I know you, like you know your Number Two, like he knows his. But *I* don't know your Number Two. And *he* doesn't know his Number Two's assistant. And so we can never fall apart if one man dies, one man deserts, even if one man defects and talks. I'm the top, so I only know one other member – you. You know two others, me and the man beneath you. And so on. The *worst* that can happen is that three men get collared. Three out of . . . how many do we have now? Eight?'

TWO: 'Nine, including you. That's the latest word coming up the ladder. But our ninth man is working on a Number Two. I gotta say it gives me the sweats, growing this way. What if we took in a shoofly?'

ONE: 'We won't. Every man is too concerned for his own skin to take in anyone he isn't a hundred percent sure of. The way I was sure of you, and you of your Number Two. That's the beauty of it.'

TWO: 'Still, we *could* make a mistake.'

ONE: 'Yes, we could. And then the remaining members would eradicate the mistake. Because the traitor won't know who we are, and we'll know who *he* is when he makes his accusations.'

TWO: 'That's right. You thought it out straight down the line, Mr Washington.'

ONE: 'My sister's calling.'

TWO: 'Wait. I wanted to ask you . . . are you *really* the very top? I mean, did it *start* with you? Or is there someone who calls you *his* Number Two?'

ONE: 'What do you tell your Number Two? About a superior, I mean.'

TWO: 'Nothing. He can't be sure *I'm* not the top.'

ONE: 'There you are, Mr *Washington*.'

TWO: Laughing: 'Jesus! It confuses *me*, so what chance has anyone else to understand it, even if they tumble to a part of it?'

ONE: 'Exactly. What chance does M–4 and the long-experienced sergeant have?'

TWO: 'A snowball's in hell. But he'll never know it. If he's lucky, he'll catch his three mothers and that'll be that.'

ONE: 'And if he isn't lucky, he'll make us, part of us, or get too close, and we'll have to eradicate *him*.'

TWO: Long pause. 'That would be lousy.'

ONE: 'Yes, it would.' Voice growing hearty: 'But the chances are still a snowball's in hell, so don't worry about it. See you at twelve.'

Radford and Corinne walked to 140th Street and turned toward Eighth Avenue. She said, 'You told me we was going riding in a new car and we're walking half of Harlem. My momma expects me back at six.'

'Fuck your momma,' Radford snapped, hands jammed into trouser pockets, long body hunched forward, walking out ahead of her with quick strides.

'Bet you'd like to. My momma still has it!'

'Oh, she sure do. Has it *big*, all over, like a trailer truck. I learn to ride your momma, I get a good job at high pay like on the TV ads.'

The slender black girl stopped dead. 'I'm going home! She told me you wasn't any good, getting thrown outa school all the time! And what you said about doing those white people downtown . . .'

Radford whirled, his fist rising. An elderly man stepped into the gutter, giving them wide berth.

Corinne quieted instantly. 'I'm sorry, Rad-honey. Please don't be mad.' Radford remained coiled to batter her, eyes narrowed and raging. He'd been uptight all day, though he'd tried to act cool when picking her up at her friend Rosanne's. He could see that she was afraid of him, even more afraid than the night he'd used force – slapping her; threat-

69

ening to knock her teeth out – to make her come across that first time.

He let out his breath and began walking again, looking ahead and across the street for the Firebird. Could've been ripped off, sharp car like that.

Then he saw it. 'There's my wheels, baby!' The scraped fender was barely noticeable; just a little blue on the red.

As they ran across 140th, dodging traffic, he also saw the officer strolling up the street toward them. Black . . . but like he'd told Ju-Ju, no pig could be a brother. They reached the sidewalk, and he glanced at Corinne. She was staring at the cop. Radford suddenly regretted telling her about Fifty-second Street and the honkies. If she wanted to, she could wipe him out in a minute. The papers and TV were full of that M–4 and a special number to call and she could pick up the phone and he'd be dead.

The pig went on by. Radford said, 'The red Firebird, see?'

'Hey, a beauty!'

He looked around and opened the door and let her in, then went around to the other side and slid behind the wheel.

'Where'd you get it, honey?' She was touching the stick shift, smiling.

He said, 'Cousin lent it to me; just for a few days,' glad he hadn't mentioned the car when talking about Fifty-second Street.

He started up and headed for Riverside Drive. 'You know that rap I was giving you about killing them honkies? Pure shit. We heard it on the radio so I thought I'd have a few laughs . . .'

She was nodding, eyes straight ahead; nodding too hard. He said, 'What the fuck's wrong with you? How could I kill three people? I mean, you know me for the loving man I am, right?'

She nodded again, just as hard, still looking through the windshield. 'I never believed it, Radford, honest.'

That 'honest' sounded like their first time together; like begging him not to hurt her. Maybe he *should* hurt her, at

70

least a little, to make sure she didn't get ideas about telling anyone.

Or maybe he should blow her away, waste her, *ice* her as Ju-Ju said.

If he told Lester and Ju-Ju she knew, they'd ice *him*, especially Ju-Ju.

He turned onto Riverside, uptown, thinking he'd like to see where that captain lived. The papers said Tarrytown, lower Westchester, and he had change for the toll and why not look around? He'd never been to Tarrytown. He'd been to Jones Beach, where they busted those two honky kids in the parking lot for their transistors and wristwatches, and he'd been to Rockaway, where there were plenty of brothers, and he'd been to Coney, sure, for the rides. Coney was where they'd almost got their nuts cut when Lester patted a Rican chick's ass and maybe eight PR's came after them. Not too good, man, but they'd backed off slow; Ju-Ju never ran; backed away and a cop car had come along and it was the only time they'd been glad to see the pigs. Later that week they'd visited Lester's brother in the South Bronx where he'd married a PR chick, foxy and with tits like not too many spics had. James was kinda square and so was his wife, but they had a nice place and she cooked good. On the way home they caught a spic and beat the shit out of him. They took everything, including his pants and shorts, and left him balls to the wind in a doorway. James later told Lester that it set off a gang hassle that killed a few people. But James didn't know it was them who done the spic, so everything was cool and they had their revenge.

He'd also been to Atlantic City to visit his father, but that was almost ten years ago, when he was small and they'd still known where Dad was. Now no one knew. Cut out somewhere. Couldn't take the hassles with Mom. Radford didn't blame him. Religious bullshit and go-to-school bullshit and work-for-your-daily-bread bullshit.

He drove onto the Henry Hudson Parkway and approached the toll booths. He tossed his quarter in the basket and the light Green-for-Go and he went, burning a little rubber, but not much because he didn't want cops looking

71

his way. Still, he opened up for a short stretch to feel the *smooooth* power.

His father had bought a big car, a Mark IV, and taken him for rides before he went to Atlantic City, 'on business' he'd told Radford, but his sister said he had himself a woman, almost white, who was 'ruining him'. Radford met the woman when he went to Atlantic City a year later. A real high-yaller knockout; even an eight-year-old cat could get the stiffs when she picked him up and squeezed him to those big jugs.

Corinne had the radio on and was singing.

His father had sung to him; he remembered it from way back when he was five or six. His father was a big, good-looking man; all the girls, even white ladies, he claimed, wanted some of his 'sweetness'. 'My sweetness is for the whole world!' he'd laughed, tossing Radford into the air.

Radford wished he could tell his father about Fifty-second Street and watch his face, see the quick, crooked smile, hear the funny laugh that sounded like a kid's, smell the cigarettes and booze and that sweet after-shave lotion when the thick arms held him close ...

It didn't feel good remembering, wanting, so he got out a cigarette and lit up and glanced at Corinne. 'Wait'll you see Tarrytown. Wait'll you see where I'm gonna live when I figure how to make the bread.' What he didn't say was, 'Wait'll you see the empty places I can dump you.'

She leaned close. She kissed his neck and put her hand on his crotch, giggling. She rubbed until she felt what was happening. 'Dy-no-*mite!*' she said, and opened his fly.

He drove. She worked him out of his pants. He groaned as she really yanked on it. 'Baby,' he sighed, 'how 'bout some head?'

'What, *here?*' She looked around at traffic.

He reached out and pulled her down.

It didn't take long. He came with his eyes half closed, crawling along in the right lane, listening to her wet sounds, loving the way her hand tickled his balls.

She spit out the window. 'Now I won't get mine.'

He said, 'Don't worry about *that*,' wondering how he meant it.

Ten minutes later he wanted her again. This time they parked behind a billboard off a small road. And took a chance balling in the front seat.

After that they drove to other roads, where there were big houses prettier than any he'd ever seen. He forgot about hurting her because he dug her and she dug him and they'd never do anything bad to each other.

He came to a dead end and drove slowly around the circle that had one motherfucker of a house; big, like from *The Beverly Hillbillies*. It was almost seven, but the light was still good and two women, one a black in a maid's uniform and the other a white bitch, were on the lawn playing with a baby. They looked up, looked right at him. He looked back and smiled, thinking he could take them; thinking he could take whatever they had, even the house.

Well, maybe not the house, he thought, driving back toward the highway. Still, he saw himself in that house, imagining what it would be like to grow up in a fucking mansion and no thousand other kids right on the same block and no your-turf and their-turf; and a big *allowance* like they said in the old movies on TV, Andy Hardy and other honky crap; and no reason for ripoffs and no one pushing for hassles and fights and maybe he'd look at the books once in a while and get through school and his father would give him a car for graduation and he'd get a girl with long hair and big tits like the high yaller and he'd take over part of his father's business and be rich and never see Harlem or the South Bronx or anyplace full of brothers and spics and pigs and trouble again.

Or maybe it would bore the shit out of him and he'd go back to the old neighborhood and pick up Lester and Ju-Ju and they'd show the man who was boss in this fucking city, who had the guts and muscle. They'd *kill* the mothahs!

'What's the matter, Radford?'

He looked at Corrine, and realized his mouth was twisted, his hands *aching* from gripping the wheel. He took a deep

73

breath. 'Nothing. Just thinking of some sucker owes me bread.'

So he'd never get the house. So *someone* was going to give old Radford his, like those honkies on Fifty-second Street gave. Maybe Ju-Ju was finished taking, but old Radford was just beginning. Maybe Ju-Ju conned himself with shit about *feeling* a bust coming their way, but not him.

He dropped Corinne at the corner of her block and drove around and found a place to park not far from where he'd been parked before, just off 140th.

He walked home, whistling. It was a warm night and the streets were crowded with kids and the stoops were full of older people sitting around. He kept an eye open for Roy and Cole and the little cat they called DDT 'cause he did a number with some kind of tear-gas spray to take you out of it – members of Big Fist, a gang that was broken up like most of this neighborhood, but these cats stuck together and they'd tangled with him and Lester and Ju-Ju.

Nothing happened and he reached his block and felt fine. He'd see his friends tonight. Have a few joints and a little coke if Lester's uncle came through like last time; and maybe Ju-Ju's girl would bring the friend she kept promising for Radford, the twenty-year-old that gave Around-the-World.

So it was a good day and could be a better night, and fuck that M–4 and Sergeant Radish or whatever his honky name was. No *way* to find them!

Still, he watched the ten o'clock news after Lester and Ju-Ju hadn't shown and he'd killed time on the street. Watched the old pig, and shrugged, and went to bed early. The car was still safe. They weren't sure of the make or the color, though they were close. But as long as they didn't have the license plate, *sheeit*, he could use it! Also, not a word about the watches and rings, and maybe he'd pawn the stuff he held and get a little more bread. Or maybe he'd wait like Ju-Ju wanted; no sweat either way. He could play *real* safe and forget the car and forget the watch and ring and forget worrying.

He dozed off, but a while later he was sitting up, rigid,

sweating, thinking the old sergeant was in the kitchen talking to his mother. He could hear the pig's voice . . .

It was the TV. His sister Margot was watching the tube, late news on one of the channels, and the old sergeant was doing his thing again.

If they came after him . . .

He got up and walked softly across the small room – his own; no one to share with since Margot said she was too old to sleep with a brother and moved in with Mom. He went to the window and the big potted plant on the sill, the geranium that Mom kept 'cause it made her feel a little more like when she was a girl in West Virginia. It wasn't doing too good. Mom kept watering it, worrying about it, wondering what had happened to it the last week.

Radford knew what the trouble was. He took the plant by the main stem with his right hand, held the pot down with his left, and pulled. The plant came up. On the bottom of the pot, wrapped in two plastic bags from the vegetable section of the A&P, was his short-barreled ·38 revolver. He'd had to cut away a lot of roots and thrown away a lot of dirt to make room for the gun, so the fucking plant was kinda sick.

Better the plant than old Radford!

No one could take him, long as he had his piece!

He put the plant back in the pot and lay down. He held the gun until he felt better, felt sleepy, then tucked it under the pillow and drifted off. He dreamt about his father walking down the street and he running after him only his legs wouldn't move right and his father got further and further away and Radford called out and his voice was a whisper and everyone was yelling like they always did on the streets of Harlem and his father disappeared in the crowd. Radford the child sat on the sidewalk and wept.

SIX

Roersch sat at the kitchen table, the plastic zipper case
open before him, and took out the abridged reports, the
half dozen sheets of paper that had the Fives boiled down
to essentials. It was one A.M. Ruthie was asleep. They'd had
dinner and gone to bed and made love and slept in each
other's arms ... and he'd known, while sleeping, that he
had to read those reports. The knowledge had eaten at him
and wakened him and he'd slipped into his robe and gone
to the kitchen and taken a beer from the refrigerator. Bad
for his diet, but necessary right now to get him going. He
began to read.

The way it shaped up from witnesses and physical evidence, Louise and Arnold Jaeker had been killed first, both
'execution' style, lying helplessly on the pavement between
parked cars. None of the bullets had been salvageable;
none had survived impact with the pavement. But weighing
what remained of the slugs, measuring the wounds they'd
made both entering and exiting the skulls, gave Forensic
the proper calibers. Besides, the same guns appeared to
have been used in the other two killings.

Richard Magris had probably been shot before Captain
Worth, but the difference in time was only seconds, the
assailants having split up – two for Magris, one for Worth,
according to witnesses. Of the three bullets that struck Magris, one had lodged against his spine and another, after
grazing his left bicep, had been found some thirty feet down
the street, almost in mint condition. They were ·22's, as
were those that killed Arnold Jaeker.

The two bullets that killed Worth, heart shot and head
shot, had been recovered, one on the street and mashed
badly from ricochet impact with brick and metal, the other
in his mouth and in good condition. They were ·38's. The

captain's ·38 caliber service revolver had not been fired.

It was a reasonable assumption that there'd been two guns among the three assailants, since Richard Magris, attacked by two of the killers, received wounds from only *one* gun. Reasonable, yes, but not necessarily factual, Roersch thought, and made a note in a dime-store spiral pad.

Identification of the victims had been simple and immediate. The killers removed money and left wallets and purse of the three on the south side of the street, and never did get to rob Worth on the north side. The wallets and purse were being dusted for prints, but not until a suspect was in custody could matches be attempted.

Relatives of the victims had been notified – in the Jaekers' case, in Los Angeles, since they'd lived in Century City – and responses received. All had been asked: 'Do you know what So-and-so was doing on East Fifty-second Street at that time?' None had been able to explain, though Arnold Jaeker's partner in a talent agency said the couple was in New York to visit CBS executives.

Magris's wife said he often worked late with his boss, Paul Mahon, and gave the address of Kromer Publications.

Worth's wife said it was a rarity for the captain to stay late in town, but when he did it was because of 'some case or other' and he generally remained overnight at the Premway Hotel.

The witnesses now numbered five, as a doorman west of the action had seen Worth fall, and had also seen the getaway. But with all the publicity, there was *still* no appearance by those who'd played host to the victims. And Roersch had expected this would have happened by now, except of course in Captain Worth's case; a payoff man would hardly be anxious to reveal himself . . .

Witness 1, Kenneth Lowery, had admitted Roersch and Jones to his apartment and apologized for being so 'suspicious' before of Jones. He said he'd seen most of what had happened, having been sitting at his second-floor window 'thinking of the past. Old men haven't much else . . .' Roersch knew he had *one* thing else – money. The apartment and furnishings would've made Ruthie turn green with envy.

Lowery became aware of the three boys when movement across the street between cars caught his eye. He didn't *hear* them, because his was a sealed, air-conditioned building. After opening a window, he heard a single loud shot, but he couldn't be sure who had fired it or into whom. He backed away in fear and horror, considered calling the police, then returned to the window to confirm that two people, a man and a woman, were lying between the cars. And that the three boys, 'who I now could see were Negroes', he said, not looking at Jones, 'were on the move. One crossed the street to my side; well, not all the way. He yelled something to a man coming west about his hands up. The man yelled back he was a police officer and began to crouch. There were shots from the other side of the street, where two of the boys were approaching a man, and then two shots, much louder, from this side. I was looking at the other side, and then leaned forward to look down and back east a ways, and saw the man who said he was a police officer falling. I looked across the street and the other man was down and the boys were running toward a car. Looked like a sporty GM – Camaro or Firebird . . .'

Witnesses 2 and 3 were across the street in two different buildings. One, a middle-aged man, saw only the bodies on the street and the flight of the three boys to their car, and ran to phone the police. Another, a young woman, saw them entering the car and driving away. She was the one who insisted it was red, though she couldn't tell the make.

Witness 5, the doorman in a building near First Avenue, had been at street level and was potentially the most valuable witness of all . . . but he'd been unaware of the action until the final two shots, the ones that killed Worth, and hadn't come out of his building until the getaway car was striking the Porsche. He'd been startled, yet hadn't thought to take down the license. No, he couldn't recall a single number or letter.

It was Witness 4, back in Mr Lowery's house, who interested Roersch the most. Mrs Amy Gleason was

78

seventy, wore thick glasses, and had opened her window 'as I do every night. The air-conditioning will *kill* you. My husband worked in an office with the air-conditioning and his lungs went bad. They said it was the cigarettes, but I knew...'

Roersch had gotten her back onto the subject. Her eyes might be weak, but only at short distances, she said. 'Put something far enough away and I'll see it perfect. And my ears are still pretty good.'

She'd heard 'strange sounds' and gone from her bed to the window and leaned out and looked five stories down to a point almost directly beneath her. 'A boy with that kind of bushy hair was pointing something – now I know it was a gun, but then I didn't – he was pointing it at a man on the sidewalk right under me. The man was saying something about being a police officer. Then he half turned around like to run to the basement entrance to this building, not far from where he was. And then there was a loud sound and the man turned *all* the way around and fell on his face and there was another shot. But the shots were really close together. The whole thing, the turning and falling, took no time at all, a second, a little more. The boy who killed him ran across the street and then I saw the other two boys and the people lying around and I got a sick feeling and went to my bed. But I came down the next afternoon when I was stronger and I told the officer...'

Roersch leaned back and thought of that crayon outline, and the parked cars, and he wondered how the second shot had gotten to Worth's head as he lay on the pavement. Between the two parked cars? Or had there *been* a car parked there? He had to check out alternate-side-of-the-street regulations on Fifty-second: had to check all the witnesses on their recollections of parked vehicles. If a car had blocked Worth's prone form, how had the bullet entered the top of his head?

And then he froze. Because if Worth were dead from that heart-shot, as the coroner insisted he was, then he wouldn't have moved once he'd fallen. And he'd been found with body, and head, turned slightly toward the building, toward

79

that basement entrance. And only someone *in* that basement entrance, on those stone steps leading down to the shadowy passageway, leaning out and aiming carefully, could have put the bullet – the *coup de grâce* into his head.

All right, bodies *did* move convulsively, in muscular spasms. So don't play Sherlock Holmes. This is New York City where cops makes mistakes like too vigorously searching, and perhaps moving, corpses. And hadn't Deverney's 'white Jew's son', Patrolman Michaelson, taken an envelope off Worth, and couldn't he have moved the body in the process? And couldn't the other responding radio-car officer, or perhaps a member of the Third, have also examined, and moved, the captain?

Still, he thought on it, made notes on it, his gut feeling growing stronger.

There were detailed reports from the coroner about things like 'a severed vagus nerve' in the base of Arnold Jaeker's head being the 'immediate cause of death' since it controlled 'cardiac rhythm' and Arnold's heart would have stopped because of that first bullet and not the two others that ripped through his brain. Important to a doctor, maybe, but not to a detective.

There were last-minute reports from Forensic updating previous reports; descriptions of partial prints other than those of the victims on wallets and purse.

There were reports by detectives of the Third Division on the results of their long and continuing canvass, which amounted to nothing (though they'd made a list of all tenants on the murder block, by address, and they'd turned up the doorman who'd watched the getaway). No more witnesses, though there had to be a dozen! No one stating they'd known the victims.

And no one was going to help him, Roersch thought, until he got his ass on that street and *made* them help him.

There was even a report by police psychiatrists – a perpetrator workup; a psychological profile of the three killers – which had obviously been produced under heavy pressure from Deverney and other Headquarters brass. It was a load of bull that used phrases like 'partial racial motivation cannot be exempted' and 'their youth indicates parental withdrawal' and Roersch felt sorry for whoever'd had to write it. Instant psychology. Instant analysis. Roersch never asked for, or used, the services of police psychiatrists.

What he *did* ask for and use was the relatively new SPRINT system at Headquarters – Special Police Radio Inquiry Network. With an average of eighteen thousand calls a day handled by radio cars and walkie-talkie-equipped officers, no one man could canvass the precincts properly in search of information phoned in by citizens . . . but the five-million-dollar SPRINT computer could – could check police files in all five boroughs for the information he wanted.

He rose to go to the wall phone and call Deverney; then realized how late it was.

Time to put away the reports and get to sleep. Time to wrap a heating pad around that aching right shoulder, give some rest to that aching chest . . .

But he didn't want to think of his heart, or that his father had died of a coronary at age forty-seven. No reason to think of it. His last physical had shown his pressure up just a little, his heartbeat arrhythmic just a trifle, his general condition good. Good enough, at any rate, for the doctor to send him back to duty, though with a vague warning about avoiding tension.

Tension? Find a murder case without it!

He was at his desk at eight. Deverney returned his call at eight-twenty, from his home, his voice thick with sleep. But he didn't grouse, and he called back again in ten minutes to say three men were monitoring SPRINT with orders to report to Roersch by noon.

Roersch began to enjoy the feeling of *clout*.

At nine, Jones, Ross, and Lauria arrived. Jones reported on his visit to Fort Apache the night before to see Joe Hooker, who had some teenage maniacs in his files. Hooker hadn't come up with any threesomes that worked together as the M-4 killers had, but he would call Roersch later in the week if anything occurred to him.

'Just don't send me back there,' Jones said, shaking his

head, smiling ruefully. 'I mean, you should have *seen* what was going on! And that station house – like poor-folks Dickens! And the neighborhood – half burned out like movies of World War II!'

He looked at Roersch, and Roersch said, 'Well, anything more?'

'Aren't you going to tell me about the racial makeup of the South Bronx?'

Roersch laughed.

Jones nodded sadly in the direction of heaven. 'Yeah, he's got me trained. Tell me about the black rabbits, George.'

Lauria said, 'What's that mean?'

Roersch told Lauria to have Xerox copies made of the tenant list compiled by the Third Detective Division and to take Ross with him to canvass every 'Martin' on the list – there were no fewer than five – to see if they could find the 'Marty' Richard Magris *might* have called with his dying breath.

A man called on his mother or God in most last-breath instances. And if this one had called on another man it set up a train of thought in Roersch's mind, a mind well-schooled in every form of human activity – sexual, social, antisocial – that explained why this particular Marty had not come forward. Richard Magris was married and had three children.

But he said nothing of his thinking to the young detectives; kept it for later, when he himself would do followup on what they narrowed down. Instead, he told Jones he was leaving and not to move his butt from the M–4 room; to send out for lunch; to have the jailer down the hall at the holding cells cover for him when he went to the john. Because Roersch wanted that call from SPRINT received promptly; he would be phoning in for it.

At nine-forty he was in his car, using siren and slap-on roof swivel light to make his way through very moderate Saturday morning traffic. He parked at a Fifty-second Street hydrant a few minutes after ten, and walked to the apartment house on the east end of the block, north side. Worth had been on this side, walking east to west, coming from somewhere to this end.

Roersch opened the glass door. A different doorman looked up from where he sat on a high stool, reading a *Daily News*. Roersch flashed badge and ID. 'Mailman here?'

'Not yet. You can catch him up the street. One house back, unless he's behind schedule. Then it's two houses.'

'That's all right. I'll wait here.' He went to the mailboxes and row of tenants' names. 'Got any Martins, Martys, maybe swish, living here?'

The doorman said, 'Another detective was around. Had a list. It told him I didn't have any Martins.'

Roersch read names off the mailboxes. He touched one with a thick finger; spoke without turning to the doorman: 'This A. Tortemango in apartment 9-G. Do you know him?'

'I know all my tenants.' Yet his voice was uncertain ... or was it *worried*?

'Good tipper around Christmas?'

'The best. How'd you know?'

'First name Angelo?'

'He says to call him Angie.'

'Good tipper all year round, correct?'

'Like I said, the best.'

'Does he work regular hours?'

'Hell, I don't check on when people leave and when they come back.'

Roersch turned. His look was heavy; his voice matched it. 'I asked you – does Mr Tortemango work regular hours?'

The doorman was in his early thirties and balding and thick of face and body. He flushed. 'Every time a cop sees an Italian name he thinks Mafia, rackets, gangsters. Well, *I'm* Italian and I'm not ...'

'There are at least five other Italian names here. I didn't ask about any of *them*. Does Angie Tortemango work regular hours?'

The doorman was off his stool, moving to usher in a tenant. He greeted the small, perky woman and nodded at her comment about the 'lovely' weather and moved with her to the elevators. Roersch and his heavy look were still waiting when he returned to his stool.

'Listen, officer, he's touchy about his name. 'Cause of the New Jersey Tortemango family, you know? But this one, he's straight, I'm sure. Rich, maybe . . .'

Roersch sighed.

The doorman waved his hands. 'No, Christ, he doesn't go out at eight or nine or come back at five or six.'

'Would he be up and around by now?'

'I don't know. Sometimes he's down at ten for his mail and sometimes he don't show till noon or later. And it's Saturday.' He paused. 'I don't want him to know I've been talking to the police.'

'He won't.' Roersch asked other questions: about Tortemango's marital status; whether he received many women visitors; whether he received any celebrity-type visitors; whether he'd ever received any of the victims, perhaps Captain Worth.

Angie was single, had 'plenty of friends, men and women, some of them maybe in show biz, I'm not sure, but Raquel Welch or Robert Redford or like that wasn't here'. And finally, 'Jesus, you mean the cop that got killed down the street? You mean *him*? You think Mr Tortemango . . .?'

Roersch said, '*Did* you ever see Captain Worth in this house?'

The doorman was standing tensely beside his stool now. 'No.' He held up his *Daily News*. 'Picture of the captain right here, big. So I'd know if I ever seen him, and I never seen him. But I'm only on days. Used to be on nights, but that was a year ago. You need to speak to Saul Gordon, our five-to-twelve man, or Lou Flecher, our midnight-to-eight man.'

Roersch made notes and turned back to the mailboxes. He considered going up to see Angie Tortemango now, and discarded the thought immediately. He had to speak to Saul Gordon and Lou Flecher; Flecher first, because that late tour was the one that made the most sense in terms of a visit by Worth.

The mailman arrived. He was short and stumpy and

84

black, and implacably cheerful. He said, '*Beautiful* day! Going to be a scorcher, but I'll be back at the post office by then! Don't I get my good morning, Marty?' He chuckled, nodding at Roersch.

Roersch turned to the doorman. '*Marty?*'

The doorman had a stricken expression on his thick face. 'The other officer wanted *tenants* named Martin, so I didn't tell him because I don't live here and I was home at five-thirty that day ...'

Roersch said, 'The other officer will be back. You tell him then.' But he really wasn't interested. This Martin didn't fit any pertinent category.

The mailman was opening a large brass panel to the mail-boxes. Roersch flashed his badge and ID and mentioned M–4. The mailman's smile disappeared. 'Yeah, *that*. Makes life easier for the rest of us, doesn't it?' He began flipping letters into boxes.

Roersch spoke to him. About tenants named Martin. Perhaps gay; perhaps not.

The mailman shrugged. 'Hard to tell.' He flipped letters. 'There's a Martin Anders across the street. Maybe he is and maybe he isn't.' The smile returned briefly. 'But if he isn't, *I* am.'

Roersch brought up Angie Tortemango. The mailman said, 'Never see him,' and flipped letters faster. Roersch felt that he'd gotten an answer, and would get no other.

'Anyone on the block work for CBS?'

The mailman rolled a magazine and stuck it in a box. He hummed a little, then said, 'Don't know if she *works* for CBS, but she gets steady *mail* from CBS. Name's Maigret. Marilyn Maigret.'

Roersch took Martin Anders' and Marilyn Maigret's addresses, and thanked the mailman. The mailman said, 'What for? The three you want didn't come from around here or have anything to do with people from around here. I'm not helping you catch them with names from around here, no matter what detective work you *think* you're doing.'

Roersch nodded. 'But maybe those three didn't kill *all* the victims.' He smiled as for the first time he got the man's full and undivided attention. 'How does that grab you?'

'In the right place, officer, the right place. Especially if it's that captain they didn't kill. And if you can prove it before Christmas-tipping time.'

Roersch chuckled with him, and gave him the M-4 number, and turned to the doors. Marty left his stool to open up for him. Roersch said, 'Thanks. Get my number from the mailman, or your newspaper. If you can think of anything, call me.'

Marty said sure.

Roersch was halfway through the doors when he said, 'As for Mr Tortemango, I won't say anything about you and you won't say anything about me, agreed?' He kept his eyes on the man as the doors closed. Marty stood there nodding; Roersch stood there looking.

Finally, Roersch walked away. He had a hunch Tortemango would be warned. The mailman's reaction indicated this was one of the New Jersey clan, and the doorman was probably into Angie for heavy tips, for women or junk or whatever turned him on. The racket boys paid to keep their doorsteps swept clean, their peepholes kept open. The doorman would reason that Angie would be more grateful for the warning than irritated that Marty had been forced to talk about him.

Roersch checked his notebook, the names of those he wanted interviewed. But it was just ten-thirty, still early for some people on a Saturday morning. It would have been early for Roersch, too, who liked to sleep late, or at least laze around, on his days off. They had been Mondays and Tuesdays his last tour, before the aborted vacation and M-4. Now all off days would be put aside, for him and his men; would accrue for future use.

Fifty-second Street was almost empty. On the south side, a young man in tan chinos, brown body shirt, and white sneakers walked a small white poodle. The dog looked across the street at Roersch, then returned to sniffing the curb. A car drove by, windows wide open, trailing a brief spray of music. Trees and hedges and an occasional window box were in full leaf. There was a long hoot from the river – tug or barge or excursion boat.

Roersch paused to look around and breathe deeply; and experienced a mild sense of *déjà vu*. Of course, he actually *had* stood on Manhattan streets, in and out of uniform, back when many had been as safe, as peaceful, as this street seemed. And as beautiful as this street *was*. Because New York – where it wasn't being vandalized, spray-painted with graffiti, soiled, heaped with garbage, and burned to the ground as in the South Bronx and other battlegrounds – remained the most hypnotically charming of American cities. And this neighborhood was the good neighborhood; these were the good streets, the rich streets, the goal of many hard-working New Yorkers. These were the streets of last refuge before fleeing to the suburbs . . . and these were the streets now being bloodied.

He thought of Wednesday night, early Thursday morning, and the senseless deaths that had taken place here . . . and perhaps one death *not* senseless; one death well planned. He wanted to crack that one more than the others, because the others were simply New York's, and America's, sickness showing, spotted past catching up with it. The Captain's death, on the other hand, was a job for what Deverney had called a 'shadow', an old-time detective solving an old-time puzzle. Something that had motive, that had reason, that didn't chill the blood and bring despair the way the thousands of slashings, shootings, *butcherings* did. Something that required more than computers and good assistants and informants and manpower and luck. Something he not only had to do alone, but *wanted* to do alone, pitting himself against whoever had stood in that basement entrance.

He was approaching that entrance right now.

And approaching *him*, having just emerged from an apartment house, was Detective Third Paul Lauria. They met, and Lauria jerked his head at the young man – now walking his dog toward Beekman and the F.D.R. – on the other side of the street. 'One of your Marties, Sergeant,'

Roersch turned to examine the man more carefully. He appraised the delicate walk, the movement of head and hands. 'Anders, is it?'

'That's right. You check him out yourself?'

'No. Just recognized a description.'

'A sweetheart. He, along with two others I checked, say they didn't know Richard Magris.'

'Go back to Anders' building. Do a door-to-door on his floor, paying special attention to immediate neighbors. Use pictures of Magris – the *News* had better shots than the coroner gave us – and find out if anyone saw him in the building. Maybe with Anders, or entering Anders' apartment. Get the names of the night staff; the doormen, if they have any. Same questions.'

Lauria said, 'Right. There's a newsstand around the corner on Beekman.'

'After you finish, check your address sheet for Magris's home – it's in Queens. I want you to drive there and find out what sort of jewelry he was wearing – watch, rings, ID bracelet, religious medal, whatever. If we can find out who he was visiting, we'll have a double-check on those items, the items stolen. And we'll also have the details surrounding the victim's last hours, so dear to the D.A.'s heart.'

The short detective hurried across the street. Roersch turned to the basement entrance of the apartment house that was almost dead center of this block, north side. He looked back, and found faint traces of the crayon outline of Worth's body on the sidewalk. He saw the angle of that head; remembered again the coroner's report. He walked slowly to the entrance and opened the iron gate. He was walking down the three concrete steps, thinking that whatever else he was doing was crap compared to *this*, when he heard Detective Third Eli Ross's deep voice call his name.

He returned to street level, unwilling to have anyone intrude on him here.

The lanky detective said he'd interviewed two of the Martins. 'Nothing, Sergeant.'

Roersch took out his notebook. 'Write this down, Eli.' He read off Marilyn Maigret's name and apartment number.

'This building; same as Gleason and Lowery. Ask her if she knew the Jaekers. Since she didn't come forward on her own, she might lie about it. If she says no, do a door-to-door of all apartments on her floor. You got copies of those CBS publicity shots of Louise Sanders?'

Ross said no one had told him to take them.

'From now on carry everything we've got on the victims *wherever* you go. Buy a *News* at the coffee shop on First. It's got the husband too.' Ross began turning away. 'Eli, you'll be driving back to the station with me, not with Lauria. If I'm not here, try that coffee shop.'

Eli Ross strode back up the street. Both he and Lauria were enthused, excited, full of energy. Roersch began to feel the juices flow himself as he finally opened that iron gate and walked down into the gloomy concrete tunnel.

He tried the door on his right, about ten feet from the steps. It was heavy metal and it was locked. He rattled the knob, used his shoulder in an experimental push, felt it would take a bulldozer to break it open.

He walked further into gloom, and saw the naked bulb set into the ceiling. It was out, and there didn't seem to be a chain or switch nearby.

He tried the second door, about halfway along the fifty-five-to-sixty-foot passageway and on his left. Same as the first; metal and locked.

Nothing unusual here. Apartment houses weren't likely to hire security doormen and then leave side and back doors open for the city thieves.

He went to the very end of the passageway, coming into a small, shadowy courtyard with brick walls rising on all four sides; walls broken only by the archway through which he'd entered, and a series of apartment windows. The windows of the first two stories were barred top to bottom.

So there was only one way in and out of this concrete tunnel, and that was via the street. Which meant a witness might be found who'd seen someone either entering or leaving shortly before or after the killings.

He returned to the street, walked east some fifteen feet, and entered the lobby of the house that held two of his witnesses, Mr Lowery and Mrs Gleason, as well as Marilyn Maigret, who could be a witness. The same elderly doorman, sitting well back near the elevators, told him the doors were 'always locked, except when Terry, the super, takes out the garbage cans. That's in the morning, around eight-thirty, nine; never at night'.

'He could leave them open by mistake, couldn't he?'

'Not really. They lock on closing, and close on a spring. All he has to do is let go. Those're steel doors with heavy Yale locks and no one's forced them yet. Not long ago some tenants complained of prowlers in the courtyard. The cops checked it out and said there was no sign of a break-in or anything.'

'How about keys to those doors? Do you have a set?'

'Not me! Not anyone but Terry and the owner. And the owner's got a rule – no duplicate sets. It's the same for every house on this street.'

Roersch made notes and came out onto the summer street. It was eleven-ten and people were beginning to show in some numbers. He walked to First Avenue and across to the coffee shop, where he used the wall phone in back to call Jones.

'Nothing yet from SPRINT, Eddy.'

He said okay, disappointed, and, 'I want a complete check run on Angie Tortemango.' He gave the address. 'Known Criminals File, and more important the office of the chief of organized crime at Headquarters. Don't forget to say it's for M–4. I want the information on my desk before we leave today.'

He went to the counter and ordered coffee and a wedge of Swiss Knight cheese. The waitress – a buxom redhead in her forties – shook her head. 'That's not enough to keep the fires stoked for anyone with hands as big as yours.'

'What've *hands* got to do with it?' Roersch asked.

'Big hands means big tool. Big tool means big lover. Big lover . . .'

'Got it,' Roersch muttered. 'My wife has me on a diet.'

'If she gets too many headaches,' the redhead said, turning to the coffee urn and bending to display her massive

90

bottom, 'come back some night around seven.' She faced him again, her bright-red mouth smiling broadly. 'I just can't resist big hands.'

When Eli Ross appeared, Roersch picked up his tab and went to the register. The lanky detective said, 'Thought I'd get a sandwich.'

'You're too young to eat in a place like this,' Roersch said, and walked out. Eli joined him on the sidewalk, looking back at the luncheonette, frowning.

'What did you get from Marilyn Maigret?'

'She said she met the Jaekers in California. The husband, Arnold, was an agent and represented her in some sort of a deal out there. She's an actress.'

'And?'

'That's it. But she was really shocked when I asked if she knew the Jaekers. She was drinking coffee and her hand jerked and she spilled it on the carpet.'

'She denied seeing them in New York?'

'Yes, after a while. I mean, she thought a while before answering my question. Like she realized she *had* to tell us she knew them out there because someone *here* knew about it and we might find out.'

'What about the door-to-door?'

'Nothing. But not everyone was home. July weekend, you know.'

Roersch had stopped. 'Why don't you get that sandwich after all, Eli? Take it to my car.' He pointed down Fifty-second. 'I'll be along in a few minutes.'

He went to the apartment house with the passageway and once again spoke to the doorman. He rode the elevator to seven and found the apartment and pressed the bell button. The door opened immediately, as if she'd been waiting with her hand on the knob. 'Now what the hell *is* this! I have a day off and I'm bullied all morning! A police officer just left ...'

Roersch said, 'Sorry. We're trying to find out who killed your friends.'

She was tall, about five-eight or -nine, and pretty in a crisp, almost hard sort of way. Her hair was dark brown and disordered; her eyes underscored by fatigue shadows and reddened by what might have been tears. She wore a long, quilted robe of bright pink and pulled it together at the neck, though it was buttoned floor to chin. 'What do you mean, my *friends*? I simply knew them from the West Coast.'

'Your neighbors saw them here.' What did he have to lose? Eli had felt her tension, and he was getting vibrations of his own. Might as well crack through in one area, unimportant though it was. He was sick of blank walls. 'Saw them more than once.'

Her mouth opened. He mouth closed. 'My neighbors?' she muttered.

'You know – people who live up and down the hall. Louise Sanders was getting too well known to sneak in and out of places unrecognized.'

'*Sneak?*' She began to bluster. 'Now listen here . . .'

'Miss Maigret, I don't care what reason you have for keeping your relationship with the Jaekers a secret . . .'

A door opened near the elevators. Marilyn Maigret stepped aside. 'Come in,' she said, voice weak.

He came in, closed the door, stood leaning against it. 'I want to be able to say that Mr and Mrs Jaeker visited you the night of the murders. That you were busy later and just didn't bother with newspapers and television; just didn't learn about the deaths. Until today, when you contacted me and gave the following information.'

She was an actress on daytime television; CBS.

Louise Jaeker had been wearing a very expensive watch, 'the band in effect a diamond bracelet. She wore a cocktail ring, also very expensive. And two rings on the right hand that I don't really remember.'

'Try,' Roersch said. 'And don't forget her wedding band.'

'She didn't always wear the wedding band, which was a wide, diamond-studded ring she said she disliked. Anyway, because of her career . . .' She shrugged. 'I'm sure she wasn't wearing it Wednesday night.'

'Those rings on her right hand?' Roersch prodded.

Marilyn Maigret sighed and bent her head and closed her eyes. 'She would take off her jewelry . . . not always the same rings . . . but the watch and big cocktail ring were *always* the same. The other two, that night . . .' She suddenly nodded, and looked up. 'A large pearl in antique gold. And a diamond-chip cluster around a deep-cut emerald.'

Roersch had caught that, 'she would take off her jewelry', and had a hunch about Marilyn's secret. 'Who was your date?' he asked, as he made notes.

'What gives you the notion I had a date?'

He looked up. He was fishing, and she was a sucker for a baited look.

'Well, as a matter of fact, I did have a friend drop over.'

His eyes went back to the notebook. 'His name and address?'

It was a newscaster named Morgan Breen. Roersch had seen him. A little too pretty, a little too involved in himself, to make the horrors that passed for today's news sound right. For that you needed a Cronkite.

'But you won't bother Morgan, will you? I can tell you everything you need to know.'

Roersch didn't look up. 'As I said, I'm not interested in your reasons for wanting the evening kept to yourselves. But I have to check out what he remembers of the jewelry against what you remember. Now, how about *Mr* Jaeker? What sort of watch? Any rings?'

'A good watch; very simple. No dates or flashing lights. Gold and thin and Roman numerals. A Longines, I believe. And he always wore a pinky ring. Good-sized diamond in heavy gold setting. A gift from Louise.' She shook her head. 'How could it happen? They had everything.'

Roersch closed his book. 'I'd like you to come to Manhattan West Homicide later today.' He took a card from his breast pocket.

She looked at it. 'Come to a police station? But *why*? I've told you everything you need to know.'

'I'll have an artist help you draw up representations of the Jaekers' jewelry. I'll also have Morgan Breen there to confer with you and the artist. If you'd like, you can call him when I leave, explain the situation, and come down together. No later than three, please. We have to get the infor-

93

mation on a sheet to go to pawn shops and jewelry stores.'

She blinked at him. 'And after that?'

'After that you're finished. I don't want any publicity about *my* home – kitchen *or* bedroom – and I accept your not wanting it either.' He paused. 'Your windows face the street. Did you happen to look out, to see if your friends had reached their car?'

She was shaking her head. 'Morgan stayed for a nightcap. We talked. We ... we were planning to see Louise and Arnold the next night too. Neither of us thought to look out the window. You simply don't expect your friends to be murdered crossing the street to their car!' Her voice was growing thick. 'Why should those boys have killed them? Arnold was a most liberal man. He had black employees and donated to the N.A.A.C.P. I think he's been a member since World War II ...' She began to cry.

It was pointless answering that it had nothing to do with the N.A.A.C.P. It was pointless standing here any longer.

He turned to the door. She said, 'I'm relieved – actually *glad* – that you found out about me. You have no idea how I worried, suffered since I heard the ghastly news from my doorman Thursday morning.'

He stepped into the hall, nodding. 'Now explain that sense of relief to your friend Morgan.'

In the car on the way back to Manhattan West, Roersch slumped low in the passenger's seat, allowing Eli to fight growing traffic. And said, 'Get an artist over to M–4 by three o'clock.' The young detective glanced at him; began to question him. Roersch said, 'Don't ask me how to do it, Eli. Find out from someone else. I want to doze a while.'

He closed his eyes, but he didn't doze. He thought. About a lot of things ... always ending up in that passageway. Because until they found the three kids, and found the gun that had killed Worth *on* those kids, the big answers lay in that passageway. Until the kids confessed to killing Worth – that head shot coming between cars, under a car, some fluke ricochet that hadn't damaged the slug – until then he had to consider the twenty thousand dollars as a motive, tied in with payoff or blackmail.

He kept his eyes closed and muttered, 'SPRINT's doing a crawl. SPRINT fucked up.'

But it wasn't, and hadn't, as he learned the minute he walked into the M–4 squad room. Jones was rising from his desk, holding a typewritten sheet. He spoke with an undercurrent of excitement in his voice. 'I'll be going to work soon, Eddy. Read it and grin.'

Roersch read it, and grinned. They had a witness who'd seen both car and boys together, maybe twenty minutes before the crime and heading toward the scene of the crime. And who'd phoned a complaint to the police.

At the time it hadn't seemed like much – just three black kids in a new red Firebird running a light and almost hitting a pedestrian at Park Avenue and Fifty-ninth Street. SPRINT and the three cops who'd audited the computer's tapes had made the connection for M–4. But it was that pedestrian, a Mr Wolfe Lowen, who had really delivered. Because he'd taken down the license plate on the spot. And it turned out to belong to a Firebird stolen Wednesday afternoon, the day before the murders, near 145th and Riverside Drive.

'That's deepest Harlem,' Jones said, when Roersch looked up. 'Those kids aren't professional car thieves – not with the dumb butcher job they pulled. Joyriders, Eddy. And ghetto joyriders don't travel far on foot. Which means they hooked that car somewhere close to where they live.'

'Maybe,' Roersch said, pushing him to refine it.

'At least *one* of them lives nearby. And at least one of them will want to use the car again. The odds favor it.'

'One is all we need, Willis. He'll get us the other two.'

'I'd forget the South Bronx and Brooklyn and anywhere else. I'd work the hell out of Harlem, between 130th and 150th, the west side. I'd hit Harlem High, maybe another school on the fringes. For that one kid. For at least a week.'

'Then do it. Write it up. I'll get the manpower.'

'*Black* manpower, Sergeant. At least on the streets. Otherwise the extra activity will be noticed and we might blow it.'

'I don't know how many black officers are available, and whether we can transfer . . .'

'*Only* blacks, Eddy.' He was very tense now, was Sergeant

95

Willis Jones. He was the compleat cop now. He knew the streets to be worked and he knew the people and Roersch wasn't going to go against his main man, not in the area of his expertise.

'Write it up that way, Willis. We'll keep the honkies in the cars.'

Jones smiled, but only briefly.

Roersch sat down at his desk. He looked at the fresh paper, the new pile of blue D.D.-5's that had accumulated since he'd left for Fifty-second Street. 'I wonder if they can *feel* our breath down their necks?' he said to Jones, who was inserting paper into his portable typewriter.

'Let's hope not. It's going to be tough enough without their having E.S.P., or African voodoo, on their side.' Jones chuckled.

Roersch picked up the phone as Jones began typing out his Harlem street plan. He got Deverney's office. The inspector was out to lunch. He said, 'Officer Nolan, my love, get the anonymous inspector for me. And don't ask if it's urgent. With M-4 it always is.'

She said right away.

'One thing, Donna. How do you have an anonymous man paged in a restaurant?'

'Funny you should ask that. I did too. He counts on being the only "Mister Inspector" there.'

Roersch laughed and hung up. He waited no more than fifteen minutes before Deverney was on the line. He explained how important it was that the media be kept from what SPRINT and Wolfe Lowen had delivered. 'I'm also going to keep the descriptions of the stolen jewelry from them as long as I can, Inspector. If they tumble to our flyer to jewelry and pawn shops, I hope the P.C. will make a personal appeal to keep the lid on it. I want those kids to drive their hot car and sell their loot.'

Deverney said, 'The officers who audited the SPRINT tapes won't be any problem. The flyers to jewelry stores ... I'll have to talk to people about that. If necessary, the P.C. *will* make an appeal. But you'd better move fast on this, Eddy. It's too big a story to control.'

Roersch said movement had begun. Now the department – a big hunk of it, and heavily black – had to be assigned to search for that Firebird. And how to keep *that* from sharp police reporters?

Deverney was silent a long moment. 'You just ruined a great lunch at "21". I'll speak to the boss right away. What about Worth?'

'Also beginning to move.'

'No shit?'

'I'm getting the beginnings of a picture.'

'Ah,' the inspector said. And then, 'Might as well tell you this right now, Eddy.' He paused. 'You're not to put a collar on anyone involved in the Worth murder until you confer with me.'

Roersch had never heard anything like that before in all his thirty-five years as a cop.

'You got it, Eddy? No collar until we talk it over. And we don't talk it over until you're damned sure you've got your solved.'

Roersch had to say *something* while he wondered how the brass could allow Worth's killer to come to trial and still hope to keep the lid on the twenty thousand dollars.

God, how he prayed those black kids had done it!

He said, 'Orders is orders, Inspector.'

'That's right, Eddy. Don't forget *this* order, for all our sakes.'

The line clicked. Roersch felt sweat trickling down his sides. And here came that gut-wrenching hunch again. Here came the feeling of being backed toward a precipice.

He belched, without getting relief from sudden heartburn. 'Oh, Christ,' he muttered, and pressed a hand to his chest. He'd always hated the thought of retirement. Now he cursed himself for having waited too long.

SEVEN

The Victims

Louise wasn't sure how Arnold would take the news that she was going to leave him. She hoped he would continue to represent her, though if it came to that she could find as good an agent. Her career was moving along on its own now. She no longer needed Arnold: not for sex; not for acting. She'd tell him when they got back to L.A.

What she wanted was her own household, with a 'secretary' (she had the girl picked out) and a woman 'friend' or two.

She leaned back, crossing her legs, wondering if the seat of the cab would soil her pale green evening gown. New York cabs were so *shabby* lately, and it didn't help to have that shield separating passengers from driver. She felt as if she were a prisoner in the back of a police car!

They were on their way to get their rental car; then on to Marilyn Maigret's Fifty-second Street apartment. Arnold was talking of books, of politics, of Solzhenitsyn. She nodded and murmured uh-huh and looked out the window. She was *tired* of Arnold, she decided; tired of his complexity, his Jewishness. The People of the Book. She wanted People of the Body – of the penis, the vagina. *Her* mind was stimulated mainly by her work. And by theater and film, a little television . . . all in privacy, experienced alone, without the need to consider the tastes and feelings of a partner, especially an unchanging, lifetime partner.

And that, she decided as the cab pulled to the curb in front of the Third Avenue Drive-Ur-Own garage where they always took their car rentals, was the bottom line. She wanted to live her life exactly as she pleased, *entirely* for herself, and basically alone. She wanted her sexual partners, her social partners, to be there when she desired them, and to be gone when she didn't.

Men had operated that way all through history. Women hadn't been able to. Because they hadn't had the financial resources. And in the rare cases where they had, they'd been forced to waste themselves, dissipate their energies, fighting an environment hostile to women being free, being swingers . . .

'Catherine the Great,' she murmured, after Arnold had signed for the Oldsmobile waiting near the garage exit. They would use the car tomorrow, and over the weekend.

'Catherine who?' he asked, as they drove off.

It was only about five minutes to Marilyn's place, though it took another five, and two trips around the block, before they found parking. They might have looked even longer, except that a car pulled out in front of them, giving them a space almost directly across the street from their destination. She explained her reference to Catherine of Russia as they walked across Fifty-second Street: 'I was trying to think of a woman who directed her own destiny and had a ball doing it.'

He shrugged, looking back at their rental Oldsmobile, and said Catherine had been a whore.

She knew he was preoccupied, had probably not heard what she'd said, but it served her purpose to explode in anger. It would be easier to break with him after a series of fights.

'That's what men call women whose sexual appetites they can't control! That's what they call any woman they fear as an equal in sex, and sometimes in society, business, *power*! A whore, or, if she's an Eleanor Roosevelt, a *dog*!'

'You're shouting,' he said mildly.

'Am I?' She turned to the lobby entrance. 'A stupid statement like yours *deserves* shouting.'

He ruined the beginning of what seemed a good argument, one that could have led to her punishing him at the gig, one that might have carried over to L.A. He said, 'I'm sorry. You're right, I've been a little . . . well, insecure lately. With you. I've wanted to discuss . . .'

Which wasn't what *she* wanted, and she took his arm and hugged it and said, 'Let's forget everything but the gig!'

99

Marilyn opened the door wearing black lederhosen and matching boots, carrying a riding crop. She said, 'Pay the entry fee, please,' and turned and bent. The bottom of those German pants had been cut out. Louise knelt to kiss Marilyn's round behind. 'The tongue, madam, the tongue!' Marilyn snapped. Louise obeyed.

When she arose, Arnold was offered the behind. He knelt, flushing, embarrassed, upset, out of it, as he always was at the very beginning. Then he hurried to the kitchen counter and the liquor, glancing at Morgan, who sat on the couch, a newspaper in his lap. The tall, well-built, too-handsome newscaster was dressed in one of his beautifully cut Cardin suits. He'd probably done his show in it. He smiled at Louise, looked at Arnold, said, 'How about kissing *this*, old man?'

Arnold turned, a glass in his hand.

Morgan flung aside the paper to reveal his penis rampant through his open fly.

Arnold flushed again, more deeply. 'No thanks,' he muttered, and poured straight Scotch.

'Then *I* will,' Louise said. She went to the couch, sat down, and took the enormous tool into her mouth. When Morgan began to get a little too ardent, she disengaged. 'Your turn,' she said to Marilyn.

Marilyn fellated Morgan for a moment or two. Then rose. 'Your turn,' she said to Arnold.

Arnold shook his head, drinking. He had yet to consent to homosexual activity. Marilyn shrugged and began to caress Louise's hip and thigh ... but Louise had her argument now, the one that would carry through tomorrow night, and the weekend, and all the way back to Los Angeles.

They all did everything in the gigs ... except Arnold. The furthest he'd gone homosexually – if it could be called that – was to grasp a penis, not Morgan's monster but a black musician's smaller job, and place it in her. That was it. Four or five months ago, and never again. And she felt he'd done it only to prove he was totally without prejudice; wouldn't have done it if the man had been white.

'It's intolerable,' she said, glaring at him. 'We extend our-

100

selves to make the gig work, and you . . . you *hover* there, an officious, disapproving asshole . . .'

'Easy,' Morgan said.

Marilyn took up the argument. 'She's right, Arnold. You make it difficult for the rest of us. And what does it entail anyway? Just sucking the damned thing for a minute! *I* do it to you. Morgan *tries* to do it to you. We do everything we can . . .'

Louise said, 'Maybe he prefers to sit the entire thing out? It's all right with me. The three of us can carry on very nicely without him.' She took Marilyn around the waist, jerked her head at Morgan, and headed for the bedroom doorway.

Again Arnold ruined the opportunity for a serious, long-lasting argument. And this time she was really surprised. She'd never thought he'd allow himself to be coerced into gay activity.

'All right,' he said.

She turned, unbelieving.

He strode to the couch, sat down, bent his big, graying, distinguished head, and took Morgan's penis into his mouth. Did it like he did so many things he disliked, in a rush, the decision made, the job to be done and gotten out of the way.

Morgan, however, loved it. His eyes rolled, his Adam's apple rippled, his organ swelled. He stroked Arnold's head and began to groan.

Marilyn was on her knees, almost completely hidden under Louise's long gown. Louise whispered, 'My goddam pants! Pull down my goddam pants!' Marilyn did, and Louise stood straddle-legged, writhing.

Arnold raised his head, beginning to withdraw. Louise said, 'To the finish! For *me* Arny! *Please,* baby!'

He looked at her, stricken. She could see it. He was being raped. And *she* was doing the raping, with the power she exerted over him. Christ, how it excited her!

He went back down. Morgan began to wail. Marilyn's tongue and fingers did what no man had ever been able to do for Louise.

101

When Morgan began to hump into Arnold's mouth, when Arnold choked and drooled sperm and fought to lift his head against the pressure of both of Morgan's hands, Louise shrieked and tottered.

It was the best kickoff to a gig ever!

Like all New York City police officers, Captain Thomas Worth had at least two hand guns – his service revolver (a standard ·38 Detective Special) and an off-duty weapon smaller in both size and caliber. Actually, Worth had *six* weapons, ranging from a pearl-handled ·45 Colt automatic to a tiny, platinum-plated, two-shot derringer.

Tonight, on leaving Headquarters at eight-thirty, he'd decided in favor of his Detective Special in its hip-pocket holster. Yes, it made a noticeable bulge, if you knew what to look for, but he preferred the weapon he'd been issued fourteen years ago to anything else he owned. Because it was his action weapon, his law-and-order weapon, what he'd used in the shootout off Washington Square when those robbery suspects had holed up in an N.Y.U. fraternity house. He'd led a rush that night; he'd killed himself a bad guy that night, and *kissed* the Special in the privacy of the station-house john two hours later and realized he was still shaking.

He'd used it to face down a nut trying to hold a super-market manager hostage a month before he made lieutenant. He'd used it the time he caught his one and only slug, aimed blindly down the stairs by one of three guys trying to get away with armloads of mink coats. He'd started up the stairs, shouting the usual stuff about surrendering-with-your-hands-above-your-head, when that bullet caught him in the right side, ripping a good-sized chunk of meat out of him. Clarise still wasn't crazy about touching the scar when they made love ... but it hadn't been serious, and he'd gotten a commendation and a year later made captain.

He'd used his Special in a dozen tough situations; and he had to consider applying the squeeze to a Tortemango a potentially tough situation. Because Angie might decide old Tom was bluffing about putting evidence down on paper, or might figure he and Auntie Maria could intercept any letter

102

to Paddy and the logical move was to erase the squeezer. Or
forget logic, forget making sense, and remember the percentage of guys who blew their cool at the critical moment,
who went bananas and tried to kill a cop, especially one
stepping on them, *hard*.

Then there were other problems. Like not leaving a
trail from Headquarters to Angie's, in case of any future
flak.

He took a cab uptown to Forty-fourth, west side, and had
a leisurely Chinese dinner with a half bottle of Chablis. He
went to an all-night movie and sat through the double fea-
ture; then he went to the back of the theater and a phone
booth. He dialed Angie's number.

'Yes?'

'Mr Tortemango?'

'Yes.'

'Two A.M. is what we agreed on, right?'

The voice sighed. 'Yeah. You can come over now and
not waste time.'

'No. Two A.M.' He hung up.

It was a quarter after one. He strolled into the street, the
·38 creating a comforting pressure on his right hip.

He got a cab at Forty-sixth and Sixth, and when the white,
mustached driver asked his destination, said, 'I'm not sure
of the address. Drive down Fifty-second east of First and I'll
recognize it.'

The cabby gave him the eyes in the mirror then, probably
sweating a little over old Tom, because light-skinned or not
he was still Negro and it was late.

He let the man drive past Tortemango's end-of-the-block
residence, had him turn onto Beekman, and stopped him.
He paid and stood on the sidewalk, fiddling with his wallet
until the cab turned out of view. Then he walked back to
Fifty-second and started up the street ... but on the south
side, opposite Tortemango's apartment house. He kept
going, purposefully, as if headed elsewhere. He looked
around without seeming to, and saw service entrances to
houses and saw the man walking his English bulldog near
the corner of First Avenue. And watched for strange moves,

funny moves, dangerous moves. And except for that dog-walker, saw no moves at all.

He crossed the street before reaching First, but the dog spotted him and growled. He turned back east before the man could look up and see his face. He walked quickly and came to the mid-street basement entrance with the steps leading down. He checked it out without seeming to and walked on; then suddenly turned, as if to light a cigarette away from the mild breeze that blew in from the river.

No more dog-walker. Nothing. All clear.

He went directly to Tortemango's house and into the lobby and towards the elevators. The doorman came out of an alcove in back, a mug of something steaming in his hand. He looked worried. Tom said, 'It's all right. I'm Charlie for Mr Tortemango.'

Letting the doorman see and hear him was a chance he had to take, but it wasn't much. The name 'Charlie' would mean nothing; without Angie's active cooperation there could be no problem. And unlike a shakedown for gambling or drugs, Angie couldn't fink out by blowing the whistle.

He relaxed just a little while the doorman spoke into a house phone and listened and turned. 'Go right up, sir.'

He stopped relaxing as soon as he got off the elevator, and tensed as he walked along the hall to apartment 9-G. He went past it, moving very lightly for a man his size, and reached the end of the hall and an EXIT door. He stepped outside, still holding the door open, looked around, and jammed the lock with a matchbook cover. He went down half a flight and leaned over the railing and looked down the stairwell. He went back up past the ninth floor, and a half flight more, and leaned out and looked up.

He returned to nine and stood on the landing, smoking for five minutes. At a quarter to two, he drew his gun, jerked open the door, and rushed into the hall.

Nothing, and he put the gun back in its holster.

He went back past Angie's door, up on his toes, silently, to the other end of the hall. He saw the door marked SER-VICE and tried the knob. Locked. He walked away heavily, and whirled around.

104

He went back to the EXIT and stood out on that landing smoking another cigarette, letting more time pass, letting Angie sweat for fifteen minutes.

At a quarter after two, the gun transferred to his jacket pocket and his hand holding it in that pocket, he walked straight to Angie's door and pressed the bell button.

When Angie opened, Tom stepped in fast, grabbed him by the right forearm, and spun him around, drawing the gun at the same time. He put the muzzle to Angie's ear and whispered, 'A little tour of the premises, please. Including closets.'

Angie said, 'Okay,' quietly, resignedly, and Tom was convinced he would find no resistance here. But of course he'd never *really* expected resistance; just had to play his Safe Game.

When they returned to the living room, Tom put the gun back in its holster and said, 'I'll have a bourbon.' And still playing safe, he *mouthed* the words, *'And the money.'*

Angie pointed at the marble-topped coffee table and a large manila envelope. 'Nice place you have here,' Tom said, making conversation for tape recorders. And was sure there were no tape recorders, no problems . . . unless Uncle Paddy had died in the last six hours; which was how long ago Tom had checked on Pasquale Tortemango's state of health. That's what it would take – Paddy's death – to turn Angie into one very tough proposition.

Angie brought him his drink. Tom was counting the sheaves of bills. He sniffed the booze, sipped it, then gulped it. When he finished counting, he put the sheaves back in the envelope, fastened the clasp, and said, 'Glad to see you're not consorting with known criminals.'

'About that letter addressed to my uncle,' Angie said in his soft voice, the reference blowing any possibility of tape recordings. 'It really isn't necessary, and it's damned dangerous. I mean, it's not fair. What if you were to have an accident?'

Tom smiled. 'You do your part and I'll do my part and we'll see that I don't.'

'Sickness . . .'

105

'Never felt better,' Tom said, rising, tucking the envelope under his left arm.

Angie waved a hand. 'You're maybe twenty years older than I am.'

'I'm insulted,' Tom said. 'You thirty-two from my forty-nine makes seventeen.'

'The odds are you'll die before me, from natural causes. What happens then?'

Tom went to the door. 'Uncle Paddy's older than me. He'll die first. The line of business you're in, the way you take chances with women, *you'll* die first.'

'Charlie, listen.' The soft voice was *very* soft now. 'A man can't take this sort of pressure for too long. You've got to give some guarantees.'

'And if I did,' Tom said, hand on the doorknob, 'why should you believe them? No, it's got to be this way. If I find I'm getting sick, I'll do something. If I live to seventy ... hell, it won't make much difference by then.' He threw the dog a bone. 'After our last meeting, I might reconsider my options.'

Angie sighed. 'Okay, Charlie. I'll play your game.'

'I know you will, Angelo. It's the only game in town for you.'

He walked out. He was breathing a bit more quickly than usual, his palms were a bit damper than usual. He was *up* for the return to Fifty-second Street, and the walk to First Avenue and a cab stand. He'd *stay* up, stay on the lookout for strange moves, funny moves, dangerous moves ... until the moment he locked his hotel door behind him. And even then, he'd only come down as far as Tom Worth *ever* came down. Which wasn't much.

That's why *no one* would take him.

Dick Magris considered it all arranged: he was to spend the evening alone with Marty. Yet when he called the young editor at his office to ask if they might lunch, he received an unpleasant surprise.

'I'm having a small gathering tonight,' Marty said cheerfully. 'Perhaps a dozen people, if all decide to show. I'll have to do some shopping, of course, during my lunch break. Try not to get there before eight. Clark Johanson will be helping me prepare.'

'But . . . you said nothing about this yesterday!'

'Didn't I? I've been planning it since Monday; I must have said *something* about it. Ah, well, it isn't much anyway. Just a little fondue, cold cuts, and wine. Since Clark has to come from Englewood – Prentice-Hall, you know – he'll be spending the night. So might Chuck Berway with that long commute to Fire Island.'

'I don't understand . . .'

Marty interrupted casually, in the same cheerful voice, 'You'll be glad to learn I'm going to get some sun this weekend. Chuck's invited me to stay at his cottage.' He laughed. 'Well, not exactly *his* cottage, since he shares it with three others, and all have weekend guests. That will make for close quarters. Or should I say *no* quarter?' He laughed again.

Dick said, 'That's . . . revolting!'

Marty's laughter ceased. 'Then I won't expect you tonight.'

The line clicked in Dick's ear. He sat at his desk, telling himself he still didn't understand . . . when in fact he did. Marty had finally decided to play the field. Or *appear* to play the field, and so apply pressure to Dick to make a decision about coming out of the closet.

He would not be coerced this way! He turned manuscript pages and didn't see a word.

Fire Island and the gay cottages and the close quarters and . . . God, that 'no quarter' joke, meaning no mercy shown any young man in bed with all those hot bodies! *His* Marty . . .

But Marty *wasn't* his, very obviously now. And Marty *wouldn't* be his until he'd fulfilled his overdue promise to leave the Kissena Boulevard apartment with his wife and three children.

All right, Marty had a point; but to lower the boom on him this way! To turn around, overnight as it were, and act as if they were nothing more than casual bedmates! To tell

107

him that Johanson and Berway were spending the night, when *both* had been Marty's lovers before Dick had come on the scene!

He leaned back, closing his eyes, trembling. It all boiled down to wanting Marty desperately.

The phone rang. It was Paul Mahon, asking if Dick was free for lunch. Dick said yes and they chatted about Mahon's secretary-cunt and about Dick's mythical advertising-copywriter-cunt; then Dick was alone with his thoughts again.

He was glad when Mahon dropped by to suggest lunching early. And dulled the vulgarity of his boss's lip-smacking, clinical descriptions of past and present amours with two vodka martinis.

Later, back in the office, going through old issues of the movie magazine for references to a recently deceased actor, he found himself blinking back tears at a photograph of the actor *en famille*, a plumpish woman sitting beside him, a curly-haired little girl in his lap, a frowning boy leaning against his leg. It was the Great Man's first marriage, one of five ... but before he'd died he'd made reference to it as his 'period of joy', had quavered in his old man's voice that leaving his stolid but faithful nonactress wife, his two 'very normal' children, had been a terrible mistake.

Dick typed a caption for that picture: THE LOST PERIOD OF JOY.

He began to write the article. He wept for the happy days, the meaningful days, thrown away for pleasures of the flesh.

He wiped at his eyes ... and was suddenly laughing. Because the old actor had almost certainly sentimentalized something he hadn't been able to tolerate at the time. Because the Great Man had been a drunk, a lecher, a grand sonofabitch all during his seventy-eight years of life, changing only in the last three months when there was no longer any doubt that his illness was terminal.

Time passed. The office emptied. He continued to work, losing himself in the Great Man's melodramatic life. Then he went to the washroom and used his toilet kit to shave and freshen up. It was nine o'clock and he was uncertain of whether he would go to Marty's, but he wanted to be ready.

He left, and went directly across the street to the little Italian place that served fine veal scallopini. He drank a glass of wine with his meal, and had a leisurely brandy with his coffee. By then it was after eleven. Anthony, the owner, was at the door to let out the last customers, and suggested he take a cab wherever he was going at this late hour.

On the street, Dick looked around . . . and realized he was totally alone. Not one other pedestrian in view, and it was a mild summer night. It hadn't been this way *last* summer, had it? Certainly not the summer before. Of course, this was a business district . . .

He began to walk toward Fifth, and thought he saw someone slouching around the corner . . . *ducking* around the corner.

He hesitated; then returned to the restaurant. Anthony said he was wise to call a cab and he'd buy him a brandy to celebrate that wisdom. After which Dick bought *him* one. They sat at the bar while a waiter set the tables for tomorrow's lunch and a cleanup man used a mop on the floor. It was after one and he was quietly high before they shook hands; then Anthony remembered no one had called a cab.

Ten minutes later, a horn honked outside. The moment the driver asked, 'Where to?' Dick made his decision.

He gave Marty's Fifty-second Street address and leaned back and told himself he'd have some of that California Chambord Marty favored – not a bad wine; not at all. He'd have *lots* of it, in fact.

But not so much that he wouldn't sober up on the subway ride back to the Main Street station in Queens.

The thought of that late, long ride suddenly bothered him.

Why not stay over? Why not get good and drunk and do what he'd never done before, what he'd never wanted to do before: take on another lover? Let Marty and his old friends wrestle in the bedroom; he had no doubt he'd be able to find some sweet young boy for the sleeper couch!

The cab had stopped. Dick paid, went into the lobby, and

pressed the button next to Marty's name. The buzzer sounded and he entered and strode to the waiting elevator.

If and when they ever got together again, got together for good, they'd pool their resources for a larger apartment in a house with twenty-four-hour security service . . .

His heart sank in direct proportion to the elevator's rise. He'd have to pay Kathy alimony and support for each child and what would be left wouldn't allow him to make such moves. He'd bring in *less* than Marty, and wouldn't *that* be good for the old ego! Besides, Marty might well have written him off by now.

The elevator stopped. He got off, as onto a scaffold, and walked slowly, reluctantly, up the hall. And stopped at the door and tensed for sounds of raucous revelry, of shrill, suggestive laughter and wild music and perhaps even orgasmic groans.

He heard nothing beyond a tinkle of music.

He pressed the bell button. Those idiotic chimes sounded, and the door opened almost immediately. Marty was there, wearing cut-off denim shorts and a Brahms T-shirt. He was barefoot and held a dish towel.

'Ah, Dickie, just in time to help clean up.'

Pushing inside, Dick was ready to hurl accusations . . . but the living room was empty. There were glasses and full ashtrays and plates with bits and pieces of food, but no people. Not even Whitey, Marty's miniature poodle. Shamefaced, he asked about the dog. 'In the bedroom,' Marty said, and turned away.

Dick followed him to the kitchen. He loosened his tie and helped load the dishwasher. He said nothing because he was grateful that his fears had gone unrealized. He said nothing because he was beginning to work back toward the feeling of love.

He started up the dishwasher and returned to the living room to continue helping Marty. They worked in silence; then Marty said, 'You've earned a glass of wine,' and gestured at the couch.

Marty served him cold Chambord. They sat side by side and Marty smoked.

110

'I didn't expect you tonight,' Marty finally said, flicking ashes into a tray.

'I wasn't sure I'd come. But I'm glad I did. I had all sorts of wild thoughts. I expected . . .' He smiled.

'Yes,' Marty said, also smiling. 'That comes later.'

'Much later, I hope. Like ten or twenty years.'

'Then you've decided to move in with me?' But his voice was too cool, his smile too cynical.

'Of course, eventually.' He put down the glass and reached for his beautiful boy.

Marty rose. 'Just give me a few minutes, please. I want to take a quick shower.' He was already moving toward the foyer leading to the bedroom. 'Help yourself to more wine. It's in the fridge.' He was gone.

Dick emptied his glass and checked the time: a few minutes before two. He'd have to phone Kathy, despite the hour, so she wouldn't expect him home.

He stretched out on the couch, wanting to remove his jacket and shoes . . . but he'd wait for Marty, wouldn't give him any reason to feel he was being taken for granted. The boy was overly sensitive today. If they could just forget Kathy for a while . . .

He was frowning, bothered by something. He sat up, and realized he'd been waiting for sounds of the shower – that faint moaning the pipes made; that slamming of the door when Marty got in or out. The apartment was quiet; the entire house was quiet.

He got to his feet, telling himself it was foolish to feel bothered. He'd been lost in thought and simply hadn't heard the sounds. Perhaps ten minutes had passed, which meant Marty had now finished showering; so he would go to him. He went to the foyer and then to the bedroom door. It was locked.

At that point his heart began pounding. At that point he knew something ugly was happening.

And heard them.

Heard Marty moan, 'Easy, Chuck-baby, *easy*.'

Heard the other voice, the deeper voice, the inflamed voice: 'Come on, loosen it up!'

111

And the bed creaked. And both voices groaned. And he knew what was happening to his Marty.

He rushed from the apartment. He wanted to tell Marty he'd leave Kathy, leave his children, do *anything* if only he'd erase those sounds.

And they could never be erased.

He came into the street. He wanted to drink himself into oblivion. He remembered a place on Beekman – the Grenadier – and there were several bars on First . . .

He heard something from the direction of First – a loud sound, like a car backfiring. But he was too anguished, too frantic to wipe out those earlier sounds, those bedroom sounds, to think much about it.

Still, it decided him. He turned toward First Avenue, toward cars backfiring, toward movement, toward life.

Louise was drained; no smallest portion, no atom of desire left. And she smiled to herself, knowing it would start again tomorrow.

'Well, it's over,' Arnold muttered, as they rode down in the elevator. 'Thank God.'

God, yet! What an incredible time to refer to that Old Testament Jehovah of his; that heavy-handed inflictor of punishment! Even her all-forgiving Christ might have trouble with *tonight's* action!

'Not *quite* over,' she said, as the elevator doors slid open. 'We'll be back again at nine.'

He groaned. 'Are you sure you want . . .?'

She said, 'I'm sure,' and laughed to herself at the way he was walking into the lobby. He swayed; he sagged; knocked out, boozed out, *gigged* out.

She said, 'It was in a good cause, honey,' and laughed aloud and took his arm. He grunted, and managed to get free of her as they stepped through the door and off the curb to cross to their car.

The first she knew that something was wrong was when she heard footsteps to her right; someone running. And then she saw them. Her hand rose to her throat and the fear exploded in her brain and she was afraid to scream and wanted

112

to tell him to talk to them, to explain how he'd helped them, how he'd never allowed jigaboo jokes or . . .

He *did* speak, but all he said was, 'Leave my wife alone.' She heard that word 'wife' and she remembered something she'd forgotten – a feeling that went with that word 'wife'. But the feeling was gone in an instant because there were three of them with guns and savage expressions, and a savage voice was ordering her between two cars and calling her 'bitch'.

And the dark street and the black men were out of her deepest nightmares, from when her mother had threatened visits from the 'boogey man' if she was bad; and she'd been bad and now they'd come for her.

She said, 'Arny,' weakly, and saw him punched in the face. Then she was being pushed down between the two cars and could see no more. But she heard Arnold being hit again, gasping, saying he'd give his money and not to hurt them.

Her bottom was clutched, and she was strangely comforted. If they had sex, made love, they might not hurt her. The respite from panic freed her tongue and she said, 'Lord God!' For some reason it was the wrong thing and the hand left her and the savage voice ordered Arnold brought over.

They did something to Arnold. She didn't see because her face was flat against the filthy gutter and her eyes were squeezed shut, but he said, 'Stop!' and she heard the pain in his voice.

After that there were snapping sounds and Arnold sighed and his hand fluttered against her arm.

Warm wetness ran from Arnold to her. Sticky wetness.

She wept. Something was pressed to her head. A voice said *go on* and she said, 'Dear Lord Jesus, don't punish me for what I've done. Be merciful.' In answer, a flaming sun rose behind her eyes and bleached out the world.

Fleeing one ugliness, Richard Magris ran headlong into another. Before he knew what was happening, two men were coming at him, guns in hand, demanding his money.

The shock, the fear, brought adrenaline flooding into his brain, and he was cold sober on the instant. And was prepared to do *exactly* as they said. And began to tell them so, because now he saw they were kids and he'd been robbed before by black kids, his senior year in high school, that night he'd stayed for the History Club and come home after dark and the two had grabbed him and held a knife to his throat. He hadn't resisted and they'd punched him out a little and taken a dollar sixteen. And he'd been back in school the next day.

Okay. He had about fifteen dollars in his wallet. So they might expect more and punch him out again. Just as long as they understood he didn't intend to resist.

And then he was falling. And then he was looking up into the sky. And he hadn't felt himself hit the pavement.

Someone moved him, tugged at him, and was gone.

Okay. He'd been slugged. Now he'd get up . . .

The period of shock – the seconds it took for shock to wear off and pain to make itself felt – passed and he screamed, or tried to. His throat. He couldn't stand the pain in his throat!

And then he couldn't *breathe*. Liquid was choking him, blocking his breathing!

He managed to roll his head a little. He eased the blockage a little.

But the pain didn't ease and God, God, he couldn't tolerate that pain! And then the blockage was back. *And* the pain. It went on and on and became his world, his entire experience; he could remember no other.

He thought of something, and wanted to tell it to Marty. Something important. Something about not caring any more about him, or Kathy, or even his poor children.

His head was swimming, whirling, and he didn't know he was being lifted onto a stretcher; didn't know he had just about bled to death, just about choked to death. He had his message to deliver:

'Marty, God, look at me! It's bullshit, all that loving and caring. *This* is where it's at. Tell Kathy too – there's nothing to care about. *Because it all ends.*'

He exhaled, and tried to inhale, and couldn't.

Tom thought he heard a sound outside the lobby doors. But when he was on Fifty-second Street, striding toward First, there was nothing. You could overdo the Safe Game . . .

Scratch that! Someone on the other side, two or three steps behind him. He checked him out. Young, a little drunk, sort of faggy. Never looked Tom's way. If Tom kept up his normal pace, he'd leave him behind; leave him his unguarded back.

He slowed until they were walking even. He watched without seeming to, the envelope under his left arm, his right hand hovering near his hip pocket and gun.

They were almost halfway up the street and he still watched, remained ready to grab his ·38, told himself that a hit man didn't have to look the part.

And that was why he didn't catch the real action until it was almost on him: a bushy-haired kid coming across from the other side and up ahead. A freak with a gun and a high-pitched voice and a ghetto accent. Stinking skell out there in the open like a target at a Coney Island shooting gallery, expecting to take old Tom. Pitiful!

He ran forward a few steps, drawing his gun, holding tight to his envelope, and reached proper cover from a parked car. And saw several things, almost at the same time. And sensed one more thing even before he saw it.

He called out, 'Drop it! Police!' and the ghetto skell began to run. Yet that sensed danger, that gut feeling, intensified and he felt he had lost control, been sandbagged.

He saw two shapes stretched out in the gutter across the street. He saw two more freaks approaching the young drunk. And he caught *something* to his right and behind him.

He began to turn, finally forgetting the envelope, trying to bring up his left hand to steady his gun, knowing he was too late yet hoping to get off a ninth-inning shot. *He'd been so careful, so fucking goddam careful, yet someone had nailed him!* He saw the head rise from the bottom of that three-step

115

basement entry; saw the pistol extended; saw the blossoming fireball as the gun went off in the darkness . . . and illuminated a man's face.

I know that face, he thought as a bullet tore through his chest and ripped apart the pump that fed his life.

The blood in his brain was functional for another few microseconds. And even as he fell, he continued to think: *Know him. Met him . . .*

There was a chance he might have recognized his assassin before consciousness ended; carried that final make into eternity. But a second bullet exploded those thinking, remembering tissues, and Captain Thomas Worth was ready for his full inspector's funeral.

EIGHT

Saturday, July 19, and Sunday, July 20

Willis Jones wore a pale gray suit with flare jacket and bell-bottomed trousers, pleated and cuffed. His shirt was pink with ruffles at the neck and wrists; his hat creamy-white with a polka-dot band and a wide brim down all around; his shoes hundred-thirty-dollar silver snakeskin ankle boots. He was worth close to five big ones, not counting the two hundred dollars in informants' payoff money in his wallet, and it wasn't a dime out of his own pocket; it was all on the N.Y.P.D. Which was *outasight*, man, to use *his* generation's patois. Which made Saturday night in Harlem not just a job but sort of fun.

No way he'd ever consider buying such clothing – this was his wildest undercover street outfit – for his *real* life. Because being black, deeply black, as he was, you could be mistaken for lots of things.

Bad thoughts. Keep on the *up* side. The world is going your way. Sergeant now, but lieutenant soon enough. He'd make captain before he was through, he was sure of it, like Thomas Worth. And being a New York cop, might end up dead like Captain Worth.

Slipping to the down side again. Keep up the swagger. *Bop* along, man, 'cause you hot shit.

A cool-looking dude getting into an Eldo nodded and said, 'How's it hangin', brother?'

Willis said, 'Heavy, man, heavy, but it get lighter by morning.' He stepped over and they slapped hands and he leaned into the Cadillac and murmured, 'Hell, Reese, we're the only action on this street and we're both cops.'

Reese said, 'Wonder what the poor folks are doing tonight? I wouldn't want to be on those goddam side streets with Chickering and Lyons and the others.'

They parted with hey-man's and lookin'-good-brother's

and Willis was strolling down 145th again. Saturday night in Harlem, and Christ the *looks* he got from certain flashy chicks! Couldn't help but warm the cockles of his heart.

He let one foxy lady give him eye action that centered on unzipping his fly, and groaned a little under his cool, disinterested smile. But he wouldn't have played her game for the two grand Eddy had landed in informants' money today. Because he valued his health. Because he knew all about 'Nam Rose, which was a form of syphilis still resistant to wonder drugs. And besides that, where would he take her, *home* where the neighbors could see? Or to *her* home, somewhere around here, where he'd met the family and maybe the boyfriend waiting behind the door with a lead pipe . . . or more likely a pimp waiting with a bill for services rendered?

He kept strolling, looking for one of several informants on his string. Not one had shown since he'd hit the streets two hours ago. And it might stay that way, it being the big date night with action at the old malt shop and dancing at the prom and holding hands on lover's lookout. Jukebox Saturday night alright, alright, alright.

He smiled a little, grimly. Oh *yeah*! This was just the place for Harold Teen, the comics his father used to read him as they sat at the table near the window that looked across New Lots Avenue to the trolley yards, which became the bus yards. Clang, clang, clang went the trolley . . . he had loved that song, later, when he'd heard it and remembered the trollies of his early childhood, which had disappeared long before New Lots had become part of East New York's black ghetto.

It hadn't been that way when the Joneses lived on the top floor of the three-storey house – yeah, *tenement* – and the block or two was all black, and it could get hairy at times with some of the bad kids. But it wasn't tenement or slum or ghetto to him. It was home, a mostly Jewish neighborhood in transition since World War II, but a *slow* transition, and still a good place to live and go to school. P.S. 190, where his father made sure he did well, even in comparison with some of those bookish Jewboys who pushed the hell out of their grades, heading for admittance to the free city colleges from kindergarten on. Morency Jones had the same goal in mind for *his* children, and he used the strap when the grades were down, and laughed and celebrated with movies and dinners and trips to Coney Island and showed such goddam *happiness* when they scored high ... so of course they scored high. Pop would come to school to talk to the teachers and even though he worked in those trolley and bus yards as a lowly cleaner and even though he hadn't had a dime's worth of education himself, he was a man of dignity, purpose, pride, tact, intelligence ... and damned if the teachers didn't see it, accept it, even admire it. He helped, old Pop did, when he came on Open School Day, or for a conference on bad grades later on at Thomas Jefferson High ... because Willis had one *hell* of a time with French and it was too late to switch. He had to fight to keep his general average in the high eighties so he could go to college, free, which was the only way he thought he *could* go.

Then came the Army. Then came two years of service in the early days of the Vietnam War, which meant he spent the time in Texas. Then came the G.I. Bill and admittance to N.Y.U. – Washington Square College of Arts and Sciences – rather than City or Brooklyn College, and life was sweeter than it had ever been.

And it had been sweet enough, truth to tell, for little Willy and his older sister Norene, because while Mom was a good woman and a great cook and spread love throughout that apartment like no one else could, it was Pop who had the *plan*. And part of that plan was to be around forever; to direct his children forever; to make certain they got everything America had to offer if he had to *carry* them to the right places on his broad back.

It became a problem after Mom died so young, after Pop lost his job during the cutback in the bus yards and went to work as a janitor – pardon, superintendent – of a Borough Park apartment house. Better pay than the bus yards, and a landlord who respected his obvious qualities and hard work, and an apartment next to the elevator on the lobby floor, a lot nicer than their old New Lots Avenue apartment.

Morency's pride, however, wasn't easy with the work. He

119

stayed, and provided a good home for his two children, but it wasn't the same. '*Nothing's* the same what with the way the world's going,' he'd say. 'Crazy, no-work, Black Power fools and dangerous, loudmouth black Muslims, and whatever happened to Jesus Christ our Lord and working hard and becoming George Washington Carver?'

Willis tried to explain the many positive aspects of the Black Power and Muslim movements. Norene, who was into black political clubs at Brooklyn College and who admired Stokely Carmichael and Rap Brown, had some real shouting matches with Pop at first ... but then she too realized he couldn't change, had lived his whole life one way and it was too late for him. Besides, as she admitted, 'He did one hell of a job with us, didn't he? How many others from the old neighborhood are where we're at? Not many I can think of.'

'Not *any* I can think of,' Willis replied.

So they stopped arguing with him, though some of the things he said while watching blacks on TV really made them mad. Norene once had to run to the bathroom, where Willis heard her shouting over the flushing toilet and running sink, 'Goddam Uncle Tom!' over and over until she was able to come back out and take more of Pop's political philosophy, which could be summed up as:

Work your ass off, pray your ass off, never complain, and you'll prosper.

Norene couldn't wait to get out of the house and on her own. Still, Pop's training told in the end. Norene went to Alabama for Martin Luther King's Southern Christian Leadership Conference, instead of staying with her college group, the radical S.N.C.C.; then on to California with a black studies teacher she'd met in Tuscaloosa, the University of Alabama. And finally she began teaching too, at Berkeley. She wrote Willis that it was 'a little too unsettled' for her, 'so we're moving to Los Angeles where we'll both teach at U.C.L.A.' And, 'P.S.: We're getting married. Not that we believe in it, but for our child's sake. Did I tell you about my daughter?'

Pop was winning every round, hands down!

And not just with Norene; things were happening inside Willis too. Things rooted deeply in his childhood, in his father's training and beliefs. He continued going to school, but he was no longer quite sure why. He got his B.A. at Washington Square in three years by taking points-heavy programs and attending summer sessions. He then moved across the street to N.Y.U.'s Graduate School of Education and prepared himself, like Norene, to teach.

And those deep-rooted things kept working inside him and teaching didn't seem to be where it was at and he listened to his father each night when he came home from school, listened to the ever-more-irascible comments and discovered in them a certain kind of truth that needed handling. That made *him*, Morency Jones's son, want to handle them.

He knew from his junior year on what he would become. Knew but didn't *admit* to knowing. Knew what he'd admired as a child, and not in a child's cops-'n'-robbers way. Continued to admire it through all stages of childhood and into adulthood. And left graduate school and became a cop.

Wouldn't Pop have a fit seeing him now in these pimpish threads! Though he would understand if told it was police work. Because he'd been proud, had *approved* (to Willis's astonishment) the dropping of teaching and the entering into the Police Academy. Never explained that pride, but nodded and said Willis had done good.

And *why* had Willis done it? If teaching wasn't where it was at, there were other things to do, less dangerous, less involved with the very essence of what divided the black community and made a middle-class black most uptight.

Specifically, he'd done it for a father who'd been mugged once and sassed often – often enough so that the old man had decided to move back home to South Carolina. Thematically, he'd done it to protect *our* kind of people from *their* kind of people.

And he was approaching Eighth Avenue and it was eleven o'clock and 145th Street was full of people and it was hard to tell *our* kind from *their* kind but he knew both kinds were present in large numbers.

121

He saw one of his men crossing Eighth, seemingly on a casual bop down the avenue; but Willis also saw the bushy-haired teenager just reaching the other side, and figured the cop was doing a trial number. Having no better leads, he had picked a kid in the general category, fitting the general description of the M–4 killers, and was tailing him.

And then he saw something much more interesting: one of his snitches was stepping out of a car, waving at a girl, and walking toward a record shop. Willis moved quickly, calling, 'Hey, Mack the Knife, where you been *hidin'*, man? I owe you bread, baby, you forgot that?'

Sam Macry (a small whipcord-lean and jerky-tough ex-con and mainline junky, turned and stepped back warily. *No one* owed him money and he owed *everyone* money and he worried constantly and that was one of the many reasons he looked ten years older than his thirty-five. His grayish-black face was lined around the eyes and mouth and his hands trembled as he stared at Jones. And then he nodded and his arms flew out and he did the exaggerated inner-city surprise act – rocking, crouching, almost dancing, caterwauling:

'*Hey*, man, you like the sun in the mornin'! Never thought I'd see that bread again! You got it on you, man, or you just singing sweet songs?'

They were close enough to each other now to slap and shake and turn away toward a closed store, and for Mac to murmur, 'You gonna *kill* me, man, dressed like that and callin' me by name! Every operator on the street gonna be watchin' us, figurin' I'm helping a new pimp move in! You *know* the Apple Man's got eyes around here!'

'No one's watching. I'm looking for a red Pontiac Firebird, scraped right fender, this year's model, maybe last year's, but new-looking. I've got the license. It's written on the twenty I'll give you.'

Mac's button eyes flickered. 'What I gonna buy with a hat, man? Ten joints? Five Q's I need a bean at least. Maybe then I can get lookin' for that Bird.'

A 'hat' was twenty to twenty-five dollars. A 'bean' was every inside hooker's terminology for a hundred.

'Twenty now. Twenty when you locate the car. What's a hot car worth to us anyway?'

Mac smiled his truly childish and engaging smile, yet he'd been up twice for homicide. He also had three armed robberies and no fewer than eight assaults, plus innumerable drug busts, on his record. He was out because he'd cooperated with the police after his last three arrests. 'That's right, Willy. What's a hot car worth anyway? Like maybe ten cops on the street, such clean-cut mothers, and the honky fuzz riding around in cabs and hogs and every fucking thing but bicycles. Just a hot car, huh, Willy? Somewhere in Harlem, but nothing to do with that M-4 shit, right?'

Jones smiled and put his hand on Mac's arm. Mac winced, because Willis worked out mornings and evenings so that when he put the arm on a bad guy, he could *break* that arm. 'Twenty now, twenty if you locate the car. Say yes like a good little junky.'

'Hey, man, you pushin' too fuckin' hard!'

Willis tightened his grip. 'You still have two charges pending, Mac. How'd you like Sunday breakfast on Riker's Island?'

'No way you can work that, man! My lawyer . . .'

'And before Riker's, how'd you like me to spread the word you're rappin' with the fuzz?'

Mac's face went a shade grayer, and he forced a grin. 'Hey, you know you my man, Willy. Can't we play the game a little? Like Jewin' the bread up, you know, man.'

Jones said, 'Sure. Shake on it, Mac.' And pressed one of the twenty-dollar bills inked with the Firebird's license-plate number into the informer's hand. After which he stepped back, bopping again, grinning broadly. 'Good to see you, brother.'

Mac headed for the curb, muttering, 'Man, you ain't *no one's* brother.' He ran across 125th, giving the finger to a car that blared its horn at him.

Jones kept walking, kept bopping, kept watching, returned a few nods and smiles and sultry looks from ladies of the evening, who were out in considerable numbers. Also

out were families: men and women enjoying the mild
summer night, many with children, stopping and looking in
shop windows, laughing and talking. He remembered *his*
family on Sutter and Pitkin Avenues, walking and talking
and shopping and laughing. Whoever tried to lump them with
the killers and the Macs and the hookers was doing the
devil's work, as Pop used to say.

'What it take to make you *smile*, baby?'

He snapped out of it, smiling quickly, automatically, and
saw his way blocked by a woman ... make that a *child*. She
was done up in klunkers and a slit-to-the-ass midi and paint
and whatnot, but she couldn't have been more than fifteen.
Actually, he guessed her at around fourteen, possibly thirteen.

'I'm huntin' a man to take me in,' she said, coming up
close against him. 'I can make us both some heavy bread.'

She'd rated him pimp, and was asking to be put to work
under his protection. Young hookers were in great demand
all over town. Pussy Posse had collared teenyboppers on
some of the best mid- and uptown streets, being delivered to
customers for 'partying'. One slight twelve-year-old had
bragged that her price was two hundred per *hour*. Of course,
she'd been light-skinned. This girl was pretty enough, but
quite black.

'I only got old ladies of eighteen and up on *my* string,'
Jones said, smiling haughtily.

'You freaked out on something, man? You know what
you *talkin'* about?' She was staring at him in complete
amazement. 'I pull in more than any *old* lady ever seen! If
Quincy – you know, the Apple Man – didn't bust my ass so
much, I'd stay put and get my hog and my mink and my
penthouse. I'll bring you four, five hundred a night every
night, and no vacations. Just you deliver the right johns.'
She moved a knee high between his legs. 'And 'stead of
bustin' my ass, jive it a little, huh, joy-boy?'

He shook his head, laughing. 'Out of the way, small stuff.
I got heavy action waiting on me.' He moved her aside,
firmly ... and thought he'd better get himself some loving,
because damned if she hadn't begun to turn him on!

124

How long had it been now? Caroline about a week ago . . . last Saturday night, in fact. That made seven full days, which was too long. But she'd taken to asking, 'Where's it going?' and he didn't know.

Other fish to fry right now. Had to walk away, escape the child-hooker's openmouthed disbelief that anyone would turn down her money-making offer to leave the well-known pimp and Mafia surrogate, Quincy Apple.

She was an ill-informed little whore. Almost no one would consider matching muscle with the Apple Man. Pimp warfare still led to bodies, male as well as female, being found in cars and vacant lots all over the metropolitan area; not to mention broken arms, legs, and stomach linings. And Mr Apple had the backing of a very powerful family, the New Jersey Tortemangos. Even a cop would think twice before he fucked around with *those* mothers.

He was crossing Broadway, taking in the heightened lights and sounds and movement, when the dark Plymouth slowed alongside him and the voice said, 'You're getting yours, *now*.' It then moved on, parking near the corner. He kept strolling, bopping heavily, and crossed to where that Plymouth was parked. He began to walk past it and up Broadway.

The two men came out and flashed shields and grabbed him and turned him and slammed him up against the car. Swiftly, they 'spread' him and did their search procedure. One pulled his off-duty ·32 automatic from its holster on his lower right calf and held it up triumphantly. People were stopping. A few mumbled 'pigs' were heard, but most simply watched. Jones said, 'Brothers, I'm being . . .'

They cuffed him and pushed him onto the back of the car. One got behind the wheel, the Plymouth screeched off, and that was that. He'd been busted. By Eddy Roersch and Paul Lauria.

Roersch removed the cuffs. Lauria headed downtown, and said, 'My brother's having a bachelor party next week. Could you provide the girls?'

Jones said, 'Sure, at a hundred a head.'

'It's not the *heads* we want.'

125

'And not the *color* you want either,' Jones said, his hours on the street having had their effect.

Roersch said, 'You've had a long day. I'm pulling the first shift off the street. Myself included.'

'I couldn't make more than one snitch,' Jones muttered, deeply depressed without quite knowing why.

'Reese made two of his. Three's not a bad score for the first night.'

'We're short of men for the late tours. Three and three, the way I had it.'

'Four and four,' Roersch replied. 'I rounded up another two darkies.'

Jones looked at him, and Roersch held up a thick hand. 'Okay, no more jokes. Not even about the call you got at the station. A Miss Andra Stennis; that reporter, remember? She wants to interview you. Wants to ask questions about how it feels to be a black cop working on a case involving three black murder suspects. Wants you to call her whenever you get off duty, at this number.' He handed Jones a slip of paper.

Jones put in his pocket. He wanted to get laid, not answer questions. He wanted fast, fast, fast relief from tension. Andra Stennis could wait.

After they'd dropped him at the station and he'd driven to Twelfth Street and his second-floor apartment in the converted brownstone, he phoned Caroline, and her roommate informed him she was out on a date. The roommate, who was stacked, laughed at his suggestion that *she* come over. 'Like to, fuzz, but I've got a friend here. *'Bye!*'

He'd probably blown things with Caroline for good by pitching the talkative roomie. Of course, he could always say he'd been kidding . . .

He went through his book. Saturday past midnight and who could he call? And Jesus, he didn't feel like being alone tonight!

He had a white girl, but that was a complicated business. Had to set it up carefully so her bigot parents, as she herself described them, didn't find out. Though it wasn't as if he was really hooked on white thighs, as the old underground

126

song went. It was more ... well, like being in step with the guys at the station. Like they all had white girls and maybe some had blacks and ... shit, he was a cop and they were cops and cops were alike ... and who gave a damn *why* he did it, he just did, a big deal once a month!

Anyway, he couldn't get in touch with Betsy except at her office, so that was out.

He hadn't returned Gea's calls for months.

And Georgette was married.

So who was left?

He took the slip of paper from his jacket pocket and studied it a moment. He remembered Eddy's description of the girl reporter and picked up the phone.

A woman's voice answered. He asked for Andra Stennis. 'Speaking. Is this Sergeant Jones?'

He slouched low in the armchair, getting into his sweet-talkin' mood. 'You were waiting, huh?'

'Yes. Can we meet someplace? Or would you rather do it tomorrow?'

'I'd rather do it right now. At my place.' He chuckled.

'Ah yes,' she sighed. 'Well, I'm talking about an interview.'

'Come now, Miss Andra. You know us hot-blooded black folk. Can't do without it.'

He'd given it a touch of his Kingfish accent, thinking to get a laugh. He got, 'Maybe we should forget the whole thing.'

'That's a deal!' he snapped, and hung up. He rambled around the apartment, muttering to himself, and fixed a Scotch and water.

The phone rang. He grabbed it, hoping Caroline had returned from her date and been given an edited version of his call.

His hopes were dashed.

'Sergeant Jones, I ... uh ... really want that interview. I've never dealt with a police officer before. Perhaps if we took it slowly, learned a bit about each other ...'

'I've been on duty since nine A.M. I've been walking Harlem streets and meeting hookers and pimps and looking

127

for three murdering *brothers*. I'm not in the mood for intellectual exchanges. I just want a warm body and some laughs. If you can provide that, come on over.' He gave her the address. 'If you can't, wait until we've solved this thing and my hours are back to normal.' He paused. 'And my temperament too,' he added more softly.

She said nothing.

He said, 'Okay, Andra, good night now.'

He had his drink in bed and turned out the lights. He tossed a few minutes, thinking of thighs, all sizes, shapes, and colors, and finally fell asleep. And was awakened almost immediately by the doorbell.

He stumbled through the apartment, picking up his service revolver en route. Because this was New York and that was the way a cop thought. He said, 'Who is it?' and a woman answered, 'Andra Stennis.'

Still somewhat befuddled by sleep, he tossed the gun on the couch and opened the door. 'Surprise, surprise,' he murmured, and stepped aside.

She hesitated, seeming to flinch, but came in.

It wasn't until he closed the door that he realized he was naked. He began to turn away. '*Oops!* Hold everything!'

She said, 'You made it plain enough on the phone, so why waste time dressing just to undress again?'

He stopped and faced her. She came directly into his arms. She took his kisses, and as they turned to the bedroom, said, 'I've had a bad romance and now I have no romance, and if this is the price I have to pay for an interview . . .'

He came to a halt. He was in a state of high arousal, and it was no secret, yet he said, 'Hold it, lady! You're paying *no* price! I don't make deals for my body!'

She began to laugh. She laughed so hard she laughed him right out of his state of high arousal. She stumbled backward and leaned up against the wall, wheezing, 'Isn't that *my* line?' And laughed some more.

He finally laughed with her. He gave it a minute or two and led her to the bedroom, where he put on the night-stand lamp and began undressing her. He sat on the bed and she

128

stood between his knees and he took off her skirt and blouse and panties and brassiere. And smiled. 'You could make a deal for a *book*, lady, not just an article.'

She began to laugh again. He stopped that fast with kisses deep into her belly. A lovely, chocolate-dark, softly rounded belly. She was firm and well-fleshed, not hard or skinny like too many young women he'd met. She had small breasts, but more than made up for them with a swelling behind. Her legs were long enough and shapely enough ... but it was her face, when he finally lay down beside her and took time to look at it, that really made him happy; a sweet-featured face, just a touch lighter than his own. 'You're a goddamn *beauty*!'

'Sure,' she said. 'I was a cheerleader at Tilden. I was queen of Bay Ridge Commerce Day. I was a much-sought-after piece at Hunter. And in the intervening years – don't ask how many, because they depress me – I've been balled by the most eligible black bastards in New York City. And by one white bastard as well. He fooled me with his sensitive approach to black history ...'

He kissed her. He used his hand between her legs. He pulled her over onto him, spreading her lovely black thighs, driving deep up into her. And took the time to pant: 'God, do you ever talk up a storm!'

It wasn't until later, when he'd reversed their positions for a second go, when he'd fallen forward onto her, gripping her ass with both hands and crying out softly into her face, her hair, that she answered him:

'You ain't heard nothing yet, racist, chauvinist pig.'

Lifting his head to answer what he thought would be her mischievous grin, her puckish smile, he found himself looking into a face devoid of humor. It was damp with perspiration, relaxed by orgasm ... but deadly serious all the same.

Willis Jones knew he was in for one *hell* of a relationship.

NINE

Roersch was exhausted, a seemingly constant condition since he'd rushed back from his vacation and Amagansett. And he was going to lose more sleep tonight.

But he was satisfied with the way things were going, and this was new. Not with what was being imposed on him from above, but with the mounting evidence and the shadow case forming far back in his mind. He suddenly wanted to talk about it. Which was *verboten*, as per Inspector Deverney's instructions. Still, it was beginning to need airing, with someone he could trust.

Someone he could trust ... Ruthie, of course. But that would be like talking to himself. She wouldn't understand; wouldn't be able to offer a second viewpoint, a *professional* viewpoint.

Jimmy Weir. Jimmy was his closest friend in the department. Or *out* of the department, for that matter. Roersch and Jimmy went back almost thirty years together, and that counted for *something*!

The pressure to speak about Worth and the twenty grand and Deverney's latest instructions grew steadily as he drove home. Still, he fought it. Maybe after he'd had dinner, kissed his wife and daughter, looked at his son, who was almost always sleeping, and relaxed for a while ... maybe then he could defuse the mounting tension.

Ruthie was in the kitchen, and something smelled marvelous. He guessed at her speciality of lamb stew with small potatoes, and she nodded as she hugged him hello.

He ate hugely. He drank two cans of beer. He blew his diet completely, and while she didn't say anything, he could see the irritation in her eyes, her round, pretty face. It had taken almost a year to lose his gut, those excess twenty-six

130

pounds. He belched softly and muttered, 'Just needed it, honey.'

'Sure,' she said.

She continued to grouch as she cleared the table, so he went to the living room where Jen was watching one of her rerun situation comedies. He picked her up and kissed her and smacked her bottom, big like Ruthie's. 'How's my baby?'

She struggled out of his arms and plumped herself back down in front of the TV. 'Not now, Daddy! Endora's gonna turn Darrin into a *frog* and he'll miss the meeting and Mr Tate'll *fire* him!'

Roersch nodded. 'Turning into a frog will cost you your job nine times out of ten. Of course, if you're a *sergeant* frog . . .'

She wasn't listening. He left her with *Bewitched* and went into the master bedroom where his son lay in his crib. Asleep, of course.

He considered picking him up for a little smooching anyway. He could say Mark had awakened and he'd had to comfort him . . .

She'd know. He'd done it a few weeks ago and she'd been one angry woman for the rest of the evening. As if losing ten minutes of sleep meant anything to an eight-month-old who was the world's champion cooper!

He returned to the living room. Ruthie was on the couch, watching TV along with Jen. 'Want to play Monopoly?' she asked, eyes glued to the set.

'Can't. Have to be back downtown by nine.'

'Not again?' she muttered, but she didn't seem surprised, or upset, as she had the first two nights he'd put in on this case. Of course, he'd explained the situation and the need for M–4 to work straight through until they'd made a collar. They had to cruise Harlem tonight.

Nevertheless, he felt some resentment at the way his family was leaving him alone to work, and slouched to the kitchen. His plastic zipper case lay on the counter, where he'd thrown it, and he took it to the table.

131

Review time. Put-things-together time. He hadn't had the chance to do it at the station; might as well do it now.

But first he went to the refrigerator, glancing through the doorway to make sure Ruthie wasn't looking his way, and took out another beer. He closed the door softly and returned to the table. Where he drank, and assembled.

He read something he hoped he wouldn't have to use – a metropolitan-area APB on the Firebird, in case Jones's Harlem operation didn't pan out. He'd give Jones three days, then call Deverney and explain he had to cast a wider net. And how to keep the news lid on *that*?

He read Paul Lauria's report. The young detective had been busy:

He'd found a witness on Martin Anders' floor who 'thought' he'd seen Richard Magris entering Anders' apartment – not the night of the murder, but on a previous occasion. And also 'thought' he'd seen them walking together on the street early one evening.

He'd gone to Magris's Queens home and interviewed his wife, as well as his mother and father, who had been there with the young widow and her children. The parents were certain Richard had been on Fifty-second Street 'conducting business'. When Lauria murmured, 'At two in the morning, and his office fifteen blocks away, and his boss's home even further?' the parents fell silent, but the widow spoke sharply:

'I'll swear on my children's lives it isn't what you're thinking – another woman.'

Lauria had assured her he'd been thinking no such thing . . . and he hadn't.

He'd gotten a description of the jewelry Magris had been wearing: a Bulova watch and a ring the wife had given him on their fifth anniversary – a small ruby in a Mexican silver setting.

He'd learned that there were no doormen to question in Anders' house, and stated that their evidence was no longer necessary.

And later he'd interviewed Magris's boss, Paul Mahon. Mahon had asked not to be quoted, 'but Dick had a lady copywriter on the side, Guess on Fifty-second, and guess it cost him his life ...'

Which just about wrapped up Richard Magris. Roersch could give the D.A. a complete picture of Magris and his reasons for being at the scene.

Same for the Jaekers, because a hotel clerk had phoned M–4 to say he'd 'suddenly realized' that the murdered couple were two guests who hadn't been seen since they'd checked their key at the desk Wednesday evening. Eli Ross had been sent to the Prince George to toss the Jaekers' suite, and had come up with a personal phone book listing quite a number of famous names in Los Angeles, and a few here in New York. Among the *not*-so-famous were Marilyn Maigret and Morgan Breen.

Maigret and Breen had come to the station and given a police artist specializing in objects rather than faces) a complete description of the jewelry the Jaekers had been wearing. The artist had drawn sketches of the rings and watches according to their specifications, and had later added Magris' items from Lauria's descriptions.

A call to Arnold Jaeker's place of business, and a return call from his partner, brought an estimated value of thirty-five thousand dollars for Mrs Jaeker's jewelry alone. Arnold's was worth perhaps another five, and Magris' about a thousand. Roersch totaled it a rough forty thousand.

It was highly doubtful that those three ghetto kids had any idea of what they'd scored, or knew that with the right buyer they could come away with twenty grand, enough to take them one hell of a distance from Harlem. If they went to the wrong buyer – which in this case meant any of the standard neighborhood pawn shops or buy-sell jewelry stores – they'd be turned in. Because no small-time operator would screw around with M–4 and the possibility of being involved in four murders. Because copies of the jewelry sketches had been sent out to all those shops. (And Deverney's lid must be working, because no word about it yet in the media.)

Anyway, so much for three of the victims; nothing about

their deaths was a mystery any longer, including who had murdered them. But Captain Worth was another story.

Roersch had to get some light onto this dark thing; had to get another opinion, to find out if he wasn't letting himself in for illegal procedure, criminal charges, a disastrous end to his career; had to discuss that persistent hunch, that gut-wrenching feeling of being backed toward a precipice.

He considered phoning Jimmy Weir at his home and suggesting they meet for a drink later on, say at one A.M. Jimmy took weekends off, and if he wasn't at some broad's house, or at a mountain resort chasing chippies, he would certainly help out his old friend.

Just as Jimmy was the only one who knew about Ruthie's past as a hooker, so Roersch alone had been in on the sad details of Jimmy's divorce from his wife of eighteen years and his marriage to a twenty-year-old sexpot who'd dumped him in five months. Eddy had kept a week-long suicide watch over Jimmy, which was the time they'd told each other everything. Which was the time he'd convinced Jimmy that while life could be pretty bad, there was no predictable alternative. '*Anything*,' he'd said, 'is better than nothing.'

Jimmy had bought it, and pulled out of the tailspin, and while he hadn't exactly been a swinger for a good six months, he'd done all right for himself the last year or two. The captain was back in shape, that was for sure ... and being his old, tough self could give good advice on how Roersch could protect himself against those special aspects of the Worth case. Roersch just couldn't leave himself entirely in the hands of a man like Deverney!

He rose to go to the phone ... but went to the refrigerator instead. He got the last beer, and Ruthie called, 'It's okay with me, Eddy. But let that gut blow up again and you can sleep on the couch!'

He put the can back, nodding sourly. 'Is that all I am to you, a body?'

She laughed. 'Better than being a trick, right?'

This was one of the times her little jokes, her references to the past, when he and Helen had lived down the hall and Ruthie was turning tricks to support her kid and Helen died and Roersch put the time-honored cop squeeze on the hooker for a little trade to dispel the killing loneliness ... this was one time he didn't want to hear it. Even though the squeeze had soon given way to a relationship, and the relationship led to marriage and Mark Roersch, his son. Even though the old cliché about an ex-hooker being the most faithful of wives had proven true. Even though wife and mother was all she wanted, and all he wanted from her. Somehow, tonight, the past wasn't all that great and jokes about it weren't all that funny and he needed that beer and maybe stronger stuff than beer, maybe a real bender ...

His blood pressure wouldn't like it. His weight wouldn't like it. And Ruthie, most of all, wouldn't like it.

He went back to the table and his work. He turned D.D.–5's and several less formal memos, and came to the information Jones had secured by phone earlier today from the Known Criminals File, and from the office of the chief of organized crime.

Known Criminals File had a very brief entry on Angelo Tortemango – his one and only arrest for felony pandering, and his three for conducting 'games of chance'. It had a far more lengthy report on Pasquale 'Paddy' Tortemango, Angie's uncle, who had, in his youth, caught twenty-eight felony arrests ... and only two convictions. The Tortemango family had excellent lawyers, but more than that a heavy 'campaign fund' to cover witnesses (both civilian and police) and jurists.

The chief of organized crime's office gave Angie better billing:

Known to conduct illegal gambling (floating crap games, poker, numbers) and a prostitution ring in the five boroughs and in black areas through surrogates Quincy 'The Apple Man' Apple in Harlem and Guy 'Ding-Dong' Brothers in Brooklyn. Angelo Tortemango's operation continues to grow steadily. In line to absorb part of his uncle's drug, loan-shark and union-rackets action. Is suspected of taking part in 'executions' of Vincent and Henry Saccoso when Saccosos attempted independent

135

narcotics operation. Angelo questioned, then released because of insufficient evidence – a key witness changed her testimony. Angelo directed 'legal' as well as criminal action against independent prostitution and gambling competition in Manhattan; 'legally' by having information delivered to certain police units concerning competition's actions and thereby insuring raids; criminally by having stores where numbers were being taken burned, runners beaten, prostitutes disfigured.

Then followed a sentence that riveted Roersch's attention. It identified the two police units Angie had used against his competition ... 'safe' or 'bought' units to any knowledgeable cop, though the report made no such judgments.

Deverney had been a power in one. The second had been Worth's last assignment before being transferred to Headquarters.

Of course, a lot of other men had served in those units. Roersch, for one, a long time ago, when he and Jimmy had been on Vice Squad operating under then *Lieutenant* Deverney. Balleau also, if he remembered correctly, and a dozen other acquaintances; good men, most of them, who'd known about the heavy pad but who'd failed to get involved either through choice or chance.

Still, it was something to remember ... and he thought and projected and played What If and so many possibilities came to mind that he had to shut them out. It *still* had to wait on what could be proved against those three kids.

He turned pages. He came to what he'd typed, personally, even though Ross was a whiz on the old Royal.

This report was for himself and Deverney and maybe the P.C. ... *if* Deverney was telling it straight and the P.C. really knew what was going on.

Which was part of what he wanted to discuss with Jimmy: being in Headquarters and knowing how to route memos and messages, an inspector could make it seem as if everyone in power was moving along with him ... when in fact he might be moving all alone.

And if he *was* moving all alone, manipulating Roersch for private reasons, what could those reasons be?

And how could a sergeant get around the enormous prestige and power of an inspector and find out what the score was?

He sighed. He wished he hadn't given up smoking. He chewed his fingernails and told himself there was no sense in worrying, no sense bothering Jimmy, until he had something definite.

The report he'd typed was on a blue form D.D.–5, all right, but it was in a kind of personal shorthand and not, as per regulations, in triplicate.

He had driven out to see Mrs Thomas Worth at her Tarrytown home at three, and been back in the station by five. Most of that time had been spent driving. Twenty minutes had been spent with a terribly grief-stricken woman. His report read:

Mrs Worth (Clarise) and eight-year-old daughter, Rita, in house. Three sons not present; in city discussing inspector's funeral for father on Monday. (M–4 attend?) Mrs Worth groggy; doctor gave pills; *very* down. Asked if she knew what Worth doing on Fifty-second. She said, 'Police work, of course. Whole life police work. Wonderful husband. Wonderful father. Life nothing without him.' Cried. Left room. I got Rita to show me around. House worth over hundred grand. Probably *much* over on current market. Pretty good for cop, even captain. (Big taker?) Mrs Worth returned. Asked her husband's feelings about leaving precinct for Headquarters. She said he *hated* it; wanted to be 'with his men'; he disliked the paper work he had to do – a report on crime in four major boroughs – but lately he'd adjusted and was cheerful again. (Check this report with Deverney? Or go straight to Worth's office; see if secretary has report?) Asked Mrs Worth if captain had any papers at home relating to job; anything might shed light on 'case' that brought him to Fifty-second. She said no. Returned to M–4.

He went into deep thought . . . and jumped when the hand touched his shoulder. 'It's eight-thirty,' Ruthie said. 'If you want to make the station at nine . . .'

He kissed her and left. His nerves were beginning to fray at the edges. It wasn't like him.

With Jones walking the streets, Ross cruising alone in an unmarked, and Lauria set to drive with Roersch in another unmarked, M–4 was left to Balleau, who nodded as Roersch reminded him that the special number had to be covered at all times. 'I'm on it, Eddy, and when I'm not I've got a detective third.'

They drove to Harlem, and up and down the crowded, noisy, dirty, dangerous streets. Lauria shook his head. 'Jesus, what skells these people are! The goddam shit goes on around here! This place could be nicer, you know that? I mean, it once *was* nicer, when whites lived here.'

Roersch cleared his throat. 'I've seen old prints of the Draft Riots during the Civil War. Irish refusing to serve in the army of a country that called them shanty and micks and said, "No Irish Need Apply." Area around here, I think Looked awfully dirty and noisy and dangerous.'

'Not like *this*, even for those rougher, poorer days. I never read anything about any immigrant group that lived like *this*. I mean, just the trash on the streets and the way the kids don't respect the older people. You can see it all around you, how *different* they are. They just don't *want* to make it better. All the others, no matter how crowded and poor they lived, they wanted to make it better and it showed in the houses and the streets . . .'

Jones had helped Roersch understand and that the not-wanting in so many of his people came from not caring. The not-caring came from something no other ethnic, slum, or immigrant group here had ever experienced: the *forced* migration of slavery. The *forced* dissolution of families by slave buyers and sellers. The *forced* abandonment of their previous land, culture, traditions, religion, with little or no replacement of those except in the area of religion.

138

Lauria went on about skells, and Roersch suddenly said, 'You're keeping me awake.' His tone of voice was such that Lauria got the drift and muttered, 'Hey, I know how many *good* ones, like Jones . . .'

'Who's out on that street. Who could use a *white* to draw attention from the haters, maybe attract one or more of those killers. I think this white should be a big mouth, a talker who can get under the skin of a black hater.'

Lauria glanced at him. 'You're kidding.'

'Someone like you, Paul.'

'You've *got* to be kidding!'

'Someone who'll find out I'm *not* kidding if he says one more word.'

After that, and until they picked up Jones, Lauria drove in complete and blessed silence.

Back at the station, Roersch grabbed his own car and made it to Fifty-second and Angie Tortemango's house by eleven-fifty. Which was just in time to catch one night-tour doorman going off duty and another coming on. His notebook told him five-to-midnight was Saul Gordon and midnight-to-eight was Lou Flecher. He showed his badge, and got them sorted out. Gordon was short, late thirties, redhaired, pink-faced. He paled when asked if he'd ever seen Captain Worth in his lobby.

'The officer that was murdered?' He stared at the picture Roersch showed him, one of a set of glossies made up from recent photographs of the victims. 'I don't think so. We get a lot of people here, right, Lou?'

Flecher didn't answer. He was a taller, older, darker man, and he was staring at the photo past Gordon's shoulder. He turned away as Roersch pressed Gordon to search his memory. Gordon tried, and failed, and called good night to his replacement. As soon as he left, Roersch went to Flecher, who was bringing a wicker-backed chair from a small room at the right rear of the lobby.

'You recognized him, didn't you, Mr Flecher?'

'Who said I recognized him? Like Gordon says, we get so many people here . . .'

139

'*I* say you recognized him. How long have you been a doorman, Mr Flecher?'

'Me?' The man was upset, unhappy, stalling. 'Just four years. But before my heart attack, I was an electrician. *That* I did for twenty-seven, twenty-eight years.'

'And you knew your business, didn't you?'

Flecher saw what was coming, and nodded weakly.

'Well, I've been a police officer for thirty-five years, and I know *my* business. I know how people react, and I know you recognized the photograph of Captain Worth.'

Flecher's stricken expression was answer enough.

'What's bothering you?' Roersch asked softly. 'Is it *who* Captain Worth was visiting?'

Flecher made up his mind. 'I never said that. I did see the man in that picture, but I don't remember when and I don't remember who he was visiting.'

'It was Wednesday night, Thursday morning; probably twice, once going *up* to Mr Angelo Tortemango's apartment.'

'I didn't say that! I don't remember that!'

'And again about two-fifteen, two-twenty, just before he was killed, coming *down* from Mr Angelo Tortemango's apartment.'

'I saw him, yes. I don't remember ... maybe Wednesday night ... but I'm not sure. And one thing I *am* sure of, I don't know who he was visiting.'

'You have to ring the tenant before sending up a visitor, don't you?'

'Yes, but I don't remember ...'

'This is a murdered police captain we're discussing!' Roersch was leaning close, voice growing harsh, personality growing tough. 'And you're concealing evidence relating to his death!'

'I've got children,' Lou Flecher whispered in a time-honored attempt to get out from under. 'I can't get mixed up with ... such people.'

'I'm going to have to take you in, Mr Flecher.'

The doorman sank to his chair. Roersch waited. The doorman dropped his head. Roersch continued to wait,

'All right, take me in,' Lou Flecher said. 'I'll tell you again: I saw that captain here one night. I don't remember what night. I don't remember who he visited.' He stood up. 'I've got to call the landlord. We've got to have a replacement. I've got to call my cousin Harold. He's a lawyer.'

'You'll *swear* to not remembering?'

'I'll swear.'

Roersch went to the door and turned. Flecher was wiping at his face with a handkerchief. 'Thank you, Mr Flecher.'

'I can't help it!'

'No, no, I *mean* it, Mr Flecher. Thank you. You've told me just what I had to know. I understand your position. But please understand mine. If the time ever comes when what you know has to be brought out in front of a jury, I'll rip your life apart to get it.'

Flecher stared at him. Roersch nodded pleasantly and left.

He stepped out onto Fifty-second Street. Cooler here than in Harlem, with that breeze coming in off the East River. He walked up the north side of the street, heading west, as Worth must have done. He tried to imagine he was the captain, it was Thursday about two A.M., he had that envelope full of money under his jacket, or was carrying it under his arm. His *left* arm, at some point, because he had died with his gun in his right hand.

Roersch reached the spot at which Worth had been found; there was still a faint trace of white crayon on the sidewalk. He suddenly crouched, reached for his hip holster, made an imaginary draw of his gun, pointed a finger with cocked thumb at the gutter. Then, moving his head a little, he found he could glimpse a portion of that three-step depression to the basement passageway. And turned toward it and tried to aim . . . and nodded, muttering, 'Too late. Went down, spinning around, and came to rest parallel to street, to parked cars but angled just slightly at that basement. And caught a second slug, in the head, from the basement.' He rubbed his hands together and added, 'Maybe.'

He looked across the street.

And again at the basement entrance.

141

And back across the street.

Almost anyone on the second to sixth floor in that house directly opposite could have seen the fire-flash of the gun that killed Worth. If he found only one witness to that flash, he'd *know* he was right instead of just suspecting it.

He crossed to the south side. He walked along that house front and looked up at windows. And stopped, seeing movement at a third-floor window – something pale; something gone now.

Had it been curtains fluttering in the breeze?

He backed off into the gutter.

No way it could've been curtains. The window was closed; almost all the windows were closed in this air-conditioned house.

And again he caught movement – someone coming to the window and backing away almost immediately. And if that someone was a chronic window sitter, an insomniac who spent considerable time looking out . . .

Of course, it was Saturday night, Sunday A.M., and no work in the morning. And many people awake now wouldn't have been up late on a weekday night, when the murders had taken place.

He went to the lobby. The outer doors were open. Behind inner glass doors was a big, uniformed man who looked like a boozy ex-cop. Roersch held up his badge, and got a wide grin and immediate entry. And immediate confirmation of his character analysis.

'What can I do for you, Sarge? Name's Dolan, detective second, retired. Took this soft touch because I'm up most of the night anyway.' He laughed, shaking Roersch's hand, and glanced around mock-conspiratorially. 'The C.O.'s not watching, so how's about a snort?' He laughed again, and proceeded to pull a pint of Johnny Walker from his hip pocket.

Roersch was going to refuse, but Dolan was already pouring into a pink plastic Dixie Cup he'd drawn from a paper bag under his stool. 'Be prepared, that's my motto. Never know when a buddy's gonna drop in.' He handed Roersch the cup. 'Off the English!' He belted down his drink. 'Ah!

One more to damn the fucking Limeys.' He poured for himself, and shrugged at Roersch's still-full cup. 'Here's to the I.R.A. Brave boys, every one of them.' He was going to say more; then suddenly stopped and muttered, 'But each man to his own side.' His eyes blinked nervously.

'The I.R.A.,' Roersch said, raising his cup, seeing a path to solid cooperation. 'Off the English.' And drank, making silent apology to his late wife Helen and her London-born mother.

He sighed. The drink had bitten sweetly, pleased him enormously. And it was all in the line of duty.

He accepted a second drink, and Dolan had a third, and again they toasted the Irish Republican Army and damned the English, in Scotland's best.

Roersch said no to a third drink. 'Still on duty. M–4 . . .'

Dolan's eyes widened. 'You're Roersch! Sure, I've seen you on the TV. I'd've called in, *come* in, if I had anything to offer. I was here, all right, but didn't hear a thing and didn't see a thing. Behind these two sets of heavy plate glass . . .' He shook his head.

And with half a pint or more in him, and maybe cooping, and definitely not interested in anything that meant trouble. If he'd been on the force and anywhere *near* Edmund Roersch, he'd have found his ass before a board of inquiry!

Roersch smiled at the thick face with the boozer's badge – an intricate system of fine red blood vessels close to the surface of the skin, culminating in a near-purple W. C. Fields nose. 'Bet you get some company from the insomniacs, the bad sleepers. A house this big's bound to have a few, right?'

Dolan nodded. 'There's an old Jewish man comes down every so often, sometimes one o'clock, sometimes later. And out for his walk by six thirty, rain or shine. But he don't drink, he don't talk much, he just farts around looking out the doors and complaining about his wife not caring whether he lives or dies and his kids not writing. There's a fine young lady . . .' he winked leered . . . 'comes down two A.M. on the button each night, and is picked up by a car. Not always the same car, but always a man driving. Pussy Posse

143

might be interested, but I'd hate to see her collared – she's the only cheerful thing around this goddam graveyard.'

They both chuckled. Roersch said, 'Was she down here Wednesday night?'

Dolan nodded.

'Before the killings or after?'

Dolan frowned. 'I'm not sure. But she didn't say anything about seeing people killed. And she sure as hell would have. I mean, a woman sees action like that, she starts yelling.'

'Not a hooker, Dolan. Not if it's going to bring the police.'

'I get it.' He thought a moment. 'Well, she wandered over to the doors like always, looking for her ride. Sometimes I cop a feel or two . . .' He suddenly laughed. 'Hell, why hide it, Sarge? She's given me a freebie in the storage room more than once. On Wednesday night the phone here in the lobby rang and it was for her. Her trick was going to be an hour late.' The big boozy grin again. 'So she took me in back and gave me the finest poontang I've had in a long time. For once we wasn't rushed and I had enough of the sauce in me not to worry about some tenant coming in and reporting me off duty. We were at it almost an hour. I had the bitch climbing the walls. She actually *thanked* me!'

Roersch nodded, disappointed. The hooker, if she'd stood at the doors, could have looked across the street and *might* have had a view between cars on the other side – *might* have seen that flash.

'You were gone from when to when?' he asked Dolan.

'Say five to two to maybe quarter to three. She used the employees' john for five minutes, and was out here waiting by three. There were plenty of cops around by then, but she just took off.'

Roersch was annoyed with this bum. And with himself for standing around wasting time with maybes and faint hopes and dirty stories and the kind of investigation that a rookie patrolman should have handled.

Should have, perhaps . . . but couldn't. Because Roersch himself had to handle everything relating to Worth and that basement entrance.

144

'The elderly Jewish man you mentioned, does he have a window facing Fifty-second?'

'Hold it,' Dolan said, and went to the row of bell buttons and tenants' names. 'My memory gets worse each week.'

Roersch chuckled sympathetically.

'Sure,' Dolan said. 'Mr Epstein faces out on the street – both living room and bedroom. That's 3-J, about twenty feet closer to First than the lobby.'

Seemed just about right for the movement he'd seen a few minutes ago ... in a window positioned perfectly for looking across the street and down into the three-step depression; maybe even further, into part of the basement passageway itself.

'What are the chances of Mr Epstein's being awake right now?'

'Damned good. He says he goes to bed at nine, nine-thirty, then has to get up for the bathroom at twelve or one. And can't sleep again till maybe four. So he's probably up the ...' He stopped because Roersch was walking toward him, looking at the bell buttons. 'Now wait a minute, Sergeant. It's a quarter to one and I can't be buzzing tenants.'

'Just a short buzz,' Roersch said, smiling into the boozer's face. 'If he's sleeping, he won't even hear it.'

'No, I don't think ...'

Roersch was standing beside him, running his finger down along the names. 'Here we are. I'll give it one little press and you'll talk to him.'

'Wait a minute!'

But Roersch had already pushed the button.

'Jesus Christ, Sergeant!'

The wall-set intercom unit spoke tinnily: 'Yes? Epstein here. Dolan?'

Dolan picked up the phone unit. 'Sorry to bother you, Mr Epstein.'

'It's all right. Something's happening?'

'There's a detective here; the one you saw on TV.'

'You mean an *actor*?'

'No, no, Mr Epstein. The real thing. Sergeant Roersch

from that special M–4 unit. You know, the four people who got killed outside?'

'Ah. The older officer. It's nice to see an older man get recognition. He looked sixty, at least.'

Roersch cleared his throat. 'Ask him if I can come up. If not, ask him to come down.'

Dolan said, 'He'd like to come up to see you, Mr Epstein. It's important.'

'Well, my wife is sleeping. But nothing wakes her. All right, tell him to come up. I'll make some toast and tea.'

Dolan hung up, grinning. 'Toast and tea! What a house! One more drink, right?' He reached for his pint and turned toward his bag of Dixie Cups.

But Roersch had already entered the elevator.

Mr Epstein's first name was Morris. He was seventy-six years old and very proud of his physical condition, '. . . with the exception of the prostate, forgive the reference. I keep running to the bathroom. But maybe a man of your years knows firsthand?'

Roersch always liked to agree with a potential witness, to stay on the good side of him, but this was getting too close to the area of his fears, his depression.

'Not yet. Now, your windows . . .'

'How about some whole wheat toast? And a good cup tea?'

'Just had dinner,' Roersch said, to cut it short.

'What, so late?'

'Night duty,' Roersch muttered, and walked across the living room to the large multi-pane window. This *wasn't* the one in which he'd seen movement.

'Do you often sit at the window?' he asked looking out and across the street. He could see the basement entrance perfectly.

'Sure. Why not? My wife sleeps and I look out the window.'

'You were looking out fifteen, twenty minutes ago, weren't you? But not from here.'

'You saw me?' The old man was tall, stooped, cadaverously thin, but his voice and hands were firm, his eyes bright. He had a full head of absolutely *white* hair, which was parted and combed meticulously, and his face seemed freshly shaven. His bathrobe, worn over pajamas, was a rich blue and looked like silk and very expensive.

Maybe Epstein dreamed romantic daydreams as he wandered his apartment sleeplessly. Maybe he longed for companionship other than the sleeping wife . . .

Roersch was annoyed with himself, and with the ache of compassion that hit him. Old men were old men. He had a ways to go yet.

Not so long a ways, the hollow thought responded.

'Yes, I saw you,' Roersch said. 'And you saw me.'

Morris Epstein smiled. 'You were playing bang-bang. Making a gun and turning and shooting and grabbing your chest. I thought you'd fall down like the captain did.'

Roersch stared at him. 'You saw Captain Worth fall? You saw him die?'

Epstein spread his hands. 'Don't be angry. I didn't think I had anything to add to what was in the papers. I didn't see the *others* die. I heard a noise and I was coming out of the bathroom so I went to the window – the bedroom window, where I have a nice chair and where I usually sit. Rose sleeps, but at least she *breathes* and that's something to make a man feel he's not alone on this earth.'

'And you saw out the window?' Roersch prompted.

'I saw a man across the street. I heard loud sounds. I saw him turning around like a dancer and falling and lying still. And I went back to the bathroom with cramp and I didn't come out again until later and I didn't look out again until morning – when it was light, I mean. It upset me. I'm not used to such things. I had a dozen relatives die in Hitler's gas chambers, but I myself never saw a person die before. Not even my father, when he lay on his deathbed and my two brothers and my sister stood around him. I *couldn't* join them. I went and hid in my shop, a grown man of thirty-two. So just like then, when I understood I'd seen the captain die, I hid in my bed.'

Roersch asked if he could enter the bedroom. 'Just for a

minute, Mr Epstein. Just to look out that window. I won't
turn toward your wife.'

The old man laughed, a surprisingly hearty, almost
bawdy, laugh. 'Look all you want! That's if you've got a
strong stomach!'

Roersch went down the short hallway to the bedroom. He
opened the door and walked softly to the windows on his
right. There were two – single-sized, metal framed, opening
outward – and the view from here was as good as, if not
better than, the view from the living room. Because Worth
would now be slightly to the viewer's right, and the basement entrance on a straight line across.

He turned to the door. Mrs Epstein groaned and moved.
Roersch fled into the hallway. Where Epstein waited. 'You
heard the sleeping beauty?'

Roersch turned quickly, hiding a grin, and they returned
to the living room. Epstein said, 'Dolan tell you about the
courva who lives on the sixth floor?'

'Courva?'

'Forgive me. That's Yiddish for whore. But she's a lovely
girl. Name of Sheri, with an "i". He told you? He brags to
people he gets her. She told me he *blackmails* her. Anyway,
she comes here sometimes when my wife visits her sister in
Valley Stream, and she tries to help the old man feel a little
younger. Not that it always works.' He shrugged. 'But I'm
not bragging like Dolan. Neither am I complaining about
my *petzel*.' He chuckled. 'What I'm saying is that Sheri was
here on Friday. It worked. I was happy, and I made us some
lunch, and we talked. She told me she was upset because
she'd seen something Wednesday night. Her client was late –
Dolan told you how she waits in the lobby?'

Roersch nodded. 'He also told me he was with her from
before two A.M. until almost three.'

'Like I said, he brags. She calls him the three-minute
wonder.' He laughed. 'Me, I could be called the three-*hour*
wonder. The poor girl has to work so hard sometimes ...'
He shook his head. 'Enough. What I mean to say is she told
me that Wednesday night – early Thursday morning, you
understand – she had to wait around the lobby a full hour.

148

Dolan was pestering her to go to the storeroom and she didn't want to because he was drunker than usual and she doesn't like him anyway. Even a *courya* has the right to like and not-like. Especially when the man never pays her a dime.'

Roersch nodded. 'I agree. What did she see, and when?'

'About two o'clock, maybe ten minutes after; she didn't check a watch just like I didn't check a watch. She went to the doors so Dolan might stop with the hands. But like I said, he was very drunk and didn't stop and then she saw it. A boy ran into the gutter and pointed a gun at a man across the street. That was the captain. Sheri got scared, but Dolan was kissing her neck and, well, such things, and he didn't notice. And then she heard the two noises – the shots, same as I heard. And saw the fire. But Dolan was still too busy with his hands and his kissing to see or hear, and drunk like I said. So she took him to the storeroom. She didn't say anything about what she saw. Because he was once a police officer. Because he would call the police. And she might be in trouble about her business. You understand her point of view, don't you, Sergeant?'

Roersch said he did; then questioned quietly: 'She saw the *fire*?'

'Yes. I saw it too. In the basement across the street. Twice, like someone using a cigarette lighter. Only rounder, brighter, quicker, like explosions. If the papers didn't say the shots came from the boy in the street, I'd think . . .'

Roersch took out his notebook, sat down on the couch near the lamp, and began to write.

He got Mr Epstein's statement.

He got Sheri's full name – 'Even the last name's not real, but she says it's on the lease: Royal.'

He thanked Mr Epstein and said the information was really helpful.

'You mean there *was* a gun shooting in that basement?'

Roersch said no . . . because Deverney was waiting and he had to do it under wraps. 'You were right, Mr Epstein. You didn't have anything to rush to the police with.'

'Ah, a *danken Gott* for that. I was feeling guilty.'

'But what you've said reinforces certain facts, makes me see things a little more clearly.'

Epstein walked him to the door. 'You're sure you can't stay for toast and tea? At least tea?'

Roersch said no thanks, shook Epstein's hand, and began to ask him for one last favor.

The old man said, 'A minute, please. What I told you about Sheri – it won't get her in trouble? Dolan tells everyone and nothing happens. She has some kind of protection. But you ... you're an important officer, in charge of a big case.'

'Nothing will happen to her,' Roersch said. 'But I *will* have to confirm what you've told me. If you'd call her and ask her to see me ...'

Epstein gave a turn of the head toward the bedroom and Mrs Epstein.

'Just keep your voice low,' Roersch said.

'I don't think I want ...'

'Otherwise, I might have to send a detective to interview her. I don't know what *his* attitude might be.'

Epstein nodded slowly. 'Ah, so there's steel under the nice face, the nice smile. I'm glad you're not after me.' He went to the phone across the room, dialed, spoke too softly for Roersch to hear. When he returned to the door, he said, 'Just down the hall apartment K. She doesn't leave until two, so she's got half an hour.'

Roersch put out his hand again. Epstein shook it, with a wry smile this time.

Apartment K's door was ajar, and opened as he began to tap on it. The girl was about twenty-five, small, busty, with shiny blonde hair falling to her shoulders. Her face was cute rather than pretty, with a broad little nose and high cheekbones and unusually deep dimples that showed as she gave him her best, albeit worried, professional smile.

'Sergeant?' She stepped aside. Unlike street hookers, she didn't wear the boots and mini, or extreme klunkers and hot pants. However, the figure-hugging red knit suit created quite a bit of excitement in him. And the spike-heeled black

150

pumps made Roersch wonder what she looked like ... in *just* those shoes.

She was obviously judging him judging her, and spoke resignedly: 'I honestly don't have time for any ... action right now. But if you want to come back later ...'

'I'd be lying if I said I wasn't tempted. But no thanks. As Mr Epstein probably explained, I just want to know what you saw from the lobby Wednesday night.'

She motioned at a couch. He shook his head. She told him what she'd seen, and it was exactly as Epstein had said ... except that it was much more fun hearing it from Sheri. Her voice was a soft, sensual delight, and when she turned to gesture toward the street, her bottom in that skin-tight knit was a true work of art.

Again she caught his eyes. This time she smiled a little. This time she said, 'I wouldn't mind,' her eyes going over him.

He found he was perspiring on his upper lip. He turned quickly toward the door, putting away his book. 'I wouldn't mind either. I'm glad you don't live in *my* house. I think it could lead to divorce.'

She was laughing as he hurried into the hall.

In the lobby, he considered ramming Dolan's dumb head against the wall. The doorman's need to brag about his sexual prowess had almost blown the most important single piece of evidence yet that Captain Worth had been killed by someone standing in that basement entrance. Not that Epstein had seen a *person* there; just the flashes. Sheri had seen only *portions* of the gunblast, because a car on the north side of the street partially blocked her view. And she hadn't seen the captain fall, since he'd crouched behind another car, which again blocked her view. But this in itself supported the death-from-basement theory, since that same car – and he finally had evidence a car *had* been there – would have protected Worth from the black kid's gun.

Now he wanted to find that car and see if it had been hit by gunfire. And on what side.

Wouldn't the owner have reported it?

Perhaps only to his insurance company. And he might not

151

even have known of it, if it was in the lower panel. Or connect it with the shooting . . .

Dolan was getting off his stool to open the doors. Roersch said, 'Thanks, you've done enough,' and went out.

A good night's work.

Now to tie Angie Tortemango to the twenty thousand. And establish a motive for wanting Worth dead. And get to whoever had stood in that basement entrance. And if it wasn't Angie himself, tie him to Angie.

He'd need *ten* good nights' work for that, and a small miracle!

On the way home, he turned his radio from the police band to AM and the all-news station. And didn't really listen, until:

'Assemblyman Terrence Albony was shot and killed in an apparent robbery on a Greenwich Village street late Saturday night. Police told our mobile reporter Albony's pockets were turned out, his wallet was missing, he was wearing no watch or rings. When asked how the assemblyman was identified without his wallet, the officer replied: "A friend had been watching his car from her apartment and wondered why he hadn't reached it. She came down and found him in the lobby of the brownstone."

'The woman, identified only as a secretary, began screaming and a neighbor called police. It was the neighbor who directed responding radio-car officers to the secretary's apartment, since she had meanwhile returned there. She at first denied having found the body, or even having known Albony, but when faced with the neighbor broke down and said he had been visiting her. Police say her attempt to hide the truth is personal and in no way connected with the crime. Assemblyman Albony lived with his wife and two sons in Oyster Bay.

'Residents of a five-block area east of Fifth Avenue in Greenwich Village have reported several instances of robbery and attempted robbery in the past two days. Police say descriptions are sketchy, and the assailants varied in number from one to three, but in all cases they have been young black males. Our reporter is still on the scene and the latest word is that Albony was shot twice, once in the stomach and once in the head. A bullet has just been recovered and it appears to be of ·38 caliber. This plus other factors will undoubtedly lead to connections being drawn between Albony and the M–4 murders . . .'

Roersch turned off the radio. He had enough problems without speculative media bullshit.

But later, entering his apartment house's underground garage, he knew he'd be up early to get the latest on Assemblyman Albony.

TEN

He'd been waiting since eight that night, and here it was almost two in the morning! Waiting to at least hear from her by phone, and what the hell was *wrong* with the bitch? He was sure she understood it was important, even though the message he'd left with Paddy's housekeeper was a bland: 'Angie called to find out how his favorite relatives are doing.' Because they hadn't spoken since the goddam insanity struck Wednesday night, and they *had* to speak. She knew about Worth and his shakedown and his letter to Paddy. No mention of the twenty grand on the news, so those black cocksuckers had made a real haul.

But more important, they'd passed a death sentence on Angie and Maria. It was only a matter of time – *days*, if Worth's wife or a son had access to his safety-deposit boxes. Which could mean the letter was in the mail right now. Which could even mean the letter had been mailed Thursday and might be sitting on Paddy's leather-topped desk. Might be waiting for Paddy and Maria to come home from wherever they'd gone. Might be ready to explode in her face . . .

The phone rang. He lunged at it, spilling his Jack Daniel's. '*Yes?*'

'Hello, Angelo, it's Aunt Maria.'

He heard the warning little laugh, and a man's chuckle in the background. He took a deep breath, and chuckled himself. Paddy might be on an extension. He was certainly nearby.

'Hi. How's my uncle?'

'A little the worse for a ton of clams and a gallon of wine. We took a few days in the mountains, and on the way home he decided he wanted to stop at Umberto's.'

'Won't keep your figure that way,' he said, trying to think of how to get her to call back, or better yet come over.

154

'My figure's fine. I had Stella D'Oro biscuits and tea. Your uncle is just now stumbling into the bathroom . . .' She paused and whispered, 'I checked the mail, if that's what's got you worried. Nothing that could be from Worth. I even *opened* a few that might have had phony return addresses. So relax for tonight, and we'll talk tomorrow.'

'Why didn't you call, dammit! We might not have until tomorrow! Worth might have set it up with one of his relatives to *phone* the letter to Paddy! If Worth's family gets the crazy idea I contracted that killing, they'll go for revenge!'

'But how could they think that? Those three Negroes . . .'

'People hear Mafia, they think anything.'

'Oh, God,' she moaned.

'God's not going to help us! We should've been talking two, three days ago!'

'I *couldn't* call! We were in the Poconos with all those relatives of his, and every damn minute . . .'

'There's always a free damn minute,' he interrupted coldly. 'You didn't want to call.'

'I . . . well, I was afraid.'

'Sticking your head in the sand won't save it from an acid bath if Paddy finds out. We've got to talk *now*.'

'I can't see what we can do . . .'

'We might have to *kill* him!' he said, controlling the shout. 'Together we can get away with it. Alone, never!'

'Mother of God. I thought it took weeks, months, before wills were read and estates probated.'

'*Estates?* You dumb . . .' He fought for control. 'Worth was a cop on the take. For years. His *estate* is cash stuck away in boxes, secret, no taxes, no lawyers, just him and maybe his wife and maybe a son. Not even a close friend because that friend would be able to rip off the whole works. So whoever had a key went into those boxes right away. That person has Worth's money . . . and the letter to Paddy. The only thing we don't know is when it'll be sent. We've got to assume that it's in the mail right now.'

She was quiet. He was about to tell her to get moving, when she said:

'I've been thinking. Worth might have been bluffing about

155

writing the letter. He wouldn't want such evidence to his dishonesty, would he? It would be dangerous for him. Did you ever think he might have made up that story?'

He sighed wearily. 'I thought of it the minute he mentioned a letter. And forgot it. I wasn't willing to test for a bluff then, and I'm not willing to now. Are you? With your life at stake?'

'Maybe . . . maybe Paddy wouldn't . . .' She faltered.

'Tell him your mother's sick,' he said. 'You have to hurry to her side.' He hung up . . . then sank to the couch. Spelling it out for Maria, he'd spelled it out for himself. He couldn't risk trying to intercept the letter. And couldn't believe an old hand like Worth wouldn't have thought of phoned readings, telegrams, hand-to-hand deliveries, maybe *all* of them, to make sure.

There were no defenses. There was only killing Paddy before he found out about them. Which meant right now.

He mixed a fresh Daniel's and water, a stiff one, and went to the bedroom and the wall safe where he kept his gun. It was a Luger, not because he dug the German automatic more than a Colt ·45, for example, or a Smith & Wesson ·38 revolver, but because it could be easily fitted with a silencer.

He had a silencer for the Luger, tooled for him by a gunsmith Paddy kept on the payroll. It was of the type called 'automobile muffler' and did one hell of a job. He'd used it twice in the past four years, and had thought with his growing eminence in the family never to use it again.

He shrugged. Not that he was committed to shooting Paddy. Maria might have a better way: pills or some kind of medication. The Luger was for whoever might get in the way. Rick, for example, his uncle's bodyguard, who lived in the guest house.

He put the five-inch silencer in his pants pocket, slipped a shoulder holster over his head and right arm, put the loaded Luger in the holster. He went to the closet and got into his jacket. And all the time he was sweating.

Back in the living room, he lowered the thermostat to get the air-conditioning going. And continued to sweat. And not just about Paddy. That cop had been around again –

first pumping Marty, then Lou Flecher. Flecher looked ready to have a heart attack. Eventually he'd admit Worth had visited Angie.

Okay. No problem. Worth was dead and no one in his family wanted his name dirtied, or his assets questioned. Worth had come to check him out about some prostie hassle or other. The Apple Man had been throwing his weight around a little; something like that. Legit police business, and the late hour was because Angie hadn't made himself available earlier.

The twenty thousand was gone and no one could know about it . . . until they caught the blacks. And they might not find out about it even then. Jewelry had to be fenced, but cash melted quickly away.

Anyway, he'd worry about them catching the blacks when it happened, *if* it happened.

But what if that sergeant thought *Angie* had put the chill on Worth? Marty said that the M–4 sergeant had told the mailman Worth might *not* have been killed by whoever killed the others.

He was sweating, rubbing his hands together nervously . . . and thought of something else, and began to come unglued.

What if M—4 had a stakeout on him right now?

He ran to the window. He pressed against it, looking down and this way and that way, cursing and wondering whether to try and stop Maria . . .

And said aloud, 'Cool it, *paisan!* No sense panicking. If the stakeout's there, you'll spot it when you leave. And shake it before you make a move.'

He opened the window, as if for a breath of fresh air, and leaned out and cast an experienced eye around for a full five minutes. And began to feel it made no sense for M–4 to waste men tailing him. The sergeant hadn't learned anything yet; he was just playing cop, checking on the well-known Mafia name. Maybe later . . .

Later, Angie wouldn't give a damn. They knew what he did for a living. Let them follow him to hell and back; they'd never get him for anything more than illegal parking.

He closed the window, returned to the couch, and lit a cigarette.

God in heaven, why had he let Maria get to him! So she had green eyes and long legs and big tits. So what the hell was that to Angelo Tortemango, who had a *thousand* chicks who'd suck the boss's cock just to make him happy? And if he didn't want pros, there was Lori and a dozen other knockouts from show biz. And if he wanted good clean Italian stuff, there was Regina, who was built like the best of them and ready to marry him tomorrow and believe-it-or-not he'd taken her cherry! Ass had *never* been a problem, so why Paddy's wife?

'*Why?*' he whispered, raging at himself.

Yet he knew why. To score the old bastard. To pay back for the slaps in the face with Rick and Chimp and the other soldiers watching. To erase the humiliation of the thin smile, the scornful, 'Angie's good for the whores, the nigger gambling.'

It was a *hate* fuck he'd thrown into Maria. A revenge fuck. Giving the *cornuto* to the *patron*; putting the horns on his bald head. Oh Jesus, how he'd *loved* shooting into Paddy's private slot!

Still, he could have controlled the hate; reminded himself he was a full-fledged *capo* now. Getting into shylocking might have been tough, but he *was* in. And there was a promise of more . . .

But no sense kidding himself. He was a million miles away from cutting into unions and drugs, where the big money lay. *Maybe* the dying metropolitan waterfronts, after he kissed Paddy's ass another five years. And took a few more slaps. The last one had come just before the wedding, when he thought his uncle might be happy enough to discuss letting him take on a little more responsibility.

With Rick helping him into his cutaway, the bastard had turned and *slapped*. Just a flick of the fingers across the lips, but the contemptuous 'Don't talk such shit on my wedding day' had burned itself deep into Angie's heart. And helped make him do what he'd done a few hours later.

Yet Paddy liked him in a *family* way. Had no sons, and

158

had no brothers left, and named him best man when he lost his fucking marbles and married the cunt he'd bought with furs and cars and jewelry. Made her his *wife*, for the love of Christ! So smart and so tough in most ways; so fucking stupid about women! Maybe he'd have been better off if *he'd* run the despised prostie racket; learned a little about hookers and how they thought. Because anyone who knew whores knew *all* women to a certain extent. Especially the ones who married men thirty years older than themselves.

A fucking fool, the *don*. An *aging* fool who wasn't giving Maria what her hot box required. She was *ass*, pure and simple, and Angie found out about it right at the reception ...

She saw him go to the john, she admitted later, and when he came out she was in the little powder room, fixing her stockings, one foot up on a chair, that short wedding gown hiked to her waist. And those see-through white panties and those garter-belt bands pressing into her bare thighs, her pink-white thighs, and the way she took her time dropping the dress, looking him in the eye and saying, 'Hi, nephew.'

He'd had a lot of champagne. He got a hard-on and wanted to use it.

But of course this was Pasquale Tortemango's bride and what he had to do was go find another girl, like the one he'd brought.

What he *did* do was go to Maria and put a hand on her breast and kiss her with open mouth and say, 'I'm going to fuck you, auntie.'

He did, at the Don Juan Motel, three weeks later. And the bitch used imagination. She wore *white* – white midi dress, white hat with white veil, white shoes. The desk clerk thought they'd just been married; Angie saw him shake his head a little at a bridegroom bringing his bride to a porno motel!

A laugh to make things even better. But the laughter stopped when he shut the door behind them and turned to see her standing with one foot up on a chair, her dress hiked to her waist, wearing those same see-through white panties with those same white garter-belt bands pressing into her bare thighs, her pink-white thighs. All of it, the same as at the reception.

She said, 'Hi, nephew,' and used one delicate finger to pull aside the panties looking him in the eye, proving she was a real redhead.

He went at her, opening his pants *wild* for it.

She said, 'Wait. This is your aunt, nephew Angelo. You *kiss* your aunt.'

He dropped to his knees and ripped those panties clean off and worked his mouth onto her and his tongue into her as she stood there, that leg still up. She began to whimper; and he spoke his hatred of Paddy, said the venomous obscenities he could never say to Paddy's face into Paddy's wife's cunt. And it was the greatest! The wildest!

He picked her up and threw her on the bed and with that wedding outfit still on, he fucked her, *slamming* her, gripping her tits and ass *hard*, hurting her in his need to hurt Paddy. When he came, he pressed his face into the pillow beside her head, smothering the 'Fucking Pasquale bastard!'

Then they had a drink and shared a joint and started all over again. And came back to the Don Juan the next week, and the next. And the last time the stinking fuzz had busted in on them.

And now? Now he was as close to dying as he'd ever been.

And so was Paddy.

It was three-fifteen when Maria arrived. They didn't embrace and they didn't kiss. That's what had gotten them into this goddam mess in the first place.

He talked nonstop for about ten minutes, explaining what they had to do ... tonight.

She sat opposite him in the brown armchair, crying and hugging herself and rocking a little. Her red hair was mussed and her big tits were hidden and it looked like the knees on her long legs were knocking together, they shook so. And *this* was what he'd risked his life for.

He said, 'I can do it with the gun. Or do you have another

160

way? Does he take medication he doesn't talk about? Something he can O.D. on?'

She shook her head; wiped at her eyes. 'He's healthy. A bull. Except in ...' She shrugged; then looked directly at Angie.

He smiled – the first time in days – and said, 'Your nephew will comfort you in your hour of grief.'

'We'll have to stick together, Angie. Maybe later, we'll ...'

He nodded brusquely. 'First things first.' The silly bitch wanted to talk marriage!

'The family will ask questions,' she said. 'Who'd want to kill him?'

'A dozen men, at least. The Polletaries. Dominic Scarness, seventy-five and still full of hate for the way Paddy gave it to his brother twenty years ago. Others. But certainly not his loyal nephew, his loving wife. You get a lot less from Paddy dead than you do from Paddy alive, you know that?'

She wasn't crying anymore. 'He made it plain enough with that stinking marriage contract!'

'Be grateful for that stinking contract. It puts you above suspicion. As for me, I can only lose with a new *don*.'

'So then what are we *doing*?'

'Saving our lives. You keep forgetting that. What the hell good is money to a *corpse*?'

She wiped her eyes again, blew her nose, asked for a cigarette. He went over the plan. She listened, smoking, watching him. Then she said, 'Why are we in this alone? You have men loyal to you and not to Paddy. Wouldn't they do it ... you know, on contract?'

He shook his head. 'Forget it.' Yes, he had men like Iggy and Morgan, and the Apple Man would lend a hand for a larger cut of the action. But one might decide to blow the whistle and come firmly into Paddy's favor. And even if that didn't happen, whoever helped would have him firmly by the nuts for the rest of his life. And would know it.

Of course, that was true of Maria, except the dumb cunt thought he was going to get heavy with her when things cooled down. When he *didn't*, she'd be trouble. So eventually Miss Big Tits would have to total her car and her dingbat head. He had just the mechanic who could see to it – friend of a friend on Brooklyn's Rockaway Avenue.

But for the present, it was Angie and Maria to the finish. *Paddy's* finish, that is.

He began to feel good about it. He hoped the bastard would open his eyes at the last second and know who was giving it to him!

Anyway, no assistants. No hit men. Keep it as simple as possible.

Maria would give Angie her house keys – there were three to handle the complex two-door security – and drive to her mother's. Angie would go for a walk and steal a car.

He'd drive to Fort Lee and the big house standing alone on the quiet dead-end street. Then in he'd go with Maria's keys, straight to Paddy's bedroom, and with no more noise than a snap of the fingers solve his problems.

Out again, leaving the keys in the mailbox on the road, and return to Manhattan, where he'd dump the car within a few blocks of home. Stroll back, hoping no muggers were around (he smiled), and into the house. A little chat with Lou Flecher about his family and how to keep them healthy, followed by a very solid tip for services rendered – say a grand – and then to bed. And he'd consider retiring Lou to Florida.

Or more permanent retirement. He'd see.

Anyway, Maria would come home *early* – say seven, seven-thirty – grabbing her keys from the mailbox. Her mother hadn't been that sick after all ... her sister would swear to *anything* the dingbat said, since Maria supported the whole shebang of sick mother, widowed older sister, and the sister's ten-year-old daughter.

Maria would enter her bedroom and find her husband dead. Screaming, yelling, Rick running around and soon other soldiers running around. Then some cops firmly in the family's pocket would close out a quick investigation and keep reporters from annoying the widow.

Eventually, they'd blame it on old Dominic and his son,

162

and knock them off. Eventually, Angie would go to the Polletaries and suggest a deal. And eventually, despite what he'd told the dingbat, he'd end up in a stronger position than under Paddy . . . and without the slaps.

'You'd better go, baby,' he said, moving her out of the chair and to the door.

She turned. 'Kiss me, Angelo.' Her voice shook. 'Make me sure.'

He was impatient to get going. He kissed her and patted her ass and maneuvered her into the hall. 'Don't worry,' he said, and closed the door.

He had another Daniel's and water, thinking it through and trying to find loopholes. There were a few soft spots – mainly the doorman – but nothing he couldn't handle.

He finished his drink and left the apartment.

Getting the car was a snap; the third one he tried on Fifty-fourth was open. He got inside and reached under the dash for the wires; then remembered what the Apple Man had told him Harlem car thieves did. He checked the sun visors, searched the glove compartment, lifted the floor covering on both driver's and passenger's side.

The key was under the carpeting on the passenger's side.

He laughed, inserted it in the ignition, and took off. Oh what a fucking dumb world this was! What a big, beautiful, ripe, idiot thing waiting for the man who knew how to rip it off!

He drove slowly, cautiously, and reached the quiet dead-end road at five-twenty. The sky was touched with light in the east as he parked near a clump of scraggly trees and brush.

He waited. He tasted the situation. No problems. He got out and moved across the road.

First door – just a brief moment of fumbling with the alarm-disconnect key; enough to place a thin film of sweat over his forehead. Then the second key turned and he was stepping into the vestibule. The inner door opened with the big key, and he was moving softly down the hall to the stairs.

To the right and near the kitchen, the Jamaican maid was

163

sleeping. Out back behind the main house and pool was the guest house, and Rick. Up the flight of stairs he was approaching was the second floor and the three bedrooms, including the master bedroom suite.

Always a sound sleeper was Uncle Paddy, as Angie had learned those nights he had stayed in the east bedroom. That was when Rick had also slept in the main house, in the room beside Paddy's.

With marriage to Maria, the house had emptied. Paddy wanted no audience to his grunt-and-groan lovemaking. A lousy screw, old Paddy, according to half a dozen girls Angie'd sent to Fort Lee.

He was at the top of the stairs, and Paddy's grunt-and-groan days were coming to an end.

He drew the Luger from its holster, the silencer from his pants pocket, and screwed the thick cylinder to the barrel of the German automatic. He had a very long weapon now, one impossible to hide. But that was all right; there was no one to see. He made sure the safety was off, a bullet ready in the chamber. All that remained was to put that bullet, and one for good luck, into Paddy.

He came to the master bedroom. The door was open. It was dark, the drapes drawn, but he could still make out the shape in bed. He stepped inside, moving on the balls of his feet, the gun extended. The shape grew clearer; Paddy appeared to be facing the draped windows, his back to Angie.

He came close in three long steps. It was too dark for niceties, so he put the first bullet roughly into the heart area and a second higher up, where the head should be.

Two tiny pops of sound. That was all.

His heart jumped. *That was all?* No sound from Paddy? No choked-off scream? No groan? Absolutely *nothing*?

He shoved the gun deep into the bedding ... and that's what it was, bedding.

And he was hit from behind and there were flashes of light and he found himself in a chair against the wall.

His head was split open. Blood ran down into his mouth.

Then he saw them. Maria and Paddy. They were sitting

164

on the bed, side by side. They were holding hands. She was crying, just like at his apartment.

Paddy said, 'You jerk. You think all women are whores. She came home fast as she could and told me everything.'

He couldn't believe it. 'Everything?' he mumbled, and his head radiated pain. He tried to lift his hands to it, and found that they were tied behind him.

'How you drugged her and took her to that motel. How you told her the story about a dead cop sending a blackmail letter.' He laughed, shaking his head. 'Who would believe that shit except an innocent girl! You wanted to keep getting her. You scum, you wanted to take over from *Paddy Tortemango?* Your own blood? Your own father's brother?'

'That's not . . .'

'She came right home as soon as she learned how far you wanted to go. She woke me and begged me to forgive her for not confessing sooner.' He smiled, that squat, bald man with the sensual mouth – a mouth much like Angie's own. 'I told her it was soon enough. We stood in the bathroom, the three of us, and waited. We watched you, Angelo.' He raised Maria's hand and kissed it.

The three of us. Angie turned his head to the right, and saw Rick. Rick was an ox. Rick had hands like hams and fingers like bananas. Rick looked at him with interest and amusement.

Angie forgot the pain in his head. 'Uncle, listen! I didn't drug her! I swear by all the saints . . .'

'Even if she went for you, for a minute . . .'

Maria cried out, 'May my mother die *tonight* if I did!'

Paddy smiled a little and nodded a little. 'It happens.' His smile fled. He leaned forward, his face turning a deep, angry red. 'But to *kill* me? To make a plan with my wife and expect her to *help* you kill me? You stinking pimp! You think she's what you peddle, a *prostitute?*'

'The letter'll come! Just wait until Monday. Maybe a call'll come sooner! Just keep me here until . . .'

'If a letter comes, *you* wrote it, *you* sent it. You and your organization of nothing trash. I'm going to give your action to Rick, if he can make you die for ten minutes.' He leaned

165

back. 'You'll be a *capo*, Rick. But ten minutes, by the clock.'

'Pasquale! For the love of God!'

The squat, bald man turned and pointed at the punctured bedding.

Angie began to scream, *'Forgive me! Forgive ...'*

A cloth was jammed into his mouth and halfway down his throat. He gagged. It was withdrawn a little.

He felt a rope slip around his neck. He felt something hard against the back of his head.

The garrote. Death by strangulation. It couldn't be happening!

He looked at Maria, trying to beg for intercession with his eyes. He remembered kissing her at the door of his apartment; remembered patting her ass and pushing her into the hall. After she'd asked for something: affection? assurance? love?

He tried to tell her he'd give her love, give her anything she wanted, if only she'd plead for his life!

She turned away, leaning into Paddy, weeping heavily. He stroked her head. 'You'll go to church every day for a month. You'll pray for forgiveness, and for him.'

She begged to be allowed to leave the room. Paddy said, 'No,' very firmly, and spoke to Rick. 'Some good will come of this. We'll get rid of Dominic and his son. We'll get together with the Polletaries. It'll be a good thing for everyone.'

Angie agreed. It was his plan exactly ... except that now *he* would be the cause, the corpse.

Maria sobbed.

Angie's mind jerked this way and that. And came to rest on a single thought.

How could he have been so wrong about her, so stupid about her, he who knew everything about women?

More than the gag was choking him now. It got worse, but very slowly ...

ELEVEN

Sunday, July 20, A.M.

Jones was up before Andra and moved quietly to the bathroom so as to allow her to sleep. It wasn't *entirely* out of kindness and altruism that he did this. He wanted hot water on his body, ham and eggs in his belly, and a quick departure to M–4.

He also wanted a sweet parting from reporter Andra Stennis, but that was not to be. When he walked out of the bathroom, showered and shaved, she was dressed and waiting. He came to her, a towel draped around his waist, and kissed her mouth briefly. 'Got to rush. Big day on M–4.' He turned to the dresser for underwear.

'Yes. Big day hunting down three black boys. *Children*, from all indications. What are your feelings, Sergeant Jones, about having them *identified* in so blatant a manner?'

He'd gotten into his shorts and was sitting on the bed to put on his socks. 'What?' he muttered. He didn't want to quarrel with this beautiful girl. He hadn't had as satisfying a bout of lovemaking in a long time. He wanted to stay friends, and have her again, and *talk*, certainly, but not quarrel; especially not about race.

'Your commanding officer, Sergeant Roersch ... and by the way, why is he commanding the operation when you're both of equal rank?'

He headed for the closet and his suit. He spoke softly, reasonably (even though he was beginning to burn a little): 'You haven't covered police procedure very often, have you, Andra? I mean, you're not a regular police reporter, are you?'

'No, thank God. But how does that answer my question?'

He zipped up his fly and bent to his shoes. 'Roersch is not only a sergeant, he's a detective first grade with a record thirty-five years of service. I'm a sergeant, yes, but I'm a

167

detective, period, and my length of service goes into Eddy's five times. His experience – and more than that, his expertise, his ability – makes him the *only* choice to head up this case. I'd go further. I think he should be running Manhattan West Homicide instead of Captain Hawly, and Hawly's damned good.'

He tied his shoes and went back to the closet, where his shirts were on hangers. He hoped she'd forgotten her first question, but she hadn't.

'Why did this experienced and admired commanding officer of yours have to identify the three suspects by color? Why inflame public opinion . . .?'

'Because we want help from the public, from witnesses, from people who might know those . . .' He swallowed an obscenity as he tucked in his shirt. 'Those three killers.'

'*Suspects!*' she snapped. 'You are not judge and jury, Willis!'

'Those three black suspects,' he said, and chose a tie and turned to the mirror. Where she was standing. 'We wanted the identification to be as complete as possible.'

'*We?* You were consulted?'

'I didn't have to be. I mention color in every report on every crime. I mention it to every reporter who asks me. I identify suspects as blonde Caucasians, pale-skinned or *negrito* Hispanics, blacks of various shades and facial types, Orientals, Eskimos, whatever! I'm a police officer and I describe *suspects* as closely, as completely, as I can! So that they can be recognized by the public! So that in this case people won't be looking for redheads, Puerto Ricans, Indians!'

'Please don't shout at me,' she said, turning away.

He finished knotting his tie. 'I'm sorry,' he said. 'I'm a grouch before breakfast. Can you cook?'

'I'll do my share, but I won't serve as you sit watching.' Then, as they walked to the kitchen: 'You really think there's no reason to eliminate mention of race in criminal cases?'

'Oh, Christ,' he groaned, and opened the refrigerator and took out eggs, milk and ham. He made omelettes, and tried

168

not to answer, tried to avoid the argument. She made coffee, and glanced at him every so often, and finally said, 'Well?'

So he answered, and with some heat. 'If you're in favor of criminals getting away with their crimes, stick to that no-mention-of-color idea. If you'd like to see more criminals caught, more punished, and a resultant reduction in crime . . .'

'Who says jail reduces crime?'

'When they're off the streets, they can't rob and kill.'

'But they get out and they're worse than before!'

He turned the omelettes. 'I give up,' he muttered. 'You want anarchy.'

'I want justice!'

'Okay. So do I. But we seem to have different definitions. Do you think catching the killers of those four people on Fifty-second Street might possibly come under the heading of justice? That's what Sergeant Roersch and I are trying to do, the best way we know how.'

'Yes, catching the murderers is justice, as we know it.'

'Okay then. That' all I want to do – bring about *that* particular justice.' He flipped the omelettes onto two plates.

They went to the table, she carrying mugs of coffee. He looked for orange juice, and realized he'd forgotten it. He sipped steaming coffee, and it had no cream or sugar as when Caroline made breakfast, as when he was able to *concentrat*e on breakfast.

She saw the face he made, and went to the refrigerator and brought back the quart container of milk. Sugar was on the table, and she moved it toward him. 'I take mine black,' she said.

'Yeah. You sure do. You take your *life* black. If you were a white, you'd hate you as a goddam racist.'

She actually jerked in her chair. 'There's no sense trying to interview anyone like you! I could get as much from your commanding officer!'

'More,' he said, stuffing his mouth with omelette that tasted like glue. He chewed determinedly. She sighed, and looked down at her hands. He pushed his plate away and rose. 'Gotta run.'

She spoke in a deceivingly quiet voice. 'You see, Willis, I'm not saying that those three boys – if they actually did the crime, and that has yet to be determined – I'm not saying they shouldn't be caught and punished. But the point is this: we, I mean blacks, have been treated like scum for so long that it's going to take time before we can adjust – in the mass, that is – and function without hatred, without, well, waging war on our oppressors.'

'War?' he muttered, staring at her. 'You're saying those three fucking butchers . . .'

She jumped to her feet. 'I'm saying those three boys committed a lynching in reverse!'

They were leaning toward each other now, shouting into each other's faces now.

'And you *approve* of these "lynchings in reverse", do you? You think it *helps* blacks to have four innocent people murdered in cold fucking blood?'

'I never approved of whites lynching blacks, and I don't approve of blacks lynching whites! But I *understand* it, damn you! And stop using your pig obscenities on me! I don't like the word *fucking* thrown into my face!'

'Those three *fucking* butchers are throwing something else into your face! *Shit!* Hatred from all the non-black people of this country!'

'*You're* getting that shit too, aren't you, Willis? That hatred? You'll *keep* getting it no matter how hard you try to act white!'

Willis had a headache. 'Good-bye,' he said.

She went to the bedroom. He stood there, waiting. A minute later she reappeared, carrying her large leather handbag, and walked past the kitchen archway. He followed her through the living room to the door.

He remembered last night's loving, and said, 'Couldn't we say good-bye like people? I mean . . .'

She faced him, smiling just a little. 'Why is it that when I finally meet a man who turns me on, he has to be a police officer?' Then, more intensely: 'Why does a smart man, an educated man, a beautiful man like you, Willis, have to be a *cop*?'

He answered without having to think. 'Because I love it.'

She opened the door and stepped into the hall. 'Don't call us, we'll call you.'

The door closed, maybe for good, on Andra Stennis.

Before he had time to feel bad about it, the phone rang. He looked at his watch as he went into the living room. Not quite eight. It had to be Eddy.

It was Balleau. 'I've been trying to get hold of Roersch, but he left home at about seven, his wife said. Didn't tell her for where. And this won't wait. We got a call on that Firebird.'

Jones forgot Andra Stennis and everything else.

'A cover message from a stoolie. "Mack the Knife wants his main man to call about the red-assed bird." I tried to get a phone number, but he just said it again and hung up. You got a clue?'

'Yes. Keep trying to get Eddy. Tell him I'll be on the street.'

He went back to the bedroom and began undressing. It was too early for his pimp threads; he'd do an in-between number. And hope Mac would make himself available.

Today could be very big in the life and times of Sergeant Willis Jones. And three ghetto skells.

Eddy left at seven-ten and drove downtown toward Headquarters. He had already phoned Deverney, at home, and explained to a definitely displeased inspector what he needed. The displeasure remained in the sleep-thickened voice: 'Okay, Eddy. I hope this is *really* urgent. Sunday at seven A.M., God *damn!*'

Now Roersch listened to the all-news station and got weather reports (it was going to be another scorcher), vacation-travel reports (the roads were clear leaving the city), and foreign news (all fucked up, as usual). Then came sports, and he tried to remember just when he'd last seen a baseball game except on television.

At one time he'd seen the Dodgers – when they'd made their home at Brooklyn's Ebbets Field – ten-twelve times a season. Helen had learned to love the game. Those exciting

171

seasons with Jackie Robinson playing up a storm; then Roy Campanella. And those great World Series with the so-called unbeatable Yankees. Reese at shortstop, Hodges a *poem* at first and a terror at the plate, and old Preacher Rowe on the mound.

So much fun then.

Was he simply growing old, growing out of fun?

He wondered when the hell they'd stop the goddam commercials and get to the local news and the followup on last night's murder. It was out of Manhattan West's territory, but if the brass decided there was a chance the perpetrators were the same as on M–4, he might get stuck with it.

More sports news. Someone had broken an ankle sliding into third and was lost for the season. Roersch hadn't caught the player's name, or his team. Baseball just wasn't important to him anymore.

Yet he had a son now. Fathers and sons went to ball games together; it was traditional. His own father had taken him from LaGrange in upper New York's Dutchess County (where they'd lived a country existence), catching the special bus at Poughkeepsie, all the way to Ebbets Field at least a dozen times during his childhood years.

He'd been about five, the first time Mike had taken him to Brooklyn.

He could take Mark at the same age and they'd watch the Mets and he'd hold his son up to see over the screaming fans.

And he'd be sixty-three, sixty-four . . .

The story he'd been waiting for was about to come on, 'after these few important messages'. He was glad he could stop thinking about fathers and sons.

And yet he had one more such thought: of how his still-young, still-blonde, still-strong father had crumpled one day in the kitchen while opening the icebox for a drink – a beer, sure; it was lying beside him when the ambulance came – and died of what the doctor called 'massive coronary'. And Mike's father, Eddy's grandfather, had also gone that way.

But Grandpa had been real old, hadn't he? In his seventies? And still strong, virile . . .

172

Well, old, anyway, and maybe Eddy took after Grandpa.

He concentrated on the radio announcer's voice.

'Assemblyman Terrence Albony was only forty-two, but had already gained a reputation for shrewd political acumen that earned him a strong voice in the mayor's and occasionally the governor's ear. He was a lawyer and quite well-to-do because of land investments.

'His wife of eighteen years, Ellen, was in a state of shock last night, but Albony's brother told the press she knew where her husband was at the time of his death, and why. Albony had used the services of secretary Ann Groomer many times for confidential business matters, and was preparing a land prospectus, on his own time, as he always did in personal business affairs ...'

'Yeah, yeah,' Roersch muttered impatiently as the announcer went on with other relatives' statements and co-assemblymen's statements and it was all shit. 'Personal *affairs* is right! He was banging the girl and he was a grift artist under secret investigation for conflict of interest and he was tied into racket money. For Chrissake get to the gun, the wounds, the perpetrators, the witnesses, *the fucking murder*!'

Hearing himself, he wondered if he wasn't wearing a little too thin. He had to get some of this pressure off his chest by talking with Jimmy Weir tonight.

He took deep breaths of already-heated morning air, and tried not to listen to the bullshit. And was rewarded with 'a synopsis of our earlier story'.

Albony had been shot twice with a ·38 caliber revolver. Once in the *heart*, not the stomach, as earlier reported. Once in the head. Either wound was enough to have killed him.

Also corrected was the information on where the secretary had found Albony: not in the lobby of the brownstone, but down a hallway behind the interior staircase, near a cellar door. Since there were no signs of a struggle, Albony seemed to have been killed 'for no practical purpose, much like the victims of the M–4 murderers', the announcer said.

Roersch groaned.

There were no witnesses. The aging couple who acted as

173

rental agents and custodians lived in the one apartment on the ground floor toward the front. The couple was watching television and had heard nothing. Albony's secretary had spotted his body on her way *back* to her apartment, catching a glimpse of his shoes.

'The only suspects so far,' the announcer said, 'are several young men who fit the descriptions of those wanted in connection with the M–4 murders.'

Roersch turned the volume dial to OFF.

By the time he parked in the Headquarters garage – not impossible this early on a Sunday morning – he'd put together the comparisons in his mind.

The Albony case was close enough to the Worth case to disturb him. But how the hell could there be a connection? Had Albony been dealing with the Tortemango branch of the Mafia? Was Angie having a clearance on associates and shakedown artists, knocking them off wholesale?

He got out of his car and walked to the elevators. Forget Albony. He had to meet Worth's secretary, if Deverney had been able to get in touch with her, and two or three police clerks, and go through Worth's report and source material. And look for references to the name Tortemango.

Yet Albony stuck in his mind.

Worth had been a cop on the take. Albony had been a politician on the take. Both had conducted their operations so as to remain untouched by investigators. Each had died with a bullet in the heart and a *coup de grâce* in the head.

But it didn't make sense for the Tortemangos to kill people they dealt with. And that included Captain Tom Worth, who *had* to have had some sort of protection, some sort of knife at Angie's throat.

It just didn't add up.

Yet he was here to *make* it add up, to nail Angie to Worth's corpse. Because what other way was there to go?

He stopped projecting and began taking one very small mental step forward at a time. That brought him to Worth's office, where a dark, cute policewoman was waiting, along with two not-quite-so-cute policemen. The policewoman looked tired and unhappy.

174

'Sergeant Roersch?'

She and the two male cops rose from chairs in Worth's anteroom.

Roersch nodded. 'Sorry if I ruined your weekend, Officer ...'

'Francine Grasso. You didn't really ruin it. Just ... shortened it.' The smile failed to convince.

'All I can say is it might help collar your boss's murderers.'

She nodded briskly. But she still didn't look as if it meant much to her. Worth hadn't been her boss that long; and he obviously hadn't made much of an impression. Which fit the picture the department had of him. He was a charm-boy with his men in the precincts. He was tough and seductive, by turns, as the situation demanded, with the bad guys. But with women he was basically cool and disinterested; very tight with his wife; a true family man.

He asked her to get Worth's report. 'Whatever he completed of it.'

'Nothing at all, as far as I know. He wasn't on it that long; was still putting together the source material. Maybe he had a few notes ...'

Roersch asked for the source material. Francine Grasso led all three men into the office proper and pointed. 'Good luck!'

The cardboard crates would have filled a normal-sized office. Even in this large corner office, they were stacked three and four high and came almost to Worth's desk.

Roersch went behind the desk and sat down. 'There are records from four boroughs, excluding Staten Island, as I understand it.'

Officer Grasso nodded.

'All right, find those from the Manhattan precincts. Bring me a case and each of you take a case. Not you, Officer Grasso. Look for those notes Worth might have made.'

A case was brought to him. He slid his chair aside to accommodate Officer Grasso's search of desk drawers, and admired her shapely calves and thighs. He told the others to

175

concentrate on one thing, one word: 'Tortemango. Any reference at all.'

Officer Grasso was the first to find it . . . in a lower filing-cabinet drawer, where she was again distracting Roersch with a display of tanned flesh. She brought the folder to him. It was, quite logically, marked 'T' on the flap. Inside was a single sheet of paper. On it was written, in pencil, 'Angelo Tortemango. Maria Tortemango. Pasquale Tortemango. D.D.-5, March 18. 4th Detective Zone. Raid on Don Juan Motel.'

That was all. Tom Worth had obviously gone ahead and learned all he needed to get that twenty thousand dollars – and perhaps more money before, or more to come – and had forgotten this minor notation. Or would have destroyed it when he'd completed his report and emptied the filing cabinet; or when, as rumor had it, he made inspector and was honorably retired this November.

And if he hadn't been murdered and become the subject of a special investigation, this note would have been too cryptic to have meant anything to anyone. It *still* meant nothing, but Roersch had faith in old Tom's money instincts.

He and his assistants narrowed the search down to one carton, and, dumping the contents on the floor, found the March eighteenth material within minutes. It was Patrolman Clark who held up a blue form. 'Angelo Tortemango. Possible possession marijuana. Yeah . . . Don Juan Motel.'

Roersch took it from his hand. 'Keep looking,' he said, and returned to the desk. He sat down and began to read.

'There are further reports on that raid,' Officer Grasso said. 'No further reference, as yet, to Tortemango.'

'Bring them all here. Then you can go home.'

Francine Grasso beamed, and Roersch envied whoever was waiting for her. The two male cops looked at each other, and one said, 'That go for us, also, Sergeant?'

Roersch caught a scam in the making. 'Only if it's your day off.'

They shrugged and left. Officer Grasso laughed. 'They

wouldn't have had the guts to try the direct-order route anyway. I'll just clean up a little.'

Roersch nodded. He heard her slamming metal filing drawers and throwing reports into cases, but he didn't look up to check her legs this time. He didn't look up even when she called ' 'Bye, sergeant.' He continued to read the D.D.–5, the report on Angie being caught with an 'ex-wife' in a raid on a porno motel. He read it twice, and scanned other reports on the Don Juan raid, and leaned back and saw several possibilities. Angie's Uncle Paddy either had a young daughter, or a young wife.

A niece? Twenty thousand was high for a niece.

He used the phone to call a contact at the *Times*. The contact wasn't working this Sunday. He got his home number and dialed. A woman said he was at church. 'Can he return your call, Sergeant?'

Roersch gave the M–4 number.

He took Worth's note and the D.D.–5 with him, not bothering with questions of whether this was legal, and drove to Manhattan West. Where he learned two things that gave him great satisfaction:

Jones was on the street in response to a stoolie's code message about the Firebird.

His reporter friend, who'd done articles on Eastern Mafia families, called and said Maria Tortemango was Pasquale Tortemango's wife.

Roersch allowed himself a few minutes of leaning back, eyes closed, thinking very lazily, very loosely. Then he used the phone, apologizing quickly in case he'd caught Jimmy in bed at nine-ten. Would Jimmy be free for dinner?

'Can I bring my date?'

'No, Jimmy.'

'Can it wait until tomorrow?'

'Well, yeah, it can . . . but I don't want it to.'

'Is it more important than my getting laid, Eddy?'

'I think so. I don't want to carry this particular load alone even one more night. There's no one but you, Jimmy.'

The captain's voice changed. 'Danziger's at nine.'

Even there, Roersch had to push his old friend. 'I'll have to call you. I don't know what time I'll be free. Things are breaking on M-4. Can you give me a number where you can be reached?'

'Yeah, but I won't. With your delicate touch, guess what I'll be doing when you call?'

Roersch chuckled, and waited.

'I'll be at home, Eddy. Watching television and cursing out old friends.' But he finally chuckled in response ... and Roersch felt an immediate lessening of pressure.

What would a man do without at least one good friend!

Roersch and his two detectives third were about to leave for Harlem when the phone rang. Eli Ross answered, and held the handset out to Roersch.

It was Deverney. 'You've got media problems building on this Albony thing. The networks are trying to arrange another conference. The *News* is pushing the hell out of all its City Hall contacts, and the *Times* is waiting one more day. They want to lay it at your door. They want you to draw parallels and give them a national-interest story. It's building into something like the Zebra murders in San Francisco, or so the fucking reporters would like to think!'

Roersch could have pointed out that the Zebra murders had claimed *fourteen* victims and the race-war overtones had been obvious from Killing One and Worth was black and going in another direction and Albony figured closer to Worth than to the Jaekers and Magris.

Deverney continued: 'You're not to be assigned Albony. You're not to discuss Albony. You're to keep M-4 just as it is, not let it blow up into M-5 or six or goddam fucking ten! Which will happen, if we allow every murder to be compared to M-4! So if a news conference is unavoidable – and I want you to try and avoid any until you have your solved – but if it's *forced* on you, then state firmly Albony is out of your jurisdiction. Refer them to the First Detective Zone. It's none of your business, got that?'

How upset the good inspector was, Roersch thought.

Was it really just because he wanted to keep M–4 uncomplicated? Or were Albony and Worth linked in Deverney's devious mind?

Did he know something he wasn't telling his M–4 commanding officer? His 'long-experienced sergeant', who'd been given a job that truly belonged to a captain, an inspector, a chief? His patsy, who could be controlled as no high-ranking officer could?

It was time, Roersch thought, he found out how far his 'long-experienced' neck was being stretched. 'If the P.C. gives the word to the networks, the papers, they won't bother me about Albony, will they?'

'The P.C. can't control the fucking world! The P.C. can't work more than three miracles per week! The P.C.'s eye isn't on the fucking sparrow! The P.C. isn't *God*, Roersch!'

'Yessir. I would, however, like to know his thinking . . .'

'You're getting it! From me! Now do as I tell you and catch those motherfucking jigs! For the money; for your promotion and pension; for your goddamn fucking *life*! Do you read me, Sergeant? *Do you?*'

He was screaming. He'd screamed before, as C.O. of Manhattan West. Sometimes it meant he was angry, and sometimes it meant he was acting, and sometimes – now, perhaps – it meant he was scared.

Roersch said, 'Got it, Inspector. Everything's moving. If you want a breakdown . . .'

'Great,' Deverney snapped, and hung up.

Yes, he'd been right to insist on seeing Jimmy tonight.

It was hot as hell in the top-floor apartment and Radford was up by nine, sweaty, sticky, wanting something cold to drink. And a good breakfast. And then a shower.

But Mom wasn't around, and neither was Margot. *Never* around. Either working or going to church. Today was Sunday so it was church. Praying for his fucking immortal soul. *Shee*it! He'd take care of his own soul, his own 'sins', as Momma called any sort of fun.

Which brought Corinne to mind. He sure could use a little

179

of her head, her sweet pussy. Ju-Ju's chick wouldn't *never* come through with that girlfriend who gave Around-the-World, so forget it. He'd spent too many nights waiting on that stupid bitch. Time to get around to nailing Corinne down as a steady thing.

He'd call her and they'd go to the beach. Warm sand and cool water.

He was heading for the shower, but the bump in his jockeys made him turn to the kitchen and the wall phone. He dialed Corinne's number, thinking her momma went to church on Sundays too. All the old mommas praying for all the kids' fucking immortal souls. While their kids stuffed it up their fucking immortal holes.

That wasn't bad. He'd tell it to Lester and Ju-Ju when he saw them.

He hadn't been seeing much of them the last few days, that M–4 thing bugging them when they were together. Easier to forget it when they *weren't* together. He didn't need them anyway.

Corinne answered the phone. 'Hey!' he said. 'This is your joyboy! Hot day, huh?'

'Yeah,' she said listlessly. 'I can't talk long. My girlfriend Rosanne is here and we're going to the movies. It's too hot to stay home.'

'Girlfriend? Movies? What you talkin', woman? This here's your man! We're going to Rockaway and *frolic* in the surf.'

She giggled a little, and he was sure he had her.

'And if you come over here, where the family's long gone and *will* be gone till eleven, eleven-thirty, you get a special surprise.' He grabbed himself with his free hand. 'Ummm, *good*!' he said commercial-announcer style. 'And so good *for* you!'

She giggled again, throatily. 'But I promised Rosanne . . .'

'C'mon, Corinne.' He was rubbing himself. 'C'mon, my sweet true love. We'll get in the shower together and I'll love you with water in your hair . . . both places.'

Again the throaty giggle. But again: 'Maybe later, after the movie. I just can't break my date with Rosanne.'

180

'*Date*? You a fucking dyke or something? I tell you, get your ass over here!'

'I'm not going to listen to that, Radford! My momma is scared for me when I'm with you. She asked at the school and they told her how you and that friend beat up on Mr Truesdale and coulda *killed* him! A teacher, and such a little man, and you beat on him and beat on him ...'

He was going to tell her he'd beat on *her*, but he was facing his bedroom and his eyes touched on the dresser and he remembered what was in the bottom drawer, wrapped in underwear, under a shirt. If she saw that ring the bitch actress had been wearing ...

'Corinne, wait a minute, huh, sweet-stuff? I'm sorry I yelled. I just feel bad because I have a surprise for you. I bought you something.'

'Bought me something?' She wasn't yelling no more.

Like his father had said, 'Feed the sweet things sweet things and you'll *always* have 'em around.'

'Yeah, baby. Something special. I been thinking, you know, after our ride up Tarrytown? That was special, wasn't it, sugar?'

'Well *yes*.'

'I kept thinking later how we should be steady-heavy. Like we should dedicate numbers to each other on the jockey request hours, you know. And for that I gotta give you my ring, baby. I gotta pledge my troth.'

He grinned to himself. She'd like that 'pledge my troth'. Lester'd taught it to him. Had a real fine rap with the chicks, old Lester did.

She giggled longer, and when someone spoke in the background, she said away from the phone, 'You just wait a minute, Rosanne! This is important! I might not go to the movies anyway!' And back into the phone: 'You mean like getting *engaged*, Rad-honey?'

'*Exactly!* Pledge my troth is like *double* engaged! Dy-no-*mite* engaged! You gotta make it eleven times a day on a pledge-my-troth!'

She was laughing hard now. 'Eleven times? You got a big brag there, honey!'

181

'You should know that ain't *all* I got that's big.'

She was quiet a minute. He let it wait. She said, 'But you *really* got a ring?'

'*The* most beautiful. *The* biggest, best ... why lady, I can't describe it, you gotta see it to believe it!'

'More of your jokes?'

'You don't see a ring the minute you walk in, you walk out and I never bother you again.'

That got her. 'The minute I walk in?'

'The *second*! Then we shower. Then we go to the beach. Then we make plans for our life. Then we shack up and do it eleven times. *'Cause I am the greatest!*' he yelled, like Muhammad Ali.

She laughed and laughed, and said, 'I'll be over in half an hour.'

'Make that ten minutes.'

'Fifteen, honey. You sure ...?'

'I'll go get it now.'

And he did. And found some Kool-Aid and cheese slices and had breakfast. And looked at the great big fucking hunk of shiny stuff. Man, man, if it was real it could be worth thousands! But even if it wasn't – and he didn't believe for a minute it was – it was still a good three, four hundred. It was *gold*! And it was made *right*! All those clear stones so nice around that big red stone and then the green stones and more whites and the whole thing like a snake curling around and building higher and higher. Only it wasn't *shaped* like a snake. More like a tiny roller coaster, some jewels on one side and some on the other and some going up. More like ... like nothing he'd ever seen!

And it was safe to give it to her because there was nothing on the news about jewelry. M–4 didn't have a clue about the rings and watches. And not much more about the car. All they knew was a red Camaro or Firebird, *maybe,* and three black cats with bushy hair. And there were a *million* such cars and such cats!

But Lester and Ju-Ju already had haircuts, the chicken bastards. Got 'em Thursday night after the movies and wanted Radford to get one too, but damned if he'd look like

182

them! Real square halfway-to-nothing style, like mother-fucking high school jocks.

If *he* decided to dump the Afro – and he'd been thinking of it long before Wednesday night – he'd go to plaits, African rows tight-braided against the scalp, and look real cool with the *latest*!

Then let Sergeant Radish of M–4 try and find him. They'd think Radford was a little old *pickaninny*.

He said the word aloud, mouth twisting in distaste. 'Pickaninny! *Shee*it! he words they make for us!' He repeated the word they'd made for black children and he thought of the other words they'd made for black people and the coons and jigaboos and spades and spooks and shines and niggers filled his heart, and his mother and sister and Corinne were 'black meat', sure, and he was *glad* he'd killed those honkies and he was going to get more bread the same way and the only time he *wouldn't* kill the motherfuckers was maybe when one carried so much bread – *hundreds*, man! – that it was like a ransom! And if it was a young honky chick he'd fuck her ass, man! He'd fuck her good and make her honky husband watch like they'd fucked all the black women, the cream-in-the-coffee! Archie Bunker, man! He'd fuck Archie Bunker's hot blonde daughter right in front of Archie Bunker's eyes!

He was pacing up and back, almost sick with the need to *do* something. He clutched the ring and wanted *more* Wednesday nights. Oh fuck, how much hate he had for whitey, for this empty world whitey'd made, this world without his father . . .

Someone was knocking at the door.

'Yeah!' he shouted.

'It's me, honey. Okay to come in?'

'Hold it a minute, Corinne. I want this to be right, baby.'

What he wanted was a minute to get the craziness out of his heart.

He put his head under the kitchen faucet. He used the dish towel and took deep breaths. He put a smile on his face and tried a little bop-walk as he went to the door. He opened the door. She came in and put down the plastic bag with her

183

bathing suit and said, 'You look . . . funny, kinda, Radford. Like when you think of that friend who owes you money.'

He smiled and smiled. He held out both hands, closed. 'Pick the ring. You don't pick it, you get eleven times first.'

She flicked her eyes to his crotch, but he wasn't with it and she was surprised. He said, 'This is *romance*, baby,' sounding hurt. 'I wouldn't mess it up. This is pledge-my-troth hon.'

She nodded, smiling and tapped his right hand.

It was in his left, but he said, 'You win either way, sweet thing,' and opened both hands.

Her eyes went big and round. She put a hand to her mouth. She didn't touch the ring.

'Go on honey, see if it fits. If it doesn't, we'll get Lester's Uncle Will to size it right. He works at a foundry, but he makes rings on the side.'

She was shaking her head. 'Oh Jesus, Rad, you stole that! Look at it! I never seen *anything* so beautiful! It's a million dollars! It's . . .' Her eyes shot from the ring to his face. 'That night . . . when you said you'd done the white people . . .'

'Shut up!' he said, and took her hand and pressed the ring into it. He turned away, composing himself. 'I told you I made up that shit about doing the white people. You hear anything about jewelry stolen that night? You *didn't*. This ring . . . I bought this ring. I had some bread . . .'

'Rad! It must've cost like . . .' She shook her head, unable to conceive of a price.

'Lester's Uncle Will made it,' he said, his back still turned. 'It cost me thirty dollars.'

'Lester's uncle made *this*?'

He turned. He smiled. 'Come on, lady! Put it on and let's go shower. I want to see you *creaming* with pretty stones on your hand!'

She wet her lips. Her eyes flickered to his shorts, and this time he was getting with it. She muttered, 'That uncle sure makes great stuff.' She tried the ring on the biggest finger of her left hand, then switched it to her right. 'It's a little loose.'

'If it's too loose, we'll have it fixed.' He was playing a game now and held out his hand.

184

'No, honey! It's fine! I *like* it loose! I'm only fifteen, Rad! My fingers are bound to grow fatter!'

He laughed and took her in his arms. They kissed and he rubbed up against her and she pulled her head and shoulders back so as to see the ring without losing contact.

'I love you, honey,' she whispered . . . and suddenly kissed him so hard she hurt his mouth. But he just laughed and led her to the bathroom and took off her clothes. She was a sweet little gal, nice little tits and nice little ass and she'd grow in more places than her fingers. But he hoped she never grew down *there*.

They were in the shower, soaping each other and kissing and looking at that *wild* ring. He spread her up against the wall and bent his knees to bring his tool to the right level. He started shoving it in, and she made little crying sounds that drove him wild. When he'd finally got it *planted*, he straightened his knees little by little, lifting her with both hands under her ass, her arms tightening around his neck, her breath pounding in his ear.

'Oh Lord,' he moaned. 'The Bible sure is right when it says, "Happiness is a tight pussy." '

'Don't blaspheme . . .' she began. He pulled out a ways and slammed in a ways and she forgot blasphemy and everything but his seven inches.

Later, he wanted to get some head and go for it again, in his bedroom. She kept looking from her ring to him, and he knew she'd have eaten his asshole inside out. But he was afraid Momma and Margot would come home and catch them. So they dressed and went downstairs.

On the street, she started holding the ring this way and that, and he decided maybe he'd better switch sides to where he could hold her right hand, cover her ring, just in case.

He did it smooth, tossing up the bag with their bathing suits and catching it on her other side. And he kept talking about Lester's uncle making her another pretty thing.

She interrupted with, 'Whew, man, it sure is getting *hot*! Maybe we should go to the movies like Rosanne and I wanted? Air-conditioning, and they got a great show. Double-feature horror!'

185

He considered it. He'd figured to stay away from the Firebird anyway, because he'd used it twice now and maybe he was pushing his luck. Last night he'd gone to Brooklyn's Bedford Avenue, cruising all on his own. But he hadn't stopped anywhere, even though some foxy chicks had given him signs at a traffic light. He'd got to feeling a little *exposed*, man, and gone home and parked it back off 140th.

Still, nothing about it in the papers, on the TV, same like with the jewelry.

He wasn't sure *what* to do until Corinne said, 'And I'll show my ring to Rosanne and the others and we'll tell them we're engaged! Hope no one tells Momma . . .'

*Shee*it! One more ride couldn't hurt! That M–4 knew *nothing*!

He turned to cross the street, away from the movie. 'No way, baby. Like I said, we gonna frolic in the surf and play in the sand. And later . . .' He looked down into her eyes. 'Well, we got ten more times to go.'

Which cracked her up, and they went hand in hand toward 140th and Eighth and the street where the red Firebird was parked.

Jones went directly to 145th Street, parked illegally, and began strolling. He bopped a little, and he looked for Mac. He tried the place where he'd met him last night, near the record shop, and he tried further west near Broadway, and he tried every place he could think of. And then, with the sun gaining height, with the heat gaining strength, with a few people – mostly kids – beginning to hit the streets with him, he started back east to do it all over again.

And there was Mac hovering in the doorway of the closed record shop.

Jones didn't waste time with the big scene; just a, 'Hey, man, where's my bread?' to cover any possibility of Mac being tabbed an informer . . . though who the hell would tab him, one of those ten-year-olds walking by?

Mac told him just where his 'bread' was, smiling easily and accepting his second 'hat' with a nod. 'No problems,' he said, and yawned. 'No word around it was anything but what you think -- three fucking dummies; kids; no muscle.' He turned away. 'Time for bed. The Sabbath. Bye-bye. Oreo.'

Mac was grinning, and Jones knew that under no circumstances should he create a disturbance. But without being able to stop himself, he sunk the toe of his high klunkers into Mac's skinny ass. And sent him sprawling near the curb.

'Ow! Man!' Mac scrambled to his feet, dusting his threads, then sucked at a scraped section of thumb. 'You goddam ...' But Jones stepped toward him, and he fled across the street.

Some kids were looking. Jones loosened his shoulders and *bopped* away, like a tough street skell.

Stupid, he told himself. And felt good, as if he'd also kicked that talky reporter's ass.

When he reached the unmarked radio car, there was a parking ticket tied to the windshield wiper. He consigned traffic patrol to the hot spot, and left the ticket where it was, protecting himself (he hoped) from further tickets for a while. He got inside, bent low to pull the mike from its concealed position under the dash, gave the special M–4 code number and his message. Then he took his walkietalkie from the glove compartment, got out, and carefully locked the door.

SPRINT now knew where the Firebird was. Within minutes, every M–4 radio car in this area would know it. Minutes after that, every plainclothes cop on the street would know it.

But they wouldn't rush to the scene. They'd move in slowly, staying several blocks away, until he could establish his stakeout.

He turned left, off 140th, strolling up the tenementlined street. He saw the red Firebird on the other side, and kept walking, and reached the south intersection. He crossed and turned back north, coming up on the Firebird from the front, and saw the license plate and scraped right fender.

He walked past it, no longer looking. He saw kids on stoops, in doorways. He saw two men setting up chairs and a

187

folding table for a card game. The street was coming to life, but it was early yet. If he could have ten minutes, just ten lousy minutes he'd be *certain* of nailing whoever went for that car.

He thought of Pop and of how Pop would say he'd 'done good' – *if* he got the collar.

But if all three skells showed and if they were armed what would it be like trying to take them in this neighborhood?

He had his off-duty ·32 automatic strapped to his left calf. He could cut them down, after the minimal warning. With Reese and Fryer and another few men who thought much as he did, he'd be sure to wipe them all and save the state the expense of a long trial, save himself and other blacks the embarrassment of having that trash on TV and in the papers.

How would Pop rate his 'general deportment' if he used any and all pretexts to kill suspects?

And what about his career? The department might approve, in private, but there would have to be an investigation in response to an almost certain public outcry. 'Children,' Andra had called the three butchers. So would others.

He watched for a place of concealment . . . and saw the basement entry and without hesitation stepped into it and used his walkie-talkie. When he came out, he figured he had five minutes before taking up a position near the Firebird. He was thirsty.

He reached the north intersection and crossed to the little lunch counter on the opposite side. And had a partial view of the Firebird.

The fat young woman came over and said, 'Morning. What'll it be?'

He said, 'Orange drink,' and stood a foot away from the counter, looking down the street.

On TV, good cops risked their lives to capture rather than kill bad guys. In New York City they sometimes did the same, out of stupidity, inexperience, or confusion due to all the cautionary lectures on using one's gun.

He wasn't stupid, inexperienced, or confused about using

his gun. But neither was he sure what he would do when he came face to face with those suspects.

He used a paper napkin to wipe sweat from his forehead.

'Hot,' he murmured as the woman served his drink.

'Just ten o'clock,' she said, making change of his dollar. 'Wait'll later!'

Roersch caught the call at ten, cruising Broadway near 145th with Eli Ross. He immediately instructed all marked patrol cars to leave the vicinity of 140th and Eighth. And, after a pause: 'All white patrolmen, too.'

Eli turned downtown, glancing at him. 'That'll leave a lot of unpatrolled streets, Sergeant. I mean, for normal crime protection.'

Roersch nodded. 'I'll bring them back in an hour or two. I want to give Willis time to set his action without some sharp-eyed cop thinking he's spotted a crime in the making.'

'You're kidding. Willis wouldn't be that obvious.'

'It's happened before. A cop who knows his beat will spot strangers and call for backup and blow a stakeout.' They were approaching 140th. 'Keep going. Don't get too close. We're of no use to Willis until the suspects show.'

Radford had twelve dollars, and figured it would give them a good day – a tank of gas and enough left for hot dogs and cold drinks. But tomorrow, he either had to sell the man's watch – which didn't look like much – or try another stickup. He sure as hell wasn't going down to the employment office for one of their shit jobs, fifty-sixty bucks a week in a supermarket, when he could make more in ten minutes in a good white neighborhood. They'd been unlucky Wednesday night. Alone, he'd do better, go cooler, hit a couple of times . . . and keep everything for himself. Splitting three ways was nowhere, man! Twenty-two dollars, *shee*it! And a lot of junk they were afraid to sell.

It was either sell the junk, or do a stickup. Or . . . yeah . . . he'd *use* the junk. The watch wasn't bad – no day or month or year, like a good Timex – and the ring the dude had worn on his pinky, well, that was one fat pinky and Radford had gotten it on his left index. He'd wait till it was all cool then use the stuff. And for bread, he'd use whitey!

He threw his arm around Corinne as they turned past the luncheonette, and began to run, pulling her across the street and down to where the Firebird was parked. Man, he loved summer!

'Your cousin letting you have the car all week, Rad?' she asked, laughing, panting.

'Maybe all month,' he said. 'He's gone to Detroit. Big-time bookie there. Like my father in Atlantic City.'

He was bending to the car putting the key in the door, when he heard Corinne say, 'Hey! You cut that . . .'

He began to turn, figuring some wise-ass was messing with her, and couldn't see her at all. Then he did, off to the right, being pulled behind a stoop by a big dude. And was that a *piece* in the dude's hand?

He hesitated not knowing what the hell was coming down.

And then another dude sitting on the stoop threw himself flat on the sidewalk! A big grownup cat, like a little kid playing soldier!

This time he *knew* he saw a gun, and heard, 'Police! Hands on your head! Down on your face! *Move!*' And the dude with Corinne had his gun poking around the stoop.

Oh Jesus Christ help me the pigs the pigs and he didn't want to die and didn't want to be in jail this hot day when he could frolic in the surf and pledge his troth and Jesus Christ help me!

He was running away from the pigs, around the Firebird to the other side, crying and screaming, 'Brothers, the pigs, the pigs!' And facing him again like kids playing, like he used to play, were two brothers pointing guns at him and yelling about hands-on-head.

He stopped in the middle of the street. He turned to 140th. And toward him came a car with a hand out the window and a gun in that hand. The hand was black. All around him were blacks. And all were pigs.

A car swung into the intersection, blocking it. They had a fucking army here and how had it happened and he turned

190

around and around. And the first black who'd thrown himself on the sidewalk, the first one who'd told him cops-and-hands-on-head, came toward him and said, 'Don't reach for a gun. It's stupid.'

'I don't have it on me!' Radford screamed. 'If I had it on me I'd reach for it, man! I'd reach...'

They had him and the black cop cuffing him was saying something about rights and the car blocking the south corner moved up and he was pushed in the back.

He looked at the big white face turned to him from the front seat beside the driver. It was that sergeant from the TV, that Radish, and his nightmares had come true and Radish had him. He took a deep breath, and looked at the black cop beside him. 'You got a smoke, brother?'

The black cop put his hand on Radford's throat. 'Call me brother one more time and I'll finish you here.'

Radford said, 'You got a cigarette, pig?' because he was dead anyway and what the hell.

The black cop slapped him. It was a hell of a shot and Radford was knocked back into the corner. And those cuffs locking his wrists behind him cut into his flesh and his arms felt like they were being wrenched from their sockets. 'Motherfucker!' he gasped.

Radish said, 'Willis, don't mark him.'

The black cop grunted, and went through Radford's pockets. He got the wallet and the driver's license, and Radford knew another part of his nightmare was going to come true – Radish would be talking to Momma and Margot.

Radford said, 'I stole that wallet. That's not my license.'

'All right,' Radish said. 'We'll just drive over there and ask...'

'No! Leave my family alone!'

Radish said, 'My name is Roersch. I'd appreciate your cooperation. Make it easier all around and give us the names and addresses of your two friends.'

'What two friends?' Radford muttered, and flinched as the black cop snapped a look at him. 'I mean, man, I got so *many* friends, which you want?'

'The two with you Thursday morning on Fifty-second

Street,' Radish who was Roersch said. He was a quiet-talking man, and he didn't look angry like that Willis, and it was funny but he wished Radish-Roersch was back here and the brother up front.

'I was home Thursday morning. I slept late.'

'Wednesday night,' said Radish – it was easier thinking that name than the other. 'When you got the ring you gave your girl.' He put his hand over the seat and opened it, just like Radford had done with Corinne, and in it was the beautiful hunk of shiny stuff. 'The officer who got her away from you gave it to me. To give back to you.'

Radford stared at the ring. 'What you gonna do with me?'

The black cop, Willis, said, 'What did you do with those four people on Fifty-second?'

'Jesus, man, I didn't do more than *one*! I did the blonde bit ... the blonde lady! I mean I *had* to, man, she was going to scream and fight me ...'

The black cop made a sound of disgust, and Radford was suddenly ashamed.

'Your friends?' Radish asked.

Radford said, 'I want a lawyer. I got rights.'

Radish suddenly looked upset. 'Before we say another word, read him his rights.'

The Willis-cop said, 'I did.'

Radish said, 'You did?' like he didn't believe him.

'Yeah, when I cuffed him. But I'll read them again.'

'That might be wise.'

'No one read me anything,' Radford said, but he remembered something with 'rights' in it before. 'I'll tell the judge ...'

Willis-cop gave him a short shot to the side, and Radford buckled, choking on pain. Willis-cop read that shit about the-right-to-remain-silent and the-right-to-have-an-attorney just like on *Kojak*. Then Radish asked, 'Your friends?'

'I don't know,' Radford mumbled, watching the Willis-pig-bastard, who was going to give him more pain, he just knew it. 'I only know my part. The others were cats I met on the street just before we got the car.'

'His girlfriend is with Reese,' Willis-pig said, 'talking her head off.'

'Bullshit,' Radford muttered, his heart sinking.

'They're right behind us,' Willis-pig said, glancing through the rear window.

'No way,' Radford said, refusing to turn. 'You can't arrest *her*. You can't take *her* in a cop car. She's not wanted.'

'Accessory,' Radish said. 'At least until she's finished talking.'

Willis-pig stuck his head out the window and waved and called to someone behind them. A car came up on the right, hung alongside them a moment while Willis-pig leaned back so Radford could see. And there was Corinne talking her head off to a young black pig and both of them smiling and the pig would fuck her later if he wanted to, goddam bitch!

Christ, why hadn't he killed her in Tarrytown like he'd thought to!

But they'd have gotten him for that too. He slumped wearily. The car with Corinne pulled ahead, passing them. Again he asked, 'What you gonna do with me?'

'Put you away for life,' Willis-pig said.

Radford watched Corinne's car moving faster and faster, leaving them behind. And this fucking car just crawled while these fucking pigs worked on him. He knew they were doing a number, so he shook his head and forced a laugh. '*Life*? Man, you can't do that! No way! I'm a juve, dig? I'm not eighteen ... not till October. I'll be out in a year, maybe two if the judge is tough. I been in juvenile court twice, man. Lady judges ...'

'It's *sixteen*,' Willis-pig said, cracking his stone face in a smile for the first time. 'Strange how many of you pisspot killers don't know that. In New York City, on a homicide charge, you're treated as an adult at *sixteen*. How does that grab you, *juve*?'

And Radford remembered Emery Dunster who'd knifed a kid messing with his girl. Sunk an eight-inch grav into the cat's chest and that was *wipeout*. Emery was just a few weeks past sixteen ... and he'd caught a full adult trial and heavy sentence.

Radford slumped even more. 'Bullshit,' he said, barely whispering.

'You'll go away for life. Or until we get the death penalty back in New York. Then we'll fry you in the chair.' Willis-pig continued to smile. 'We'll see that you and your friends don't get out on parole. You killed a famous actress and her husband. You killed a young man with a wife and three children. And you killed a cop, a *brother*. That last one will keep you off the streets forever. That last one will ruin your every chance for parole.'

Radford suddenly believed him. 'I hear they make deals,' he said, 'if someone helps the police.'

'Help us,' Radish said, 'and we'll see.'

'No. I gotta have a *guarantee*.'

Another shot in the side sent him sprawling into the corner. 'Oh, *man*!' he screamed. 'That hurts!'

Willis-pig said, 'Imagine how those people on Fifty-second Street hurt. Now tell us about your friends.'

Radish said, 'Your girl will tell us anyway.'

'She don't know,' Radford gasped ... but Corinne *did* know and he was sure she'd already told them. So why shouldn't he try for a deal?

Willis-pig leaned close. 'What were you thinking of, to butcher four people that way?'

'I told you, I only did the woman!'

'All right. Shooting her through the head. *Why?*'

'I don't know why,' he said, giving it all the *honest* he could muster.

'A minute ago you said she was going to scream; you said she was going to fight you.'

'Yeah, that too. But ...'

Radish said, 'Now, son, the names and addresses of your friends.'

'Don't know. Ain't friends. Just guys I met on the street.'

They kept talking to him, Radish calling him 'son' a few times. Son! *Shee*it! Was no cream in the Johnson family coffee!

194

Still, Radish kept Willis-pig from punching his gut, and Radford got back a little courage. Maybe Corinne wouldn't remember his telling her *who* was with him that night, and back on the street he'd be famous 'cause he hadn't told, and his friends would spread the word and in the slammer he'd find more friends ...

But when they walked into the police station and began the shit with the pictures and forms and all, he saw Corinne in a room without a door. Radish went there, and in a minute he came out and leaned over a cop at a typewriter. 'Lester Cole, about eighteen,' he said, and he gave Lester's address. 'Albert Wyins, about eighteen, called Ju-Ju' and he gave Ju-Ju's address.

Radford yelled, 'Corinne, you snitch-bitch! You gonna end up dead! You gonna ...'

Willis-pig grabbed him by the hair and dragged him to another table, where they took his fingerprints. Willis-pig hurt him, and Radford yelled, 'Police brutality!' and damned if everyone in the place didn't break up. He looked around while Willis-pig held him by the hair, and there were lots of brothers in hip clothes ... and he realized they were cops who'd been in the street. They were looking at him, and they were *laughing*! 'Oreos!' he screamed.

Radish came over and he had pictures – big pictures, in color – and at first Radford didn't know what they were. When he did, he turned away, no matter how Willis-pig twisted his hair. It was the white actress he'd shot, her blonde hair black with blood. And worse in front, where the ·38 slug had come out, tearing open her face, a big hole where her nose had been and one eye gone too ...

He began to gag. Someone brought over a basket and he vomited his cheese and Kool-Aid into it. Then Radish showed him the rest of the pictures. Then he looked, to see what the cops were seeing, what the lawyers and judges and juries would see. And it was the worst.

He and Lester and Ju-Ju had done *that*? The young guy with his throat torn open and his tongue out and his eyes all crossed. The older, bigger guy who'd been lying near the actress – her husband – he had *three* holes, smaller than the ones the ·38 made, but still *three* of them and they ripped the shit out of his face.

And the cop. They held that picture in front of him longest; not Radish, who'd walked back to the office and Corinne, but Willis-pig. Held it there and said, 'Here's your brother.'

A piece of the cop's head was blown away, but his face was okay and he examined it.

The black captain didn't look very black; lots of cream in *that* coffee. But the hair and some of the features showed he was a brother. And Radford suddenly hated Ju-Ju's guts for killing him, pig though he was, drawing on Ju-Ju though he had. Hated Ju-Ju even more for *lying*, trying to get from under by saying he'd never fired his piece.

Okay. They'd get Ju-Ju. And he, Radford, hadn't been the snitch. He, Radford, would keep his cool. But Ju-Ju would catch the worst shit, in and out of the slammer. Ju-Ju would get it up-the-ass-without-no-class ... and serve the mother right!

There was a lot of noise at the front desk, and Radish came running, saying, 'Keep them out! We need at least ten more minutes free of reporters! I don't care if you have to *draw* on them, no interviews until the squads leave to get the other two. And even then, just a quick statement by Jones ...' He stopped and said, 'Willis for Chrissake, *let go of his* hair! You remember those pictures of Chief of Detectives Seedman holding a suspect by the head? He almost didn't *become* Chief of Detectives!'

Willis-pig let him go.

Radford was given a chair. He sank into it, his head whirling, not able to care anymore.

Then he heard crying and looked up and Momma was there and Margot was there and he was able to care again. Momma came over to him. 'You didn't *kill*, did you, Rad? Not *kill*?'

He didn't answer. He didn't look at her. She began to *scream*. Willis-pig took her away. She kept *screaming*, and her voice blew his head apart. He tried to shut it out with his hands to his ears, and couldn't.

Margot just looked at him, sitting across the room and talking to a detective who wrote on a pad. Margot talked and looked and he finally covered his face.

He was glad when they took him down a flight of stairs and put him in a cell. They moved two white dudes out and put him in all alone, even though the other three cells were now packed, four to a cell. The cop sitting on a chair got up and came over and looked at him. Radford lay down on a lower bunk.

The cop said, 'So you're one of the M–4 killers? You sure must hate us. C'mon, admit it. You hate us, don't you?'

Radford sat up. 'You mean cops?' he said to the pink-faced pig.

'No, not cops. I mean Mr Charley.'

'Mr Charley? Don't know that dude, honky.'

The cell next to his held four blacks and they laughed. They hee-hawed and one said, 'All *right*!'

Radford saw the flush moving into the pig's face. And listened to the continuing laughter; and some from the other cells too, where they were mostly whites. He began to feel a little more alive.

*Shee*it, where he was going no mommas and sisters and pigs counted! What counted was the brothers, and there were lots in the slammer, the majority he'd heard, the ruling class, man. What he'd done wouldn't make any of *them* get uptight. What he'd done would be like what lots of *them* had done.

When Radish came down and held up a clear plastic bag with a gun in it, Radford asked for a smoke. When Radish said, 'We found this in the flower pot. It's the ·38 that killed Mrs Jaeker, isn't it?' Radford said, 'Get my lawyer to get me a smoke.'

Again the cats in the other cells hee-hawed.

Radish said, 'We found Mr Jaeker's watch and diamond ring. Your girl, Corinne, was wearing Mrs Jaeker's cocktail ring.'

'Filter-tips, man, with brown paper like Nat Shermans. And a brown lawyer too.'

Ho-ho hee-haw, went the cells. Radford bopped a little and grinned a little.

Radish said, 'We're bringing Lester in. We haven't found Albert . . .' He stopped. 'Ju-Ju – haven't found him yet. Would you care to give us a little help?'

'No, sir,' Radford said, bopping and slapping on the English accent. 'No, I would *not*. I pledge my troth, sir, I definitely would not care to help.'

Cracked up the cells like Bob Hope man!

But didn't crack up Radish. He just kept showing Radford the gun. 'An important bit of information, Radford: Captain Worth, the murdered officer, was also shot with a ·38. We think it's this gun. So by admitting to Mrs Jaeker's murder, you've probably admitted to Captain Worth's.'

Radford had more funny rap all ready, but it stuck in his throat. 'Hey, man, that's pure shit! I never went across the street, and I never lent my piece either. Me and Lester went to the young dude . . .' He stopped then.

Radish was nodding. 'And Ju-Ju went to Captain Worth. Ju-Ju has a ·38 too, does he?'

Radford backed away. He was getting sucked in here. He'd said things, and he didn't want to say things. The other cells were listening and no more Bob Hope time. No more hee-haw, man. He backed another step, and his legs hit the john. 'I don't know about guns. I don't . . .'

The old cop was beginning to smile. And Jesus that smile scared him more than Willis-pig's threats and shots to the gut. Those cold gray honky eyes and that smile, man, that smile . . . like the Muslims said, a white devil!

'We got you, Radford. Jewelry and gun and confession. And no lawyer will ever get you off. Yours, by the way, will be assigned from the Public Defender's office, unless your family decides to hire one. You can probably get a fellow black. Whoever you get, he'll work hard for you. And he'll lose for you.' He turned to the staircase. 'Brower, give this stupid bastard a smoke.' He was gone.

Radford tried desperately to think of something to call after him, to bring back the laughter, the hee-haws. The guard came over and *threw* a cigarette into the cell. It landed

198

at Radford's feet. He wanted to step on it, contemptuously, but Christ how he needed a smoke!

He picked it up. The guard struck a match. Radford came to the bars and got lighted. The cop walked back to his chair. Radford listened to the other cells. Sighs. Coughs. Someone in the next cell whispering things that made him sick: 'Hey, Radford, you got a nice ass, hear me, baby? Want some cigarettes? Want to suck . . .'

The guard said, 'Cut that out,' and turned the pages of his *News*.

In another cell, someone said, 'Lumpy fucking mattress!' Someone else said, 'You wake me up one more time, man . . .' Then the sound of fist on flesh and a cry of pain. The guard got up, drawing his nightstick from a side holder, whapping it into his hand, saying, 'Can't you skells wait for Attica to begin killing and fucking each other?'

Radford began to sweat. Hot in here.

He sat down and sucked smoke. Too soon he was burning filter. He put it out under his shoe. Some tough mothers in the slammer. He looked around the cell. And wondered what would happen next.

What happened next was lunch – hamburger, mashed potatoes, coffee, and a stick of Juicy Fruit gum. The guard said, 'This comes from a cafeteria. Wait'll you taste the stuff at Riker's Island, your next stop.'

Somewhere, a church bell began tolling. Radford found himself counting; found himself thinking of time; found he couldn't eat. It tolled twelve and stopped. Again he sat and wondered what would happen next.

And realized he would be doing that forever, for the eternity that twenty or more years represented.

Sitting and wondering what would happen next.

TWELVE

VOICE ONE: 'Yes?'

VOICE TWO: 'Well, did my Number Two do a good job, or did he do a good job?' Chuckle.

ONE: 'If you mean is Albony dead, he is. If you mean did we accomplish the task of throwing suspicion toward the M–4 blacks, we didn't.'

TWO: 'But the papers and the broadcasters . . .'

ONE: 'Are not whom we have to convince. It's that long-experienced sergeant, or have you forgotten him since our last conversation?'

TWO: 'What would bug *him* about Albony?'

ONE: 'The same thing that's bugging *me*.'

TWO: 'We hit Albony just like we hit Worth. And Worth is M–4, isn't he? And we picked the right spot, in his broad's house, and in a neighborhood where blacks have been robbing . . .'

ONE: 'Only this time there was no mugging going on as we stalked our prey; no coincidence to cover a perfect murder perfectly. By duplicating the Worth killing so exactly, you've made *me* uncomfortably aware that they're carbon copies of each other . . . and totally different from the Jaeker and Magris killings.'

TWO: Unconvinced: 'Yeah, Mr Washington, but you *know*. The sergeant doesn't, and can't.'

ONE: 'Don't ever underestimate him. He's always mistrusted so-called open-and-shut cases. Where there doesn't seem to be contrary evidence, or mystery, or even slight doubt, he pushes, pushes, and *intuits*. That's the real reason he's still in the Bureau when most men his age and years-of-service are long retired.'

TWO: 'Even so, there's nothing here for him to push.'

ONE: 'But something to intuit.' Sigh. 'Well, Albony's done. And maybe I'm wrong to worry.'

TWO: 'It's seven-thirty. Gotta head for work.' Pause. 'And I think you *are* wrong to worry, Mr Washington. Worth and Albony are both perfect. Worth because witnesses pin it on the three blacks. Albony because no one can pin it on anyone else.'

ONE: Still unhappy: 'Those two blacks in custody are denying anything to do with Worth. I'd hoped at least one of the three would be killed to take the fall for the captain.'

TWO: 'Could still happen. The third one could make a fight of it. Or get clean away, and take the fall anyhow. The radio says those two in custody are hinting the third one did it.'

ONE: 'I hadn't heard that.' More cheerfully: 'Of course, everyone *expected* they'd try to squirm out of the cop-killing. So even if the third is captured and the D.A. never gets nail-down evidence or confessions on Worth, he's going to place him at their door. They'll go up for life, and the file will be closed.'

TWO: 'That's the ticket, Mr Washington!'

ONE: 'But no more heart and head shots. We might have to abandon the luxury of firearms for a while and go with a knife. Or even the infamous blunt instrument.'

TWO: 'Well, the next assignment is for my Number Two's assistant, so I won't sweat it.'

ONE: 'Unless we have to perform a protective rather than corrective execution, which we'll do personally.'

TWO: 'What?'

ONE: 'That sergeant.' Deep breath. 'Well, we'll know more by tomorrow. Keep your eyes and ears open.'

TWO: 'Don't I always?'

It was eight before Willis Jones reached home. He was sweaty and hungry and dead beat. They'd worked on Radford Johnson, and later on Lester Cole, and as far as those two were concerned it was all sewed up. An airtight solved. Confessions, with lawyers present. The D.A. would be able to *sleep* through this one.

Albert Wyins, called Ju-Ju, hadn't been apprehended, and despite everything Eddy had tried to do about the reporters – calling Deverney and pleading for a little more time – they'd held a goddam news conference with lights and cameras and bringing the two kids up for quick appearances. But, thank God, not for statements.

Not yet, that is. Soon enough they'd be talking to America, the dirty, cocky little killers.

He began climbing the stairs.

Tired. A frozen TV dinner, a few cold beers, a shower, and the sack. Tomorrow would be better.

Or would it? Eddy was pissed off at the news conference. Couldn't hold back on the name of the third suspect. Besides, a few reporters had made contact with their special guys on the force and the Ju-Ju nickname had caught on and now the radio and TV were blaring about 'the hunt for Ju-Ju Wyins'. Soon the first edition of tomorrow's *News*, sold the night before, would hit the streets. The *Post* was already out. And tomorrow morning the *Times*.

Anyway, Ju-Ju would be warned; Ju-Ju would be twice as hard to find now, despite the media's theory that citizens would be able to spot him more easily. Citizens in this town weren't statistically important in collaring suspects. Citizens in this town tended to their own business, hoping to forget that bad guys were out there in *droves* trying to kill them. Citizens in this town would let a *dozen* Kitty Genoveses die without lifting a finger, so why take the chance fingering a killer?

Only if Ju-Ju tried to sell the jewelry in his possession did he run the risk of being turned in. Mainly because more than a few Harlem fences were on the string on the N.Y.P.D.; could be sent away if they didn't play the snitch game.

He reached his apartment and put the key in the lock . . . then saw that the door was ajar. He stared, thinking he *couldn't* have forgotten to lock it . . . and heard voices.

He jerked up his right pants leg, drawing the ·32 automatic from its calf holster. He kicked the door open and lunged in and to the side, throwing himself to the carpeting.

Andra and Mrs Cohen, the landlady, were sitting on the couch, staring at him.

He got up and they looked at his hand and he went to the telephone table and put the gun in the drawer.

'I'm sorry we startled you,' Andra said. 'I made sure to leave the door open so you wouldn't ...'

'What *is* this?'

Mrs Cohen, a slender and rather pretty woman in her mid-forties, stood up. 'She said you'd be exhausted. She said she wanted to make you dinner ... and I helped.' She looked at Andra, and Andra smiled a seemingly warm smile, and Willis wondered what Mrs Cohen would think if she could see inside Andra's flinty heart.

He said, 'Oh yeah, thanks. Excuse me a minute.' He went to the bathroom, took off his jacket and shirt, soaked his head in cold water, washed himself from the waist up and splashed on cologne. He went into the bedroom, put on a pullover shirt, brushed his hair, and returned to the living room.

Where Andra was just closing the door on Mrs Cohen. She turned to him. 'I was at the news conference.'

'I didn't see you.'

'I made sure of that; I stayed near the front desk. But I got what I needed, called it in, and was free. If you've eaten out, you can sit and watch me demolish a stew you won't get in any restaurant. No wine or other nonsense, Sergeant. Just beef and onions and tomatoes and potatoes and carrots. And secret herbs and spices handed down by my Haitian grandmother.'

'You Haitian? I thought that face was kinda fine for an American plantation nigger.'

She winced. 'You *do* have a way with words. But no words can keep me from dinner.' She came over to him and took his hand and led him to the kitchen. Where the aroma was fantastic!

She told him to sit down. The table was set and she brought a big orange pot from the stove – a pot he didn't recognize.

'I came prepared,' she said, 'including a Beaujolais of

noble character and low price.' She spooned out steaming portions of the stew, took the pot back to the stove, and opened the refrigerator. She removed his salad-tossing bowl, and it was already filled and the salad tossed and dressed. She also brought out a bottle of wine. 'Never chill red,' she said, before he could. 'What the hell – I mean, what the *fuck*, to use your favorite word – does whitey know about soul food?'

'This is soul food?'

'When two soul mates eat it, it is.'

He nodded, smiling, and picked up his fork.

It was great stew. It was great salad. It was great wine, and he *liked* it chilled on a hot summer night.

They finished the wine in bed. They finished it beautifully, with a few drops for her nipples and a few drops for his penis. And after the frenzy of lovemaking was over, and after he'd kissed her gently and thanked her for this very beautiful evening, she got up and went to her clothes.

'Aren't you spending the night?'

'No.' She began dressing quickly; almost frantically, he thought.

'Got someplace to go?'

'No. My Haitian grandmother never stopped talking and I take after her and sometimes I wish I'd taken after my American plantation nigger grandfather.'

'I don't understand.'

She was hopping toward the door, getting into one shoe. She was through the door and hopping on the other foot now. He followed her into the living room.

'If you've got no place to go, why are you going?'

She was at the hall door, her big purse hooked over her arm. She stepped to the left, to look into the oval mirror, and groaned. 'Well, can't be helped. Good night.'

'Andra, if you don't explain . . .'

She opened the door, and hesitated, then *whirled* rather than turned. 'That news conference! Those two boys! The way Radford flinched when you came near him! The way you shut Lester up . . .' She shook her head. 'I want to be with you, and I can't *stand* being with you! I want to love

204

you, but when I think of your job and discuss your job I end up *hating* you! *Now* do you understand why I have to go? *I can't keep still another moment!*' She went out, slamming the door.

Somehow, he found himself laughing.

The doorknob rattled. He went over and said, 'Who is it?'

'Oh, stop that!' Andra snapped.

Controlling fresh laughter, he opened the door.

She looked at him, and he finally understood that old bookish expression, gritting one's teeth. 'I'm afraid to walk alone to my car. I'm ashamed of myself, but I'm afraid. Our wild brothers don't ask whose side their victims are on.'

He could have laughed in her face right then. She'd earned it with her insults, her criticism, her dumb racial approach to crime. But his laughter was gone and he turned to get his clothes.

He was back in time for the eleven o'clock news. He smiled at the way Eddy pulled him in front of the cameras, smiled at the things his friend said about him ... and frowned at some of the shit those reporters threw at Roersch. Pushing him to draw parallels to Albony, when he'd asked, specifically, that they shouldn't bring that up, that it was in another detective division, that there were *orders* to be obeyed. And when he *pleaded* for twenty-four hours of silence on Albert 'Ju-Ju' Wyins, he was ignored. Fucking media crap! The locals were the worst! Pushy, noisy, treating cops like *slaves* of their goddam boob-tube audience!

He got up and darkened the set in the middle of Roersch's attempts to control a particularly obnoxious jackal.

Roersch was at least able to defend himself, being a knowledgeable cop. But the way they came at victims, and families of victims, with their sickening pseudo-sympathy: 'And how do you feel about the death of your husband, Mrs Magris?'

That one had almost made him vomit!

He shook his head. The day had been too long, too full of tension.

*   *   *

205

Roersch called Jimmy Weir at ten and asked if he'd mind eating in the all-night cafeteria on Broadway.

'Yes,' Jimmy said. 'I'd mind. You know Mel's Steak House on East Forty-seventh where we went last month?'

'Nice, but I won't be there for at *least* half an hour . . .'

'Their bar is open until midnight. And they'll serve dinner, for me.'

'You're on, captain.' He hung up. He was alone in the basement M-4 squad room, and walked out into the hallway, putting on his jacket.

He'd already phoned Ruthie, for the third time, and asked her not to wait up for him. She'd wondered aloud how much longer 'this crazy way of living' would last. He had no answer.

He intended to go right up the stairs to the main floor and the washroom. He intended to consolidate his thoughts on Worth and the twenty grand and Angie and Deverney, and on his gut feeling of something terribly wrong, for presentation to Jimmy. He couldn't wait to shift part of that load to his old friend.

But he went past the staircase to the first of the four cells, a spot he'd come to at least half a dozen times today. He stood outside the bars and looked at the two boys, one in each of the cell's two lower bunks. The double-deckers stood opposite each other against the unbroken side walls. The far wall held the sink and toilet; the front wall was the bars. It was a grim, tiny world, that cell . . . and yet it was better than most at Attica, where they were headed.

They'd killed in cold blood, viciously. He'd hated them for the destruction they'd wreaked, the lives they'd ended, the anguish they'd caused.

Yet here they were, two tall, skinny kids, sleeping peacefully; Radford curled on his side, his hand at his mouth; Lester flat on his face. Here they were, seventeen and eighteen years old, respectively, and it was hard to believe what they'd done or to hate them for it.

He must have sighed. Lester Cole sat up abruptly, face frightened. He was a kid waking out of a nightmare . . . *into* a nightmare.

'*Shee*it, you again? I told you, we didn't do that cop! Maybe Ju-Ju, but he says no. And about that Baloney guy ...'

'Albony,' Roersch said, smiling in spite of himself.

'Whatever. We didn't do it. I told you to ask my aunt Elsie ...'

'She gave her statement. So did your brother. So did a counterman at that candy store. You seem clear on Albony. So does Radford.'

At his name, Radford also sat up, rubbing his eyes. 'Radish,' he mumbled. 'He closer than my daddy. All day, all night, he with his baby boy.'

'You have enough cigarettes?' Roersch asked.

Radford nodded. 'Lawyer got me three packs. Wrong brand, the turkey. I don't like him.'

'You asked for a black,' Roersch said.

'Sure, man, but I wanted a *smart* brother.'

'Jew lawyers smarter,' Lester said, touching a scar on his chin in what had already become a familiar gesture to Roersch. 'That's why I got myself the Epstein man. And he got an Afro just like mine!' Then he shook his head ruefully; rubbed his short-cropped hair. 'Keep forgetting. Real waste of time and bread.'

'Well, I want an Epstein-man too,' Radford said, taking cigarettes from his shirt pocket. 'I demand a motherfucking Jew lawyer of my own!'

Roersch was chuckling now. 'You tell Mr Epstein that tomorrow when he comes to counsel Lester. I'm sure he'll do something for you.'

Epstein was good; among the best Public Defenders Roersch had ever dealt with. But despite his lawyer's mask, Roersch had read the complete despair with which he approached this case. He'd be begging for plea-bargaining of *any* sort ... and there wasn't a prayer. The D.A. himself would make an appearance on this case before allowing a second-or third-in-command to take over.

No bargains. No reduced charges. This was for the maximum sentence.

'Are you sure you can't help me find Ju-Ju?'

207

Both boys showed disgust. Radford said, 'Give up, man. We don't know.' Lester said, 'And if we did, we ain't telling. You know that by now, so why'd you wake us up?'

Both boys lit cigarettes. Roersch said, 'Just want to save his life. Just want to bring him in here in one piece. Otherwise, some cop will kill him.'

Lester glared at Radford. 'You bring Ju-Ju in here, you gonna have to save *this* sucker's life! I mean, man, driving around in a hot car after what Ju-Ju said! Coming back and using it like a goddam . . .'

'I did it,' Radford interrupted, rising. 'I said once it was dumb. I ain't saying it again. And I ain't listening . . .'

'You'll listen, man, when Ju-Ju gets here!'

Radford blustered a little, muttering, 'He don't tell *me* what to do.' But Roersch could see he was frightened.

'What you hangin' around here for, Radish!' Radford suddenly shouted. 'Man, I'm sick of looking at your face! I'm sick of you asking and asking . . .'

'Don't raise your voice,' Roersch said, 'or I'll put Ju-Ju and you alone in our isolation cell in the subbasement. No one will hear you there.'

Radford laughed, a high-pitched giggle of pure shock, and sat down.

There *was* an old cell down there, but they hadn't used it in Roersch's memory, and wouldn't. Besides, Radford was right to ask why Roersch was standing here.

Why *was* he?

He had all he needed from these two.

He knew they hadn't killed Worth; knew Ju-Ju hadn't killed him either.

So why stand here, why look at them, talk to them, find it so hard to leave them?

He began to move to the staircase . . . and then surrendered to what had been lurking in his mind from the moment he'd turned to look at Radford Johnson in the car this morning. It was a way out for Eddy Roersch. Perhaps the *only* way out.

'What if you'd heard Ju-Ju confess to killing Worth; would you tell me?'

208

Lester laughed. Radford flicked ashes into the butt can at his feet.

'What if it could make a difference to *you*?'

They both looked at him. Lester said, 'You got my piece and you got those rings and the watch. I got two honkies on my scorecard, and everyone says *life*.'

Radford nodded. 'Like with me. You say it too, a hundred times.'

Roersch took a deep breath. He hated doing this. 'There are life sentences and life sentences. Maximum life is twenty-five years before you can look at parole. Minimum life is fifteen and with the right word, I mean if an understanding is reached, parole *wouldn't* be impossible. The D.A. would speak to the judge. The judge would make notations on your court record. Some day . . .'

'Yeah,' Radford muttered. 'When we're eighty.'

'In fifteen years you'd be thirty-two, thirty-three. It could be sooner. Say *ten* years, when you're twenty-seven, twenty-eight.'

They stared at him, and Radford wet his lips. 'But we already told you Ju-Ju says he never fired his piece. How can we . . .'

'You want us to *lie*, Mr Policeman?' Lester said, beginning to smile. 'The famous *Radish* wants us to break the law – like *perjury*, man?'

Roersch nodded very slightly. 'At the least, Ju-Ju will go up as an accessory. Nothing you do can save him from getting the full treatment. And you both know he killed that cop, no matter what he says.'

Lester glanced at Radford, and Roersch went silent, giving them time to search each other's faces. Radford muttered, '*Ricochet*, he give us. I mean, man, he want to leave us alone in this.'

Lester went to the sink. He ran water into his hand and drank. 'I don't know. It's *telling*, man. And if he ever got to us . . .'

Quite suddenly, Roersch didn't want to do this. Not only because it would leave a hole in his case, a question forever unanswered ('Who stood in that basement entry?'), but

209

because he couldn't come through for these kids. The D.A. wouldn't care *what* Radford and Lester said; he was certain to get his three convictions, his three maximum life sentences.

Ju-Ju had jewelry and a ·38, according to his friends. Ju-Ju was on the run. Ju-Ju had been seen aiming and – so they thought – firing at Worth by at least three witnesses, and ballistics wasn't the exact science TV and movies made it out to be. Besides, they probably wouldn't get to examine Ju-Ju's ·38. If he'd read the papers or heard the news (and a New Yorker almost couldn't avoid it!), he'd react by dumping gun as well as jewelry, a right move in most cases, a wrong move in Ju-Ju's. Anyway, Albert Wyins was finished and there'd be no deals for him, or the others. So it was cheating these two ...

This whole gambit, Roersch realized, had been a clutching at straws, a last-ditch attempt to avoid the need to work harder, think harder, guess harder, and take more chances than ever before in his life.

Lester was beginning to say something about 'thinking' he'd heard Ju-Ju admit to shooting Worth. Roersch held up his hand. 'Forget it. Just testing.' He felt like hell when the faces, which had begun to reflect some hope, turned from him.

Both boys lay back down. Radford muttered, 'They play with us, man. We goddam toys to the pigs.'

Lester pulled the pillow over his head.

Roersch said, 'If you're hungry, call the guard.' He went down the hall to where Grimes, the night man, was dozing in his chair. He gave him a five and told him to phone out for whatever the boys wanted. 'Use any change for their cigarettes,' he said, and went back past the cells. He was very tired.

He went upstairs to the washroom and began shaving off his ten o'clock shadow.

And Angie made no sense to him.

Worth and Albony *did* make some sort of sense ... but not as Angie's victims; not as *any* racketeer's victims. Unless someone had gone bananas. Which was always possible.

He splashed on after-shave and went into the main squad room. Harry Balleau was on the phone, catching a squeal. He hung up and called to the desk sergeant, 'Get a car over to Tenth and Thirty-first to investigate a report of a body hanging from a lamppost.'

'Hanging from a lamppost?' the desk man repeated incredulously. 'It's a rib, isn't it?'

'Third call in the last ten minutes. All different people. I figured three was the magic number.'

Roersch and Balleau grinned at each other, and Roersch kept going. He heard Balleau say, 'Gotta be a dummy, a mannequin, but what a gas if it's real, huh?'

Clarise Worth, who still thought of herself as Cappy, the name her father had called her to the day of his death, the name Tom had refused to call her, opened one of the two big briefcases and looked at the money. 'Cappy,' her father had said, 'be honorable, be honest, be happy.'

It was easy for Pops; he'd been a mortician in Three-Towns, Georgia, and done well. It was another time. It was another life back there, back then, and Cappy had thought she would never have to go against Pops' wishes.

She *had* been honorable, been honest, been happy with her Tom.

But she'd suspected . . . and closed her mind and heart to the suspicions. She'd been proud of Tom's refusing help from Pops, but confused by how he'd been able to manage so well, to provide so well, on his patrolman's pay, later his sergeant's, and after they'd moved to Tarrytown his lieutenant's and captain's salary. Because they had a big family and they lived in a big way. And the few times she'd opened her mind and heart to *wonder*, she couldn't make his income fit their expenditures.

But he'd had 'outside investments that had done very well,' hadn't he? And lots of men didn't discuss their investments, their businesses . . .

She put her head down on Tom's desk; on the rich, red Moroccan top. She surprised herself by having still more tears left. 'I miss you,' she whispered; then looked up, looked into the darkness beyond the open window, beyond the lawn and the woods. The whole world was dark; would remain dark. She was a one-man woman and her man was dead.

And her man had been a thief.

On the desk were the two briefcases into which she'd emptied his safety deposit boxes. At the bank in Greenwich, Connecticut, which he'd used even before they'd moved to Tarrytown. Which he'd used since he'd been a patrolman. Because he had begun thieving then – going on the pad, on the take, as the police called it. Because he'd planned well from the very beginning, knowing that New York had estate-watchers who read obituary notices and opened safety-deposit boxes. And he couldn't allow that. Had to avoid that. With the boxes in another state; with the signature cards in the name of Tom Farris and/or Clarise Farris . . . Farris being her maiden name. 'For luck,' he'd said, 'so your investments will prosper.' And he'd kissed her head as she'd bent to sign the card.

But it wasn't *luck* or *investments* that had filled those boxes. It was her Tom, like the stories that came out of the Knapp Commission on police corruption. It was the note he'd left her, warning that she mustn't declare the money in the safety-deposit boxes.

Corrupt, her Tom.

Corrupt, so ugly a word for so loving a man.

Had he also been corrupt with women?

She thought of it, and it was a natural assumption to make for a man who'd acted with such contempt for the law he'd been sworn to uphold . . . and she didn't believe it. Because what they'd had between them as man and woman could *not* be corrupted. She would know; she was sure of it; and she hadn't known.

What should she do with the money? She had four children: three sons and her baby, eight-year-old Rita. Her oldest, Johnny, was going into his sophomore year at Brown. Her second oldest was hoping to be accepted by either Syracuse or – slender chance but much prayed for – Princeton. The tuitions were steep, and both boys had to live on or near campus.

And there was this house; big, and with a big mortgage.

And all the cars, and all the insurance on the cars, and Tom's death payments and pension wouldn't cover that. His life insurance had shocked her; just twenty-five thousand. For this, she blamed herself. She remembered when he'd taken out the policy, just after joining the force. She'd never asked if he'd increased it; had assumed a man in his position *would*.

He'd left those safety-deposit boxes instead. He'd thought to handle them himself; make their lives comfortable as he always had, without bothering his wife or children with details.

What should she do with the money?

That question had been tormenting her since Friday, when she'd gone to the bank as instructed by the letter he'd told her was in the top drawer of his desk, to be opened only in case of his death. A strange, almost funny letter, revealing he just didn't believe he could die abruptly, violently, without having time to make the letter obsolete. So he joked about her having peeked before his death; told her to seal it up again and wait until she was 'seventy-five, at least'. And added the warning not to declare the money, tacitly admitting his corruption.

Her signature had held up. Maybe anyone who had the keys, and knew the name to be signed, would be admitted. She had taken two briefcases along with her, as the letter instructed, had taken them into the little room, and gasped when those three boxes – not the normal size, but *big* ones – gave up their contents.

As close as she could tell – and she'd not yet found the time, the patience, the period of calmness, to count it thoroughly – she had between three and four hundred thousand dollars. Illegal dollars. Tax-free dollars. Dollars she couldn't tell anyone about ... unless she decided not to keep them.

She could go to the man who had found her husband's killers. She could talk to that sergeant who looked wise, understanding, honest ...

And what if he too was 'on the pad'?

213

Tomorrow was the full inspector's funeral and the police commissioner would be there and the chief of detectives and the mayor and some said the governor, election time drawing close and this being a good way to appear in the media in a sympathetic role. And inspectors and captains and lieutenants by the gross. And New York City patrolmen, hundreds on hundreds, silver shields striped across by black tape as a sign of mourning.

And how many of them knew her Tom was a thief? Some, certainly.

And how many of them were thieves themselves? Some, certainly.

And sweet Lord Jesus, how could she get through tomorrow with her lover being put into the ground and her children all depending on her to be strong and her strength being sapped by this money, what it represented, her confusion over what to do with it?

She wanted to give it away.

And yet, life would be so much easier with it than without it.

She wanted to give it away.

And who could she give it to? If the newspapers, the television, got hold of it – and they would, eventually – then her Tom would lie stinking in his grave, his name in ruins. And that name, Worth, was carried by his four children. And by herself.

There was only one way she could get rid of the money, and that was to destroy it. And Tom had risked his career for it, for her . . .

She put her head back down on the desk. She couldn't destroy it. She couldn't flush it down the toilet into the septic tank; couldn't burn it one fall day with the leaves; couldn't even send it, anonymously, to some charity. He had worked – well, thievery was work too – his entire adult life for this treasure, and she couldn't reject his life.

She heard the delicate Swiss clock she'd bought on their last trip to Switzerland – two years ago, a lovely second honeymoon, or rather a third, a fourth, he was forever finding time, and money, for new honeymoons – she heard it

214

strike eleven. Everyone lay in exhausted slumber. Everyone but Cappy.

Her father's words were still in her ears: 'Be honorable, be honest, be happy.' Her father had been a simple and very naïve man. Also, very lucky to inherit the 'dark-town' mortuary, and have it grow along with the town, the state, the entire South, in population and in riches. Her father had died with his naïvetés, his enthusiasms, his beliefs intact. Lucky little man.

Her Tom had worked in a bigger mortuary, he'd often said. Her Tom had done whatever he'd done in New York City, and her father wouldn't have lasted a week where Tom conducted his 'outside business investments'.

She suddenly stood up and carried both briefcases to the floor safe behind the cabinet door. A moment later, she left the study.

She would hold onto her home, for her younger children and herself.

She would provide the very best educations for her older sons; for *all* her children, in time.

She would ease the money from the safe into her daily life, as Tom would have done. It was *her* money now, and she wouldn't be honorable, wouldn't be honest . . . and wouldn't be happy without her Tom.

All pain passes, all memory fades, the mortician's daughter knew.

Knew, but didn't believe.

She walked through the first floor of her beautiful home. She looked at shelves, tables . . . places where at times she'd tried to put some sign of their race, their heritage. He allowed only her family's photographs, and those only in her dressing room. He had no family of his own; not in pictures, not in words.

She still didn't know where he'd been born, except for that long-ago muttered, 'In hell, and I'm not going back.'

She still didn't know if he had mother or father, sisters or brothers, aunts or uncles or cousins alive anywhere, because all he'd said was, 'There were nine of us kids, and that was eight too many for me.'

She'd met him as a man, loved him as a man, and tomorrow she would bury him as a man. A self-made man. Even his name, Worth, was self-made; legally changed from something she didn't know.

She went upstairs to bed. She lay there, and knew she should take one of the pills her doctor had given her for sleep, and didn't want to sleep.

He was in the mortuary, her Tom ... still above ground. Her father's craft hadn't gotten him yet. This was his last night in the summer air.

Foolish, she knew, but she talked to him, said good-bye to him as she hadn't been able to in the shock of identifying his body; as she wouldn't be able to at the grand circus of his funeral – which was for his city, his department, his Bureau, not for the Worths.

Finally, she said something she'd been wanting to say to him since the moment they'd told her he was dead, killed by three black youths.

'You always hated them, Tom. You must've been something like them yourself, early in your life. I know they killed you, but please don't hate them anymore.'

She listened for his 'stinking ghetto skells' and heard nothing and knew it was irrational to expect answers from a dead man. And still was comforted.

He no longer hated them. He no longer hated himself.

Jimmy was seated in a booth at the rear of the small, almost-empty restaurant sipping a martini on the rocks. He called to the bartender for a Scotch and water, Roersch's usual – though he'd also liked bourbon and branch back in the days when he'd really indulged.

Jimmy was in full uniform, and looked great. Except for the brief period of despair after his second wife Teresa had left him, he'd always kept himself in shape.

He was about Roersch's height, not as broad-boned or heavily muscled, not quite as old, with graying blond hair cut medium short, a high forehead indicating the only area of hair loss, small features except for a full, firm mouth. He'd come into the department with more education than most had thirty years ago – a B.A. from C.C.N.Y. He'd gone on to get his master's from Columbia after making lieutenant. He read a good deal, and he knew a good deal.

More than that, he'd been one hell of a partner on Safe and Loft, and in Worth's old precinct when they'd gone up against that nut on Houston Street. Special Forces had backed them up and they somehow found themselves outside the nut's door and the nut was holding his wife hostage with a shotgun at her head.

The nut had come busting out and killed a Special Forces guy on the stairs, despite a bullet-proof vest, by blowing his head off. And turned on the surprised detectives – very surprised and caught off guard. With luck, they'd killed him. They'd run into more shit later in the month, at the riot in Columbus Circle, where that heist artist had tried to use the confusion as cover for a robbery ...

Jimmy said, 'You've really got something on your mind, haven't you?'

'I have, but I wasn't thinking of it. I was thinking of the old days.'

His drink came. They toasted the old days and exchanged reminiscences. Jimmy said, 'Have you heard about Danziger's?'

It was their favorite restaurant, good German food, way downtown on Erickson Place where they'd first served together in the old fourth precinct. As venerable as the precinct house itself, Danziger's had never been robbed while the founder, Herman Danziger, lived ... because he encouraged cops to eat there, for nothing. The old kraut used to say it was a hell of a lot cheaper serving a dozen meals a day on the pad than being robbed, especially since he limited the freebies to the inexpensive specials. And as New York became less and less safe, Danziger's record of no stickups, cops always there, and a station house close by, actually *increased* business and profits.

Then the old man died, and his two sons took over. Quickly, they let it be known they didn't approve of the pad. Oh, if a *captain* came in, he'd get an electric-chair dinner, as the cops called a huge banquet style meal. But no more freebies for patrolmen. And so the cops stopped coming; they couldn't afford Danziger's.

'They were robbed twice last week,' Jimmy said.

Roersch chuckled a little.

'The second time the younger son got his skull fractured.'

Roersch finished his drink.

'I hear they're putting out the word they want cops back, on the pad.'

Roersch laughed.

Jimmy suggested a second drink. Roersch said no thanks. Jimmy looked at him, giving him a chance to speak. Roersch said nothing. Jimmy called the waiter, and they ordered.

Roersch ate quickly, seriously, enjoying the New York cut of beef, ignoring, with difficulty, the pan-fried potatoes Mel's was famous for, sipping water instead of the dark Danish beer Jimmy sipped.

Quite suddenly with Jimmy still eating, Roersch put down his fork and began to talk. He talked in a low voice, leaning forward. He started with his first day on Fifty-second Street, and he went through *everything*.

When he reached the interview in Deverney's office, Jimmy stopped eating. When he drew a connection between the twenty thousand and Angie Tortemango, Jimmy gave an involuntary little grunt.

Roersch told of the witnesses to the gun flashes in the basement entry, *proving* the blacks hadn't killed Worth, and of Deverney's phoned order not to effect a collar before consulting him. He was going to continue into the grayer areas – his feelings that Deverney was threatening him, his doubts that Angie would have *dared* kill a sharp, self-protective, experienced squeeze artist like Worth – when Jimmy said, 'You've got to protect yourself.'

'Against Deverney?'

'Yes. Against his setting you up for a fall. Illegal procedure is in the offing, Eddy. You're not writing proper reports, not going through channels, not letting anyone but Deverney know what's happening. He's the only one who suspects Worth wasn't killed by Albert Wyins, correct?'

'And you, now.'

'I mean in your proper line of command. You just can't *do* such things in the Bureau, unless you're working with a buddy.'

'Hardly a buddy, the gray shark,' Roersch said. 'So what now? Blow the whistle?'

Jimmy leaned back. 'Only if you're certain the P.C. *isn't* behind Deverney.'

'I don't know that. And I can't find out without disobeying the inspector's orders. I've got the money riding on his good feelings, and a promised promotion, and if I go over his head ... hell, I just don't see how I can win.'

'Deverney could be getting ready to set Angie up for a fatal fall. If you give him the right evidence, and he doesn't want Angie talking in open court, he'll move with some close friends and Angie will die resisting arrest. Which wouldn't be a tragedy to anyone but Angie. But there *you'd* be, the man who gathered the evidence, and no D.D.–5's to back you, and how would you explain it to a board of inquiry in case there was any heat?'

Roersch thought a moment. 'No good to tell the truth. My word against Deverney's. And I'd be the one who'd broken the law.'

'Right,' Jimmy said. 'So you're going to make up a full set of D.D.–5's. You're going to date them properly, and you're going to keep one set in your desk at Manhattan West, and give one set to someone you can trust ... just in case things get really rough.'

Roersch nodded slowly. 'I should've done that from the beginning.'

'You couldn't know what was developing.'

'Yes, I could. And did. *Almost* from the beginning. Certainly from that meeting in Deverney's office.' He paused. 'Is there any talk about Deverney's having been on the pad?'

'There's talk like that about everyone.'

'I mean like there was about Worth.'

'Not like there was about Worth. But Deverney had a bagman or two. His precinct filed the fewest Green Slips in

219

one of the city's biggest gambling areas. One month, only two U.F.–45's on KG's were handed in. That meant that Known Gamblers were paying off at a higher rate than anywhere in the city. Of course, it's possible the precinct captain didn't know about it.' He smiled a little.

Roersch said, 'It *is* possible. When we were in the Sixth, serving under Worth, it took *me* a long time to find out just what a pig heaven we were in. Did *you* know about it right off?'

'I was a sergeant to your detective third, Eddy. I heard more, so I knew more. Knew it was a precinct with heavy payoffs, with unusual opportunities for getting on the pad.'

'Did you know Balleau at that time?'

'Harry Balleau? Sure, he was called The Kid then, remember? Youngest detective in the division. Whatever happened to him?'

'He's on night tour at Manhattan West, didn't you know?'

Jimmy shook his head. 'Harry was always a bit coarse for my taste. Is he still cheating on that pretty wife of his?'

'No. She divorced him.'

Jimmy chuckled, then said, 'If Harry is dependable enough – and he was always a good man, on the job – give that set of reports to *him*. I presume that's why you brought his name up?'

'I thought of it. But I want to give them to you, Jimmy.'

Jimmy shook his head. 'I'm not part of Manhattan West. I'm not part of M–4. I don't see how much validity I'd have coming forward . . .'

'I don't trust anyone else, Jimmy. If something happens and my ass is up on charges . . .' He paused. 'Or if someone tries to wipe it out, then I want *you* to have the ammunition.'

Jimmy didn't look happy. Roersch didn't blame him. But he needed his old friend and he didn't care if he was pushing him into an unpleasant task. 'I'm probably making more of it than there is. I probably shouldn't consider Worth and Albony as belonging to the same perpetrators . . .'

'But you said the blacks didn't do Worth. And if Albony was done by muggers . . .'

'No evidence at all on that, Jimmy. Just talk. Media talk.'

Jimmy was incredulous. 'I know you've put some wild cases together in the past, Eddy, but you're not suggesting Angie Tortemango is knocking off all his contacts, no matter *what* sort of pressure they've put on him?'

'Deverney would like me to think so.'

'Ah. Then you don't?'

'No. But I've got to follow through on Angie. Cross him off the suspect list and I'm in left field without a glove.'

Jimmy smiled a little. 'Haven't heard that one since Durocher left Brooklyn. Well, if it's not Angie, maybe it's another Tortemango – Paddy?'

'Why? They're both in the same family, the same business. They both stand to lose if anything hanging over their heads falls as a result of these executions.'

'Then how about another family entirely?'

Roersch slowly nodded and slowly smiled. 'That could be, Jimmy-boy. Why didn't *I* think of it?'

'You would have, Eddy. In your own time. And when you did, you'd have had a *reason*. I'm just throwing out ideas.'

'No problem finding a reason. If another Mafia family wanted to bring the Tortemangos down, they'd kill some of Angie's and Paddy's contacts and hope that on-my-death letters would begin to move to the authorities; that it would bring heavy pressure on the Tortemangos and leave openings for others to move into their hustling . . .'

Mel came over to the table. 'Sergeant Roersch?'

Roersch looked up.

'There's a call for you. A Sergeant Balleau.'

Roersch nodded, and followed the short man to the end of the bar and the phone. And wondered just when it was he'd told anyone he'd be eating at Mel's.

'Eddy, we got a very hot squeal here. Concerns a resident of East Fifty-second you may not have known about. Angelo Tortemango.'

'Don't tell me *he* was swinging from that lamppost?'

Balleau laughed. 'That was a dummy, just like I said.

221

Angie was found in a car parked on First Avenue. Foot patrolman noticed someone slumped over a wheel and checked and there's this guy with his tongue sticking out and marks around his neck. The old Sicilian necktie party. Reporters are already bugging the desk sergeant, and because of Tortemango's address, they're asking for an M–4 connection. And they're asking for *you*. Thought you should know.'

Roersch thanked him, and returned to Jimmy.

Jimmy said, 'I don't believe it! You mean they're starting what the newspapers call a gangland war? It doesn't make sense, given today's realities!'

Roersch was rubbing his face. 'And what does it do to my line of investigation on Worth? There's no place to go.'

'May be for the best, Eddy. Deverney will almost certainly call it quits here. The D.A. will put all four Fifty-second Street deaths on the blacks, who can't get tougher sentences than they will for *three*.'

'But those gun flashes in the basement entry; do I forget about them?'

Jimmy looked at him a long moment. 'With anyone else, I'd say certainly. With you . . .' He slowly shook his head. 'I doubt it, Eddy.'

'You think I *should* forget about the flashes?' He almost hoped Jimmy would convince him; ease him out of further struggling, further sweating. But Jimmy shook his head again.

'You wouldn't be able to do it, even if you swore to it on Mark's life. Eventually you'd go back to that basement and pick and shove and get someone to say something. You'll work up another case, Eddy. Don't worry.'

Jimmy had a brandy. Eddy sipped black coffee. They didn't talk until Mel brought the check. Jimmy waved Roersch back. 'You should have been a captain, at least. Let me make up for the department's stupidity in this small way.'

A few minutes later, they walked to the door.

'What if you're given Angie as a case?' Jimmy asked. 'What about your Five Commandments? Don't you go on sick leave every time they try to hand you inter-racketeer killings? And doesn't that include Assemblyman Albony?'

'I don't know, Jimmy. I'm too tired to think right. But there's something different here. The non-Mafia contact men are getting killed, and that's not usual. Worth and Albony ... as for Angie ...' He rubbed his face. 'I think we've got two different perpetrators, at least.'

They came into the street and shook hands. Roersch said, 'Thanks for dinner, for listening, and for the advice. I'll get on those D.D.–5's in the next few days.'

'Good. Get some rest, Eddy. I've never seen you look quite so tired.' He turned up the street to his Caddy.

Roersch walked to his Plymouth, smothering a belch. He'd never *felt* quite so tired. He intended to sleep until ten or later tomorrow.

Back home, he found Ruthie asleep and a note on the kitchen table. 'Call Inspector Deverney at home, no matter how late.'

It was a quarter to one; not too bad. He dialed. Deverney answered on the first ring.

'Did you hear about Angie Tortemango?'

Roersch said he had.

'Now we forget the twenty thousand, we forget there was ever any doubt as to who killed Worth, and we go with a straight, simple solution. Ju-Ju Wyins did it. Whether we catch him or not, he did it. No matter what he says, he did it. The three spades take the fall for all four victims. And you get the money as of tomorrow.'

Roersch muttered, 'Thanks.'

'I know. I promised you gold bars. Resolve Ju-Ju Wyins, one way or another, and you've got them.'

'One way or ...?'

'He'd be better off dead, Eddy. All three of them would, but with Wyins it can still happen.'

'Yes.'

Deverney made a deep, sighing sound. 'I think we're out of the woods. With the wops knocking each other off, with M–4 ready for the D.A. it's home free for the department.'

'Yessir.'

'Goddammit! Show some *enthusiasm*! We've kept the police *clean*! You'll be getting over twenty-three thousand a year, starting tomorrow! After your promotion comes through, there'll be a year of duty to nail down your pension, then you're off to the Keys, or wherever you like to fish, You *do* fish, as I remember, don't you, Eddy?'

'Yessir I do.'

'What's wrong ...?'

'I'm just about out on my feet, Inspector. I've been averaging four, five hours of sleep a night and the days have been murder.'

'Of course. Thoughtless of me. You've done a great job.'

Roersch couldn't see where, but said thank you. He wanted to shower, but couldn't face being on his feet another moment. He dropped his clothing on the floor and fell into bed and mumbled, 'Good night,' to whatever Ruthie said. And slept like a dead man. Until the phone woke him at eight.

His promotion was going to come even sooner than he'd thought. Albert 'Ju-Ju' Wyins was in a Harlem apartment over a jewelry store, offering Louise Jaeker's diamond bracelet-watch for sale. The jeweler-fence had a heavy rap hanging over him to be erased in the next six months. He'd erased it with a sneak call to M-4. The desk sergeant who'd informed Roersch said he would now call Jones. 'It's still Willis's baby, right, Eddy?'

'Not with a suspect who might split at any moment! What the hell are you thinking of? Get radio cars over there immediately! A quiet approach, Hank, but have them cover all exits. *Then* phone Willis.'

'Well, we've been working black on black ...'

'*Get those units over there!*' Roersch shouted and slammed down the phone.

Mark began screaming in the bedroom. Ruthie's voice climbed as she said, '*Must* you yell that way, Eddy? You're hardly ever home and then you scare ...'

Jen began to cry at the kitchen table, round face screwing up, streaking.

Roersch fled to the bathroom, where his right shoulder ached, his chest ached . . . his fucking head ached!

What the hell was wrong with him? He was going to get his third collar; he was going to sew up M-4; he had the money and he'd get the lieutenant's bars. His kids would stop crying and his wife would stop grousing once he explained that they could now move to the suburbs and leave the Radfords, Lesters, and Ju-Jus behind.

Life was a fucking bowl of cherries!

THIRTEEN

Monday, July 21, and Tuesday, July 22

VOICE ONE: Sharply; angrily: 'Why didn't you call last night? We have to set up another job, and fast.'

VOICE TWO: 'Christ, I thought we were going to skip a few weeks, let the heat die down. Who is it?'

ONE: 'Not now! You know where I am!'

TWO: 'Easy, Mr Washington. I just didn't think.'

ONE: Deep breath. 'We've got to do it ourselves. But I want a backup man; your Number Two.'

TWO: 'He left on vacation Sunday morning, right after we did Albony, and I have no address for him. We figured on two weeks of coasting, at least.'

ONE: 'Well, the situation is changing and we have to change with it.' Pause. 'I wouldn't like doing this with just the two of us.'

TWO: 'Don't get mad ... but I know the name of *his* Number Two. He told me, and I can reach this guy.'

ONE: 'Against the rules! And dangerous!'

TWO: 'Yeah, but it'll come in handy *now*, won't it?'

ONE: Explosive exhale.

TWO: 'What's the big sweat anyway? No one has a clue about us. First I was nervous, but now I don't see a thing coming near us.'

ONE: Resigned: 'Nearer than you think.' Pause. 'All right. Meet me at the coffee shop inside the Pfizer Building.'

TWO: 'When?'

ONE: 'Noon. And alert that man you shouldn't know. Put him on standby. You and he will have to take turns tailing.'

TWO: 'No problem with *him*. He was laid off work during one of those small cutbacks leading to the big one we got now. Did they call it default then?'

ONE: 'Whatever they called it, or call it now, it's because of union greed; public mismanagement and dishonesty; racketeer influence underlying too much of our political structure. That's why we're blowing away the *official* scum. The racketeers come later. And then we'll rehire all those ex-cops and more; we'll build law enforcement to a high point, a point it's never reached before.'

TWO: 'Yeah, well, he's been waiting to get back in, collecting unemployment and taking tempo jobs and living with his folks. My Number Two, the guy on vacation, is another one who was kicked out back then.'

ONE: 'Excellent. Their motivation should be of the highest.'

TWO: Chuckle. 'Oh, my Number Two is a blood-thirsty bastard, all right.'

ONE: 'Which is what we need. However, I can't help wondering how many of our seven associates know more about each other than they should.'

TWO: 'Human nature, Mr Washington. But we're a tight group. We'd rather die than talk to *outsiders*.'

ONE: 'That remains to be seen.'

TWO: 'What?'

ONE: 'Only when the choice between dying and talking is at hand will we know for sure. Now get in touch with your ... what shall we call him ... your Number *Three*.'

Albert 'Ju-Ju' Wyins wouldn't come out. He'd shouted obscenities and fired shots from the second-floor window above the little jewelry shop about halfway down the street. And Inkie Baker, the jeweler-fence, had been shoved half out of that window, a rifle at his head. Inkie had screamed for the police to withdraw.

The police couldn't do that. At least not further than behind parked cars across from the jewelry shop. And, in back, behind a fence dividing a tiny courtyard into two garbage-littered halves.

Ju-Ju shoved the aging big-gutted Inkie from front window to back window. And was accurate enough with that rifle to keep officers pinned down behind cars and fence.

Roersch and Jones stood talking at the corner. Jones said,

'Those damned fools drove up almost to the store's front window in patrol cars! What sort of way is that to approach a suspect? What the hell's *wrong* with this department?'

'In this case, lack of specific instructions ... which might be my fault.'

'No way. The radio dispatcher's call was explicit enough in stating that Wyins was to be approached carefully, without sirens or flashers. They came without sirens, all right, but used flashers right up to the store! And Ju-Ju must've been keeping his eye out as Inkie examined the loot.'

'Too late to blame anyone now.'

'Once this is over. I'm going to put those dumb bastards on report!'

'We'll see, Willis.' But Roersch too was upset, because Deverney's fondest wish seemed about to come true. Which made him more determined than ever to capture Ju-Ju alive.

A shot sounded. A cop tried to aim over a car hood, and ducked without firing as Ju-Ju used his rifle again.

'He couldn't have walked *in* with that rifle,' Jones said, staring down the street. 'I thought he had a ·38 revolver?'

Roersch nodded, preoccupied. 'Must've taken it from Inkie.' It was nitty-gritty time for M–4; time to earn your pay-and-pad, as they used to say when he and Jimmy were at the old Fourth. And no pay was enough and there was no pad at Manhattan West Homicide. And standing here thinking of old times and old friends wasn't going to get the job done.

It was almost eleven. The block was sealed off to all traffic, foot and auto. But kids still darted in and out of houses, almost under the guns of officers, laughing and calling to one another. And adults were in every window.

There was a holiday atmosphere ... and an occasional shout of encouragement for Ju-Ju. His was a famous name now. Roersch just hoped no one decided to aid the celebrity. It had been a relatively quiet summer in terms of mass movement of ghetto blacks against property, whites, and the police. It could change quickly if a resident got hurt, or even hassled, on this Harlem street.

A patrolman came trotting up. 'He says he'll kill the jeweler in exactly ten minutes if we don't pull out completely ... off the block.'

Roersch sent him back to his position. And remembered how Jimmy and he got to the nut's apartment on Houston Street some twenty or more years ago. So how come Jimmy was behind a desk now and he, Roersch, was still putting his ass on the line?

He shrugged. 'Willis, those roofs are all flush against each other, and all on a level ... I think. Maybe one narrow gap on the *other* side of Inkie's building, but none on this side.'

Jones shielded his eyes against the morning sun. 'Maybe a small gap on this side too, and a small drop. Hard to tell until we get up there.' He looked at Roersch. 'Want me to do it with Eli?'

Roersch had already begun crossing the street, heading toward the first of the three-story tenements. 'Thanks for the vote of confidence.'

'I was only ...'

'My vast experience, as Hawly puts it, will carry me through.'

'Yeah, through the roof, if you have to jump half a story.'

Roersch looked back at him, and Jones muttered, 'Okay, sorry, lead on.' But Roersch was smiling when he entered the hallway. Just might happen that way.

The smile was gone by the time they reached the roof. They'd drawn their guns in case Ju-Ju decided to use the roofs too and doors were open on each floor because of the growing heat, and the *looks* they got from people! He was glad Jones was there to say, 'No trouble, brothers. Just here to protect you from a very bad customer.'

They crossed the tar-and-pebble roof to a low – perhaps three-foot-high – barrier made of brick. They stepped over easily onto the next roof, which wasn't in as good shape, having patchy tar and no pebbles. There were two young girls in bikinis sunning themselves on a blanket. One sat up and said half nervously, half jokingly, 'We surrender.' She looked at Jones. 'To the young one with the great tan.' Her friend wasn't as gutsy, putting a hand to her mouth and eyeing the drawn guns.

229

'It's all right, ladies,' Roersch said. 'Just passing through.'

Jones smiled at the one sitting up; she had a very full top and very pale skin. 'Stay here long enough,' he said, 'and you'll be just as tan as me.'

They both laughed then, and the one sitting up lay down again.

The next barrier was even lower than the first, perhaps two feet, but on the other side was a five- or six-foot drop. Jones went over, landing easily, lightly. Roersch said, 'Geronimo,' and jumped, and thought he'd fulfilled Jones's prophecy about going through the roof. From a window beneath came a shout: 'It's a fucking earthquake!'

Another two roofs and they would reach the house in which Ju-Ju was holding Inkie. 'How're we doing on time?' Roersch panted approaching the third barrier.

Jones looked at his wrist. 'We've got a good five minutes.'

They climbed over onto the next roof and trotted toward the next-to-last barrier. And saw the gap between buildings. No more than three feet – but a wrong move and they'd fall three *stories*.

Jones never hesitated: up onto the low barrier; a leap forward; an easy landing.

Roersch stood on the barrier, tensed, and overjumped by a good two feet.

'Olympic tryouts for you, sergeant,' Jones said, chuckling. 'Your style, however, could use some refinement.'

They were crossing the last barrier onto Inkie's roof, approaching a metal-paneled door. Roersch prayed that it was open.

It was locked. But it gave a bit, and he figured it was held by one of those old hook-locks. He said, 'Stand behind me,' and put his gun away. He grabbed the big curved handle with both hands; then lunged backward, jerking in with his arms at the same time.

He was caught by Jones. Both stumbled a little, but kept their feet. The door was now wide open. 'Grace and style have their place, Willis,' Roersch said, as they moved from bright sunlight into deep shadow, 'but so have beef and brawn.'

Willis laughed very quietly.

And then there was no more joking, laughing, talking. Then there was only getting down that first half-flight of steps as quietly as possible.

On reaching the third floor, Roersch stopped Jones, gestured at his feet, then removed his shoes. Jones did the same.

In this beleaguered house, all doors were closed. But as they started down to the second floor, Inkie's floor, one door opened and a little girl came out and stared at them. Jones put a finger to his lips and smiled conspiratorially. The little girl bellowed, '*Mommy, a man is here!*'

A young woman came out and looked at the guns and yanked the little girl back inside. Jones whispered, 'I hope they *like* Inkie in this building!'

They reached the second floor and acclimated themselves and Roersch pointed at one of the four apartment doors. No child came out on this floor. Ju-Ju probably checked the hall regularly, along with the front and rear windows.

Roersch motioned Willis to the knob side of the door and took the hinge side himself. They flattened there. And waited.

Inside the apartment, they heard a voice shout, 'Motherfuckers! Two more minutes and this *sucker* gets it! Two more minutes!' And the sound of a shot.

Then footsteps – a mixture of firm tread and stumbling scraping – went past the door. The same voice shouted the same message out the back window. The mixture of footsteps returned, and stopped, and the door clicked and began to open. 'Fink on me?' Ju-Ju raged. 'You die no matter *what* happen!' The door opened toward Roersch, which meant it revealed Willis first.

Inkie came out, a hand gripping the back of his neck. He saw Jones and made a gasping sound ... and the door opened further and blocked Roersch's view.

He stepped away from the wall, no longer thinking normally but in the manner of an animal hunting, a soldier fighting, a cop out to protect his buddy and screw everyone else.

Ju-Ju was sticking his head past Inkie's shoulder, looking

231

right at Willis. Willis began to say, 'Don't be a fool . . .' but Ju-Ju reacted quickly, a blur of vicious motion. He threw Inkie forward, shoving so hard that the big man hit the railing, screamed and flipped over into the stairwell. And with both hands now free, Ju-Ju swung the rifle onto Jones.

Roersch knew what was going to happen. Jones hadn't fired when he was supposed to – the very instant Inkie had been out of the way. Jones had hesitated a split second too long. Now he and Ju-Ju would fire at the same time, and *both* could die.

Roersch wanted Ju-Ju for questioning. But he couldn't save him; was squeezing the trigger; was angling the Detective Special's barrel just the fraction of an inch he had time to angle it. And was waiting to hear if Jones would scream along with Ju-Ju . . . or whether the angling had been enough to send the bullet into the apartment. Because the bullet could go through Ju-Ju into Jones.

Ju-Ju bucked forward, shrieking. He fell into Jones, and both went down.

But Jones got up immediately, face twisted, backing off.

Ju-Ju moved his legs. Roersch knelt and turned him over. Ju-Ju wailed, 'Oh, *man!*' And then, focusing on Roersch, 'Never shot the pig. Never . . . just pointed . . .' He vomited blood over himself and Roersch, but Roersch bent even closer. 'Ju-Ju, did you see who shot Worth?'

'Didn't shoot mother . . .' More vomiting.

Roersch said, 'Willis, get an ambulance.' To Ju-Ju: 'But behind Worth . . .'

Ju-Ju was choking, vomiting, strangling. Ju-Ju had a horrendous hole in his upper stomach where the ·38 slug had emerged. Ju-Ju went limp.

Roersch looked up. Jones still stood there, service revolver hanging in his right hand, left hand touching a bloody spot on his chest.

'Are you *hit*?' Roersch asked.

Jones shook his head, still staring at the stocky boy in Roersch's arms.

'Then get your ass downstairs for an ambulance!'

Jones seemed to awaken, and turned to the staircase.

Before he could start down, two white officers appeared, guns extended, faces tense.

'Cool it,' Jones muttered. 'Call for medical help. The suspect is wounded.'

'The suspect is dead,' Roersch said, rising. 'What happened to Inkie?'

'He's a lot shorter than he used to be,' one fair-skinned cop said, grinning. 'Hit feet first. From six-one to one-six without surgery.'

His companion chuckled.

Roersch said, 'Get the fuck out of here.'

The cops looked hurt. The first one said, 'The fence is alive, Sergeant. I think he broke both legs.'

His companion said, 'The ambulance should be here in a minute. We were just kidding ... relieved, you know, that you guys are okay.'

Roersch sighed, nodded. Jones said nothing, looking down at the blood on his shirt. Ju-Ju's blood. Roersch was soaked in it. And now he felt warm liquid puddling around his feet.

He said, 'Shit,' and came up on his toes and took long steps back toward the up-flight. 'Our shoes, Willis.'

When they got to the third floor, their shoes were gone. They knocked at all four apartment doors. Only one door opened, to reveal the young mother and little-girl-with-loud-voice. The little girl's eyes widened as she saw the blood. The mother said, 'God!'

Jones said, 'Take the child away.'

The little girl said, 'You're *dirty*! A boy came and took your shoes!' She pointed at the open roof door. 'You're too dirty to come in *our* house!' She smiled.

They went to the staircase in their blood-soaked, stockinged feet. Jones glanced back at the child smiling after them. 'That one must be Andra's.'

Roersch remembered the name, but he didn't ask about the reporter, didn't care about her. He was too tired, disgusted, and sticky with a kid's life's blood to care about anything but a shower and a change of clothes.

In the street, the media people now outnumbered the

cops. Roersch kept his head down and got himself and Willis into a patrol car with a driver, ignoring repeated questions about their lack of shoes. A popular local TV reporter stuck his head in the window. 'That's not fair, Sergeant! We've been good to you . . .'

'In an hour,' Roersch said. 'At Manhattan West.' And got the cop – who kept saying he had to wait for his partner – to take off.

It took closer to two hours before he was washed and changed and back at Manhattan West. Then he stood in a corner near his cubicle and told the reporters and cameras that with the death of Albert 'Ju-Ju' Wyins, the M–4 case was closed. From here on, they could go to the district attorney's office for their information.

He denied there was any connection between Worth and Albany. 'The M–4 killers did *not* have anything to do with the death of Assemblyman Albony. Radford Johnson and Lester Cole have been cleared of it, and Ju-Ju Wyins is in the process of being cleared posthumously – witnesses giving statements.'

He refused to answer questions about the death of Angelo Tortemango, saying it wasn't assigned to him. But that popular local reporter called out, 'Captain Hawly says it *will* be.'

Roersch said, 'Good news is hard to suppress,' and waved his hand in a cut-off signal as the room laughed. He walked toward the staircase leading to the cells and the M–4 squad room. Several reporters tried to follow, but he turned, said, 'No more,' and said it in such a voice and manner that there were no arguments. He went down, thinking he'd finally learned how to handle a news conference. Fat lot of good it would do him in retirement.

A message to call Deverney was on his desk. He called Jimmy instead. The captain was out to lunch, the desk sergeant said, but would return his call. Roersch said, 'No hurry,' because all he wanted to do was chat. Wanted to tell his friend about the action today.

Wanted to exchange words with Captain Jimmy Weir because something was bothering him. *Something . . .* the way something had bothered him when he'd first looked down at that white crayon outline of Captain Worth's body.

He remembered the doorman in that building with the basement entry saying that tenants had reported prowlers and the police had checked the doors off the passageway. With a key borrowed from the super.

Something, something . . .

He still didn't call Deverney. He looked up the number of the Third Detective Zone and dialed and tried to think of an old buddy's name . . . and by the time a voice answered, he had the name.

He got through to Detective First John Maugham, who was pleased to tell Roersch he was retiring in one month at age fifty-five.

'Great, John. But before you head for the Golden Age center, do me a favor. Go through your files for a complaint about prowlers . . .' He explained, gave the address of the house on Fifty-second, asked for the name of the officer who had checked the basement doors. 'Two or three weeks ago, according to the doorman.'

John said it would take a day or two. Roersch thanked him.

SPRINT and Deverney could do it in an *hour* or two. But he couldn't use them anymore. He'd lost that clout.

Something bothering him – something wrong – and his chest was hurting and he wanted to stop right here and tell Hawly he was sick; wanted to stay home until Angie was assigned to someone else and he could take off for Amagansett and finish his vacation.

And then finish out his year as a lieutenant, behind a desk somewhere, off the streets forever, never having to use his gun again, forgetting what was bothering him and what was making his chest ache . . .

The phone rang. It was Deverney. 'Didn't you get my message, Eddy?'

'Just now, Inspector. Just sat down . . .'

'Tremendous job! Exactly what we wanted, right?' He chuckled in answer to his own question. 'You'll take the lieutenant's makeup exam next Monday. Forget the

235

Delehanty books ... don't worry ... you'll pass high.' He chuckled again. 'Call it a hunch.'

Roersch managed to put some satisfaction into his voice. 'Thanks, Inspector!'

And why *shouldn't* he sound satisfied? He'd waited a lifetime for those bars! And he no longer had to worry about D.D.-5's and protecting himself ...

But when Deverney said, 'That twenty thousand was a fluke; nothing to do with racketeers or payoffs or the department,' Roersch almost laughed. 'Lucky we didn't jump the wrong way, Eddy. Maybe he was gambling. Or in on some sort of slightly illegal stock deal. Anyway, it wasn't connected with the department or his death. So forget it, just as I am. Get back to your normal duties, just as I am.'

And he concluded with one other bit of information, which turned Roersch's stomach:

'Do you know why Ju-Ju didn't get the chance to run? Why he wasn't likely to surrender? I had a very heavy call in to central dispatch. Those first two radio cars called *me* on the way to Lenox Avenue. I told them to make themselves seen, if not heard ... in order to pin down the suspect, of course.' He laughed heartily. 'And it worked out just as I hoped. Though I must admit I never thought you would have to do the job yourself. It'll earn you a commendation. Number four, right?'

Roersch said right.

'Take the wife out and celebrate one hell of a job, *Lieutenant*.'

'Yeah,' Roersch said, after the line had clicked. 'One hell of a job.'

Jones stopped typing reports to look at him. 'You okay, Eddy?'

Roersch nodded, but he was nauseated.

After a while, he shrugged it off. It was over.

But that *something* was still eating at him.

Jones was standing beside him. 'You look sick, Eddy. I think you should ...'

Roersch smiled. 'You're not a farm boy, are you? You've never watched an old bull standing under a tree on a

236

summer day ... *ruminating*. That's the way we old bulls look, Willis. Now finish your typing and go home. You've earned an early evening.'

He told Ross the same thing. Lauria had caught the unenviable task of taking Radford and Lester to court – which meant complaint room, detention room, court room, back to detention, and possibly back to court again before the formal charges were completed and the prisoners were left in detention or shipped to Riker's Island, the city's prison. But after that, Lauria too would go home. And soon his crew would be back on regular schedule, with regular days off, living normal lives. Soon M-4 would be disbanded. So it was time to drop all the questioning, the doubting, the risking of money and promotions for nothing.

He would go home now. He would take his wife to dinner and make love to her and sleep late tomorrow and call in sick and follow the plan he'd made to get back to Amagansett, to spend a soft year at a desk, to retire and live the good life ...

But he didn't go home. He went to Fifty-second Street. He walked through that passageway once, twice, and he *thought*. And on the way home, still deep in thought, he realized he'd been glancing into the rearview mirror for the past ten minutes, watching a black Chevy sedan, which was now almost a full street back, that had been directly behind him at times and three or four cars behind at other times.

He made a detour. He parked at a supermarket, went inside, bought razor blades and after-shave lotion. He came out and got into his car, never looking around. He started home again.

The black Chevy showed up in his mirror.

He parked in his numbered stall in the underground garage, walked to the pay phone near the elevators, and hesitated. Jimmy hadn't returned his call; had probably never returned to the station ... which was something a captain could get away with.

He lifted the handset, put a coin in the slot, heard the dial tone, and still hesitated. Then made his decision. He called Willis.

They talked briefly. He said, 'Thanks. I'll fill you in tomorrow.'

He went upstairs and kissed his wife and daughter; and played with his son, who was miraculously awake. Ruthie called the teenaged girl on the second floor to baby-sit, and at eight they left for their favorite Italian restaurant. It was east a few blocks and south a few more. He glanced into the rearview mirror only once, to establish that the Chevy was there, and nodded to himself, satisfied.

He pleased Ruthie by ordering fish, barely tasting his side order of pasta, and skipping dessert entirely.

She rewarded him in bed, and promptly fell asleep. He was awake a little longer, but not because he was upset. If anything, he was relieved. The agonizing was over. The decision had been made for him. Like America after Pearl Harbor he was at war, choose to be or not.

He was being tailed. The three blacks were finished; he hadn't gotten into the Tortemangos; the tail had to be because of Worth ... maybe tied into Albony. But Worth for sure. So he would continue the investigation, and Deverney be damned.

He settled on his side. His gun usually lay on the dresser, but tonight it was under his pillow. That's how he would sleep from now on, keeping it from Ruthie if he could. And he would drive differently, walk differently, live differently ... while appearing not to.

Because he was getting close to someone. And with caution and a little luck, he might stay alive to find out who it was.

Jones parked down the street from his home. It was just two A.M. Not as bad as it might have been. The guy could have lived in upper Westchester, or way-out Long Island.

He'd lived in Queens. At least that's where he'd led Willis, to a two-family house on a street lined with identical houses.

Willis walked from his car to his brownstone, wondering if Andra had tried to get in touch. He was dead tired ... but still would have liked some of that action.

He was also puzzled as to what he'd been doing tonight.

Eddy wouldn't have asked if it weren't important. Yet he'd added, 'No reports on this.'

Would the goddam night work never end?

He was upset. Not really with the night work; with the way he'd performed in Harlem. He'd *frozen* when Ju-Ju had turned that rifle on him. He doubted that he would've been able to fire at all. Yet he'd always thought the *least* of his problems would be killing a skell.

Of course, with all his experience, he had yet to fire a shot in the line of duty.

It was true of the vast majority of police officers. He'd seen the statistics. Most cops *never* used their guns, except on the range, during their entire careers.

Cops like Eddy Roersch were the exceptions. Cops like Eddy Roersch were the blood and guts of the force.

He climbed the stairs to the second floor, wondering if cops like Eddy knew it.

Know it or not, Eddy had saved his life today. They hadn't discussed it. He hadn't, and *wouldn't*, thank him for it. Because if Eddy didn't know how he felt, he was too dumb to be thanked. And he was the opposite pole from dumb. He was so fucking special, Willis Jones didn't know how to express it.

That's why there'd been no hesitation in doing a nonofficial job of tailing for Eddy. That's why he hadn't asked questions; wouldn't ask even if Eddy never explained.

He'd have been lying in that hallway along with Ju-Ju if not for Eddy.

He'd be in the morgue if not for Eddy.

He stopped at the top of the stairs. His door was ajar.

He smiled and started forward; then stopped.

It might not *always* be Andra. He was tailing someone for Eddy. Someone whose last name was either Keers or Moore; he hadn't been able to determine which apartment the man had entered.

Keers or Moore could always tail right back. And be waiting. And he thought of the look on Ju-Ju's face as the bullet ripped through his body.

He drew his gun, pushed the door all the way open, and flattened at the side.

Light on in the living room. But no greeting.

He jerked his head forward and back, getting a quick glimpse of the room. And of the couch with the girl sleeping on it.

He put his gun away. He came inside and closed the door. She stirred, sat up, said, 'What time is it?'

'Time for bed.'

She smiled sleepily. 'Made you a great chocolate mousse.'

'We'll have it for breakfast,' he said, still tense.

'I don't know if I should stay over.'

He turned to the door. 'It's after two. If we're going to walk you to your car, let's do it right now. Because once I hit that sack ...'

She came to him and took his hand. She led him to his bedroom. Then she took off her clothes.

Then he was looking at her, seeing again the remarkable beauty of her.

Then he was allowing her to undress him.

She knelt at his feet to remove his shoes, his socks, and finally his undershorts. She cupped his testicles and murmured, 'So big, so black, so beautiful.' And still murmuring things about his blackness, his beauty, she took him into her mouth.

He shivered in sudden overwhelming excitement. He stroked her hair, crisply cut, thick and strong. He caressed her cheeks, her neck.

And finally raised her, wanting to see *her* blackness, *her* beauty.

In bed, he returned the compliment of oral love. The lips of her vulva were like the lips of his white girl's vulva. The pink-red flesh within was the same too. But in the contrast of that redness to chocolate-brown thighs, deep black genital hair, they were different.

He moaned, thinking black was indeed more beautiful, knowing he'd always preferred black girls. He reveled in the contrast, the beauty, pulling the lips apart and examining and stroking and only occasionally kissing and licking. Until she said, 'Willis, damn it, get *going!*'

He laughed, and got going, and brought her to quick climax.

Then he came up beside her, fondled the small, perfect breasts, pressed the satiny stomach, clutched the swelling buttocks. Then he kissed her mouth, and wanted to kiss, to penetrate, to ejaculate over *all* of her – face and breasts and belly and ass and thighs – wanted to do it *now*, this instant!

He cried out, '*Spread*, you bitch!'

She did, face twisted, understanding the passion, responding to the passion.

And he'd never fucked so hard before. And he'd never come so hard before. And he held her afterward and wanted to say she was the only woman who had ever made him feel this way.

And somehow didn't. Somehow knew what was coming.

She said: '*Why* did you have to kill him?'

He got into his shorts and went to the kitchen. He was eating the chocolate mousse and drinking milk when she joined him, wearing just panties. Very nice, but the wildness and passion was over, and his anger mounted.

'I *didn't* kill that boy. Eddy Roersch did, to save my life. I was unable ...'

She smiled and sat down quickly. She took his free hand. 'You were unable to shoot your brother, is that it?'

He jerked his hand away. 'I don't mean I couldn't because I didn't *want* to! I mean I froze, I panicked. Dammit, I turned yellow!'

'*That* I'd like to have seen,' she murmured, still smiling.

He put down his spoon. He stared at her and shook his head. 'You don't understand anything about me. You grow denser and denser ...'

'Your manhood, your macho, has been wounded, is that it? You couldn't do the ritual killing ...'

'That fucking skell was aiming a rifle at my heart! It has nothing to do with race, with philosophy or sociology! It has to do with *survival*! I turned into, into ...'

'A Stepin Fetchit?' she offered calmly. 'A Mantan

241

Morland? The way you've been trained by the white racists to think of yourself? Could it be that you thought, 'Feets, do yo' stuff!' and were unable to act courageously? Because your white masters have trained you via film, writing, every sort of communication . . .'

He stood up. He stared at her. He wanted to laugh hysterically. ' "Feets, do yo' stuff"?' he muttered. She was insane!

At the same time, he wondered if she might not be right. Was *that* why he hadn't done his job?

And then he was appalled. He was allowing her to contravene Pop's lifelong teaching of self-reliance and accomplishment.

He sat down again, waited for her to hit him again with something new.

She said nothing . . . until morning, at breakfast, which she cooked alone and served alone.

'Willis, you could be a teacher, couldn't you?'

'I could complete my master's in education, yes.'

'It pays every bit as well as being a police officer; perhaps better.'

'I guess so. But I'm not a teacher and I am a police officer.'

She served him scrambled eggs and toast and coffee. It was all very good. They sat side by side and ate. After a while, she said, 'I don't think you'll be a police officer much longer.'

He tried to keep eating. His insides twisted. He thought of Ju-Ju and that dark hallway and his doubts as to *ever* being able to use his gun on another person. His hand trembled raising egg to his mouth.

'Your black consciousness is growing, Willis. I can actually *see* it!' She reached out and touched his face. 'And the more it grows, the more I love you!'

He kept his eyes down. *Was she right?*

Suddenly, with his mouth full of egg, he began to laugh. He choked and turned his head and sprayed egg and toast all over the kitchen. He got up, coughing, laughing deep belly laughs. He tried to say something, and couldn't for the laughter.

When he was able to gain some bit of control, she was standing, her face a mask of rage. 'I'm sorry,' he said. 'But you *do* look much more natural now.'

'You can't deny your black consciousness! You can't deny caring for blacks no matter what they've done or how they're categorized by the pig brutality force!'

'I can't deny I'm black,' he said, still chuckling a little. 'But as for the rest ... let me give you an example. Back a few months, on March fifteenth, the papers and TV covered the end of the Zebra killers trial – which, as you probably know, concerned a cult of Black Muslims who killed fourteen whites as an initiation rite.'

She nodded impatiently, tried to speak, but he went on.

'It was a Saturday when they were convicted; Sunday when the story hit hard. I was on night tour. I called in sick Saturday. I stayed on sick call, stayed locked in this apartment, for three days. On Tuesday night, I forced myself to face my fellow officers. And even then I could barely look them in the eyes. Is *that* what you mean by black consciousness?'

'*Your fellow officers?*' she shouted. 'What the hell do you think you cops *are*, anyway?'

He shrugged. He was regaining his cool, as she was losing hers.

'Cops are a bunch of generally undereducated, unintellectual, strong-arm clods who if they weren't cops would be gangsters, bouncers, bartenders! They're *low*, Willis! They're the butt of jokes when intelligent people meet! Yet you act as if they're something special!'

'Very special,' he said, certainty returning.

'You actually think cops are *better* than the rest of us?'

He nodded without hesitation. 'Because we do one of the most important jobs – maybe *the* most important – in modern society.'

She couldn't speak for a moment. Then: 'You *dare* compare yourself to ... to a doctor?'

'A doctor saves one person at a time. A cop saves streets, communities. And without milking them dry.'

'Incredible! And I suppose lawyers ...'

243

'Like stickup men, baby. Don't kill you, but strip you naked.' He chuckled. 'Next comparison.'

She stammered in rage. 'What's the use! You're elitist! Fascist! *Mongoloid!*'

'Elitist from elite, yes. The others ... you're too upset to think straight.' He sat down at the table again; began to eat again. 'Mmmm,' he said. 'Good, even though it's cold. You're some sort of cook, know that?'

She left the kitchen.

A while later, as he was finishing his third cup of her coffee, she returned, dressed and carrying her big purse. He rose and spread his hands. 'We just think different,' he said.

She didn't answer.

'Maybe too different to keep seeing each other. Not that I wouldn't like to ... but why continue to quarrel and trade insults?'

'We're both black ...'

'Yeah. A black dog and a black cat.'

'No matter what you say, it's obvious to anyone with a knowledge of history that the U.S. is dying of racism, of the wounds left by slavery and oppression and hatred ...'

'Well, if it *does* die,' he interrupted quietly, 'the best the world has ever known is gone.'

'According to whom?' she asked. 'Thomas Jefferson, or his slaves?'

'How about Eldridge Cleaver? He tried a lot of places, and came back to face the rap in the one country where he felt freedom had a fighting chance.'

'A turncoat,' she said, but said it weakly and walked away immediately.

He followed her through the living room to the front door. 'Thanks for breakfast,' he said.

She stood with her back to him. Her head was down ... and he realized she was crying.

His first instinct was to move to her. But she'd said too many things, and he'd said too many things. 'I'm really sorry, Andra.'

'You ... you're always so *sure!*'

'Aren't you?' he asked, surprised.

244

She left then, surprising him even more with a quick shake of the head.

A complex lady, Miss Andra Stennis. Too complex for Willis Jones.

But later, after cleaning up the kitchen and making the bed, after sitting down with his sample-question booklet for the lieutenant's exam, he suddenly missed her.

A pain in the ass, Miss Stennis. A great piece of ass, Miss Stennis. A mind-blower and a gut-wrencher ... and he'd never been bored a single minute.

Roersch came awake quite suddenly. It was six-thirty.

He got out of bed, careful not to waken Ruthie, and went to the dining room and his folder and the blank D.D.-5's, which he'd thought to fill out at home. But that was before Angie Tortemango's death ... and more importantly, before the black Chevy showed in his rearview mirror. Protection via forms, via words, was no longer possible. A bullet-proof vest made more sense. Finding the person who had stood in that basement entry was the only real protection. Nailing him – or *them* – before *he* was nailed was the only protection.

His pajamas were summer weight, and morning coolness made the apartment comfortable, but he was suddenly flushed with heat, with impatience to get things going. He unbuttoned his top and sat down with pad and pencil and began writing, scribbling in his haste to put down thoughts, glimmerings, bits and pieces of what had been tucked away in the back of his mind since his first day on this case. He was at that moment of quantum leap forward, in that area of instinct, of hunch.

He played his old game of What If, projecting in any and all directions, and quickly moving into the single area that felt right. He played intensely in this area, pausing to wipe sweat from his upper lip several times ... then leaned back, coming to a sudden halt. 'Enough bullshit,' he said, as he always did when the period of raw instinct was cooling, dying.

He tore the sheets of paper from his pad and took them to the kitchen. He poured a glass of cold orange juice and gulped it down and read over his jottings. And shrugged.

Now he had to get back to putting one foot in front of the other. And a moment ago he'd been *flying*.

Now he had to make sure.

He went to the wall phone. This was the day of Captain Worth's funeral. Roersch and M–4 were excused, but Mrs Worth wasn't. Mrs Worth would be suffering today.

It might be just the right moment to ask this of her; perhaps the *only* moment.

He dialed area-code 914 Information: Westchester County. He had Worth's number in his little book in the bedroom. But he didn't want to risk waking Ruthie; didn't want her talking to him and breaking his concentration.

He was given the number and hung up and dialed immediately. The woman answered in a near whisper, but he recognized the voice.

'Mrs Worth, this is Sergeant Roersch. I hope I didn't wake you?'

'No.'

'I won't be at the funeral. I'm still trying to find out who killed your husband. Because none of those three boys did it, despite what you might have read, or seen on television.'

He gave her time to respond. She said nothing, but he heard her breathing, hard.

'Your husband must have had an enemy. If you could give any idea of who it was?'

'Tom told me nothing.'

He was struck by the obvious truth of that statement. Worth would *be* like that.

'If you're in possession of any records, notebooks, personal phone books, address books?'

She was quiet a long moment. Then: 'There *is* a notebook in the safe; one of those dime-store spiral things, if you know what I mean.'

Roersch did. Most police officers of the old school did. It was what they used to list evidence, stoolies, expenses, suspects, dates, times, everything.

'It's in the safe,' she said. 'I simply glanced at it. Just some names, some numbers. But if it will help you ...'

246

'I'd like to drive right over. I can be there in about half an hour, if I beat morning traffic to the parkway.'

'... and not hurt Tom,' she continued, as if he hadn't spoken, 'you may look at it. It's important you understand me, Sergeant. I like what I've seen of you. But I'm burying my husband today, and I won't let you or anyone else hurt him. You can look at the notebook *here*, in front of me. I hope it helps you, but you'll leave without it, if I have to use Tom's service revolver to stop you.'

He believed her. There was a dullness, a pain, a *depth* to her voice that he'd rarely heard. Perhaps once at Sing Sing when he'd spoken to a prisoner about to die in the chair. Perhaps his sister's voice, describing their mother's sudden death. Perhaps Jimmy Weir's, speaking of his Teresa toward the end of his week of suicidal madness.

'I'm leaving now, Mrs Worth. Thank you.'

'Don't thank me. It's for Tom ... so he can rest.'

Roersch dressed in a frenzy of haste, and Ruthie woke and stared bleary-eyed at him. He said, 'Important,' and ran.

He used siren and slap-on roof flasher. He showed a disregard for traffic signals and speed limits dangerous even by police standards.

And behind him was a car as he approached the parkway entrance. Not the black Chevy. A blue Pinto with rental plates that had a hard time keeping up with him, but managed to. With a driver he at first thought was a woman because of long blonde hair. Then he jammed on his brakes to get a closer view, and the Pinto almost hit him, and he saw it was a man with a wig, with a beard, with a mustache, with a raincoat and collar up around his neck, with a wide-brimmed hat which he quickly pulled down.

So it was someone he would have recognized under all that phony hair, all that heavy disguise. He was tempted to give chase as the Pinto swung past him and turned right, *away* from the parkway entrance. If he could catch that car ...

If he could catch that car, what would he have?

A man he knew. Who would give some funny excuse for

his getup. Or pull a gun to kill or be killed, making a fight of it. And either way Roersch would know no more than he did now; could prove no more than he could now. And if there was more than one perpetrator, as there almost certainly had to be, he would be just as far from nailing the other. *Further*, as one piece of the puzzle leading to that unknown would be eliminated.

A waste of time, chasing the Pinto. Better to go on, until he had the whole picture.

Or until they tried to stop him, dead.

He continued on to the parkway, and then to Tarrytown, without a tail.

Mrs Thomas Worth was already dressed – a simple mid-length black dress, black nylons, black shoes. The hat and veil lay on a table in the foyer.

Her children were having breakfast, she informed him. They would all be leaving for the undertaker's at nine; the services were scheduled for eleven and they wanted some time alone with Tom.

He nodded, and followed her to the study he'd seen the first time he'd been here, when the young daughter had shown him around. A beautiful room, with a particularly handsome desk. On it lay a dime-store spiral notebook, opening from the top.

'It's five after eight,' she said. 'I have to help the children, especially my little Rita ...' Her voice broke, but just for an instant. 'You have half an hour.'

He said he didn't think it would take that long. And the phone on the desk rang.

She picked it up and said, 'Hello,' and listened and held the handset out to Roersch. 'For you, Sergeant.'

He blinked, because absolutely no one knew where he was. He took the phone and said, 'Roersch here,' and heard the click. Mrs Worth had walked to a high-backed chair against the bookcase wall, and was sitting down. Roersch held the phone to his ear and said, 'Yes, thank you,' into a dead line, because Mrs Worth had enough to occupy her this morning.

So they knew where he was, even without a tail, guessing

in the area of their strongest fears. He opened the note-book and began reading. Most of it meant nothing.

One or two pages meant quite a bit.

There were names he knew. Names from the precinct Worth had led, a 'pig heaven', as cops called a precinct heavily on the pad. Worth had listed those men, some now powers on the force, who had accepted money under his aegis, or had helped him to collect money under theirs.

He wasn't surprised. He had already made that assumption during his What If game; that's why he was here.

He reached for pen and his own notebook. Mrs Worth said, 'Please don't.'

He didn't really need to. He'd needed only confirmation. A few dates listing particularly heavy payoffs weren't that important to him.

To Worth, they had been very important. Because then he could call on men in high office to support him if the shooflies became too bothersome.

And how those men must have sweated when the Knapp Commission was on Worth's tail! How they must have rooted for their old underling, comrade, or commander ... and how they must have wished him dead.

He rose, leaving the pad on the desk. 'I suggest you tear it up; flush it down the toilet.'

Mrs Worth preceded him to the study door. 'Did you learn anything?' she asked.

'Yes.'

She searched his face. He said, 'Not about your husband.'

She kept searching his face another moment; then nodded, smiling slightly. She retained the smile as she showed him out of the house.

He hadn't lied. He'd learned nothing from the notebook about Tom Worth that he hadn't known since the meeting in Deverney's office.

Deverney, whose name wasn't the only one Roersch had recognized on that pad, but who was definitely the highest in rank.

He drove directly to Manhattan West Homicide. Hank Colburn had just come on duty and took the opportunity to

249

hit the john as Roersch began going through the sign-in-out book. He checked Wednesday and Thursday, then jumped ahead to Saturday. He went back and double-checked and nodded slowly to himself, without satisfaction.

Hank returned and wanted to offer congratulations and talk about M-4, but Roersch walked off with a wave.

He went down to the M-4 squad room. It was nine thirty, and Eli Ross and Paul Lauria were at their desks. But no Jones.

He was immediately worried. 'Did Willis call in this morning?'

Lauria said, 'If one-thirty qualifies, yes. Balleau took a message for you. Willis said the tail entered a house . . .'

Roersch said, 'Give it here,' and took the slip of paper. It read: 'Willis Jones, Tues., July 22, 1:28 A.M. The tail entered a two family house, bell listings – Wilbur Keers and Christopher Moore. No way to determine which apartment entered.' The address of the house, in Queens, followed.

Roersch stuck the note in his pocket and sat down at his desk.

'What case is that?' Lauria asked.

Roersch said, 'An old one,' and picked up his phone.

Lauria's phone rang before Roersch had finished dialing. Lauria said, 'Sergeant, the captain wants . . .'

Roersch held up his hand. 'Be right with him.' He waited as the phone at the other end rang three times. When the voice said, 'Hello?' he sighed in relief. Because he, Roersch, was beginning to know the score and could try to guard himself. Jones, as yet, knew nothing and was in the thick of it by tailing the tail . . . and calling in the message. Roersch now knew he should have had Jones call it in to his home, no matter how late, no matter if Mark would have yelled his eight-month-old head off . . . but that was second-guessing himself.

'Okay, Willis. I know I told you to take a few extra hours. Just wanted to hear your sweet voice.' He swung his chair away from the two young detectives and murmured, 'Watch yourself. Make believe someone's out to blow you away.'

'That tail last night?'

250

'Yes. I don't think they'll do anything in daylight, but I could be wrong.'

'*They?*'

'Later. Get here by one.'

Jones said he'd come right down, if Roersch wanted him to. Roersch said, 'No. Even one might be too early. I want you getting here about when I do. I don't want you getting stuck with any fresh squeals.'

He hung up as Jones began questioning again. He went to Lauria's desk and took the phone. Hawly wanted to know when M–4 could vacate the basement room and get back to their regular desks.

'End of the week okay, Captain? We've got some details to finish up.'

'I don't see *what* details, but all right. Just as long as you get on Angelo Tortemango. You can use one of the thirds. I want Willis for another case.'

'I'd like Willis for Tortemango,' Roersch said, and anticipated Hawly's reply.

'You know I have to split my sergeants and my thirds . . .'

'Until Friday, Captain. Might even be sooner.'

Hawly grunted. 'Don't turn prima donna on me, Eddy. Friday, the very latest.'

Roersch thanked him and hung up. Lauria was turning on the air-conditioning. It was a hot, muggy, overcast day, with rain forecast to break the heat spell later in the afternoon. Roersch hoped the weathermen were accurate for a change. He hoped it wouldn't rain too soon, on Mrs Worth and her children.

Lauria said, 'Got a call from Forensic. Latent Prints made a match on both Radford Johnson and Lester Cole – Radford two partials on Arnold Jaeker's wallet, Lester an almost perfect thumb and index partial on Richard Magris's.'

Eli said, 'So now they can put them away for *two* lifetimes.' He grinned.

Lauria said, 'It *might* be important. We *might* get the death penalty back. Every bit of evidence could help strap those skells into the chair.'

'But once a life sentence has been passed . . .' Eli began.

'If you two squad-room lawyers will shut up,' Roersch said, 'I'll give you your assignments.'

Eli was to question the doorman of the Fifty-second Street building in which the Jaekers had visited; the one with the basement entryway. He was to try and learn if any resident of the house had reported his car damaged by bullets. If he failed to strike paydirt in this most logical of all houses for that car-owner to live, he was to try every doorman on the block. If he still got nothing, he was to do a door-by-door.

'You mean,' Eli said, 'every apartment . . .'

'On the whole fucking street, yes. And where you don't get an answer, you come back later tonight and try again.'

Eli shook his head. 'But what's the point of all this now?'

Lauria said, 'The death penalty, right, Sergeant? Getting more and more evidence in case . . .'

'You got it,' Roersch said. 'And for being so brilliant, here's *your* assignment.' He sent Lauria to the Third Detective Zone to both goose and help John Maugham find the complaint on prowlers in the courtyard of the same Fifty-second Street house. And to get the name of the uniformed officer who had responded to it. 'Don't come back until you have it, Paul. Don't go home, either.'

'A patrolman out of a detective zone?' Lauria asked.

Roersch looked at him a moment. 'They probably referred it to the local precinct. Or the doorman got the story wrong and it was a detective who responded.' He leaned back in his chair. '*Or*,' he said very softly, and didn't finish. Then he reached for the phone. 'Get moving.'

He spoke to Hawly about a contact on the New Jersey police for questioning of Pasquale Tortemango. A New York officer had no jurisdiction in another state, even in Fort Lee, which was just across the Hudson and part of the Metropolitan area.

Hawly referred him to Lieutenant Murray. Murray said he'd have a name and number for Roersch within the hour. 'You want the local cops – Fort Lee? Or the state troopers?'

'I want a very *honest* cop, to throw a little scare into Pasquale. If I get someone in his pocket, I might as well question him by phone.'

Murray said, 'Easier said than done, but we'll try.'

Roersch left the squad room. He hadn't told Eli, but he too was going to East Fifty-second Street. He wanted to walk that basement passageway again. He wanted to unlock those two steel doors and find out where they might lead. He wanted to question the superintendent, Terry. And, as per his instructions from Deverney on handling Worth's murder, do it himself, *personally*.

He smiled a little as he drove away from Manhattan West. He doubted the inspector would approve.

Terry Pomsten was a medium-sized black man, maybe fifty, with a strong chest, shoulders, and arms, the last revealed by his sleeveless underwear-top as he wrestled a full trash can out to the entryway. 'Incinerator does most of the work, but we get between four and six cans of ash and stuff that won't burn every day. And pickup every day too. They'll be here before noon. Now, about that officer was around here three weeks ago ...'

Roersch nodded, feeling fat and out of shape by comparison with this far-from-young man. 'Was he a detective, or in uniform?'

'Uniform, just like I told the doorman. A *cop*, you know.'

Roersch took out his notebook. 'Could you give me the names of the tenants who complained about prowlers in the courtyard?'

'I *could*, if there was any. But there wasn't. This cop just showed up and told the doorman, Bert, he'd been sent about prowlers and could he have a key to the basement doors, to check things out. Bert don't have a key, and sent him to me. I told him I thought he had the wrong house, but he said sometimes people don't like to give their names on a complaint and stuff like that. So I gave him my key. You know, that man was around maybe two minutes. Then I turn my back and he's gone. I didn't get my key until next morning! Lucky it was almost five and I was finished.'

Lucky, or well planned, Roersch thought, and made notes. And was beginning to sweat again, as he had back in his apartment. With excitement. Because he was about to find out how the murderer/murderers had escaped.

He and Terry were talking on the street near the basement entry. He asked for the key to the steel doors. Terry said, 'You're not going to disappear on me like that other officer?'

Roersch said, 'Play safe. Open the doors yourself. Give me a quick tour.'

Terry said, 'Fair enough,' and led Roersch down to the passageway. They approached the first floor, about ten feet from the steps and on the right. As Terry took a key ring from his pocket, Roersch glanced down the shadowy tunnel toward the courtyard, noticing that bare ceiling bulb about halfway between. 'How do you put on that light without a pull chain?'

Terry pointed at the wall a few feet back toward the stairs. 'Switch there, kind of blends in with the concrete.'

Roersch nodded, and followed the super into a gloomy basement that held furnace, laundry room, major plumbing, and the like. He learned that there was a single elevator near the room with washers and dryers, and that anyone who got into the basement could come up into the lobby or the upper floors. 'But no way out 'cept through the lobby, or back into the passageway and out on the street.'

They returned to the passage and walked about halfway down to the second steel door, which was almost even with the ceiling light. 'This is all storage area,' Terry said, opening the door with the same key. They walked inside; Terry threw a switch; four hallways lined on both sides by wooden bins, partitioned areas with doors and padlocks, lay before them. 'Every tenant gets a bin. Nothing much stored here but junk.' He shrugged.

'Is there another way out?' Roersch asked.

'No sir. There's a few small ventilator windows, barred and grilled like no prison you ever seen! Same on the other side. Anyone want to get out of here, they got to use the passageway and the street. Anyone want to come out the other side, they got to use the lobby, or back to the street. That's why we don't have trouble with prowlers.'

Roersch thanked him. They left the storage area. Terry reopened the first door as Roersch headed for the street. Then Roersch stopped. 'Could you describe that officer who borrowed your key?'

Terry spread his hands. 'White. You know how it is with uniforms. You remember them, not the man. Unless the man's sort of special – say mustache or beard or what.'

Roersch climbed the steps to the low ironwork gate.

He tried the doorman, but Bert also said, 'Normal-size, you know. Nothing special. Just a cop.'

Roersch came outside and stood near the entryway. He felt a few light drops of rain, and checked the time. Not yet ten-thirty. Mrs Worth's day was going to be bad all around.

As for *his* day, it wasn't at all bad, so far. He felt he knew how Worth had been stalked and killed, and how his killer(s) had escaped.

The cop had either been a phony – someone in costume – or, more in line with what Roersch had been learning, a patrolman in on the slaying. Which brought all sorts of interesting possibilities to mind in terms of *motive*.

He'd made a copy of the key, and either passed it on to the actual killers, or was one of those killers himself. Again, interesting . . . and frightening, since it indicated an organization; one that used police officers.

He wiped sweat from that sensitive upper lip, remembering with distaste that one of his least favorite presidents often had to do the same.

The killers had known there was a good chance Worth would be on this street late at night. Which meant that they'd seen him here before; felt the odds favored his being here again. Which in turn meant they probably knew he'd been seeing Angie Tortemango.

He rubbed his face. He thought of *motive* . . . and how the killers seemed to have made no attempt to get Worth's envelope of money. And they must have suspected he'd come away from a shakedown.

Cops killing cops. Not for money.

To silence Worth? To keep him quiet forever?

But Worth had lived a long time, and been quiet. There were other officers who had taken and seen others take, and were quiet. Quiet was the *rule*.

So why, suddenly, kill Captain Tom Worth? Not for money . . . and not to keep him quiet . . .

He was getting into fuzzy areas here. Back to one step before the other. Back to how the killers had escaped.

They could have come up into the lobby, and walked out that way. But then there would always be the chance that a tenant would be coming or going and would remember them later . . . no, they were too professional to take such chances. Not when they could stay safely hidden in either basement or storage area – the storage area was best – and come out later, much later, when all was quiet. Perhaps even after sunrise.

He nodded. Coop a while in the storage area; then emerge through the passageway, up the three steps, out the gate and onto the street. Into a rainy Manhattan morning with people going to work and no one the wiser.

Christ, how to get witnesses to *that*!

He heard his name, and Eli Ross was waving from a car across the street. 'Just about to go back to the station, Sergeant. Got your man for you. Only wish it *meant* something.'

Roersch walked over to him. 'You found a car with bullet holes?'

'One bullet hole. Elderly man in the first house this side off Beekman – where Marty Anders lives – said he'd parked right near the spot Captain Worth was killed last Wednesday night. He complained for half an hour about parking regulations . . .'

'Nitty-gritty, Eli.'

'He said he didn't hear the shooting, but maybe three-thirty A.M. he heard sirens and commotion and stuck his head out the window and realized his car was somewhere near where a group of officers was bending over a body. He said some of them were leaning on his car, and he worried about it. He's about seventy, retired, a real sour . . .'

'Eli,' Roersch said heavily, 'if you don't learn to give the facts, I'm going to flop you to street patrol at Fort Apache.'

Eli Ross took out his leather-bound notebook. 'Mr Joel Trammel. Owns a Ford Granada, this year's. Came down about six-thirty, seven, he isn't sure, and examined his car. Found a puncture under the body molding running across the driver's-side door. Which means the side facing north. Which means Ju-Ju Wyins' bullet ricocheted off the brick wall of the apartment house into Mr Trammel's car.'

Roersch nodded, though it hadn't happened that way at all. The bullet had come from the basement entry, passed through Worth, perhaps hitting cartilage, bone, whatever, and *then* struck Mr Trammel's car.

'Thank you, Eli. We'll keep you from Fort Apache for another few weeks, at least.' Eli chuckled. Roersch said, 'Stay put here until I return. Might have something for you to do.' He took Joel Trammel's apartment number and strode east toward Beekman. A few more drops of rain fell, but nothing more. Maybe it would hold off for Mrs Worth.

He didn't think of *Tom* Worth. The man had taken his chances in a dirty business, and been wiped out by something he'd never figured on. Something Roersch couldn't figure either.

Joel Trammel, a sour apple indeed, irascible and bad-tempered in spades, had seen more than a bullet hole in the door of his car.

'Two detectives come out of the basement across there and nod at the patrolman who's standing over that body outline. I try to complain to them about the hole in my car. I ask them who I go to for compensation, and they never look at me, just walk away. I ask the officer, and he says go to my insurance company. Sure! So they can raise my rates!'

Mr Trammel was small, chubby, pink-faced, and if stereotypes held true, should have been the most affable of men. Instead, he was a real prick. Yet Roersch could have hugged him. Because he went on and on, and it was all pure gold.

'Those fools weren't even wearing raincoats or carrying umbrellas. Showers on and off and everyone else . . .'

Because they'd gone into the storage room on a dry night

and either been screwed by a bad weather forecast, or simply slipped up in their otherwise tight plan. It might even have been that they hadn't intended to stay quite so long . . .

But he was wasting himself on this point. He asked the vital question, the question that had him sweating on that upper lip again:

'Could you give a description of either of those men?'

'Why not? *Both* of them, the surly fools! Police like them . . .'

'Are you *certain* they were police officers? After all, they weren't in uniform.'

'You must be joking! I was partners in three bars before I retired. I made a lot of money, and I *paid* a lot of money. And I know a plainclothesman as well as you do!'

'Maybe,' Roersch said, controlling irritation. 'But *I* can't always tell who's a cop and who isn't.'

'Then what were they doing poking around the basement at six-thirty in the morning, behind where a man was killed? *Tenants* don't waste time like that, especially without raincoats or umbrellas when it's pouring. Police officers, running in and out of cars at taxpayers' expense, yes.' He smiled triumphantly; a very unpleasant smile. 'They were either cops, or they were crooks.'

Roersch nodded slowly. Mr Trammel's smile faded.

'You mean they might have been . . . but those blacks . . . how could . . .?'

Roersch asked Mr Trammel if he'd ever heard of a Minolta.

'Of course. It's a Japanese camera. One of the best.'

Roersch said he was right. But that in police terminology, a Minolta was an electronic mechanism made by that same Japanese firm; a machine that used photographs of facial features taken from mug shots, flashing them onto a closed-circuit TV screen as a witness either accepted or rejected them. Little by little, a face could thus be constructed, until the witness was satisfied he was looking at his man. From that, photographs were made, far more accurate and more easily recognizable than police artists' sketches.

'Remarkable,' Mr Trammel said dryly, already beginning

the process of what Roersch thought of as 'I-can't-get-involved,' sometimes called, 'I've-got-no-time.'

'Yes, remarkable. But it rarely works the way it should, because most witnesses can't describe a suspect to save their lives. Now you say you saw both these men at reasonably close range ...'

'Five or six feet,' Mr Trammel interrupted irritably. 'And I could describe them to the glasses on one man's face – tinted like a hippy's, the clown – to the older man's ...'

'If you can, then you're among a tiny minority,' Roersch shrugged. 'Well, it's an expensive business. We'd have to drive you to the Rockland County Sheriff's office in New City, buy you a good lunch, have you take the time of a valuable operator ...'

'You mean with all the taxes we pay they don't have one here in the city?'

'We have machines *similar* in type, Mr Trammel, but the Minolta's the most sophisticated, the best, in my opinion. And the Japanese stopped exporting it for some reason.' He turned to the door. 'Maybe because so few witnesses can serve that sophisticated and accurate a machine.'

'You want pictures of those two men, I'll give them to you! We can be in New City in forty-five minutes, this time of day. It's only thirty or so miles up along the Palisades Interstate Parkway. And I'll get those descriptions down and those pictures made in no time! You walk out of here, I'll report you to ... to the *commissioner*!'

Roersch faced him, holding up his hand. 'All right, Mr Trammel. Not that I think it'll work ...' He held up his hand again as Trammel's face turned deep red. 'May I use your phone?'

'Not to New City, you can't. That's a toll call. You reverse charges ...'

'Local, Mr Trammel.'

He called John Maugham at the Third. Maugham said Lauria had already left with the information.

'Or the *lack* of it, Eddy. We got no complaint from that address on Fifty-second. No prowler complains on that street for over two months, and that one at another house. I

259

even checked the precinct ... no complaint and no cop authorized to check the basement. There's some sort of mistake ...'

Roersch said yes, but knew there wasn't. Far from it. Part of a very tight operation. And under normal circumstances, they'd have gotten clean away with it.

But Deverney had sweated over Worth. And pushed for a solution that would keep his name from popping up in a shoofly investigation. And then, with Ju-Ju dead, with Angie dead, with nothing hitting the fan from Worth's home or estate, he had felt secure and said the case was closed. When he damned well knew it wasn't.

Roersch thought of that as he dialed again; Captain Hawly this time. Mr Trammel muttered about 'using up my local limit'. Roersch asked Hawly to set up an immediate session with the Minolta.

'We have to give them two or three days' notice ...' Hawly began.

'We don't have two or three days,' Roersch said intensely. 'This is a real break and we have to move on it. For a collar and a solved.'

Hawly assumed he was speaking about Tortemango, M–4 having *had* its collars and solveds. 'Christ, I'll have to plead ...'

Roersch said he was sending a witness to New City with Eli Ross, and hung up before Hawly could complete a warning that he might get turned down by the sheriff's office.

He dialed again, and Mr Trammel said, 'They take and take and *take*!'

Roersch got Lieutenant Murray. Murray gave him the name of a Fort Lee officer. 'A lieutenant who would love to see Paddy get it up the ass. Some sort of family problem with drugs, and Paddy's Mr Hard Stuff, as you know. Roy'll try to get a search warrant based on an old drug-storage complaint.'

Mr Trammel put on a natty straw hat and said he was ready. They went downstairs and over to Eli's car. Roersch explained, and finished with, 'Take Mr Trammel to lunch – the best restaurant up there. You got enough cash?'

Eli said he'd manage.

'It'll be replaced, Eli. Now move. And the minute you're done, bring those photographs to me. If I'm not at the station, bring them to my house. Just don't leave them anywhere with anyone but *me*!'

Eli stared at him. 'I *got* it, Sergeant.'

Roersch watched them pull away; then hurried to his car. Fort Lee wasn't his favorite spot in the world. He'd tried living there for a while, and found it had almost as much crowding as Manhattan, with few of the amenities. Nor was his errand of truly vital importance.

Still, he wanted to see Mr and Mrs Pasquale Tortemango for himself; wanted to look at them and talk to them and get whatever feeling he could about them. No confessions or mistakes or breaks could be expected from a Mafia *don* and his wife ... but then again, he didn't care about any of that, because he didn't care who had killed Angie, and that was the crime he felt Pasquale was involved in.

He just wanted to be convinced that Angie and his loving Aunt Maria hadn't had anything to do with *Worth's* death. Wanted to clear that near-to-last area of doubt from his mind.

Because if Angie and Maria *had* panicked, if it was they who were behind the captain's execution, if they'd somehow worked with the men who'd been in that basement entry ...

It would change everything. It would leave him floundering.

VOICE ONE: 'You'd better come wide awake.'

VOICE TWO: 'I wasn't sleeping. I ... I have someone here.'

ONE: 'Don't you *ever* stop?'

TWO: Laughing: 'Not by choice.'

ONE: 'We've got to do it *tonight*.'

TWO: 'You're kidding.'

ONE: 'Get rid of that girl.'

TWO: 'Wait.' Several minutes of silence.

TWO: 'She's in the bathroom. I can see the door from here. We can talk.'

ONE: 'He's going to make us soon. Maybe he has already.'

TWO: Flatly: 'I don't believe it.'

ONE: 'You don't know the man as I do! He spotted two tails. You made it easy for him, using a rookie who was fired after only four months' duty . . .'

TWO: 'I had no choice. Either my Number Three, or *you*. I had to work.'

ONE: 'You can forget work. Our necks are on the line. Call in sick. Tell your Number Three to stand by. We've got to get Roersch before morning. One more day and he'll have enough to go to his captain, if he doesn't already.'

TWO: 'And how do we do it? Walk into the station house and shoot him?'

ONE: 'The man travels through the city. We'll get him the way we got Worth and Albony. At night. On the street; in a lobby; in his garage . . . wherever we can catch him.'

TWO: 'He's not a swinger, Mr Washington.'

ONE: Irritable: 'Forget that Washington crap. If we're not quick, *these* founding fathers will end in prison.'

TWO: 'Then how do we proceed? Car tailing is going to be impossible. Once Number Three fucked up, Roersch was watching and made me real quick in that Pinto. I thought he'd go for me.'

ONE: 'The fact that he didn't shows the way he thinks. We can tail him, even if he spots us. Put Number Three in another car, for after-dark tailing. You float around between his house, the station, and the basement on Fifty-second where he spends so much time. I'll work the phone, the way I did when he lost you and went to Worth's house. The odds are he won't go for your Number Three, even if Three does his usual lousy job. He doesn't want one man giving him explanations he can't disprove, or shooting it out with him. He wants as many men as there are.' Pause. 'He wants *me*.'

TWO: 'Ever think of asking him to join us?'

ONE: 'Constantly, the last two days. It would solve everything.'

TWO: 'Then why not try?'

ONE: 'Because it entails my confessing accessory to

murder!' Long pause. 'Well, if we get the time before blow-ing him away ...'

TWO: 'I still don't see how we're going to set him up this fast. Like I said, he doesn't date other broads, or go out drinking, or have a dog he walks, or do anything much. He does go out to dinner, but always with his wife.'

ONE: 'Wife or not, he gets it the first time he puts his nose out on a dark street.'

TWO: 'With her there?'

ONE: 'With her getting it too, so there won't be a close-up witness.'

TWO: 'Damn, that's rough!'

ONE: 'No great loss, that ex-hustler.'

TWO: 'His wife was a *whore*?'

ONE: 'It's not important. Only one thing is important: we silence him before he has time to blow the whistle on us. Which means *tonight*, if we have to knock at his apartment door.'

TWO: Brief laugh. 'Yeah, sure.'

ONE: 'I mean exactly what I say. If no other means presents itself before Wednesday sunrise, that's what we do. Because he won't expect it. Because if I come to his door, he'll open it. And there we'll be.'

TWO: Shaken: 'God!'

Roersch and Lieutenant Roy Apner walked through the lower part of Paddy Tortemango's house, opening a drawer here and looking behind a vase there, as Paddy muttered disgustedly and his bodyguard, an ape named Rick, watched impassively. *Mrs* Tortemango had been in the dining room, dining, when they arrived, but she quickly went upstairs. A most impressive specimen of femininity, Maria Tortemango, especially in the mammaries, and Roersch was properly impressed.

As they came through french doors onto a terrace with a large pool beyond, Roersch put his arm around Roy Apner's shoulders. The Lieutenant was about six-four and string-bean lean; he looked like one long piece of rawhide. Roersch murmured to Apner. Apner said, 'Sure,' and turned to Paddy and Rick. 'I want to ask you two some questions,' he said, and motioned at four wicker chairs and a love seat.

Paddy, short and blocky and bald, and very annoyed, said, 'I'll stand.'

Apner said, 'You'll sit, or would you rather I got a crew together and tore this place apart cushion by bed by dresser by ...' He was waving the search warrant as he spoke, and his voice was very hard, with an undercurrent of pure hatred. Paddy and Rick both took chairs.

Apner said, 'Sergeant Roersch, check the upstairs for me, please.'

Rick began to rise. Apner said, 'Sit *down*, damn you!'

Rick wasn't impressed with the hatred. It would take an *army* to impress the monstrous bodyguard. But Paddy said, 'Let him go, Rick. The lawyer's on the way. Besides, what have we to hide, good union leaders like us?'

Apner smiled. Paddy smiled. Rick lowered his massive frame back into the chair and didn't smile.

Roersch went up a long flight of stairs and looked in a guest bedroom and a bathroom and then another bedroom. The door to the third bedroom, the master, furthest on the right, was closed. He tried the knob. Locked. A woman's voice called, 'Paddy?'

Roersch grunted.

The woman said, 'You're not Paddy. How *dare* you come up here!'

Roersch spoke in a loud voice, spacing his words carefully for maximum clarity. 'I've got a New York City Police report on a motel raid in which you and your nephew Angelo ...'

By that time footsteps had raced across the room and the door was being flung open. Maria Tortemango wore a low-cut white blouse and tight white chino-style slacks. Long red hair at one end and high-heeled red shoes at the other completed the picture of a very sexy woman. Very frightened, too.

She stepped past him and looked down the stairs.

Roersch came inside. There was a chair against one wall,

a door leading to a dressing room and a bathroom beyond on the opposite wall. Roersch went to the chair. Maria Tortemango seemed to flinch. Roersch looked at the chair, bent to the cloth seat, touched several brown stains. And looked up at Maria ... who was no longer flinching; *determinedly* no longer flinching.

Roersch sat down. He glanced around and said, 'Very nice. This house must be worth close to half a million.'

'You're short two hundred thousand. There's a guest house, and a tennis court ...'

'Marvelous. I wonder how many kids shooting H pay the mortgage. And how many hookers pay the taxes. And how many busted heads ...'

'I'm not interested in finances,' she interrupted. 'What you were saying about me and Angie ...' Her eyes darted to the door, left open. 'Are you asking ... is it money again?'

Roersch shifted weight in the chair, gripped the arms, looked down at it. Then suddenly contorted his face, wrenching his mouth open as far as he could, sticking out his tongue and bugging out his eyes.

She'd been standing near him. She jumped back, hand rising to her mouth. *'Stop!'* She began to cry.

Roersch smiled pleasantly. 'I figure Angie died somewhere in this house. Could have been right here, in this chair. Do I win the prize?'

'I don't know what ...' She shook her head, wiped at her eyes, began over again.

Roersch said, 'Forget it. I don't care where he died. But I think we both know *why*. Because Paddy found out about you and Angie. How'd you manage to get off the hook?'

She was in control again. 'I haven't the faintest idea ...'

'Does Paddy know you were fucking Angie for *months*?' He was guessing, but it was a good guess; the odds favored its being true. And her fear flashed a signal that it *was* true, and that Paddy had been given a different story.

'And in that same motel?' Risky, but she had moved to the bed and sat down, head in hands. 'And that we have samples of his handwriting from the register?'

'I don't have much money,' she said, through those hands.

'Paddy gives me enough for clothes and a few extras. He buys all the expensive items himself. It'll take me some time to arrange ... I can sell my rings and say they were stolen.'

'A minute ago you asked me, "Is it money again?" *Again.* That was Captain Worth. Angie was paying him.'

She nodded. 'Paddy thinks because Angie drugged me and took me to that motel once ...' She was whispering and kept glancing at the door, and froze, thinking she heard someone.

'Relax,' Roersch said. 'The lieutenant won't let anyone interrupt us. So Paddy let you off because he either bought that being-drugged story, or figured once was not enough.' He liked his little joke, though he was beginning to feel this was a waste of time.

'Or,' he said, 'you turned things around somehow. You went from Angie's side to Paddy's side. You helped husband eliminate lover, and earned your life.'

She was staring at him. He said, 'There are only so many possibilities.'

'But what is it you *want*?'

'The truth about how Angie killed Thomas Worth.'

'How Angie killed ...' She rose. She shook her head until the red hair flew. 'No! That's wrong! We were terrified of a letter ... we would never ... please don't think that and think I'm lying and show Paddy the proof about the Don Juan Motel! *Please!* He'll ... I swear it, he'll kill me!'

'Like he killed Angie?'

She nodded. 'But I'll never say it!'

He rose. He believed her. And he was already thinking of something else.

Without asking permission, he went to the princess phone on the bedside table and dialed New York's area code 212 and Jones's number. 'Willis, I want you to check the names of the tenants in that Queens two-family house. You know, Keers and Moore. Try Known Criminals File. And then ...' He stopped. 'I'll explain everything later tonight, so just listen. And then try the five-borough police roster at Headquarters. Members present, and past.'

Maria Tortemango stopped him on the way to the door. 'What are you going to tell Paddy?'

'Nothing.' He went into the hall.

She ran after him, grabbing his arm, whispering. 'But I still don't know what you *want*!'

'You never will,' he said, and wondered what another cop might do to this piece of baggage.

He made a decision then, figuring what the hell, and took the D.D.–5 from his breast pocket. He showed it to her, tore it up, and put the pieces in her hand. 'Go to the bathroom, auntie.' Before he reached the bottom of the stairs, he heard the toilet flush.

He walked to the terrace. 'All clear upstairs,' he said, and sat down with Apner, Paddy, and Rick. 'Did you kill Angelo?' he asked Paddy.

Roy looked at him. Paddy laughed. Rick smiled a small smile made even smaller by his big face.

'Answer the question,' Roy finally said.

'No,' Paddy said.

Roersch asked it of Rick.

'No,' Rick said.

Roersch stood up. 'That's what I was sent to do,' he said, and walked to the front door.

Roy followed. They heard Paddy laughing as they stepped outside. Roy Apner said, '*That*'s what I got a search warrant for? That's what I pushed a judge . . .?'

'No,' Roersch said. 'I got what I wanted, upstairs. You helped the New York City Police plenty today.'

Apner looked back at the house as they stood near their cars. 'I'd give my life to send him away!'

'That's about what it would take, Lieutenant.'

'But *someone's* got to rid us of scum like that! My own brother, ruined by a needle . . . by Tortemango.'

They were both quiet. Roersch felt he had to say something comforting. 'Every so often they kill each other. Someday, Roy, you and I will figure a way to start them doing it on a big scale.'

Roy smiled. Roersch shook his hand, thinking it might be more than just a placating word for a nice cop; might even

be possible. If what Jimmy had said at dinner had been true
- that Worth and Angie and Albony had been killed by
racketeers trying to bring down the Tortemangos and other
Mafia fat cats in order to step into their action – If that had
been the case, Roersch might have walked away from it all,
waiting for the war to take *more* scum.

But it was too simple and too pat and Jimmy didn't believe it and didn't expect Roersch to.

He waved and drove toward the George Washington
Bridge.

Some day, when pipe dreams came true, he might step
outside the law and along with a few good cops start a war
amongst the rats, the racketeers, the Mafiosi, that would fill
the cemeteries and clear the streets . . .

He'd been reaching for his wallet as he approached the
toll booths. He slowed, held his breath, let the thought
expand . . . let the pieces fall into place.

Horns blasting behind him, a voice shouting in his open
window, brought him out of it. He paid and went over the
bridge. And knowing what he now knew, wondered if he
had any time left at all.

Back at the M–4 squad room, Willis was waiting. Also
waiting were a dozen telephone messages – from Ruthie and
reporters and Eli and Jimmy and Deverney. Deverney's was
URGENT.

He read Eli's. It said, 'Minolta in use by Brooklyn officers.
I might be late.'

He put the others aside. He didn't return Deverney's call,
despite that URGENT.

He asked Willis about the search for Wilbur Keers and
Christopher Moore.

'It was Keers,' Willis said. 'Keers followed you, and I
followed Keers. He was a cop, Eddy. A rookie cop, until one
of the early cutbacks.' He kept looking at Eddy; kept waiting.

'I'm going to take you to lunch, Willis, but no questions.
Eli's coming back with two pictures. *Then* I'll tell you. Because someone out there doesn't like me, and I need help.

FOURTEEN

Wednesday, July 23

Roersch approached the basement entry. It was a few minutes after two A.M. and the rain that had been threatening all day was finally coming down. He wore his raincoat and old hat and remembered his first day on this case; it had been raining then too. Pausing, he took his gun from his hip holster and put it in the coat pocket.

He opened the wrought-iron gate. Dark down there, and seemingly as deserted as the storm-swept street. Deserted for now, that is . . . but not for long. Because he'd been tailed, badly, blatantly, when he'd left the station for home at seven P.M., after Eli finally arrived with the composite photographs. Been followed just as blatantly from his home to within a few blocks of here, where he'd zigzagged around the streets a little and either lost the tail or made him give up.

He closed the gate behind him, to allow for some warning sound if anyone did show up, and walked down the three stone steps . . . and immediately realized he wasn't alone. His heart began to pound heavily. He made out one dark shape opposite the first door, leaning against the wall on his left. He stopped and flattened against the wall on his right, feeling around behind on the rough concrete. And saw a second shape further down the passage, moving from Roersch's side to the opposite side. Now both shapes were on the left wall . . . and had an oblique angle of fire at him.

'You moved fast,' Roersch said, judging the distance to that second shape, its position in relation to the ceiling bulb. 'I thought I'd beat you here, but that tail must have had a radio car. And it wasn't too difficult to guess where I was going, was it, Jimmy?'

Laughter came from the first shape. Jimmy Weir said, 'What did I tell you, Harry? You wondered why we had to be running around in the rain. He made us days ago.'

269

Roersch said, 'No,' still figuring distances, his heartbeat not quite as heavy now. 'It could have been Deverney. But then I got two Minolta photographs, and even though they're far from perfect ...'

'That old bastard,' Harry Balleau said from beside the second door. 'The one whose car got hit.'

'You're a great shot, Harry. You've got citations for marksmanship. Want to let Forensic run ballistics tests on the slug from Worth's mouth and your gun?'

Balleau said, 'Wouldn't be conclusive.'

'You were out sick Wednesday night. I checked the precinct book. You were off duty Saturday night. Opportunity, ability, and ballistics.'

'And me?' Jimmy asked. 'What have you got on your old friend? Who advised you to protect yourself with D.D.–5's on Worth?'

'Yes, one set to you, and a backup set in my desk, where Harry could clean them out.'

Jimmy chuckled.

Roersch said, 'Harry phoned me at Mel's Steak House when we were having dinner Sunday night. To tell me about Angie Tortemango's body being found. I didn't tell him or anyone else where I was going. You were the only one who knew, the only one who could have told him, and you played dumb about Harry ... even as to where he was stationed. "Whatever happened to him?" you asked, and why lie about a thing like that?'

Jimmy said, 'I told you Harry. We should have done this Sunday night, right after I left him.' He paused. 'I'll bet you don't have *one* thing, Eddy.'

Eddy moved a little, back toward the stairs, left hand feeling the concrete wall. Jimmy said, *'Don't,'* and metal glinted in his hand.

From Harry Balleau's position came the soft *click* of a revolver's hammer being snapped back.

Roersch stopped moving. 'What don't I have, Jimmy?'

'*Motive*. Not that you'd need it. Not that it will stop us from what we have to do. But you're not *that* good, Eddy.'

'How about wiping out a bad mark? Worth was your

270

captain ten years ago in that pig heaven precinct. And Harry's. And mine. You went on the pad. So did Harry. Your names were in Worth's book. Or did you suspect that, when you or Harry called me at Mrs Worth's this morning?'

'*I* called you,' Jimmy said. 'Just to know where you were. As for being in Worth's book, being on the pad . . .' His voice turned harsh. 'Five lousy months, because my sister was too dumb to carry medical insurance, and her kidney operation and expenses afterwards . . . you remember, Eddy. But do you know what a dialysis machine costs? Seventeen months? Do you know how much money I spent, and how little I took on the pad? Just enough to get out of debt. Now she cooks me dinner once a week instead of rotting in Marymount Cemetery with our mother.'

'I took because Jimmy was my lieutenant,' Balleau said, then chuckled. 'And because three different broads a week costs, baby. I went along, for the same five months. But that's not why we blew away Worth. And you'll never guess it.'

'How about being the good guys who eliminate the bad guys?'

Both Jimmy and Balleau stayed silent. Roersch probed the darkness beyond Balleau, where faint gray light was the courtyard archway.

'How about doing what the law couldn't do? The daydream cops have had since the beginning of the force. Vigilantes. Wipe 'em out when the courts can't.'

Jimmy said, 'That's very good,' voice quiet. 'If you know that, you know that the Hit Squad is your kind of people.'

'Hit Squad,' Roersch repeated. 'Catchy, but still against the law.'

'*For* the law. We're just beginning. There are dozens on our list. Scumbags, Eddy. Skells. In high positions. Bad guys in good-guy hats, who think they can't be touched. Who play ball with the rackets. Who make the rackets *strong*. We're going to get them, Eddy, every one. Then we'll hit the Mafia, the other trash. And after we clean out this city, we'll move nationally, bringing justice . . .'

Eddy couldn't let that word go by unchallenged. '*Justice?*

271

That means working with rules agreed on by a majority of the people, in public. You can't go public, Jimmy, so you have no justice. You have a conspiracy. *I'm* justice here. You and Harry are just plain perpetrators.' And as he spoke he moved a few more inches . . . and found what he was looking for.

Jimmy said, 'You can't get out that way. Your tail . . .'

'You mean Wilbur Keers, ex-cop?'

Balleau said, 'Jesus!'

Jimmy raised his voice. 'Wilbur, come down two of those three steps.'

The wrought-iron gate opened. A big man made even bigger by a long raincoat came down and sat on the second step. His gun was out. 'Well,' he said, 'there'll soon be another opening on the force. Maybe I'll get it.'

Roersch's heart was hammering again, because the odds were getting bad and he worried about Jones and he worried about himself.

'Was Keers in on Worth?' he asked, hoping that he could talk them into a collar . . . and knowing there was no way . . . and trying to put death off another few minutes. 'Was he the patrolman who got the key to these doors?'

Balleau said, 'That was Schwin, another ex-cop. He was my backup on the Albony hit.'

'Harry!' Jimmy snapped.

'Well, he's not getting out of here unless he's with us right?'

'A good officer doesn't give evidence away! No matter what the situation!'

'You mean a smart bad guy,' Roersch said. 'Officers don't worry about things like that.'

'I'm not going to give you a big sales talk,' Jimmy said. 'You've guessed what we are. The Hit Squad's the beginning of a national movement. The army is discredited since Vietnam. The Feds are too square, and too tightly controlled by congressional committees watching their every move. Besides, who patrols the streets, the cities, the towns? The *police*, Eddy. We're the only ones who can do the job, first in small squads, like ours, undercover. Then in larger units, coming into the open all over the country.'

'Cops' pipe dreams,' Roersch said. 'You can never come into the open, never become a national force, unless you first destroy the way we now live. The Constitution forbids . . .'

'All reform movements are pipe dreams, at first. All successful revolutions, including ours against the British, break existing laws.'

'Okay,' Roersch said, beginning the last play. 'What if I say I'll join you?'

Jimmy didn't answer.

Balleau said, 'Captain, if he means it . . .'

'Too late,' Jimmy said, voice dull. 'I can't make a decision like that. Can't take the chance, the responsibility . . .'

'But why not?' Balleau interrupted. 'You're Number One. I'm Number Two. If we say so it *is* so. Roersch can be right up there with us. Third in command. Christ, he'd be so useful!'

'Didn't you listen to what he said a moment ago?' Jimmy's voice remained dull, and Roersch knew his old friend was getting close to the painful decision.

Roersch said, 'Give me a minute, Jimmy. I'm considering it.' And knew that Jimmy knew he was lying. Because disregarding all other reasons, how could he walk out of here with the Hit Squad and their pipe dreams when it meant letting a case go down the drain? A case this big, this complicated? A case he'd cracked?

He simply couldn't let his collar, his solved get away!

And said, 'If I knew a good cop like Willis Jones could join with me . . .'

'We have a dinge on the squad,' Balleau said.

'We're not racist,' Jimmy said. 'We're elitist.'

Roersch had to bring things to a head. The odds no longer mattered. Jimmy wouldn't let him walk out of here anyway. He called, 'Willis, get ready!'

Jimmy jerked forward, looking around. Balleau said, 'He's bluffing!' Roersch said, 'If you'd had time to check the courtyard . . .' Jimmy said, 'Stay put, Harry!'

And no voice called from the courtyard. And Jones had to be afraid, as Roersch was afraid as any sane man would be afraid. And Jones had heard that the Hit Squad wasn't racist, was elitist, and might believe it. And Jimmy would accept Jones where he couldn't accept Roersch, a man he knew too well.

And time had run out.

Roersch said, 'Jimmy, if you didn't actually take part in a physical homicide ...'

'I was with Harry, right here, the night he killed Worth. I gave him the order to fire. I named Albony as the next subject.'

Roersch gulped air. Jimmy's gun seemed to be moving out from his body catching what little light came from the entry. A hissing, rushing sound from the street made them all tense – the rain had become a downpour. Keers was beginning to rise into a crouch, both hands on his gun. Roersch prayed, *Willis get off the dime!* and clutched for the last few seconds.

'Jimmy, Harry, Keers, I arrest you for the murders of Captain Thomas Worth and Terrence Albony and order you to drop your weapons and put ..'.

He drew then, twisting towards Keers because he had to cover his back first, and fired. The explosion was incredibly loud inside the concrete tunnel, and he heard no groan, no scream and Keers still seemed to crouch. Without being sure he'd scored a hit, he jerked around toward Jimmy, bellowing, *'Willis!'*

And saw three flashes from around Jimmy's middle, and heard the deafening, reverberating roar, and felt a hammer blow in his right thigh.

With his left hand still behind him on that light switch, still poised over the lever, he said, 'Christ!' and slid down to the floor, throwing the ceiling bulb on. The tunnel was illuminated ... *glaringly* ... over Harry Balleau.

Balleau was crouching, aiming at Roersch in the approved police manner, gun extended in both hands, ready to fire. But he squinted in the sudden glare. Roersch had no time for him; he fired twice across at Jimmy. The captain, in full uniform as always, proud of being a cop as always, seemed to explode around the lower chest, pieces of uniform and flesh and blood blowing outward. And fragments of lead ricocheting off the wall bounced into him, so that he jerked first back then forward, arms flapping.

Roersch ducked as low as he could, trying to turn toward Harry, seeing Jimmy falling, more uniform and flesh and blood splattering out of him. Jimmy's face was a child's face, filled with wonder, with surprise.

Roersch tried to aim at Harry then, and knew it was too late. He heard Keers sucking air, moaning. He heard Balleau say, 'Good-bye, you sonofa ...'

Jones stepped out of the courtyard. 'Harry, one move. Just one. I promise you a very slow death.'

From the entry, a shot sounded. Roersch saw Willis crouch and aim, and turned to see Keers leaning against the wall, clutching his bloody groin with one hand, firing blindly, stupidly down the passageway.

The roar and echo of gunfire was stupefying. Roersch tried to get off a shot of his own, and saw it wasn't necessary. Keers had slammed back against the steps. He slid down, sitting there, his head sagging ... or what was left of it. A bullet had caught his right eye.

Balleau was standing with hands high, and empty. 'Don't shoot, Willis! For the love of God, we're buddies!'

Jones came toward him, gun extended. 'Sure, you and the *dinge*, buddies.' He bent and picked up Balleau's gun. He looked down the passageway. 'Eddy,' he said, voice changing, 'if you're dying, I'm going to kill him.'

Balleau babbled. Out of the babbling came promises of names. 'The whole fucking lower echelon, Willis ... everyone beneath me ... I got the names of two Jimmy doesn't know about! They'll give you more ... just let me talk! If Eddy's dying, it was Jimmy did it, not me! I never fired ...' He began to gag, to vomit.

Roersch didn't blame him. The place was a butcher shop. He said, 'Bring him here, Willis, where I can cover him. Then use your notebook for those names.'

'You need an ambulance.'

'It's a clean wound. Didn't hit bone or artery. Get those names.'

'I'll just call ...'

'Your notebook, *now!*' Roersch snapped. He couldn't add, 'Before Balleau loses the panic of this bloodbath. Before the law he ignored comes to his aid with the Fifth Amendment and rights and lawyers; with everything the Hit Squad pissed on.' What he did say was, 'The longer you wait, the more I bleed.'

Jones shoved Balleau forward. Eddy raised his gun as Jones put his away. He found it difficult, and he found it painful. Not his leg; his chest. Just trying to breathe...

He heard Jimmy say, 'Teresa,' once, twice, maybe a third time into the pavement before raising his head and making a belching sound.

Jimmy's head fell with a thunk. Looked like no more Jimmy; no more pain over Teresa. And maybe that runaway wife had been the *real* reason for the Hit Squad. Maybe all the political theory was shit and Jimmy had been striking out at a world that refused to give him what he most wanted.

Roersch felt sick about Jimmy.

Roersch felt sick, period.

So fucking hard to *breathe.*

Willis wrote. The gun in Roersch's hand was too heavy. Felt like fifty pounds. A hundred pounds...

He dropped it. He screamed and forgot the Hit Squad and collars and solveds and everyone but Edmund Roersch. Whose heart was being crushed in a vise.

He didn't pass out. Not that he knew of, or all the way, or for long. He saw Willis cuffing Balleau, and then he didn't see anything but pavement close up, and then he didn't see.

He was being moved. He was being taken somewhere in a squad car, siren whooping, whooping. Never got used to that new sound as opposed to the old wailing...

Not a squad car. An ambulance. Oxygen mask on his face. Chest being crushed and his father had died this way and he was his father's son and he would never see his own sweet son again. He knew he was dead, and descending darkness confirmed it.

A room. White ... bright ... people rushing past, forward and backward.

No, *he* was rushing ... on a wheeled table.

Black man in white coat bending over him, putting needle into him.

Darkness.

White woman with twisted face looking at him through strange fog.

Ruthie. Ruthie seen through a fog.

He tried to raise his arm. It was full of needles attached to tubes. And pads on his chest. And an oxygen tent of clear plastic around him, which was the fog.

He looked at his wife and she didn't know it. She stood far back from him, near the door, that young woman with the twisted, tear-streaked face.

Then she turned and almost ran from the room. He tried to call her. Instead, a black woman in a nurse's hat came. 'My wife,' he said, wanting someone to hold onto; to say good-bye to.

'She'll be right back. Try to be calm. Try to breathe easy. You know how important it is, don't you, Sergeant?'

He said yes. She bent lower, where he couldn't see; she bent past the plastic tent which covered him to the waist. He felt his right thigh being touched. No pain, though he'd been shot there. No pain, except in the chest.

Not much pain there either anymore, but a *feeling*, a feeling he'd never experienced. His heart beat slowly, heavily, erratically, with an underlying ache that promised eternity.

One wrong beat, he knew. One missed beat, he knew.

He mustn't think that way. Because thinking that way made the fear rise and the heartbeat more erratic.

Made death come even closer.

Willis Jones had much to do. Booking Balleau, and getting Hawly out of bed and down to the station. No way he could handle this alone: a list of five active officers and one ex. Plus the dead – Jimmy Weir and Wilbur Keers. And Harry Balleau, screaming for a lawyer now.

'Where's Eddy?' Hawly asked.

Jones told him, voice straining, but not shaking. Never again shaking.

He'd found out about himself in that courtyard. He'd

277

been the safest of all, and he'd been terrified. Shooting from cover wouldn't have answered his questions. And he couldn't live, couldn't ever write or talk to Pop again, without knowing whether he was what he'd always thought he was ... or what Andra had said:

'*Feets, do yo' stuff!*'

Hearing Captain Weir say they weren't racist but *elitist* had given him as big a way out as Andra had.

But Eddy had fired and there were no more excuses. And Willis Jones had stepped from cover and become what he'd always known he was – a good cop.

He worked with Hawly and with Lieutenant Murray, and then with a member of Headquarters Internal Security. They weren't happy about bad-guy cops, about forthcoming publicity, but they were impressed with the collar.

They said it was a *big* case; he'd done a *tremendous* job. He said, 'Christ, not me! Eddy Roersch!'

They told him yes, they knew, but him too. They told him to go home and rest. Because while his voice didn't shake, his hands did. For Eddy. Who was dying ... maybe already dead?

He ran to a phone. He called Eddy's home, hoping for a miracle – that he'd be there, resting, no real problem ...

Ruthie answered. His heart leaped with joy. He asked for Roersch.

She said, 'Here? He's ... he's in the hospital. A heart attack. He looked ... so *terrible*. He's dying, Willis!' She began to cry, hysterically.

He waited, impatient to speak again. He said he'd pick her up and they'd go to Flower Fifth Avenue together, which was the name on that ambulance. She said, 'I can't! I have to take care of my children! Later ...' Crying, she hung up.

He was soaked with perspiration ... and with Eddy's blood too, gotten after he'd put him on his back and run for help. He couldn't go to the hospital this way.

He drove home, using siren and slap-on roof light. He ran to his apartment and washed and was changing when he heard the doorbell. No time, dammit!

But it rang and rang, and he opened the door.

It was Andra. She said, 'I wanted to . . .'

'Not now. Roersch is very sick. I have to go.'

He ran back to finish dressing. She came to the bedroom. 'We have to talk, Willis. About *your* life, *my* life, not some stranger's.'

He had finished and was striding past her. He stopped. 'That stranger saved my life. Twice, really. Once from a bullet. And last night from something almost as bad – killing self-doubt. If you cared anything for me, you'd care for him.'

She was held a moment by his eyes, his *look*. Then she began to say something about, 'White masters . . .' and he left.

Driving toward the hospital, he realized she was full of grand generalizations, that little black chick, and life was made up of specifics, of unique relationships, one on one. Like his with Roersch. His with Deverney. And his with Radford.

She'd said she had to talk about his life, her life . . . and she didn't know what the word *life* really meant. Life was what his friend Eddy was fighting for, breath by breath.

If his friend hadn't already lost the fight.

At the hospital they tried to stop him downstairs, and again near Eddy's room. He used his badge, and at one point he drew back his fist on a big, surly orderly – who decided not to risk it.

A nurse finally said, 'All right! Only his family should be here, but until the doctor throws you out personally . . .'

She took him to the room, where Willis finally understood Ruthie's words. Roersch *did* look terrible. His hair was plastered damply against his big head. His beard showed gray against mottled, splotchy skin. His mouth gaped open, gasping for air. His eyes were closed, the lids trembling. Everything sagged.

Willis stared, wanting to do what Ruthie had done – run and hide. This *couldn't* be Sergeant Edmund Roersch!

But it was, and he drew a chair up to the bed.

Later, he realized Eddy was looking at him. He said, 'We got the case solved, Sergeant. Balleau spilled and another

279

two members of the Hit Squad spilled and we collared all six of them, not counting Jimmy, Harry, and Keers. Which seems to be the lot.'

Eddy nodded slightly. 'Is Jimmy dead?' he asked in a weak, rustling voice.

'Yes. Keers too. But Harry Balleau was in fine voice.'

Roersch closed his eyes. Willis sat and waited. He wanted to put his hand under the plastic – wanted to touch Eddy – but was afraid he'd disturb the tent, a tube, something.

Eddy slept. Willis went to the john. Returning to the room, he met the doctor coming out. 'How's he doing?' he asked.

'Holding his own,' the stocky young man said. 'For a severe myocardial infarction, that is. He could use company. Does his family know he's here?'

'*I'm* his family,' Willis said, daring the white man to laugh with a flinty look.

The doctor didn't laugh. 'Then get in there. Don't be pushed out by the night shift. Tell them Dr Werner said you could stay until it's over, one way or another.'

Willis said, 'Thanks,' and went back to the bed. And sat. And dozed.

He heard Roersch say, 'Ruthie?'

Willis looked through the plastic tenting. 'She's finding someone to take care of the kids. Your son's too young to leave with just anyone.'

Roersch spoke in his weak, rustling voice. 'I scared her. She didn't turn out to be much for the nitty-gritty, did she?'

Willis said, 'Well, I didn't turn out to be much for the nitty-gritty either, my first shot at it in that Harlem hallway. But you gave *me* a second chance.'

Roersch looked at him for what seemed a long time, then nodded. 'Yeah. She's young, and with two kids to support ...' He swallowed dryly.

'You're going to make it, Eddy. The doctor said so.'

Roersch smiled slightly.

'Well, he said you were holding your own. *I* say you're going to make it.'

280

Roersch smiled again, a little wider, a little more like his real smile.

Without thinking about it, Willis put his hand under the tent, taking Roersch's hand. Roersch closed his eyes, and they remained that way.

Later, he found Roersch looking at their hands.

Black hand, white hand.

Later, as Roersch slept, he too looked at their hands.

White hand, black hand.

The light faded from the room. The color faded from those hands. The men slept, one in the bed and the other in the chair.

At nine, the doctor – who'd looked in earlier and told the night nurse to 'leave things just as they are' – returned and put on the lights. He checked his patient, and said, 'I think we've got it made.'

Willis left, telling Eddy he'd be back in a few hours.

He went home, where he found a note on the kitchen table.

Thank you for the love, and for all you taught me about differences between blacks. And especially about the black police mentality. You *are* black, aren't you? No offense intended, and none taken, knowing you. But from now on, Willis, stick to your own kind. If you ever find out what that is. Andra.

He threw it in the garbage can under the sink, and dialed Ruthie's number. She answered after eight rings, voice sounding dull, drugged. He said, 'Eddy's much better. You'll be surprised if you go to see him.'

Her voice came alive. 'Oh, I'm so glad! And I will ... soon. I just got in touch with my mother. I'll take the children there. She lives in Queens, so it might be a while.'

'Okay. I'll tell him that.'

She was quiet a moment. 'I'm ashamed of myself, but I couldn't face seeing him that way – so *old*-looking; so *sick*-looking.' She took a deep breath. 'Do you think he hates me for it?'

281

'No way! But he does need you.'

'Tell him I'll be there later tonight. Tell him . . ; well, I'll tell him myself.'

Willis went to the kitchen. He made a lettuce and tomato sandwich . . . and fished Andra's note from the garbage. He smoothed it out and read it again. And thought that if she really wanted to end things, she'd simply have left.

And she had never simply left; always worked him over . . . as she'd done in her note.

He folded the sheet of paper and put it in his wallet. He had the damnedest feeling that he was close to changing her. A hunch. A gut reaction. Something a good detective relied on.

He went to the bedroom closet for his exercise equipment. Time to get back on the old schedule, now that M–4 was finished. He worked out with barbells, handgrips, and torsion bar, plus sit-ups and push-ups, for almost an hour.

It was ten-thirty when he came out of the shower. He dressed and slipped his off-duty automatic into his leg holster and checked himself out in the bathroom-door mirror. 'Feets,' he said, 'do yo' stuff!' And went to sit with Eddy.

EPILOGUE

New Voice ONE: 'Hello?'

New Voice TWO: 'It's me, boss. Thought I'd better check in.'

ONE: 'You could have waited more than four days, considering that goddam mess. Still, we have to start reorganizing sooner or later.'

TWO: 'Are you sure? I thought maybe we'd forget the whole thing. How many of us are there left, anyway?'

ONE: 'That's none of your business. They wiped us out *down*ward, not *up*ward. But as far as you're concerned, there's you and me. Our job now is to rebuild downward. You'll recruit a new Number Two to take Weir's place. And he'll do the same. And so on, until we've got a dozen or more again.'

TWO: 'Christ, I hate putting my neck on the line a *second* time.'

ONE: 'Are you turning yellow on me?'

TWO: 'I didn't say I *wouldn't* do it.'

ONE: 'I want you to consider a patrolman named Michaelson. He'll make sergeant soon, is very ambitious, and should go along with us. Let me figure out how to get you two together.'

TWO: 'I guess you feel as bad as I do about Jimmy Weir.'

ONE: 'Actually, I don't. The damned fool recruited Harry Balleau, didn't he? And that fucking skell blew the works! Who knows what would have happened had Jimmy lived? Might have wiped us out *upward*, too. Which includes you and me, my sentimental friend.'

TWO: 'Listen, I'm giving a lecture at the Academy at one-thirty. Couldn't we run into each other afterwards? I'd really like to have a long eyeball-to-eyeball talk.'

ONE: 'I phoned Roersch and told him I'd be at the hospital this afternoon. Couldn't put it off any longer. Couldn't act angry, with the newspapers calling him one of the city's great police heroes.' Pause. 'Imagine a fucking *sergeant* taking it on himself ...' Sigh. 'I'd've been a lot better off letting Captain Hawly head it up, even *without* control.'

TWO: 'Roersch is going to be a continuing danger, isn't he?'

ONE: 'Not at all. He's still a very sick man. Probably die on his own in a year or two. Besides, he's due for retirement, medical or chronological. I'll see that the retirement takes place within six months, which will be just about the time we're ready to begin operations again.'

TWO: 'Even so ... if *he* could make us, why couldn't someone else? Maybe the whole plan needs rethinking.'

ONE: 'Maybe. I'll try to work up a new angle to protect the ranks. But there aren't many Roersches around. I've known the bastard for ten or more years, and *still* didn't realize what a fucking great shadow he is. If only he had the right attitude!'

TWO: 'Making lieutenant, having a duty roster of his own ...' Pause. 'He'll have muscle and he's liable to poke upward, above Jimmy.'

ONE: Sarcastically: 'Please tell me how the hell he can do *that*?'

TWO: 'I don't know. I don't know how he did it the first time, either.'

ONE: 'Mistakes. Jimmy and Balleau fucked up badly.'

TWO: Long pause. 'I don't think I'm going to rejoin the squad.'

ONE: Unbelieving: '*What?*'

TWO: 'I'm sorry. I've decided against it.'

ONE: Raging coldly: 'Let me remind you of some past history, Mr Jefferson. Let me ...'

TWO: 'Don't remind me of anything. Don't threaten me. *Your* past history is worse. I don't need you for my promotions. And I certainly don't need you to help me end up like Jimmy. Good-bye, Inspector.'

ONE: 'Wait a minute! It's just me and you now, I admit it! I *swear* it!'

TWO: 'Even more reason for dropping it.'

ONE: 'We can't let a great idea like the Hit Squad die! We owe it to the city, the country ... and we'll be the ones running the cities, the country! Think of it! Think of the power ...'

The line clicks in his ear.

ONE: 'Damn you, Roersch, you fucking kraut! Damn you, Jerry cocksucker! Damn you, Fritz mother ...' Begins to weep.

Bestsellers available in paperback from Grafton Books

Emmanuelle Arsan

Emmanuelle	£2.50	☐
Emmanuelle 2	£2.50	☐
Laure	£1.95	☐
Nea	£1.95	☐
Vanna	£2.50	☐

Jonathan Black

Ride the Golden Tiger	£2.95	☐
Oil	£2.50	☐
The World Rapers	£2.50	☐
The House on the Hill	£2.50	☐
Megacorp	£2.50	☐
The Plunderers	£2.50	☐

Herbert Kastle

Cross-Country	£2.50	☐
Little Love	£2.50	☐
Millionaires	£2.50	☐
Miami Golden Boy	£2.50	☐
The Movie Maker	£2.95	☐
The Gang	£2.50	☐
Hit Squad	£1.95	☐
Dirty Movies	£2.95	☐
Hot Prowl	£1.95	☐
Sunset People	£2.50	☐
David's War	£1.95	☐

To order direct from the publisher just tick the titles you want
and fill in the order form.   GF4081

All these books are available at your local bookshop or newsagent, or can be ordered direct from the publisher.

To order direct from the publishers just tick the titles you want and fill in the form below.

Name _____

Address _____

_____

Send to:
Grafton Cash Sales
PO Box 11, Falmouth, Cornwall TR10 9EN.

Please enclose remittance to the value of the cover price plus:

UK 60p for the first book, 25p for the second book plus 15p per copy for each additional book ordered to a maximum charge of £1.90.

BFPO 60p for the first book, 25p for the second book plus 15p per copy for the next 7 books, thereafter 9p per book.

Overseas including Eire £1.25 for the first book, 75p for second book and 28p for each additional book.

_____

Grafton Books reserve the right to show new retail prices on covers, which may differ from those previously advertised in the text or elsewhere.